THE QUADRANT CONSPIRACY

THE PLOT TO KILL FDR

JAMES H LEWIS

CONTENTS

THE QUADRANT CONSPIRACY

James H Lewis

To Philip Padgett, my college roommate, lifelong friend, and historian, whose history, *Advocating Overlord*, inspired this story.

DER WOLFSSCHANZE, EAST PRUSSIA: JULY 29, 1943

Joseph Goebbels hated mosquitoes. The Minister of Propaganda for the Third Reich despised the blood-sucking devils. The Wolf's Lair, Adolf Hitler's reinforced command headquarters in East Prussia, lay in a swamp. The Führer Escort Command (FBK), which supervised the forest complex, had tried everything to get rid of *die verdammten Mücken*, even spreading oil on the surrounding ponds. All they achieved was to kill the fish that fed on the pests.

As he slapped at the bugs this morning, Goebbels would have given anything to be at his summer home on the Berlin island of Schwanenwerder in the Wannsee rather than in this dank concrete fortress. Not that he dared share his preference with the men gathered around him in the anteroom as they awaited the Führer. They sat in cloth-covered wooden chairs around an oak table, eyeing each other without disclosing their thoughts. Five meters of reinforced concrete surrounded them, with more than eight meters above their heads, protection against what their leader was certain was an impending Allied bombing mission.

Goebbels wondered why Hitler had brought them together. When he had summoned them at midnight, each dropped whatever plans he had for the day to fly east. They might all resent being ordered to this forlorn hideaway, but none were imprudent enough to speak out.

As though on cue, party chief Martin Bormann asked, "Do you know why we're here?" All professed ignorance, yet Goebbels trusted none of them.

He had pleaded with the Führer to leave this Prussian hideaway for months, but he refused, appearing in Berlin only twice that year. Goebbels missed the attention Hitler lavished on him during their private meetings, always building his confidence and assuring him he alone enjoyed the Führer's trust. His continued absence left Goebbels in the dark as to the leader's military and domestic plans and, consequently, unsure how to influence public perceptions. Moreover, Hitler's self-isolation and quarrels with his generals were affecting his judgment.

When his pleas fell on deaf ears, Goebbels resigned himself to the situation, rousing the German Volk through his own speeches and his control of every means of communication—radio, films, books, and newspapers.

"What is the news from Sicily?" SS leader Heinrich Himmler asked.

Army Field Marshal Wilhelm Keitel shrugged as though he had nothing new to report, but as usual, Hermann Göring, commander of the Luftwaffe, could not hold his tongue. "Lost," he said. "The fucking Italians won't fight."

Goebbels let no reaction cross his ascetic features. Whatever his faults, Göring was correct in this appraisal. It had been a mistake to ally the Fatherland to this loose collection of fiefdoms the Italians called a nation. They weren't fighters, didn't believe in the cause, and refused to deal with the Jews.

An air of defeat permeated the room. As the nation neared the fourth anniversary of the war, nothing was going right. General Patton had just taken Palmero, forcing Hitler to cancel Operation Citadel, the summer offensive on the Eastern Front to transfer panzer divisions to Italy. General Erick von Manstein protested, insisting his army could break through the Russian lines at Kursk and seize the initiative. The Soviets had lost eight times as many tanks and four times the men in the battle. If forced to withdraw, van Manstein warned, his forces would begin a retreat that could take them back to Prussia and beyond.

But Hitler insisted. "We have no choice in the matter."

And now our backs are to the wall, Goebbels thought. Two days before, US bombers attacked Hamburg, killing hundreds, leaving entire blocks in ruins. They returned the following day. There might be no end to it. To the south, five hundred American bombers dropped over a thousand tons of bombs on Rome, hitting the rail marshaling yard and dozens of plants manufacturing steel, textile products, and glass.

Goebbels's bland expression concealed his deep misgivings. He had been one of Hitler's earliest adherents, rising from an aide to Nazi leader Gregor Strasser in northern Germany to *Gauleiter* of Berlin, to minister for propaganda. While Göring's office made him the nominal second-in-command, position and power within Hitler's circle were not always synonymous. The Führer's habit of playing his lieutenants against each other made it unclear who was ascendant on any given day. Goebbels had no doubt, however. He shaped public opinion, he had built Adolf Hitler into a national icon, and he maintained the people's commitment to the war effort despite their growing deprivation. Since he had added civil defense to his long portfolio, his position was clear. He was the second most powerful man in the Third Reich.

At last, an officer of the FBK, the only armed soldiers allowed near the Führer, directed them into the bunker. Goebbels held back, allowing the others to precede him, a habitual effort to conceal the limp resulting from botched childhood surgery to correct his club foot.

"Heil Hitler!" A chorus of groveling greeted their leader as the entourage paraded into the map room. Goebbels flashed Hitler a rare smile and inclined his head in the semblance of a bow, hiding his shock at the man's appearance. He looked older and frailer than just weeks before, when last Goebbels had visited him. His hands shook

—his handwriting had become indecipherable—and his skin had assumed a yellowed pallor. Goebbels had once marveled at how this slight figure projected such a commanding presence before a crowd; it was an effort both men had practiced for years, observing themselves in mirrors as they roared and gesticulated. But as Hitler's physical appearance had deteriorated during the past year, he refused to allow newsreels to carry his image, even clips showing him at a distance. His likeness and voice had been the most powerful propaganda tools Goebbels possessed, but he could no longer wield them.

As Hitler spoke, however, Goebbels sensed a return of his old self-confidence. "Today, I am announcing an action that will bring about the collapse of the Western Alliance." A collective intake of breath greeted these words. Whatever most were expecting, it was not this. What was coming, a revelation or another harebrained scheme? Goebbels took the sense of the crowd and detected trepidation.

"At this moment, the future of the Reich turns on events in Italy. Traitors have arrested Il Duce and installed a puppet, Marshal Badoglio, in his place. Now, despite his personal assurances to me, this swine is negotiating with the Americans over terms of surrender."

As his audience listened with unease, Hitler shouted, "Let them! The Italians lack national will. They are weaklings, lacking the resolve of the German Volk."

He lowered his voice and pointed at the map of the Italian boot displayed before them. "The moment Badoglio surrenders, I will pour our reserves into the peninsula. When the British and Americans land, I will spring a trap. I am luring them into *ein Sumpf*," a swamp.

"*Wir kämpfen an allen Fronten ...,*" he said—we are fighting on all fronts, in the south and the east. "These efforts will keep the war away from the Reich, giving us time to develop our secret weapons."

The Führer paused, displaying a triumphant, self-satisfied smile. "Churchill is now irrelevant. Our true enemy is Roosevelt, backed by his cabal of Jewish bankers and financiers."

His voice rose. His face turned scarlet. Spittle formed around his lower lip, a bit of it clinging to the underside of his toothbrush mustache. As his hatred of the American president bubbled and frothed, his hands trembled. It was a familiar spectacle. Hitler railed against all enemies of the Reich, but in Roosevelt, he had a name, a face, and the same aristocratic background as those who had mocked him from the time he was a struggling painter in Vienna.

"Roosevelt is the true leader. Churchill is his mere pawn."

Hitler looked toward Goebbels as he spoke, a silent accolade that made the propaganda minister feel inches taller than his five-and-a-half feet. In his closing remarks at the Casablanca Conference in January, Churchill had said of Roosevelt, "I have been his active lieutenant." On hearing this news account, Goebbels wrote to Hitler that this was an about-face, a "humiliation unparalleled in British history." Hitler had now reached the same conclusion and gave Goebbels credit for the insight.

"Without American tanks, planes, artillery, and personnel, the British are *ein Mundtuch*," Hitler said. A mere napkin. "But the tissue is beginning to shred."

He revealed to the five men what intelligence services had picked up over the past few days. For over a year, the Abwehr's Technical Group had monitored conversations the two Allied leaders held via trans-Atlantic radio-telephone link. "The Americans are trying to force England to invade Europe through France next spring, but Churchill resists, insisting on moving against us through Italy, Turkey, and the Balkans. In this way, he intends to preserve the decadent British Empire."

The Führer sniggered. "When they met in May, Roosevelt forced the British to agree to invade across the English Channel. We now know," Hitler whispered, as though spies could infiltrate the three rings of security surrounding the Wolf's Lair, "Churchill is reneging. He insists on concentrating their forces in the Mediterranean."

Goebbels stood stony-faced as Hitler continued, fighting to conceal his thoughts. *If only he had taken my advice and not declared war on the Americans. If only he had listened.*

"They meet again three weeks from now in Québec, where

Roosevelt will try to solidify the US position. But," he hissed, "Americans are an impatient people. They see Japan as their true enemy. They are clamoring to withdraw forces from Europe and transfer them to the Pacific. If we remove Roosevelt, the Congress will force his successor, Henry Wallace, to focus on Japan. Churchill will get his way; there will be no cross-Channel invasion. But he will fight alone."

He glanced around the room, commanding their attention, and slammed his fist on the map table. "We must eliminate Roosevelt before he meets again with Churchill. Herr Himmler has devised a plan to do just that."

The head of the SS, who only a half hour before had professed to know nothing about the purpose of the meeting, stepped forward to stand alongside the Führer, a smug expression plastered across his face. "Roosevelt is going on a fishing trip to Canada before the conference," he said. "We know where he will be and when. We have assigned an agent to intercept Roosevelt and assassinate him before he reaches Québec. We shall not fail."

1

AUGUST 28, 1942

BRANDON ARMITAGE STOOPED to pick up the just-delivered newspaper and read the headline on the front page of the *Toronto Daily Star*, "Casualties at Dieppe Now Reach 671." Grasping the wood railing on his front steps for support, he lowered himself to a sitting position. A breeze ruffled his thinning, prematurely gray hair and sent the leaves of the silver maples shimmering in the morning light.

National Defence Headquarters had just released its fourteenth report on the dead, injured, and missing from the previous week's raid. Armitage ran his finger down the list of names, pausing at two he recognized. He turned to page 3, wrestling with the newspaper as it blossomed in the breeze. It would have been easier to study it over a cup of hot coffee at the kitchen table, but he relished these few moments of peace before returning inside to deal with his wife's grief.

His face betrayed no emotion as he reached the end of the list. The military had not yet released the name of one of his two sons, whose identity lay concealed in a yellow envelope on the demilune mahogany table at the front door.

When the telegram had arrived the previous morning, Margaret Armitage had forbidden her husband to open it, as though ignorance of its contents would change the outcome. She took to her bed, spurning calls from neighbors who recognized what the delivery of the communication must mean. She declined to speak to her husband, who brought her meals she did not touch. He heard her weeping behind the locked door. She refused to open it, which was just as well. He didn't know what more to say.

A black McLaughlin Buick turned onto Langford Avenue, beginning its grim journey southward. This harbinger of doom had traveled the street daily during the week following the Dieppe raid, but its visits were becoming less frequent. It stopped before the home of Fred and Valerie Pierce. Armitage shook his head. The Pierces had only one son, now sacrificed in an ill-fated operation with the ironic code name Jubilee.

He watched with growing dread as the dark-coated delivery man climbed back into the Buick and headed down the block. It pulled to the curb at the house opposite theirs. That couldn't be right. Roger Marquardt was not in the service—not yet, at least. The driver must be delivering some other urgent message. Fishing for one of the many yellow envelopes stacked in a long metal box on the seat alongside him, the man emerged, walking not toward the Marquardt house, but toward Armitage.

He pulled himself to his feet, his face set, his thin frame trembling, his head shaking in denial. The courier extended the hand containing the hated message, his eyes communicating his sorrow. Armitage tried to give him a reassuring smile—it wasn't his fault, this painful mission—but it came off as a grimace. He accepted the envelope with quivering hands, turned, and entered the house without acknowledging receipt.

He placed it on the entry table alongside its twin, looking from one to the other, wondering which to open first. What difference did it make? Two young men, Henry, the adventurous elder brother whose independence so verged on recklessness that it had long been a source of anxiety, or Richard, the more cautious son, who invariably followed his brother's lead.

Armitage had a sudden memory—Henry, straddling the first-floor railing of their home before leaping onto the entryway rug below, sensing the surge of pain in his right heel, and shouting, "No, Dickie, don't do it." And Richard blindly following him, only to join his brother as both writhed in agony.

Heaving a deep sigh, Armitage opened the first envelope.

DEEPLY REGRET INFORM YOU PVT RICHARD ARMITAGE 2ND CANADIAN INFANTRY DIVISION OFFICIALLY REPORTED DIED AUGUST 19, 1942. DIRECTOR OF RECORD.

Armitage leaned against the wall and choked back tears, an emotion he had denied himself during his three years in captivity during "The Great War." Dickie, whom he had never admitted was his favorite, dead at nineteen. *What a waste! Will we never see the end of these Hun bastards?*

He opened the second telegram, but his hands so trembled he had to lay it on the table to read it.

REGRET TO ADVISE THAT YOUR SON HENRY JAMES ARMITAGE 2ND CANADIAN INFANTRY DIVISION IS REPORTED ...

He stopped, unable at first to comprehend the words on the rows of tape affixed to the yellow page.

... REPORTED MISSING AFTER LAND MISSION OVERSEAS LETTER FOLLOWS. DIRECTOR OF RECORDS.

The forbidden tears tumbled from his eyes. He wiped his cheek on his sleeve and retreated to the kitchen, scooping up tap water in his hands and ladling it over his face.

"Brandon, come here." From the upper floor, Margaret spoke the first words she'd said to him in twenty-two hours. He dried off with the towel meant only for dishes and limped to the bottom of the staircase.

"What is it?" she said. He picked up both telegrams and climbed the stairs toward her, stepping first with his left foot and dragging the right after it.

She looked from one of his hands to the other. "Oh, no!" She had to have seen the hated car pull to the curb, had to have heard him weeping in the entryway.

"Dickie's gone." His voice quavered as he spoke, and for a moment, he couldn't choke out the rest of his message. "But Henry— he's missing. He's not dead, Margie, just missing." Armitage took the last few steps and tried to embrace her, but she loosened her grip on the newel and stepped back, bracing herself against the wall.

"He's dead, too," she said. "You know what they're saying. They retreated in such haste they couldn't bring back all the bodies."

"No, Margie. He's just missing." He forced a smile he did not feel. "There's hope. Don't you see?"

"Both my boys, gone," she said, her voice breaking. "And you did it. You let them go."

He stood mute, unable to defend himself. Henry enlisted, and his brother followed, as he always did. How could he have stopped them?

Again, Armitage reached out to his wife. "Don't touch me. You men and your stupid, senseless wars. I hate all of you."

THE FORD PICKUP lumbered down US 87 toward San Antonio, carrying a load of hay. Horst Becker, an old German farmer from Fredericksburg, hunched over the steering wheel, his eyes shifting from one side of the road to the other. Alongside him sat a young man whose papers identified him as Hans-Rudolph Meier, a Swiss national studying European history at the University of Chicago.

While his documents appeared authentic, Hans-Rudolph Meier was not. His true identity was *Oberleutnant* Jörg Schumacher, a Luft-waffe pilot shot down in a field in Kent during the Battle of Britain. Schumacher escaped his Messerschmidt 109 without a scratch, even joking with the village residents who came forward to arrest him. He'd done time in two British POW camps, escaping from one and getting as far as an airfield where he tried to steal a plane to fly back across the Channel.

With fears growing of an imminent German invasion, Churchill's government had appealed to Commonwealth nations to take Axis prisoners off its hands. Britain had an international duty to keep their captives out of harm's way, but their self-interest was even greater. Keeping German prisoners in Great Britain represented a threat. Able-bodied soldiers, sailors, and pilots, once freed by an invading army, would be turned against the British people. Transported to Canada among the first wave of prisoners, Schumacher was interned at Bowmanville, north of Toronto.

He hadn't minded life there. The food was better than the fare in the British camps. On his first day, the guards issued him a loaf of bread about the size of a baking potato. He ate a third of it and stashed the rest away, fearing another prisoner would steal it. The next morning, they gave him another, and still a third on the following day. Schumacher hadn't seen so much food in years.

The prisoners were content and the old guards tired, so they left each other alone. Since many of his fellow captives were former Luftwaffe pilots, he enjoyed the camaraderie. If there were a place where one could take pleasure in confinement, it would be Bowmanville.

Schumacher didn't intend to spend the war lounging around in a POW camp, however. He longed to return to action, to be back in the air, the only place where he felt free. Thus, he had spent every minute at Bowmanville plotting his escape, a quest that had now taken him within two hundred miles of the Mexican border.

"*Es ist so verdammt heiß,*" he said as the pickup chugged past scorched fields.

"English," the farmer said. "We must speak English in case they stop us. And, yes, it is hot."

"You're German. I'm Swiss. What else should we speak?" Schumacher said. "Can't you go faster?"

"We mustn't attract attention. The speed limit is thirty-five miles per hour, and I'm pulling this heavy load. I wish you'd crawl under the pile as we agreed."

"I'm a German officer. I will not hide in a pile of *Scheiße*. My papers have brought me this far. They'll get me the rest of the way."

Schumacher had escaped from the Canadian prison camp two weeks before, hiding in a laundry bag in the rear of a delivery truck. Fellow POWs answered to his name as the guards conducted 11:00 p.m. and 8:00 a.m. roll calls. The ruse gave him a twenty-hour head start before his captors discovered he was missing.

He traveled by train to Toronto and on to Niagara Falls, aided by railway route maps prisoners had borrowed and copied during their sixty-hour trip west from Halifax dockside. His fellow captives had fashioned a suit of clothes and forged the documents that allowed him to pass muster at the US border. Escape planning was a community enterprise, and with nothing else to do, every prisoner with a necessary skill pitched in.

Once in the US, Schumacher hitchhiked to Chicago, then Davenport, Iowa, and down the Mississippi via open boxcars and unsuspecting drivers. Along the way, he took refuge in the homes of German sympathizers—former members of the American Bund or relatives of those still living in the Fatherland. A group of Germans organized as the Chicago Knitting Club had smuggled lists of these safe houses into Camp Bowmanville, concealing them in the toes of socks masquerading as relief supplies.

"Please hide under the load for a few miles," Becker pleaded. "We're about to pass Camp Bullis, an Army training ground. We can't afford to be stopped there."

Schumacher pretended not to hear him over the roar of the unmuffled engine and wind whistling through the open windows. A hail of dark missiles attacked the front windshield, splattering into yellow-green globs. "What the hell are these things?"

"Crickets. We get them every fall, but they're early this year. Hear them?"

"That whirring racket? And the smell. I hate this damned place. How do you stand it?" Becker ignored him.

They passed the camp without incident, the farmer drenched in sweat and gripping the stirring wheel. "What will you do once you reach San Antonio?" Becker said.

"Hitch rides to the Mexican border. Then through South America until I get to Montevideo and can fly home."

"How will you cross the Rio Grande?"

"I can't tell you that. We have a plan in place and may need to use it again."

In fact, Schumacher had no such plan. He would get by on his personality and wits, as he had throughout his journey. It would all work out.

He was eager to rid himself of this man. Ever since his arrival, Becker had complained that it was he who bore the risk. If the authorities caught them, they would send Schumacher back to Canada, where he'd do the full twenty-eight days of detention allowed under the Geneva conventions. But they would arrest him, Horst Becker, a second-generation German-American, try him for treason, and perhaps even hang him.

As the farmer whined for the third time that day, the tail of the truck swerved, and they heard the steady thump-thump-thump as a bald, rationed rear tire succumbed to the miles, the heat, and the weight.

Becker pulled to the side as traffic whizzed by. "You must help me. We have to get out of here."

"I'll leave you now," Schumacher said. "You're safer without me." He ambled down the highway, his thumb stuck in the air.

Swearing to himself, Becker jacked up the truck, then noticed that the spare had lost its pressure. "*So ein Misthaufen,*" he said, discarding his warning to *sprich Englisch*.

A blue Chevrolet Master pulled up behind him, and a beefy man who, despite the heat, wore a denim jacket and a Stetson hat emerged. "Need help?" he offered.

"No. I can—*Ja*. My tire is flat, and so is the spare. Can you take me to the nearest gas station?"

"You German?"

"My parents, yes, but I was born here. I'm a loyal American."

The man looked him over. He rolled a toothpick from one side of his mouth to the other. "All right. Get in. The spare looks in better shape. Bring it with you." Becker tossed the tire in the trunk and joined the Texan in the front seat as he engaged the gears and moved onto the blacktop. A half mile down the road, a tall, blonde figure stood on the shoulder with his thumb extended.

"This seems to be my day to be a good Samaritan." The Texan pulled over and let Schumacher in. "Where're you from?"

"Switzerland," Schumacher said. "Hans-Rudolph Meier."

"Your English is pretty good for a foreigner."

"I'm studying at the University of Chicago."

"Uh-huh." They rode in silence, the hot wind collecting dust that crept through the windows. The driver twisted his rearview mirror to study Schumacher. "You folks are neutral, aren't you?"

"Yes, Switzerland has been nonaligned for a century."

"Pretty easy, sitting it out while everyone else does your fighting for you."

Schumacher considered touting the many services Switzerland provided to both sides in the conflict but said nothing. The man's questions made him nervous. He struggled to maintain an impassive expression.

"You know this guy?" he said.

"Never met."

"Seeing as you both speak German." The mirror reflected the Texan's frown. "What're you doin' down here?"

"Enjoying your beautiful country before classes begin."

The Texan continued to observe him. Schumacher considered how to reach forward and grasp the man's neck in the crook of his arm, but he wasn't certain Becker would be bright enough to grab the wheel. And the driver's eyes never left the rearview mirror for more than a second.

"There's a service station ahead," Becker said.

"I have to make another stop first."

The Texan drove on for three blocks, made a hard right turn, and stopped in front of a Bexar County sheriff's substation. Schumacher's long journey toward freedom was at an end.

"You're under arrest," he said, reaching under his denim jacket for a revolver. "One move and you're dead." He leaned on his horn until an officer stepped outside to see what the fuss was.

NORTH OF FREDERICK, Maryland, a Lincoln convertible climbed into the Catoctin Mountains. Chauffeur Monte Snyder shifted into low gear as the 12-cylinder engine struggled to haul the vehicle with its armor plating, bulletproof tires, and inch-thick windows up the pass. Such an automobile would have been an anomaly in this rural patch of northern Maryland only weeks before, but the locals had now become accustomed to it.

A farmer halted his thresher to watch as the car nicknamed *The Sunshine Special* carried President Franklin Roosevelt on his journey to Shangri-La, the presidential retreat the Navy had finished converting from a camp for federal agents only weeks before.

In the back seat, Roosevelt, who often kept a running conversation with Snyder when they were alone, smoked in silence, reflecting on his busy day. After a brief meeting with White House reporters, he'd met with senators and labor leaders, the administrator of price administration, and both the Argentine minister and Venezuelan ambassador.

After lunch with his close friend and advisor Harry Hopkins and Army Chief of Staff George Marshall, Roosevelt joined them in an hour-long session with the three other military chiefs. They brought depressing news from the Pacific, where Marines were engaged in a bloody battle at Guadalcanal that showed no sign of ending. The news from Europe was equally disheartening. The Russian Army was in retreat, Germans were bombing Stalingrad, and Rommel's panzer divisions were pushing back the British at El Alamein. Thousands of Canadian soldiers had either died or been taken prisoner in an abortive raid on the French port of Dieppe, a debacle reminiscent of the Gallipoli Campaign during the First World War.

Gallipoli had cost Churchill leadership of the Admiralty in 1915. The lesson he took from the disaster and the memory of ghastly losses in the trenches cast a shadow over current strategy. As Marshall and Secretary of War Henry Stimson had pressed to open a second front with a cross-Channel invasion of France this summer, Winston had balked. Too soon, he insisted. We're not ready. Roosevelt had agreed. While the decision may have averted a repeat of Dieppe, Soviet leader Joseph Stalin was furious when Churchill informed him there would be no second front in 1942.

At home, the public clamored for American action in Europe. The previous December, weeks after America had been dragged into the conflict, Roosevelt and Churchill had agreed that the Allies would focus the war effort first on Germany before turning their full attention to Japan. The Europe-first strategy made sense to the public only if the United Nations went on the offensive in Europe.

On that front, the joint chiefs had presented Roosevelt with the day's only encouraging news, updating him on plans for an invasion of French Morocco and Algeria in late fall. They intended the North Africa campaign, code-named Operation Torch, to relieve pressure on British forces in Egypt. It might even mollify Stalin. The planning was going well, and Roosevelt welcomed the reports. Along with the nation, he was hungry for action.

It had been a busy day at the end of a busier week, and the president was exhausted. Every waking hour was filled with meetings, conferences, and decisions, forcing him to shift his attention between the war and the economy, domestic and political considerations, all while serving as the nation's cheerleader at a moment's notice. He had earned the forty-eight hours he would spend at his retreat, away from Washington's oppressive heat and humidity. On Monday, the unceasing grind of responsibility would resume, but for these few hours, he would leave it all behind.

The vehicle's undercarriage creaked as it passed under the rustic sign reading *Shangri-La* and up the gravel driveway to the shingled

Mountain Park Lodge. Snyder parked at the entrance and helped the naval orderly transfer the president into a waiting wheelchair of his own design. While Roosevelt used his muscular arms to wheel himself inside, the chauffeur returned to the car for a leather satchel containing correspondence his secretary, Grace Tully, had prepared.

Roosevelt waved it away. "Let me watch the starlings and jays fight for dominance while I enjoy what's left of the day." He sat on the back deck for an hour, smoking cigarettes, sipping a martini, and enjoying the solitude. As the evening breeze stirred the surrounding branches, the president reflected on his political predicament. Americans were restless, grumbling about the slow pace of the war and whining about the inconvenience caused by rationing. Since they would not know of Operation Torch until after the November election, Roosevelt feared he would lose much of his congressional majority.

"Sir? Sir?" Roosevelt looked up to see the orderly standing over him, his hands locked together and a frightened look on his face. "Are you all right, Mr. President?"

Roosevelt grinned. "I must have dozed off. Did I frighten you?" The attendant exhaled, a wordless answer to the question. "You'd best call Senator Vandenberg and tell him to cancel the party. I'm still here." The president guffawed, but he could tell the orderly didn't follow politics enough to share in the joke.

The dinner of Catoctin Mountain trout, parsley steamed potatoes, and fresh green beans prepared by the Navy cook refreshed him. He spent an hour with his beloved stamp collection. The Venezuelan ambassador had brought a gift from President Medina Angarita, one bolivar and five centimos stamps. They were worthless, but that was not the point. Roosevelt enjoyed philately for its links to history and geography. It had been his hobby since he was eight. After he'd contracted polio as an adult, it occupied the tedious hours while he tried to recuperate.

At ten o'clock, he opened the correspondence Grace Tully had sent along. Most of it could wait until tomorrow, even Sunday, if the weather was fine. He tore into one envelope bearing the return address of Zenith Radio Corporation in Chicago. Its president, longtime friend Eugene F. MacDonald, Jr., was a giant in electronics who had developed the Trans-Oceanic radio, used at military installations worldwide. MacDonald had stood by him when other business leaders wanted to hang him from the nearest gallows. Roosevelt had not forgotten.

He unfolded the letter, noting its salutation, "My dear Mr. President."

It occurs to me that after nine years in office, you deserve time away from the responsibilities of guiding our nation. You have led us through a depression and are guiding us through an attack on our nation and a war that has consumed the entire world. You have earned a vacation.

I suggest that we plan a fishing trip next summer. I know of a delightful spot in Ontario, McGregor Bay on the northern edge of Lake Huron. It is isolated, the fish are plentiful, and it is as far from the cares of the world as you can get in North America.

Please consider this and let us make plans to be together next year at this time.

With all good wishes, believe me.

Laying the letter aside, Roosevelt picked up his pen and took a sheet of writing paper from the desk. There could be no vacation for the commander-in-chief this year ... but next? FDR was hopeful. "What a capital idea," he wrote. "Let us plan on it. Yours, FDR."

He went to bed and fell asleep at once, more at peace than he had been in days.

Four hundred miles to the north, a solitary figure lay awake. Behind her locked door, Margie Armitage wept with no one to comfort her, no one to witness her anguish.

"My boys. My beautiful young men." She rose and stared out the window to the street painted yellow by the overhead lamps. A lake breeze floated in, carrying with it the sweet smell of the summer phlox she'd planted in pots along the front porch.

"Gone," she said, fingering the blue-and-black chintz curtains.

She heard the front door open and close. Her husband left the house, strolled to the corner, stood under the streetlamp for a few minutes, and wandered back. Although no lights were on in her room, she retreated from the window so he wouldn't notice her.

Henry. September 1925. His first day of school. Walking alongside her, his hand grasping hers, withdrawing it slowly before taking his hesitant steps up the concrete entry, turning at the door and looking back at her, his lower lip trembling.

Richard and Henry. September 1928. Walking hand-in-hand to the schoolhouse, Margie trailing behind them. "C'mon, Dickie. You'll love it. Mrs. Nielsen is great. You'll learn to read for yourself, and I won't have to. You can read to me." His brother's light brown eyes looking up at him from beneath his thatch of bright blond hair, not yet faded into a more muted sandy color. Still holding Henry's hand as he mounted the stairs and entered the door. If Henry said it was okay, that was good enough for him.

Scenes passed before Margie like clips from a newsreel. Attending the boys' hockey matches, sometimes with Brandon, more often on her own. Christmas pageants. School plays. Henry's first date with a girl named Laura. What had become of her? Dickie making fun of him, only to decide he wanted a girlfriend of his own, three years before his time.

Where had it all gone? Margie heard Brandon return and kept silent so he would not know she was awake. She lay back on the bed, staring at the faint shadows of the maple leaves painting patterns on the ceiling.

Sometime around his high school graduation, Henry gaining a serious side. She recalled long conversations over coffee at the dinette. Posing questions she couldn't answer, while Dickie tried to keep up. How long would the depression last? Why wouldn't the royal family allow Edward to marry whomever he liked? Why had Germans allowed someone like Hitler to assume power?

Henry discussing his future, his difficulty finding work amid the economic turmoil, laboring at jobs that were beneath him, worrying about how he'd find his place in the world. Man-to-man talk, only she had played the role of father as Brandon spent long hours at work.

"Brandon, please stop them. Don't let them go."

"How can I do that? They're adults. And there's nothing for them here. Not right now."

"Please do something. I don't want them to go."

Now they were gone. Both of them. Her boys had been her life, and now their lives—theirs and hers—were over.

2

SEPTEMBER 11-18, 1942

"God our Father, by raising Christ your Son, you destroyed the power of death and opened for us the way to eternal life." Walter Houghton, the pastor of East York's Church of the Resurrection, intoned the same benediction he had given for other sons of the church during the past week. "As we remember before you, our brother Richard, we ask your help for all who shall gather in his memory."

Margaret Armitage sobbed while her husband gripped the end of the pew, staring at a point beyond the stained-glass windows that bordered the apse. He vowed to record everything about this moment in his memory, from the sunlight projecting colored tiles onto the organ pipes to the cloying aroma of wood polish. While the organist trumpeted "O God, Our Help in Ages Past," an usher moved forward, stood aside as Brandon left the pew, reached for Margie's arm, and escorted the couple up the aisle under the arches of the church known affectionally as The Rez.

Mourners followed them. Margie's mother, Brandon's parents, brothers and sisters, aunts and uncles, coworkers, and neighbors, some of whom had attended other memorial services during the past week. And there would be more. The landing on the beach at Puys had gutted the Royal Regiment, most of whose members were from Toronto. Only a tenth of the original force had returned to England, the rest captured, killed, or like Henry, missing.

After accepting condolences outside the church, Brandon and Margie entered the limousine. They rode in silence from Bloor Street and Avenue Road to their home, and close relatives followed. Neighbors had laid out a table of cookies and tea service in the dining room. Most of Brandon's family clustered there, while Margaret's relatives gravitated toward the living room, the polarity underlining the tension between the couple.

Brandon's mother placed a hand on her son's arm. "Couldn't they have had the decency to return his body?"

"Perhaps later. There's no time for that now. They buried him at Brookwood Military Cemetery in Surrey. After the war ..." He trailed off, not finishing the thought.

"And Henry? What's the news of Henry?"

"The same, Mother." Did she think some miracle had occurred during the past forty-eight hours, something he was hiding from her? They hadn't received the customary letters from their sons' commanding officers. Armitage was more willing to make allowances for the omissions, for these officers might also be among the missing. Who was left to write?

"If he had died, we would have heard," he told his mother with an optimism he did not feel.

"What will you do now?"

"I go back to work Monday."

Armitage had returned from The Great War to find his banking job, his intended career path, closed. Fortunately, Ottawa had given veterans priority for government jobs. He found work as a postal inspector, rose through the service, routing the mail on rail routes throughout the nation. He now supervised contracts between the Royal Mail and private carriers such as Trans-Air Canada.

"I may not stay," he said. "I need to help the war effort somehow."

"You won't enlist. Not at your age."

"Not at my age and not with this game leg. I have something else in mind."

"Nothing dangerous?"

"Not in the least. It's not a desk job, but it is in uniform." She poked and prodded, trying to get him to say more, but he first needed to share his decision with Margie. That would not be easy.

It wasn't until the following morning that he broached the subject. As they sat over coffee, Margie still in her housecoat, Brandon said, "I want to avenge Dickie's death."

"Haven't you done enough?" There were two ways to take that; her sullen expression told him which one she meant. "Have you forgotten about Henry?"

"I haven't forgotten either of them, and I won't. That's why I'm doing what—"

"You've decided. This isn't a discussion. You're telling me what you're about to do."

He rotated his coffee cup with his index finger. "Yes, I'm joining the Veterans Guard."

"What's that? Patrolling Indian villages?"

He caught himself before telling her not to be silly. "The guard is a group of veterans like me who are disabled from the first war or too old to serve. It's not just a bunch of old duffers trading war stories, though. They have important work to do."

He waited for her to speak, but when she didn't, he forged ahead. "We—" He corrected himself. "*They* are guarding the camps where we hold German prisoners."

A faint stirring of interest. "You'll deal with the men who killed my boys."

He had spent days reminding her that Henry might still be alive, but now gave up. "Yes."

"You can get back at them for what they've done."

"I will not torture them, but neither will I make their lives easy. I'll treat them with all the kindness and respect they offered me." He spat out the last few words. "What do you think?"

"What does it matter? You've decided."

"It's something I want to do, but I haven't signed up. I can still change. Should I do it, Margie?"

"Can we afford it?"

He opened a large pad on which, as he did at the Royal Mail, he'd recorded credits and debits—expected income offset by obligations. "It will be tight. We can't purchase anything extravagant, but there's nothing much to buy with this war on. When it's over, I can regain my job. Yes, we can make it work. What do you think?"

For the first time in two weeks, she gave the slightest of smiles. "Do it for Henry and Richard. We owe it to them."

"I REQUEST A TRANSFER TO ANOTHER CAMP," Jörg Schumacher said as two guards escorted him from the Union Station entrance on Front Street West. Travelers in uniform and plain clothes bustled in and out of the Toronto depot as waiting taxis spewed fumes into the air, their horns blaring at each other.

Getting no response from the grim-faced pair, he repeated his request. "As long as I'm here, I'd like to take in more of Canada."

"You've already seen half the United States," a guard said. "What more do you want?"

"Québec, perhaps? I hear it's beautiful in fall."

The guards snorted as they turned onto York Street, supporting his elbows as they led him into the back of a closed personnel carrier. They padlocked the metal door. Their prisoner had escaped twice in England and now in Ontario, and the Canadian military was giving him no chance to slink away again.

After his arrest two weeks before, Schumacher spent three days in a San Antonio jail. It was hot as a Finnish sauna, and flatulence from the daily diet of beans and rice filled the cell block. Despite his disappointment at being stopped so close to the Mexican border, he was relieved when the FBI collected him. They took him on a troop train to Chicago. He spent another two nights in a cell before US military police drove him to Detroit and turned him over to Canadian officers.

After another train ride to Toronto, he was on his last leg, a forty-seven-mile trip to the front gate of Bowmanville.

Until two months before, he wouldn't have minded being back in this camp. If he had to be in captivity, this wasn't bad duty. The guards left prisoners to their own devices, and they returned the favor. He'd renewed friendships among fellow captured fliers and made a few new friends.

The casual atmosphere had changed in late June with the appearance of *Major* Reinhardt Kretschmer. The officer was a dedicated Nazi who'd been a magistrate before enlisting in the Luftwaffe. On his arrival at Bowmanville, Kretschmer assumed command of the military tribunal that maintained order among the prisoners. He insinuated himself as an "advisor" to the formerly easygoing *Lagerführer*, the German officer responsible for discipline within the ranks.

"Sieg heils" replaced the heretofore relaxed atmosphere. Lieutenants were required to salute senior officers, who were so numerous that Schumacher's arm tired from the effort. Kretschmer imposed courts of honor, illegal under the Geneva conventions, to mete out punishment to those who failed to adhere to camp discipline ... and to the party line.

He cross-examined incoming prisoners about their political views. When he found one of Schumacher's fellow pilots guilty of some unexplained transgression, he ordered other officers to shun him. No one was permitted to speak to the man, sit with him during meals, or deal him into a round of skat.

Bowmanville—Camp 30 to the Canadians—was no longer a pleasant place to wait out the eventual triumph of the Fatherland. It had become a true prison camp, with Kretschmer and the two other officers of the tribunal, the jailers.

"It's good to be home again." As Schumacher climbed down from the back of the armored vehicle, he grinned at his guards.

"Move along," one said, unimpressed by their prisoner's geniality. Law enforcement agencies from two nations had chased him eighteen hundred miles. With a war on, they had better things to do.

"And thanks for the portal-to-portal service." Schumacher

stretched and looked around him. "Last time I arrived, you made me walk from the train station."

On that day in 1941, he and his fellow POWs had marched two and a half miles to the former boys' school that was now Bowmanville Prison Camp. Townspeople had lined the sidewalks, whistling and jeering.

Now, the guards led him into the camp and turned him over to two others, who escorted him to the single cell that would be his home for twenty-eight days of confinement. Disinfectant did little to mask the stench of urine. The only sound he would hear until a guard delivered his daily meals were his steps echoing off the concrete walls.

He lay on his cot and stared at the ceiling, picturing the camp's layout as he plotted his next escape. Until now, his sole motivation had been to return to his unit and get back in the air. Kretschmer and his fellow Nazis gave him fresh impetus. He had to get away from them before they got to him.

There were only three ways out of the camp—over the wall, under the wall, or through it. He would find a way.

MARGIE'S MOTHER showed up unannounced, entering without knocking. She had asked the woman innumerable times to call when she was coming to visit, to no effect.

Florence Jamison stormed into the kitchen where her daughter sat over a cup of coffee while paging through a large, rectangular notebook whose pages bore small black-and-white photographs held in place by cream-colored triangular stickers. Dropping a stack of flour sacks at her feet, she said, "What are you doing?"

Margie closed the book and shoved it to one side, as though her mother had caught her reading a racy dime novel. "Nothing." Florence sat across from her and reached for the book. "Leave it be."

"Marge," her mother said.

"I hate when you call me that. It's Margie," she said, emphasizing the hard *g* sound.

"I've called you Marge from the time you were a little girl. And 'Margie' sounds so … French."

"Yes, well …" Her mother disdained French-Canadians. In her view, they were disloyal to the Crown, having rioted to protest conscription during World War I. Moreover, they should speak English, just like everyone else. "Mother, why are you here?"

Florence reared back as though shot. "To help you clean up."

"I'm perfectly capable of—"

"I brought bags we can use to collect Richard's clothing."

"We will *what*?" Color rose in her pale features. She shook her head, her straight brown hair flowing from side to side. "I am not getting rid of anything. Whatever made you think …?" She buried her face in her hands, her body heaving as she sobbed.

"There, there. I'm only trying to help. All his things must be a constant reminder."

Margie regarded her mother through reddened eyes. "They do. These 'things,' as you put it, remind me of Dickie and remind me of Harry, and they're all I have."

"Henry."

"What?"

"You said, 'Harry.' You mean 'Henry.'"

Made conscious of having invoked the name of her late first husband, Henry's father, Margie reddened under her mother's accusing gaze. She hastened to regain control of the conversation. "Everything they wore, everything they touched, every dish from which they ate—it is all important to me. Vital. Do you understand?"

Florence pursed her lips and pushed her straight gray hair away from her face. "Brandon was selfish to leave you alone."

"He has things to do."

"He always has things to do, like sending his sons off to war. He had no right to do that to you. Or to them."

Margie knitted her hands and massaged her forehead. "Mother, he didn't send them. They went." *Why am I defending him? I feel the same.* "You're always on his case."

"I just wish you hadn't remarried in such haste. But what's done is done. It's too late to change it."

"Yes," she said, curtailing further discussion. She never won an argument with her mother. The closest she came was postponing it until Florence could marshal fresh arguments.

"Do you want some lunch?" Without waiting for a response, she left the table, took a jar of chicken stock from the refrigerator, and chopped onions, carrots, and celery.

"Nothing for me, thanks." But when the fragrant odor of sautéed vegetables and poultry filled the room, she helped herself to a bowl and sat down, slurping until she got to the bottom, mopping the bowl with a slice of rye bread. "Waste not, want not," she said to her daughter's disapproving glare.

Margie cleared the table and washed dishes as her mother dried, clutching each plate with hands gnarled by arthritis. *Is this what will become of me*, she wondered, *crippled, lonely, and angry?*

"I'm worried about you," Florence said after a long silence.

"I'm fine."

"You haven't left this house since the funeral."

"Yes, I have. I go down the street to the market."

"You know what I mean."

Margie stopped, dried her hands on her apron, stared out the kitchen window for a moment at the maples' yellowing leaves, and burst into tears again. She turned and embraced her mother, who held on as though she feared she'd escape. "I am so damned lost and alone. Those boys were my life."

"I know. Marge, baby, I understand how you feel." She waited until her daughter's body stopped heaving. "You know what you need?"

"No." Wiping her eyes and nose on a small handkerchief. "What do I need, Mother?"

"You need to go back to church."

"I'm not up for it."

"Not that church. Not Brandon's church. Your church. You need to attend Mass. I'll go with you."

Through her tears, Margie laughed. "Oh, Mother, I'm really not ready for *that*."

AT MIDAFTERNOON ON FRIDAY, September 18, a ten-car passenger train pulled into a siding near an enormous building in a flat field thirty-five miles west of Detroit. Men in dark business suits were the first to pile out into the chilly weather, a harbinger of an early fall.

After the agents took their places around an open limousine, President Franklin Roosevelt emerged, along with his wife, Eleanor, a host of federal and state officials, two unmarried cousins Laura Delano and Daisy Suckley, and Captain Ross McIntire, his physician.

The president was on the first day of a two-week transcontinental trip. Few people knew where he was. After ten years in office, Roosevelt enjoyed disappearing from public view, even as he performed official duties. It was a game he played with the Congress and the press. For the last half of September, official Washington would ask, "Where is the president?" His trip cloaked in secrecy, FDR would travel from Detroit to the West Coast and back, witnessing American industry turning out tanks, weapons, ships, and aircraft, beginning with this one, owned by the irascible Henry Ford.

Ford Motor Company's Willow Run assembly plant was the largest building in the United States, a mile in length, covering three-and-a-half million square feet. Its architect, Albert Kahn, called it "the most enormous room in the history of man." The US had invested two hundred million dollars in the project, designed to produce B-24 Liberator bombers at lightning speed.

There was but one problem: the complex had so far produced only one plane. Roosevelt had started his inspection trip here to spur production. He also hoped to bridge a gap with Ford himself. They had tangled two years before when the automaker appealed to the president to break a strike at his plants. Not only had Roosevelt refused, but Eleanor had worked with labor leaders to persuade black strikebreakers to join the walkout. Ford had neither forgotten nor forgiven.

As the presidential limousine approached the building, the president said, "Wow!" Few things impressed the man, but this structure was different.

Ford was not present to greet them. He was somewhere off in the factory tinkering, so it was left to his son, Edsel, to welcome the president and first lady while he sent minions in search of his father. Roosevelt was neither surprised nor offended at the snub. Henry Ford was Henry Ford.

The old isolationist and anti-Semite finally joined the party and, sandwiched between Franklin and Eleanor in the rear of the limousine, conducted a tour through the sprawling facility. From the front seat, Edsel and plant supervisor Charlie Sorenson described the operation, the first time the company had applied its mass production techniques to aircraft. Planes in various stages of assembly stretched as far as they could see. Nearly completed bombers formed the front of the line, many with wings off to the side, ready to be mounted. Further on, Roosevelt could see the skeletons of fuselages.

The air was filled with the rat-a-tat of riveting, the pulsing of power tools, and the chattering of hundreds of workers. A garlicky odor enveloped the party as an acetylene torch spewed sparks across the floor. Workers cheered and waved as they recognized the President and First Lady. Henry Ford stared straight ahead, refusing to acknowledge the tribute.

Women young and old, black and white, stood within frameworks, on wings, and beneath landing gear wielding heavy tools. "It is great to see these women doing their bit," Eleanor said. Ford, who had resisted the call to put "girls" on the assembly lines, merely grunted.

"Who's that?" the president said.

Turning his head toward the open tail section of a B-24, the Danish-born Sorenson said, "Those are midgets, Mr. President. That area is so narrow no full-grown person can fit in there."

"I want to meet them," Franklin said.

Edsel passed word to the driver to stop the vehicle, and the two small men clambered down to shake the president's hand. "You're doing a great service to your country," he said. "You are giants." The pair smiled, bowed slightly to the First Lady, and waved as the limousine resumed its slow crawl.

As it drew to the end of the line and made a right turn into another wing of the building, the president leaned toward Ford and said, "This must be the county line."

Ford let a rare smile slide over his face. He'd built the complex in an L-shape to keep it within Washtenaw County and avoid the higher taxes of Wayne County, which lay beyond the property. Roosevelt grinned, a twinkle in his eye, and patted him on the knee. For a moment, Henry Ford appeared charmed by the man's personality.

"Your country has a lot riding on this facility. When will we see more results?"

Ford's smile dropped. "Tomorrow. We're eliminating bottlenecks and speeding production. Ford will do its part, as it always has."

"Fine," Roosevelt said. "I know you're a man of your word."

As dusk fell, the limo returned to the trackside, and everyone climbed aboard. A locomotive backed the cars down the spur and onto the main line, to Ypsilanti and on to Chicago, where Eleanor would leave the train.

Buoyed by a sense of optimism, Roosevelt ordered champagne for his guests. In the Soviet Union, the German Army had stalled at Stalingrad. Among the allies, planning for Operation Torch was progressing. The only stumbling block was a French general who felt he should be in charge of the North African landing. Only two days before, the president had written Winston Churchill, "I consider it essential that de Gaulle be kept out of the picture and be permitted to have no, *repeat no,* information whatever regardless of how irritated and irritating he may become."

Roosevelt and his entourage sipped at their drinks as they sped through the night, confident that Henry Ford would come through for them and ready to witness the rest of the Arsenal of Democracy in action.

3

OCTOBER 9-21, 1942

FAVORING HIS RIGHT LEG, Brandon Armitage alighted from the Ontario Northland Railway coach at Gravenhurst, a small town 100 miles north of Toronto on Lake Muskoka. He took a deep breath, luxuriating in the frosty air, devoid of city traffic smells. Drawing his heavy woolen coat around him and slinging his carryall over his shoulder, he stepped into the terminal building, whose bay window overlooked the concrete platform.

He glanced at a notice on the bulletin board alongside the timetable. "All pleasure and unnecessary traveling should be ruled out for duration if our transportation facilities are to be available for war purposes." To emphasize the point, a smaller placard affixed to the entryway depicting an infantryman asked, "IS YOUR JOURNEY *REALLY* NECESSARY." Yes, he thought, it is.

"Sergeant Armitage?" A middle-aged man in an ill-fitting uniform advanced. Armitage smiled and held out his hand, but the man saluted.

"I'm not in uniform yet," Armitage said, returning the salute, "and out of practice."

The man introduced himself as Corporal Durham Smith. "Do you know this town?"

"My father brought me through the area as a child, and I took my sons fishing at Hardy Lake, but I've not spent much time in Gravenhurst."

"It's the gateway to the Muskoka Lakes region, so most people start from here." Smith explained he was from Bracebridge, ten miles to the north. Tossing Armitage's bag into the back of a Jeep, he said, "Welcome to Camp 20. The locals call it the Muskoka Officers Camp, but to us, it's just Camp 20. How long have you been in Number 2 Company?"

"Less than a month. I just joined up, and they sent me here."

Smith pushed his foot to the floor, and the Jeep took off with a jerk. He played tour guide as he careened along Muskoka Road, pointing out the turn-of-the-century Victorian Opera House. "The camp used to be a TB sanatorium, so it's pretty swanky compared to some others. You'll like it. It's easy duty."

"I'm not here on holiday."

Smith continued as though he hadn't spoken. "Gravenhurst is a pleasant little town, and the prisoners are self-sufficient. Many were professionals before the war, scientists, teachers, and doctors. We also have everything from farmers and electricians to carpenters and tailors. They look after themselves, grow their own vegetables, even make their own sausage. It's damned good."

"This doesn't sound much like a prison camp," Armitage said.

As Smith made a left turn onto a residential street, he glanced from the road to study his passenger. "We get along well. The Germans know they have it good. Not like out in Medicine Hat; that's hard duty. Here, they can play soccer and swim in summer. We have an area of the bay chained off so they can't float away."

He laughed as they entered the outer perimeter. "There's a girls' camp on the opposite shore. They paddle over in canoes to flirt with the men."

"You're kidding."

Smith pulled off Louise Street and parked in front of a two-story block building. A hundred yards away, behind a chain-link fence topped with barbed wire, Armitage spotted a three-story brick building. "The old sanitarium." The corporal rested his arms on the steering wheel. "Weren't you taken prisoner yourself?"

"They captured me at the Second Battle of Ypres. That's where the Huns first used gas. The Algerians took the brunt of it, suffocating in the trenches, poor bastards. We went in after them, peeing in our handkerchiefs and holding them to our faces. We held the line for a while, but our Ross rifles kept jamming—"

"Pieces of junk," Smith said.

"Not even *that* good, those sorry weapons. A man next to me was blinded when it backfired on him." The Ross Mark III had been Canada's answer to Britain's Lee-Enfield rifle. It was over four feet long with a thirty-inch barrel. When loaded with Mark 7 ammunition, it could be deadly accurate at distance, but it had two problems. It clogged easily in wet trench warfare conditions, and after being disassembled for cleaning, it was easy to seat the bolt shank incorrectly in the sleeve, sending shell casing back into the shooter's face.

"The Germans overran our trench, mowed down most of my fellows, and took me prisoner," Armitage said. "They say I was *lucky*." He uttered the word as though it were a curse. Public opinion in Canada at the time held it dishonorable to be captured. Armitage spent three years in captivity, some of it at forced labor in German coal mines, only to have acquaintances treat him as a pariah on his return. Even worse was the bank where he'd worked since graduating high school and had planned to spend his career. They slammed the door in his face, they and many others. He was fortunate to have found a government job.

"We treat Germans better than they treated us," the corporal said. "We set an example we hope they'll follow with our men."

Armitage got out of the Jeep, grabbed his kit, and entered the administration building without another word. He reported to his superior, Lieutenant Neil Morrison, a rangy man in his late forties who appeared much younger. The officer gave him a quick tour of the facility. "Our headquarters, administration, and mess hall are on the outer perimeter, surrounding the chain-link fence."

He led Armitage through the guarded gate into the prisoner's enclosure. "The camp itself consists of three buildings. The old sanitarium houses the officers, which is most of the population. The smaller barracks is for the two dozen or so non-coms. And this," he said, entering the third building, "is the prisoner's mess and rec center."

A few prisoners looked up as they entered, but the kitchen staff ignored them, bent over their preparations for lunch.

"Until May, we had 435 prisoners, all huddled together in a facility designed for half that many TB patients," Morrison said. "The situation has eased since we finished the barracks. Now, our biggest issues are insects and vermin. We can't keep them out."

Nevertheless, the camp seemed like a palace compared to his own experience. The prisoners had outdoor recreational facilities, a canteen, and a library. They had constructed steps leading down to the enclosed swimming area. The prisoners wore uniforms of blue and dark gray with large circles in contrasting colors on the back. "Those aren't sewed *on*," Morrison said, "they're sewed *in*. If you tear the circle out, the outfit comes apart. It's pretty hard to escape running round in your skivvies."

Guard towers surrounded the property, one even overlooking the bay. While the atmosphere seemed relaxed, Armitage suspected a prisoner who tried to escape wouldn't get far.

Following the tour, Corporal Smith escorted him to Calydor Cottage, a former guest house that now served as the officer's mess and quarters. Armitage called Margie after dinner to tell her he'd arrived. Their conversation was perfunctory, giving him the impression she didn't much care where he was or what he was doing. His last thought before he fell asleep that night was that Camp 20 might provide a pleasant vacation from his wife and that it was too much so for the prisoners.

The following morning, the commanding officer, Lieutenant-Colonel Arthur Wallington, assembled the men in the mess during breakfast. "This may prove to be a tough day," he said. "The war office has ordered us to handcuff senior officers. I expect we'll meet resistance. If so, be firm but not cruel. You are to abide by our Geneva commitments."

During a raid on the German-occupied Channel Island of Sark in late September, British forces had tied the hands of several captives. In retaliation, the Germans manacled over a thousand POWs captured during the abortive raid on Dieppe. In a tit-for-tat escalation, the British asked Canadian authorities to restrain hundreds of German prisoners held in its camps. The Ottawa government selected those sites at which to enforce the order, Camp 20 among them.

"Many of you have formed close relationships with the prisoners," Wallingford said. "I expect you to do your duty."

Minutes later, Armitage approached Lieutenant Morrison. "Since I'm new here, I don't know any POWs. I'm more than willing to help."

Morrison seemed relieved, and Armitage got the opportunity he'd longed for.

AT CAMP 30 IN BOWMANVILLE, 110 miles to the south, Schumacher emerged from detention. Twenty-eight days in "the cooler," as prisoners called the concrete cell in the Canadian guardhouse, had not been onerous. He missed the camaraderie of his fellow flyers and hated hearing nothing except the flat drone of Canadian English, but the four weeks of isolation had given him time to plot his next getaway. In his head, he had planned a means of prying open two strands of barbed wire with the open legs of a stepladder, squeezing through the gap, and making his way to Toronto, where another prisoner had a sympathetic relative. He would remain in hiding until the heat was off before making his way to Montréal to board a neutral freighter.

As his captors marched him back into the compound, he grinned and said, "*Danke*. After all that time on the road, I needed the rest."

"Maybe you'll consider that before you try again," a guard said.

Schumacher laughed and clapped him on the back. Someone

with a sense of humor, someone who could give as well as he got. The German pilot liked him.

He goose-stepped his way back into the compound, taunting the guards, and burst into Building 10, ready to show the mandatory twenty-eight days had not diminished his cockiness. He expected a day of routine debriefing, senior officers quizzing him on every aspect of his escape to build their intelligence for the next prisoner who attempted it.

Instead of greeting him, however, his fellow prisoners welcomed him with solemn gazes.

"*Was ist los?*" he said.

"We're preparing for a siege," Leutnant Kurt Müller, a downed bomber pilot, said. He described what had happened during Schumacher's captivity. The camp commander, Lieutenant-Colonel James Mason Taylor, had met with the Lagerführer and Major Kretschmer to inform them he was under orders to restrain sixty of their senior officers. "We are to present them at 1500, but Kretschmer refused, telling him we shall meet force with force. He has ended all communications with Taylor until he relents."

"That's crazy," Schumacher said. "They may not outnumber us now, but they can call in reinforcements."

"Don't let Kretschmer hear you say that." Schumacher didn't need the warning. The man was dangerous.

Schumacher returned to his room, where his bed, one of six grouped in three bunks around the walls, appeared untouched. He changed into a clean uniform, slipped on a pair of boots, and made for the front door.

"Where are you going?" a *Kriegsmarine* prisoner guarding the entrance said.

"I'm touring the grounds. I've been in solitary for four weeks."

"Major Kretschmer says no one must leave."

"I'm just taking a short walk."

"That is an order, Leutnant."

"So we are prisoners in this prison?"

The prisoner, who was equal in rank, scowled without responding. Schumacher retreated, walking back and forth in what had once been a boys' dorm for exercise. After fifteen minutes of this, he prowled the building, searching hallways and closets for the stepladder that would be his key to freedom. He found nothing, returned to his room, and waited for whatever was about to happen.

MARGIE CREPT into the church just before evening Mass. Not Holy Cross, her mother's church. Not Holy Name, where she might run into a neighbor. But St. Johns Church on Kingston Road, a sandstone, gothic structure far enough from home to provide a reasonable chance for anonymity.

As the massive bell in the steeple peeled the call to worship, she picked a pew two rows from the back, kneeled and crossed herself, and took a seat along the aisle, ready for a quick escape if she needed one. The cloying scent of incense returned her to her childhood. The pipe organ's bass notes beat against her chest and reverberated between the marble walls and the terrazzo floor.

She had not set foot in a Catholic church since the priest at Holy Cross had refused to marry them. Brandon was a Protestant; the church would not bless their union unless he converted, and, although he offered, she declined. He had brought enough to this marriage, and she was not about to exact this from him. They married in a small ceremony in the chapel at the Anglican church, just close friends and family in attendance, her mother scowling through the entire fifteen minutes.

Is that when Florence had begun to hate Brandon? No, it was earlier than that. Was it when Florence learned he wasn't Catholic? No, she had taken a dislike to him the moment she discovered he'd spent the war in captivity. "There's still time to reconsider, dear," her mother said on the morning of their wedding. "You can change your mind today, but tomorrow will be too late."

It spoiled the day for her, and their relationship had never recovered. Florence didn't relent. Whenever she found Brandon guilty of some slight, she seized on the moment, telling Margie she "could have done much better." Now, with her two sons gone and Brandon having "abandoned" her, her mother renewed her attacks with a smug aura of self-satisfaction. "I've always had a feeling about him. Mothers are seldom wrong."

For years, Margie had enjoyed her time at Church of the Resurrection, finding in the Anglican faith all the meaning but none of the oppressive cloak of judgment. That ended the Sunday after Brandon's departure for Gravenhurst, when the rector preached a sermon on grief, proclaiming, "God has a reason for everything."

Oh, really? I have lost a husband and both sons, and this is all part of God's plan? Arising, she stalked from the sanctuary, ignoring the stares of fellow worshipers. In the days following, she hung up on the rector twice and refused to answer the door when he paid an unannounced visit.

Now, as the young Catholic priest entered the cavernous sanctuary and intoned the words, "*Introibo ad altare Dei, ad Deum qui lætificat iuventutem meam,*" she wondered what she was doing there. *Same God, same plan.*

But she needed something; she couldn't say what. She had cut herself off from most of her friends—even Bernice Oberholzer, whom she had known since grade school, after she parked herself in the parlor, drank two cups of coffee, and downed muffins as though she hadn't eaten in a week. "I know how you feel," she said.

"No, you don't."

"When I lost my Walter ..."

"He'd suffered two heart attacks before his last one. You had time to prepare. I didn't."

"You have to get over this, Margie. You can't change it. You need to be strong, for yourself and for Brandon."

"Please leave."

"I only meant—"

"Get out."

Beneath the five vaulted arches of the tabernacle, each containing its own arched inset and stained-glass window, the priest turned toward the worshippers and intoned the words, "*Dominus vobiscum.*" The servers responded, "*Et cum spiritu tuo.*"

"Dear Lord, we ask your prayers for the sick and grief-stricken. They have lost so much, and no mere mortal can understand their pain. Only you know their hearts. Only you can comfort them in their hour of need ..."

Margie silently wept, and as the priest continued his words of consolation, a measure of peace settled over her. Her abject loneliness lifted—not disappearing but rising as if she was peaking from beneath a blanket at the thin light seeping into her room on a cold winter morning.

She did not take communion. This was not her parish, and having married outside the church, she was uncertain what the rules were. But she vowed to return.

At Bowmanville, three o'clock came and went, the hour when prisoners assembled on the parade ground for afternoon roll call. Today, no one left the buildings. At four, Kretschmer ordered men in outlying huts to assemble in the kitchen, the only brick building in the camp, bringing anything they could use as weapons. Schumacher grabbed his hockey stick. Others carried poles scrounged from the netting surrounding the vegetable garden. Once inside, they barricaded doors and windows. A smaller group assembled in a large building opposite the kitchen. Still others remained in their huts, ready to mount what resistance they could.

Schumacher watched through cracks in the barricade as Canadian guards strolled the grounds in pairs, rifles at the ready. They had never carried weapons in the past.

At eight o'clock, Schumacher heard vehicles come to a stop outside the fence, followed by loud footsteps and conversation as a force of unknown size entered the camp. Young men, from the sound of their voices, better able to deal with the prisoners than the aging guards.

Minutes passed, then shouting and breaking glass. "They've attacked Building 5," someone called out. "After them."

Schumacher joined the others as they tore down the barrier to burst through the kitchen door, wielding poles and hockey sticks. They advanced on the attacking force but were too late. The Canadians had taken over the building. The prisoners' counterattack sputtered, and they retreated to the kitchen. Moving prep tables, stoves, and even pushing a huge refrigerator into place, they reinforced the entrance.

As darkness descended, the men fed on rumors. Armed troops were coming in from Toronto, bringing machine guns. The Canadians had mustered Norwegian airmen from a training field up north with orders to strafe the building. But there was only silence.

The Canadians cut power to the camp. The men waited in the darkness. At ten o'clock, they heard more reinforcements enter the compound. Pulses quickened. Those who'd found makeshift weapons gripped them.

"Is it all right if I strike a senior officer?" Schumacher asked.

A voice called out, "As long as it's one of theirs." A few quiet chuckles.

"Silence." Kretschmer asserting his authority again.

Instead of a hush, however, the front door groaned as an unknown number of bodies attempted to force it. The door held. Another assault, but it remained shuttered. They heard shouting from outside and the sound of boots retreating. Five minutes passed. Ten. A loud crash as something solid smashed against the entrance. A pause, followed by another onslaught.

"They're battering their way in. Get ready."

One more crash, and the door heaved. The refrigerator toppled over with a thunderous din. The lights came on. Bodies poured through the opening, wielding truncheons. One advanced on Schumacher, who stepped inside his swing and brought the hockey stick down on the young man's shoulder. He shouted in pain. Three more Canadians came at him. Schumacher retreated, along with several companions. Regrouping, they attacked again, only to be forced back.

Schumacher grabbed a heavy pot and hurled it at the Canadians. Others followed his lead. Others threw metal dishes, silverware, glasses, cups—whatever they could lay their hands on. The attackers withdrew, taking several prisoners with them.

As the Germans attended to their injured, the night grew quiet. The metallic odor of blood filled the air while prisoners mopped the floor and their wounds with towels.

At one o'clock, Kretschmer sent out a small reconnaissance force, Schumacher among them, to ransack nearby huts for lumber to reinforce the barricade. They crept toward Building 6, where they had stacked timbers days ago for a raised garden.

Canadian soldiers approached from around the corner of the structure. The two groups looked at each other in surprise, and the soldiers withdrew. The prisoners also retreated. An officer cried out an order. Searchlights in every guard tower homed in on them. The Canadians turned and advanced, wielding truncheons. Schumacher got under one man, hit him in the stomach, kneed him in the groin, took his weapon, and swung at anyone moving. A *Kriegsmarine* officer went down alongside him. As Schumacher reached down to help him, a heavy blow caught his left arm. Stifling a cry of pain and using his good arm, he dragged his fellow officer out of harm's way as men on both sides flailed at each other. Guards in the tower shouted instructions, directing the attack.

Minutes later, it was over for the night, the two sides withdrawing to lick their wounds. A fellow prisoner, a flight doctor, fashioned a splint from a long wooden spoon for Schumacher's fractured left arm.

On Sunday morning, none of the prisoners appeared for roll call. An hour later, a Canadian staff officer advanced, accompanied by a corporal who carried a white flag. He called out for Kretschmer, who appeared with three fellow officers. "Watch me," he said to his companions. "We're going to take them hostage." At his signal, the Germans attacked the two would-be negotiators and subdued them, knowing that the only way the Canadians could retaliate under the Geneva Convention was to put them in detention. As they marched their captors toward the kitchen, a guard in the nearest tower fired toward their feet, the first live rounds used in the fight. The Germans retreated while the Canadians pulled their officers to safety.

For twenty-four hours, the prisoners responded with catcalls and jeers to Taylor's orders to surrender. At eleven o'clock Monday morning, more reinforcements arrived, armed with unloaded rifles with fixed bayonets. The prisoners fought back with bottles, stones, and bricks. The armed men stormed one building after the other, assault guards rushing in first, followed by bayoneted reinforcements.

The fight raged for six more hours as Schumacher lay on the floor of the kitchen. It was the last building to yield. At 10:15 Monday evening, the Veterans Guard conducted roll call. Schumacher joined more than a hundred Germans and Canadians at first aid stations.

Taylor's officers selected sixty uninjured German officers and shackled them. The Battle of Bowmanville was over.

PRESIDENT ROOSEVELT SAT before his desk in the Oval Office and penned a note to Churchill. "I confide my Missus to the care of you and Mrs. Churchill," he began. After two years of wishing and many dashed plans, Eleanor was about to embark on a trip to England to visit areas of the war-torn country devastated by the Blitz. She would meet with King George VI and Queen Mary, the Churchills, and General Dwight D. Eisenhower.

"I know our better halves will hit it off beautifully," Roosevelt wrote. After finishing the letter and hand addressing it, he wheeled himself into the family theater, a converted cloakroom in the East Wing where the president watched newsreels, his beloved cartoons, and, with invited guests, Hollywood films.

Tonight, on the eve of Eleanor's departure for New York on the first leg of her month-long journey, they and fifteen family guests watched *The Adventures of Tom Sawyer*, after which they dined on cook Henrietta Nesbitt's interpretation of poached salmon, rosemary roasted potatoes, and winter squash. Mrs. Nesbitt had been a member of the Roosevelt staff for years, time enough to ruin every dish she set her mind to. Tonight the "poached" salmon was boiled, the potatoes charred, and the squash squashed.

Ignoring another of the cook's celebrated failures, the guests raised glasses of champagne to toast Eleanor and wish her success on her visit.

The president held the glass to his mouth, allowing the bubbles to tickle his nostrils.

"How goes the war, Mr. President?" Louise Hopkins, seated at his right where she could access his good ear, had married his friend and advisor, Harry Hopkins, months before in the White House study.

Hopkins, secretary of commerce prior to the war, had been one of the New Deal architects, supervised the Lend-Lease program providing military aid to Great Britain and Russia, and now functioned as Roosevelt's *de facto* secretary of state. He was so close to the president that the couple lived in private quarters in the Executive Mansion, an arrangement at which Louise chafed.

Her husband was no more open-mouthed than Roosevelt, and Louise, a former editor of *Harper's Bazaar*, was an inquisitive journalist. "How are we doing?"

"The Russians have beaten back the Germans at Stalingrad," Roosevelt replied. "I foresee a long winter for them."

"But our forces? When will we engage?"

Roosevelt smiled. "Soon, I hope, and when we do, it will be something to remember."

Louise pushed a bit more, but Roosevelt gave no hint of what was to come. At that moment, General Mark Clark was on his way to Algeria to persuade the Vichy French to lay down their arms once the invasion commenced. At Hampton Roads, General George Patton's soldiers were boarding troop ships as the Navy's Task Force 34 prepared to embark for Operation Torch.

But the president could say none of this. The assault, in which 107,000 men would storm ashore in Morocco and Algeria, was shrouded in the strictest secrecy the military had ever imposed. And despite his hopes that General Marshall could move the date forward, the landings would not come until after the Congressional elections on November 3.

The public's perception of inaction in Europe, coupled with the rationing of staples like sugar, gasoline, and fuel oil, would threaten the Democratic majority in both the House and Senate. The narrow margin would increase the pressure from isolationist Republicans and those in his own party who feared losing their seats in 1944.

Then there was Stalin. So far, the Soviet Union was fighting alone against Hitler, and "Uncle Joe" was enraged at the postponement of a second front. Neither Churchill nor Roosevelt had informed their Russian counterpart of the impending invasion in North Africa. When it came, would it be enough to assuage him?

Roosevelt had lofty plans for the postwar period, determined that this would become, as The Great War had not, a war to end all wars. He needed Stalin's cooperation.

As his wife boarded her 11:30 train to New York City, the thirty-second President of the United States had a great deal on his mind.

GERMAN OFFICERS at Gravenhurst also resisted the order to handcuff them, but their opposition was less confrontational. Their Lager-führer, Major Kuno Fischer, stood at attention as he quoted Article 2 of the Geneva Convention: "Prisoners shall at all times be humanely treated and protected ... Measures of reprisal against them are forbidden. Furthermore," he said, quoting Article 9, "They shall not be confined or imprisoned except as a measure indispensable for safety or health."

"Thank you, Major," Wallingford said. "I am well aware of the terms of the agreement. I assume your own government is as well, yet your officials have violated the terms by shackling our senior officers. My orders are to follow their example until such time as they abide by the agreement, nothing more."

With that, the German officers lined up in the long first-floor corridor of the main building, their backs against the wall and their hands behind them. Armitage followed the example of his fellow guards, placing their hands on the shoulders of each officer and turning him around. The Germans offered little resistance until Armitage approached a major. As he prepared to turn the officer around, he said, "Get your filthy hands off me."

"I order you to turn and face the wall with your hands behind you," Armitage said.

"I am a senior German officer. I refuse to submit."

Other guards clustered around the pair, wondering how this new guard would handle the situation. "Leave him for the moment," Lieutenant Morrison said. "Let's get the rest of them shackled before others get the same idea."

Armitage and three other guards completed the task while Morrison and another lieutenant looked on. When they'd finished, Armitage returned to the major, whose name, he learned, was Leon Wilhelm. "I order you to face the wall," he said.

The major raised his head, jutted out his jaw, but said nothing.

"I am ordering you one last time," Armitage said, his voice louder and deeper than before.

"Perhaps I should ...," Lieutenant Morrison began, but Armitage had already acted, sweeping his weak leg across the man's ankles and sending him sprawling on the floor.

As he reached down, grasping the major's hands and slapping cuffs on him, he heard Morrison gasp. "We don't treat our prisoners like that," he said.

"I gave him four chances to comply," Armitage replied. "We had to carry out Colonel Wallington's order, didn't we?" He reached down and helped the German to his feet. He seemed no worse for wear.

"We did," the lieutenant said. "Good work."

His fellow guards clapped Armitage on the back as they left the building. "Wilhelm has given us nothing but trouble since he arrived. He got what was coming to him," one said.

The following morning, the camp commandant summoned Armitage to his office. He saluted and suppressed a smile, relaxing in an at-ease posture, ready to accept accolades for subduing one of the most obstreperous prisoners, a Wehrmacht major who had refused to submit.

"Stand at attention, Sergeant." Armitage did as instructed, wondering about Wallington's stern tone. "I want your version of yesterday's events."

My version? "You ordered us to shackle the prisoners, sir. We did so."

"I'm referring to your altercation with Major Wilhelm."

"Altercation? I merely—"

"Stand at attention, Sergeant."

Armitage drew himself up to his full height, doing his best to straighten his right leg. He puffed out his chest, presenting a caricature of a private in a recruiting film. "We had no issues with most of the officers, *sir*. But Major Wilhelm resisted, *sir*. He clasped his arms across his chest and refused to turn around, *sir*. When Lieutenant Morrison asked me to shackle him, I gave him four chances to obey the order, *sir*."

"The other guards say you kicked his legs out from under him. Is that so?"

"Only after I tried to gain his cooperation, *sir*."

"When you signed up, we gave you a copy of the Geneva convention and told you to study it. Is that not correct?"

"Yes, sir."

"And in that document, you read instructions on how to treat prisoners, did you not?"

"Sir, Major Wilhelm refused to—"

"I asked you a question, Sergeant."

"Yes, sir," Armitage said, dropping the mocking emphasis. "But Major Wilhelm—"

"Major Wilhelm is in the medical center this morning, suffering headaches and dizziness. You gave him a concussion."

"Sir, with your permission ..."

"Go ahead."

"I believe he's faking, sir. His head never hit the wall. He threw out his arms to cushion his fall."

"You may be correct, Sergeant, but you were out of line and have created a *cause célèbre*." Armitage slumped. "I have no choice but to reassign you to a position in which you have no contact with the prisoners."

"But, sir—"

"Dismissed, Sergeant."

He had been at Gravenhurst for less than a week and, at that moment, considered packing his kit and boarding the next train to Toronto. Only his desire to get even held him back.

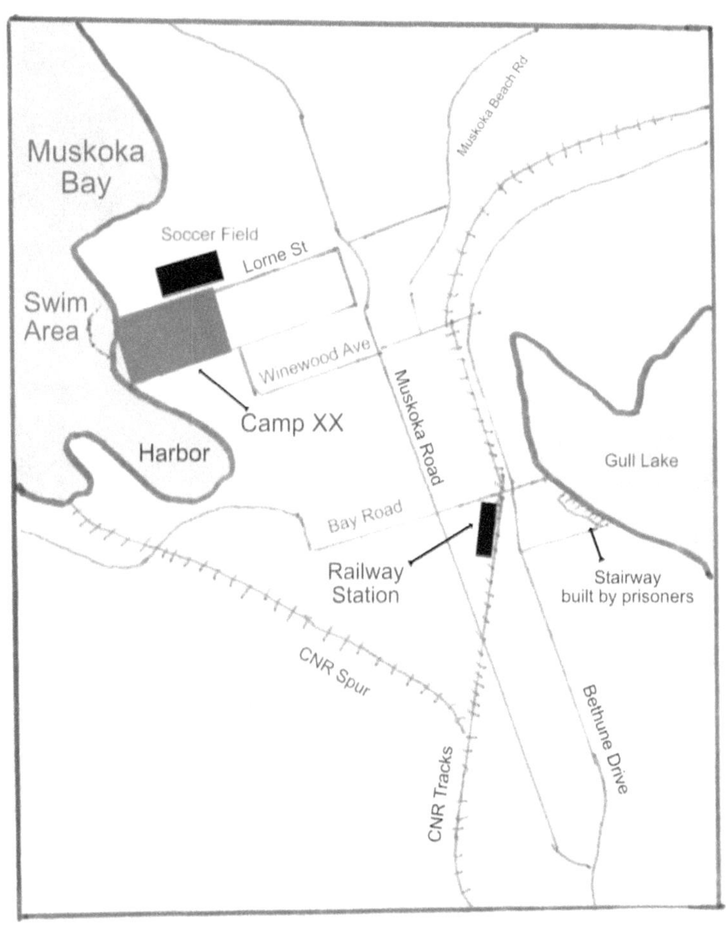

Gravenhurst - 1943

4

NOVEMBER 6-13, 1942

Lieutenant Morrison found Armitage a desk job at headquarters, outside the perimeter and as far from the detention center, barracks, and mess hall as one could get and still be within the camp. For three weeks, he recorded the delivery of clothing, food, and supplies for the quartermaster. Then Morrison read his record and discovered that he had spent three years as a prisoner of war.

"You speak German?" the lieutenant asked.

"I'm rusty, but yes, I speak, read, and write it."

The officer reassigned him to censor incoming and outgoing prisoner mail. The work was tedious. From the prisoners, endless assurances to parents, wives, and girlfriends that the writer was well. From home, scattered tidbits, all upbeat, the German censors having already excised any hint of negativity.

His sole diversion was uncovering bits of code concealed in the letters. *Sie geben zu viel Wurst in die Suppe*, one read.

"Sergeant Crowell," Armitage said, "does the mess serve sausage in the prisoners' soup?"

"What?"

"I thought not. Leutnant Moser is telling his wife we overdo it. 'They put too much sausage in the soup.' I wonder what that means?"

"Maybe she wants sausage and can't get any. *Gib mir deine Wurst*." Crowell called out in a loud falsetto. "*Bitte, Bitte*," he said, accompanying it with a series of deep-throated moans. Everyone but Armitage guffawed. He blacked out the curious passage and moved on.

The odd message stuck with him, and he'd found a few others, but neither Morrison nor anyone else seemed to care.

Daisy Suckley was overjoyed when Roosevelt invited her to join him, friends Catherine and Margaret Hambley, Harry and Louise Hopkins, and his secretary, Grace Tully, at Shangri-La for the weekend. She enjoyed the presidential retreat and reveled at being in Franklin's presence.

The Congressional elections three days before had been, if not a bloodbath, a profound disappointment. With Eleanor still in England, Daisy assumed Franklin wanted nothing more than to get away from it all for a few days. As they entered *The Sunshine Special* for the drive into the Catoctin Mountains that first Friday in November, however, Roosevelt said, "We may have to return early. The hen is about to lay an egg."

Tossing back her dark curls, she giggled. "Who is the hen, and what is the egg?"

"We shall see, Daisy. We shall see." He said nothing more for nearly an hour, staring out the window of the limousine as though lost in thought.

When they arrived, rather than relaxing before the fire with the others, Franklin retired to his bedroom, where he and Harry Hopkins spent the late evening sequestered.

"Does it seem to you," Daisy asked Louise Hopkins, "that there's more than the usual degree of security this evening?"

"I hadn't noticed," the former journalist replied.

"There are just—I don't know—more men around."

"Nothing wrong with that." The two women laughed, though both knew there was only one man in Daisy's life.

The president reappeared without explaining why he'd left his guests alone, and the three couples gathered in the dining room for a dinner of grouse caught on the compound that very day. As Daisy picked at the delicate white meat, savoring every bite, Secret Service agent Mike Reilly entered the room. "Remain inside and stay away from the windows, please. We've spotted two armed men on the perimeter."

Daisy's fork clattered to her plate, but Roosevelt gave her a reassuring pat on her arm. "Not to worry. Mike and the boys have things well in hand."

As they resumed dining, Roosevelt said to his guests, "Eleanor's visit has been a complete triumph. She's visited with royalty, heads of state, and our generals. She's charmed them all."

Daisy knew that even the *Chicago Tribune* had good things to say about the first lady's trip. Eleanor had visited enlisted men down to army privates, including a company of black GIs, a fact the southern press had not reported. She'd met with children in day nurseries and with victims of the German bombings.

"Just today," Roosevelt continued, "Londoners lined up—or queued, as they say—outside the American Embassy just to get a glimpse of her. The press is eating it up." This, Daisy knew, did her friend good after the disappointing election results.

Reilly reappeared, wearing what passed among the agents as a smile. "You can relax. We have the pair in custody. We're questioning them now."

Before the president could bite into his dessert, an aide called him to the phone, and Hopkins followed him from the room.

"What's going on?" Daisy asked Louise.

"I have no idea. I've learned not to ask."

"But something," she said.

"Something. We will know in the fullness of time."

When the pair returned five minutes later, neither gave a hint what the call was about. The president lit a cigarette and blew the \ smoke across the table, ignoring the bowl of ice cream that had now melted into a milky slurry.

The agent reappeared and whispered into his right ear. Roosevelt reared back and laughed. "It turns out our armed invaders are a pair of local teenagers hunting skunks. I daresay they could find more in Washington than up here."

The group joined in the laughter and raised their glasses to salute the secret service. Nothing more was said about the frequent interruptions, and if there were more phone calls later, Daisy slept through them, lulled by the crisp, clear mountain air.

The following morning, Roosevelt failed to appear for breakfast, once more leaving his guests in the dark. Hopkins kept popping in and out of his bedroom without explanation. Even after he joined the group at mid-morning, the president and Hopkins would leave the guests whenever a new telephone call summoned them.

As night fell on Saturday, Roosevelt joined his guests for a dinner of musk ox, which his son, Elliott, had brought back from a trip to Greenland while scouting for potential air bases. FDR glanced at his watch every few minutes, stroking his forehead with his fingers. He did not conceal his anxiety, but when Daisy asked him what was wrong, he waved her away without responding.

At nine o'clock, he said, "It's time. Follow me into the living room." Daisy led the way as an aide turned on a radio.

"Something's about to break," the president said with a mischievous grin. They waited in anticipation, only Hopkins and Tully aware of what was about to come.

Midway through a piece of dance music, an announcer interrupted with a news bulletin. Turning to the guests with a triumphant smile, Roosevelt said, "That's it. We have landed in North Africa. We are striking back."

Operation Torch, as Daisy was later to hear it called, was underway.

Brandon Armitage raised his glass of Carling Black Label and clicked it with Corporal Smith's. It was seven o'clock on Sunday night, and the pair had downed pork chops at Sloan's Restaurant before heading to the beer hall for a round. "Next one's on me," Smith called over a couple quarreling at an adjoining table.

"I'm only good for one tonight. I have letters to get through."

Smith stared into his glass for a moment. "How's it going?"

"Not so bad," Armitage said. "It beats booking lard, flour, and boxes of salt pork." On this bitter Sunday night, with a wind whipping snow off Georgian Bay, Smith drained his glass. "You're sure I can't get you another to celebrate the invasion?"

"Not for me, thanks, but go ahead. I'll keep you company."

Smith ordered a second beer while Armitage settled for a glass of water. "You're staying, eh?"

"Yes," he said without elaborating. Only Smith knew how close he'd come to resigning. He was not essential here; thousands of veterans had applied to join the guard, far more than were needed. But he'd kept his rank and still hoped to avenge the loss of his sons.

And there was Margie. Since his arrival, he had called her twice a week, but he had not returned home. They had last seen each other the morning after Thanksgiving, which they shared with two middle-aged couples from their church. It had been a subdued affair, for no one wanted to raise the most obvious topic—the absence of the two Armitage boys.

Their phone conversations were banal. Margie would tell of a film she'd seen with a friend—*The Magnificent Ambersons* was a recent favorite. "We came in late so I wouldn't have to hear Lorne Greene narrate one of those dreadful war shorts."

They avoided anything of consequence. If she still blamed him for their sons' fates—Armitage could not bring himself to think of Henry as dead—she didn't say so, but neither had she apologized. She gave him her civility, and that was enough. The closest they got to discussing anything of substance came one evening when he complained of the early sub-freezing temperatures. "I regret you have to do this," she said.

"I'm sorry for what war has done to both of us—this war and the last. You—*we've* both given so much."

He heard her sharp intake of breath. "Things never work out how you plan them. We just have to take what we are given."

"Each other. War has given us each other. That's something."

"Yes," she said, "I suppose so."

He told her he loved her. She told him to take care of himself. He contented himself with what she offered.

"When are you going to take leave and see your wife?" Corporal Smith asked. "I go home every other weekend."

"She's fine. She has her mother and a circle of friends to keep her company." Armitage was not about to confide that he didn't know how to handle his wife's grief and feared his presence would rekindle her anger.

They walked back to camp, the snow blinding them. Armitage returned to his office and the last of a stack of letters that had appeared in his in-box Saturday afternoon. Sighing, he opened the first. More banalities. Several to parents assuring them the writer was in good health. A letter to a girlfriend bragging about how fit he was. Another note gave him a moment's pause. "Most of the Canadians are kind and respectful. One is a complete bastard, but Major Wilhelm got rid of him."

Report me, prick! Armitage crossed out the latter sentence, allowing the first to stand. He yawned and stretched, the words on the pages dancing before his eyes. Three letters remained. Two were unremarkable. He read each twice, searching for anything hidden between the lines, but found nothing. The last caught his attention. "Today's news is but a temporary setback. *Der Fuchs wird sie ins Meer treiben.*" The fox will drive them into the sea.

This letter had arrived on his desk hours before last night's CBC bulletin announcing the North African landings. Armitage leaned back, running a hand through his thinning hair. *How the hell did he find out before we did?*

He needed to get back in touch with these men. He spent the night considering how he might redeem himself.

ALONG WITH FIFTEEN OTHER PRISONERS, Jörg Schumacher was herded aboard an unheated railway car in the middle of the night. Its windows were painted over to keep them from studying their surroundings and barred to prevent their escape. As though anyone would be foolish enough to make a run for it in the darkness of night, in the middle of nowhere, with the temperature hovering close to zero.

An hour after leaving Bowmanville, they felt the engine decouple them. They waited as locomotives moved back and forth along adjoining tracks, sounding deep-throated ricochets as they coupled cars together. Toronto, he thought. Another hour passed before they were jolted awake as they were hitched to another engine. Their car moved out of the switching yard in what Schumacher sensed was either a westerly or northerly direction—certainly not the way they had come. They rolled and jostled for two hours more before their car creaked to a halt. Armed guards opened the door and herded them onto a concrete apron before a train depot. A sign below its twin pitched roofs read Gravenhurst.

Schumacher pulled his leather flight jacket around the sling on his left arm as he stepped from the carriage onto the platform. Dawn tickled the eastern horizon. A lone eagle soared far above, searching for its breakfast among the rabbits and rodents emerging from their burrows.

"Move along," a Canadian sergeant said. "Into the terminal. You'll wait there until the camp guards arrive."

Schumacher and the rest of the prisoners obeyed the instructions and entered the long, heated room. "Where are we?" he asked.

"Gravenhurst," the sergeant responded.

"Ja, but where is that?"

"*Stille.*" Schumacher was among a group of suspected instigators of the Bowmanville insurrection who the Canadians had transferred to other camps. He had welcomed the change, hoping it would afford new escape opportunities and leave Major Kretschmer behind. Instead, he found the Nazi barking at him.

"I was just—"

"*Halt die Klappe,*" Kretschmer ordered. Shut up.

The sergeant watched the pair bicker and made his choice. "You're about a hundred miles due north of Toronto, at the south end of Lake Muskoka."

"Ja," Schumacher said, as though that made things clear. Cocking his head, he looked out the window toward the town that lay in monochrome hues in the thin morning light. "They've told towns-people to stay away," the sergeant said in response to Schumacher's unasked question. Recalling the catcalls that had greeted him when he'd first arrived at Bowmanville, he decided it was the Canadians' attempt at establishing goodwill.

He felt a hand on his shoulder, and Kretschmer steered him away from the sergeant, shoving him against a wall, alongside a window that looked out on the street. A movement caught his eye. He turned to find a young woman staring at him. She could not have been over eighteen, with chestnut hair and pale green eyes. Schumacher smiled at her, and she withdrew from her side of the window in shock. He smiled again. This time, she returned it.

"Turn around and leave her alone," Kretschmer ordered.

Schumacher stood erect, half a head taller than the major, and stared at him with open contempt. Turning toward the window, he winked at the girl. Though he could not hear her, he saw her giggle, lower her eyes, and blush.

A dun-colored jeep pulled alongside the building, forestalling whatever Kretschmer was about to say. Four armed guards piled out, surrounded the captives, and marched them up Second Street to Brock, past shops still shuttered against the early morning cold. Several prisoners chatted among themselves, making disparaging remarks about the small town. A laugh rang out as someone told a joke about two German farmers arguing over the provenance of a one-eyed piglet.

Schumacher watched Kretschmer stare straight ahead, taking no part in the banter. *Is humor verboten among party members?* He let the thought pass, scanning the pharmacy and other businesses as they were herded north onto Muskoka Road. They passed a row of wood-framed houses, weathered from rain, snow, and wind. His eyes took in the spaces separating each structure, the position of every overhead light, and the names of cross streets.

At Winewood Avenue, they turned left toward a body of water several blocks away, then right again—north, he was sure—on Austin Street. Schumacher recorded every street and turn as he formed a mental map.

Another four blocks to Lorne Street, where they turned left again toward the bay and entered the compound, ringed by a high barbed wire fence with guard towers at regular intervals, then toward a sprawling facility of some sort, perhaps a hospital. Its sloped roof shed the snow that now lay knee-deep, an easy drop from any of the windows. Ice covered the shoreline, a forlorn watchtower overlooking it.

Schumacher studied it all. Over the wall, under the wall, or through it. Those were the options. One of them would work. No place was escape-proof. As long as a person could enter, there was also a way out. It was his job—his *duty*—to find the pregnability of this camp and exploit it. He would begin after breakfast.

───────

"I CONFESS to Almighty God and to you, Father, that I have sinned." Margie sat on her side of the dark oaken confessional, her head bowed. She kept her blue woolen coat buttoned and wore her gray scarf and gloves against the frigid November morning that had followed her into St. Johns.

"My last confession was ..." She struggled to recall how long it had been. From the opposite side of the screen, she heard the priest breathing as he waited. It was the only sound within the sanctuary. Even silence echoed against the marble walls.

"It has been two decades, Father ... and more. A long time ... I can't recall." She took a deep breath before racing on. "Since then, I have committed a mortal sin. I have dishonored my mother. She doesn't like my husband and constantly criticizes him. I overreact. I shout at her. I've even wished ..."

She didn't complete the thought. "I apologize to her, but when next she starts on me, I react again. Also, Father, I married outside the church. My husband is a good man, but he isn't a Catholic. We were wed in a Protestant church, and I worshipped there until a month ago, when I started attending St. Johns. I've attended faithfully ever since, but I am not of this parish. I don't even know if you can hear my confession."

"It is perfectly acceptable, my child. God does not care who hears your confession or where you make it. What is important is that you do so. Please continue."

Margie trotted out a host of venial sins, most involving envy. No greed. No lust. She stopped short of anything that had occurred since losing her sons, uncertain whether her reactions constituted sins. Was she unjust to resent her country, even God, for taking from her all she loved? Others were enduring similar pain, but she hadn't reached out to them, thinking only of herself. Was that wrong?

The priest waited without speaking. Did he sense there was more on her mind? "For these and all the sins I have committed during my life, I am deeply sorry."

He gave her a penance of three Hail Marys and three Our Fathers, and told her to sin no more. His voice was warm, sympathetic, almost as though he shared her pain at having to confess. Her penance didn't seem like much, but she accepted it dutifully.

"These are difficult times," he said. "In our despair, we decide that God has abandoned us, tempting us to wander. But He is here. He mourns the loss of decency in this world. He asks us to keep the faith and do what we can to create peace—within ourselves and in those around us."

Never had a priest spoken to her in such a personal, heartfelt way. She felt he knew her other secrets, sensed what was in her heart.

"I absolve you of your sins."

Margie crossed herself.

"Give thanks to the Lord for He is good."

Through choked tears, she said. "For His mercy endures forever."

She left the confessional, knelt, crossed herself again, recited her penance, and departed with a lighter step than when she had entered.

Roosevelt returned to Washington Sunday night in a buoyant mood, as though he had emerged from a fog of worry. Throughout Monday, news reports showed the landings were going well, and on Tuesday, he met with the press.

When a reporter asked if he could reveal anything about "the planning and execution of this African expedition," Roosevelt joked, "I discussed it with two or three people this morning. It probably will come to you secondhand, so I might as well make it firsthand."

After basking in their laughter, he told them he and Churchill had met in Washington two weeks after Pearl Harbor to discuss what joint military action they might undertake. Logistical concerns had ruled out an immediate cross-Channel assault, but at another meeting in June, they settled on North Africa.

"You know that many of my Congressional critics have been pushing for a second front. Mr. Churchill and I have had to sit quiet and take it with a smile—or perhaps you might say take it on the chin —as to what all the outsiders were demanding."

"Mr. President, can you tell us why the date for the invasion wasn't set for before the election?" a reporter asked.

"Jimmy," he said, referring to Justice James Byrnes, head of the Office of Economic Stabilization, "said if we had been smart, we would have recalled that I shifted Thanksgiving Day one week ahead. Why, therefore, didn't I shift the election date to one week later?" The journalists laughed, but Roosevelt didn't reveal he had pleaded as much to Marshall. The need for silence had cost his party forty-four seats in the House, nine in the Senate, and several governorships—an election not helped by the announcement a few days beforehand that coffee was about to be rationed.

Roosevelt jollied his way through the rest of the press conference, silently counting his days to the end of the week, when his private railway car would carry him away from the viper's nest that was post-election Washington to Hyde Park.

Before then, he had one last task to complete. On November 11, enduring his ten-pound leg braces, Roosevelt stood on the steps of the Memorial Amphitheater at Arlington National Cemetery to deliver his Armistice Day address. Although the temperature was in the high forties, it was a blustery day. The president stood draped in a long woolen overcoat alongside General John "Black Jack" Pershing, commander of the American Expeditionary Forces in World War I, covered in a coat that reached his ankles and whose collar encircled his throat. The pair watched as forty-eight servicemen bore US flags, fluttering in the northwest wind, into the amphitheater. An honor guard laid a wreath at the base of the neoclassical white marble sarcophagus containing the remains of the Unknown Soldier.

"Today, as on all Armistice Days since 1918," the president said, "we remember with gratitude the bravery of the men who fought and helped to win that fight against German militarism. But this year, our thoughts are also very much of the living present and of the future which we see opening before us—a picture illumined by a new light of hope."

With the fall colors receding and the White House and Capitol standing before them across the Potomac, the president said, "Germany and Japan, opponents of decency, face inevitable, final defeat. The forces of liberation are advancing. Britain, Russia, China, and the United States grow rapidly to full strength."

Directing his message to the French as well as to the American public, he told the crowd, "We are fighting on French soil, joined by the fighting men of our traditional ally, France. On this day, of all days, it is heartening to know that soldiers of France go forward with the United Nations."

Lowering his face and taking on a somber tone, he concluded, "God, the Father of all living, watches over these hallowed graves and blesses the souls of those who rest there. May He keep us strong in the courage that will win this war, and may he impart to us the wisdom and the vision that we shall need for true victory in the peace which is to come."

The peace which is to come. That was Roosevelt's preoccupation as he traveled north the following day. He envisioned the world beyond the war, a world in which a few international leaders, led by the United States, would restore and maintain tranquility.

He knew not all his partners would accede to his vision. Both Churchill and Stalin would resist. But as he took refuge at his home along the Hudson River that cold weekend, Franklin Roosevelt was determined to win them over.

5

DECEMBER 22-28, 1942

Président Roosevelt had retired by the time Canadian Prime Minister William Lyon Mackenzie King arrived at the White House on December 4. He was shown into a guest room for the night, and in the morning, the president summoned him into his living quarters. The Canadian leader found his friend sitting up in bed, wearing a gray sweater, smoking, with newspapers strewn around him.

"Good morning, Mr. President," King said. As Roosevelt reached out his hand, the prime minister could not help but notice the tremor in his arm and the gray cast to his skin.

In 1935, shortly after King took over from the conservative government of Prime Minister R. B. Bennett, Roosevelt invited him to the White House. While King, who'd earned a doctorate in economics from Harvard, considered the New Deal dangerous policy, the two had known each other for years and renewed a warm bond. Roosevelt declared at dinner on the second day of King's visit that he was "an old personal friend."

Since Winston Churchill had taken the reins in Great Britain, King had come to serve as their go-between, helping to bridge differences in the Atlantic Alliance. This morning, with the wind making it seem colder than the thirty-three-degree temperature, King said,

"That's good news from Tunisia. We appear to have Rommel's forces on the run."

"We're making progress on Guadalcanal, too," Roosevelt replied, "but that's not why I asked to see you. We need to begin thinking of the world after the peace."

King pulled his armchair closer to the president's bed. "We call our alliance the 'United Nations,' and indeed we are, but I envision a time when the United Nations will formalize our agreement and bring lasting peace to the world."

As King listened, interrupting his friend with an occasional question, Roosevelt outlined a design for an international organization, led by a "security council" composed of the four powers that would dominate the post-war world—Great Britain, the Soviet Union, China, and the United States.

"Sumner Welles and I have been working on this for more than a month."

"What does Churchill think of the idea?" King asked.

"Oh, you know our Winston." Roosevelt stared out the bedroom window as he spoke. "He thinks I'm getting ahead of myself. He wrote me, 'We should not overlook Mrs. Glass's Cookery Book recipe for a jugged hare: First catch your hare.'"

The president laughed at Churchill's joke, but his chortling collapsed into a coughing fit that brought King out of his chair. Roosevelt waved him away. "It's just the onset of a cold," he assured him. "It will pass."

To King it sounded more ominous.

"I'm going to share a secret," Roosevelt said when his coughing subsided. "You're to tell no one about this until it happens. Winston and I are meeting next month in North Africa. I'm going to lay all this out for him. I'm sure I can bring him around."

King doubted their British ally could be so easily manipulated.

"Now that we're in it," Roosevelt continued, "I'm not going to risk the lives of American boys to protect English and French empires."

The prime minister held his counsel. He would speak with Churchill and gauge the distance between the two.

"I cabled Stalin two weeks ago, asking him to join us," Roosevelt said, "but he doesn't feel able to leave his armies with the expulsion of the Germans so near at hand."

"He's important to the alliance," King said. "Nothing will happen without him."

"I dream dreams. You know that. I'm convinced the essential first step to peace is total disarmament of the aggressor nations. We must follow this by day and night inspections of that disarmament and a police power to stop any evasion of the rules."

King agreed. "We tried doing this without a means of enforcement. We're living with the result."

"The Versailles Treaty was a mistake," Roosevelt said. "We can't repeat it. There will be no negotiation with Germany or Japan. No chance for them to cheat. The only way to end international aggression is to strip them of their ability to wage war."

With that, he laid out an end-of-war strategy in two words—"unconditional surrender"—a phrase Mackenzie King was the first, outside the president's tight-knit circle, to hear.

The letter Brandon Armitage held in his hands intrigued him. Hours before, the CBC had reported German forces had begun a chaotic retreat from the Caucasus. Operation Winter Storm, the effort to reinforce General Paulus's Sixth Army at Stalingrad, had failed. The news had broken too late for the *Toronto Daily Star* to carry it. Yet the day before, a Luftwaffe lieutenant had written to his parents. "I hear things are bad for us at Millerovo. I pray daily for Helmut's safe return." Armitage blackened the first sentence, leaving the second.

He stared out the window for a moment, watching the snow outline the muntins. Reaching a decision, he placed a copy of the letter in a manila folder that contained several others he had been collecting. The commandant's office censored incoming news reports, a holdover from earlier days when things were going poorly for the Allies. But the news was somehow finding its way to the prisoners.

Armitage made the slow, step-by-step climb to the second level, his uneven footsteps echoing in the concrete stairway. The adjutant sat behind a sparse metal desk outside the lieutenant's office. "Request permission to speak to Lieutenant Morrison," Armitage said. "I have something he should see."

"He's quite busy, I'm afraid. What is this urgent business?"

Armitage laid out what he suspected, and the adjutant quickly ushered him into the lieutenant's office.

"This morning, the CBC reported Soviet troops were withdrawing from the middle Don," Armitage said. "But Leutnant Shriver wrote this to his parents a day earlier." He displayed the letter which, since his superior officer was monolingual, might have been written in Braille.

"On December 11, he referred to Rommel's withdrawal from El Agheila, but we didn't learn that until the following day." Armitage presented three more examples that showed prisoners were getting war information from an outside source.

"And your conclusion?" Morrison said.

"The prisoners have a radio, sir."

"We know they have a still somewhere. They make their own vodka using potatoes from their garden. It's quite acceptable," he said with a trace of a smile. "Since submarine radio operators are spending their prolonged vacations with us, it's not unlikely they've pieced together the components for a receiver."

The lieutenant removed his glasses and massaged the bridge of his nose. "Given the disruption caused by handcuffing their officers, I question whether it's worth a search. What harm does it do?"

"My concern is that if they can receive signals from Germany, it's only a small step for them to transmit."

Seeing the look of doubt cross the face of his superior officer, Armitage backtracked. "Perhaps that's more difficult. But if they are receiving radio signals on troop movements, they may also be getting instructions."

The lieutenant drummed on his desk with the eraser end of a pencil. "You may be on to something, Sergeant. Lieutenant-Colonel

Wallington has mentioned similarities in the pattern of resistance at all the camps—before we'd even issued the orders to manacle the officers, they were exchanging uniforms with lower ranks; and each Lagerführer used similar wording when refusing to comply. He suspects they had advance knowledge."

Morrison rose from his chair and stared out the window. "I need to consult with the commandant about the best course. We don't want to cause unnecessary upset. This is excellent work, Sergeant."

Armitage suppressed a smile. "Thank you, sir."

He returned to his ground-floor office, basking in the praise. Should he seek permission to resume contact with the prisoners—a *mea culpa*, an abject apology, and a promise to do better?

No, not yet. He'd done well to keep his mouth shut. Armitage would bide his time and await the right moment.

Schumacher spent his first few days at Gravenhurst exploring the compound and its surroundings. The four hundred prisoners were housed in three buildings enclosed by a barbed wire fence. High-ranking officers occupied the large three-story building, the main detention center, where he found a crude sign painted on the basement wall, "*Herzlich Willkommen Deutsche Soldaten*," Hearty Welcome, German Soldiers. The Canadians were attempting to be civil, he thought. The building was bright, airy, and well heated.

The two other buildings were the recreation and mess hall and a smaller barracks for prisoners of lower ranks. It was as he strolled through the lower level of this building that someone shouted, "*Offizier Sorglos.* "Schumacher turned, beaming as he heard his nickname, Officer Happy-Go-Lucky.

"*Faulpelz*." he responded. Lazybones.

Schumacher had flown with Christoph Helbig before the war; Hermann Göring had pinned their wings on during the same ceremony. Schumacher held his friend at arm's length. The left side of his face was rough and an ugly red, as though it had been blistered.

"Fire," he said. "They shot me down over Dover. I was fortunate to crash into the sea. Otherwise ..." Helbig didn't finish the sentence. "And you?"

Schumacher raised his left arm out of the sling. "We had a little misunderstanding with the guards at Bowmanville when they handcuffed our senior officers. It's coming off tomorrow." He described the pitched battle that had led to his transfer and that of other dissidents.

"Before the Canadians ordered the restraints," Helbig said, "our senior officers exchanged uniforms with us. I was a major for a day or two, and they shackled me. We picked the locks on the handcuffs and hid them. We'll find a use for them. Many of the guards aren't too bright."

"Veterans of the last war. We had the same type at Bowmanville."

"They're pretty easygoing, most of them. One bastard tried to throw his weight around two months ago, but I think they got rid of him."

They stood together in the cold hallway, trading news about their families. Helbig had a young wife and child at home, while Schumacher had never settled down. There would be time for that after victory. "And your father," Helbig said, "still serving in Norway?"

"*Ja.* He loves it there, and so does my mother since she's Norwegian." Schumacher's father was a captain in the German army, serving on the general staff of the *Oberkommando der Wehrmacht*. He had tried without success to persuade his son to join the *Heer*, arguing that flying was unsafe. He was right, of course, but at the moment, nothing was safe.

"But why are you down here in this cold barracks rather than in the officer's quarters?" Schumacher asked.

"There was no room there when I arrived. Now ... let's just say I'm more comfortable where I am."

Helbig took his friend on a tour of the compound, his walk off-kilter. "Life isn't bad here. We have football and other sports, theater, music, arts, and reading. You can attend classes if you like, learn English or French, although my French is better than these English-speaking Canadians."

Walking as close to the perimeter as the snowdrifts allowed, Schumacher found that the compound resembled an arrow pointed west, with a guard tower at each corner. The north, south and east fences formed three sides of a rectangle, while two angled barriers to the west overlooked Muskoka Bay.

Reaching the southwest corner of the enclosure, they peered through the fence and across a ravine separating the camp from the bay. A seventh guard tower overlooked it. "Did I tell you we go swimming in the summer? You can't see it now, but a boom fence extends into the bay. We built a stairway at the end of Lorne Street to make it easier to get down to the beach."

He led Schumacher to the eastern edge of the enclosure, to what looked like a small skating rink. "They let us build a fishpond, iced over now. In summer, we grow our own vegetables. The potatoes aren't like home, but the green vegetables taste better."

They continued up the macadam road toward the entrance, flanked by a gatehouse and sentry post. As they neared the main entrance, Helbig said, "There's a hockey rink outside the fence, where we play football in the spring and summer. A guard tower overlooks it."

The prisoner's mess lay just west of the gate, close to the fence. Schumacher strolled around it, his arms behind him as though he were out for morning exercise. The corner of the long building was in full view of both the sentry post and guard tower. Beyond it, Helbig's barracks could also be seen from the guard tower, but its northwest corner lay close to the fence.

"I see why you prefer to stay down here rather than the officers' quarters," Schumacher said. Helbig looked away without speaking. "You can trust me. I'm no informant."

Helbig sighed and turned toward his friend. "We had one for a while. He was always sewing discord, trying to get the *Luftwaffe* and the *Kriegsmarine* at each other's throat. His wife used to visit, and they'd have these huge fights. It was all an act. He turned out to be a Canadian officer who spoke perfect German with a Heidelberg accent. We figure he'd studied there."

"There's also the other kind," Schumacher said in a whisper. "One of the worst came up with me from Bowmanville. Major Kretschmer, a committed Nazi."

When his friend didn't respond, Schumacher looked him in the eye and repeated his earlier statement, drawing out each word. "I see why you prefer the barracks."

Helbig again took stock of his fellow fighter pilot and seemed to decide. "We're so near the fence here. We haven't started yet. The ground is frozen. But come spring ..."

That afternoon, Schumacher asked the Lagerführer for permission to transfer from the three-story, well-appointed detention center to the smaller building that afforded no view and was cold in winter. "You're an officer," he said. "It is your right to be here with us."

"With respect, Major, I have friends in the barracks, fellow flyers I came up with."

"Officers? They belong here. Ask them to transfer."

"With your permission, sir, I'd prefer to be down there."

The Lagerführer narrowed his eyes. "We must authorize any escape attempt. You must present your plan, not only for how you will get out, but where you will go when you leave these walls."

"*Jawohl*, Major," Schumacher said.

Three days before Christmas, the Canadian authorities approved the transfer. As his fellow officers gathered in the mess hall singing *Stille Nacht, O Tannenbaum,* and *Leise rieselt der Schnee,* the two friends prowled through the basement of the barracks. Helbig carried a cup of water on which a small piece of cardboard floated, a needle threaded through it—a makeshift compass. Schumacher brought a heavy spoon from the mess kitchen. As one guided their way to the northeast corner of the building, the other tapped the concrete bricks above the walkway, listening for the dull thud indicating earth lay behind it.

"You need help, Marge. You look tired. You're pale. You've lost weight."

"Is there anything else, Mother?"

"I don't mean to be critical. I'm concerned about you."

"I know. I'm sorry." Margie slumped at the kitchen table, combing back her dark hair with her hands.

"Put on some lipstick and a pretty dress. Go see a movie."

"I do that all the time, Mother. I've seen everything worth seeing. Except for the war movies."

"Have you told Brandon how you feel? Perhaps if he knew how badly you're taking this ..."

She looked up at the woman standing over her with her arms folded. "We talk twice a week." *About nothing. We spend three minutes on the phone and discuss nothing of importance.* "But we can't speak for long. It's expensive," she said, unwilling to add any arrows to Florence's well-stocked quiver.

"He should come home. Take leave, or whatever they call it. He needs to care for his wife."

"Brandon is doing what he must. Everyone is sacrificing. He deals with his pain by treating those German boys the way they treated him."

"Revenge, is it? Where in the Bible does Jesus say to take vengeance on your enemies?"

"Let's drop it, shall we?"

Her mother glared at her. "You can't just sit here feeling miserable. You need to see someone."

Margie would not give Florence the satisfaction, but on Tuesday, three days before Christmas, she joined a dozen other women in the St. Johns parish hall as they prepared Red Cross gift boxes for prisoners held in German camps. Each package contained dried milk, butter and cheese; tinned meat and fish; an assortment of dried fruit; tea and chocolate; honey and jam; and soap.

The women, ranging in age from early twenties to two nuns who appeared to be well into their seventies, had arranged themselves on both sides of a long table. They formed an assembly line, each volunteer placing one or two items in a basket while the woman across from her did the same before passing it on.

"I wonder if these will actually reach our boys," said a young woman seated to Margie's right, who introduced herself as Sarah Tice. "I'd hate to think we were going to all this trouble just to feed Germans."

"I think they will," said the woman across from her named Patty Ryan. "My Larry writes to tell me how welcome they are. He doesn't care for sardines and trades his for cigarettes."

"The Americans put fags in their boxes," Sarah said. "It's too bad we don't do that."

"Mr. Leather doesn't approve of smoking," Patty answered, referring to the chairman of the Red Cross parcel committee.

"How long has your son been a prisoner?" Margie asked Patty.

"Dunkirk. Larry volunteered with the BEF. When the evacuation came, they captured him before he could make it to the beach." She shook her head and continued to place tins of potted pork and corned beef in the boxes as they were passed to her.

"It must be difficult for you."

"It is. But one gets used to it. He's safe there. Safer than he would have been during the Dieppe Raid. I give thanks he didn't go through that."

"I lost both my boys at Dieppe," Margie said. "One is dead. The other is missing, but I suspect—"

"Don't think like that," Sarah said. "The prisoner count goes up every week. You must have faith."

"Say, ladies, have you seen the Christmas tree in the sanctuary?" A commanding voice from down the line interrupted the conversation. It belonged to one of the two black-clad nuns. Patty looked down, trying to ignore the loud intrusion.

"It's beautiful this year," said the other nun, equaling the loud tone of the first. "It's a Fraser fir. Lovely, broad branches."

Margie ignored them. "They were my only children. I just can't—"

The first nun spoke again. "We have all suffered losses—some in this war, some in the last. But we have a job to do. We're here for the living. And to celebrate Christ's birth."

Margie rose, her face crimson. "I came here for friendship and support. I'll seek it elsewhere." Without another word, she picked up her handbag, took her coat and hat from the rack, and climbed the stairs to the entrance.

Sarah pursued her. "Wait. Margie, wait." Catching up to her as she struggled into her wool overcoat and pulled a stocking cap over her head, she said, "Let's go for coffee. I'll sit with you."

They trudged together through the bitter cold. Snow from the previous week's blizzard was piled high, blackened and topped with coal cinders, blocking in vehicles and leaving only narrow lanes at corners. Toronto, Margie thought, was the most beautiful city in the world the day of a snowfall and the ugliest two days later.

Sarah pulled her into a café two blocks from the waterfront and waved off her offer to pay. "It's on me. You're a lost little lamb, and I'm the shepherd."

An odd way to put it, but Margie took the small table at the front window, a narrow space behind the door that afforded both a view and an icy blast whenever a customer entered. A waitress appeared, and Sarah ordered coffee black and a serving of whatever pastry they had on hand. The server offered a selection, but Sarah waved her away. "Something sweet. You decide."

They sipped their coffee for a few minutes, still wearing their coats. "I apologize for making a scene in there," Margie said at length. "It was uncalled for, and now I've left the others shorthanded."

Sarah waved it away as she had the pastry selection. "You've lost two sons. You're hurting. I doubt anyone blames you for letting it out."

"I made a spectacle of myself. I don't like that."

"Do you want to talk about it?"

She did, and for half an hour poured out details of her life and her frustrations. She began at the center, discussing her sons, her fractious relationship with her mother, and her loneliness with Brandon's absence. Encouraged by Sarah's silence, Margie moved out in concentric circles, gradually revealing more, reaching back to her marriage to Brandon, their first meeting, and beyond that to her life during the First World War.

Sarah said not a word in judgment. She just listened, a gift no one had given her in years.

FRANKLIN AND ELEANOR hosted a Christmas Eve party in the East Room for nearly three hundred White House employees, police, and their families. An hour later, the president moved to the South Portico for the annual Community Christmas Tree ceremony.

Draped in a cloak against the forty-three-degree weather—the rain had paused for his address—he told Americans listening on radio that he was speaking not only to them but also to men and women in uniform from all nations.

"I give you a message of cheer. I cannot say Merry Christmas, for I think constantly of those thousands of soldiers and sailors who are in actual combat throughout the world. But I can express to you my thought that this is a happier Christmas than last year in the sense that the forces of darkness stand against us with less confidence in the success of their evil ways."

Roosevelt had reason for his optimism. That morning, General Marshall had provided an upbeat report on the state of the war. In North Africa, Field Marshal Erwin Rommel had abandoned El Agheila and retreated to Tripoli. After the British Navy had sunk seventeen of her ships in Oran, the Vichy France Navy had scuttled the rest of her fleet, keeping them out of German hands.

In the Pacific, the US had won the naval battle at Guadalcanal. Marines had stormed ashore, bottling up Japanese forces at the west end of the island, while the Navy had cut off Japanese resupply ships, starving the enemy out of hiding.

The most hopeful news came from Stalingrad, where Soviet forces, having endured the loss of over a million men, now encircled General Paulus's Sixth Army. An Axis rescue effort, Operation Winter

Storm, had failed. A Russian victory to the months-long siege seemed only a matter of time.

"The tide is turning," Roosevelt told his Christmas Eve crowd, "thanks not only to our armed forces and merchant sailors but those who toil in industry for the common cause of helping to win the war."

Bringing his message to a close, he said, "On Christmas Day, our plants and factories will be stilled. The war effort has caused us to cancel every other celebration, so this is our only holiday of the year. Christmas is a holy day. May all it stands for live and grow throughout the years."

With applause echoing in his ears, the president joined Eleanor and other guests for tea in the Monroe Room, slipping out before dinner to meet with his doctor. His health was a concern he shared with no one, not even his close friend Harry Hopkins, but he wearied quickly, and his hands shook when he reached for objects. In the days since Mackenzie King had returned to Ottawa, Roosevelt had visited his physician three times a week, but this, like his impending visit with Churchill, was a secret he kept to himself.

Following a Christmas Eve dinner of turkey with stuffing, mashed potatoes, gravy, cranberry sauce, carrots, and parsnips, the prisoners launched an impromptu concert of German carols. Armitage couldn't tell if they had rehearsed or reached back to their memories of singing in church choirs, but the sound was cohesive and polished. One young officer sang descants in a crystalline falsetto.

Fighting back tears, Armitage joined in, reliving his first Christmas as a prisoner. The Canadians had sung English carols, and their captors had answered with their own. It was not just his first, but his last decent Christmas in captivity, for weeks later, they sent him to work in a Silesian coal mine. He'd put in seventeen hard months until a cave-in trapped him beneath timbers. As he lay writhing in pain, his right ankle jammed under a wooden beam, a fellow prisoner, an Ojibwe named Nick Cadotte, came to his rescue. He braced a support beam with his back as other prisoners worked to free him. Despite Cadotte's assurances that they should take their time, the helpers pulled with such force that they snapped his right fibula, a compound fracture. He heard the bone give way before he felt it, and when the pain seared through his body, he passed out. A German doctor did his best to treat him—he couldn't complain about the care—but the damage was so severe that the leg never mended correctly.

Cadotte was the only one of his fellow prisoners with whom Armitage had maintained contact. He had once visited them in Toronto, Dicky and Henry amazed to meet "a real Indian." Far from taking offense at the boys' unintended slurs, Nick sat on the living room floor with them, teaching them how to make corn husk dolls. Now Armitage had let even his rescuer fall away, closing the doors on his years of imprisonment.

As the Germans filed out of the mess hall, an apparition brought him back to the present. *Dickie.* His son was among the prisoners, his fine sandy hair dancing across his forehead as it always did when he moved quickly. Armitage struggled to his feet and chased after the man. As the prisoners filed out of the mess hall, they split into two groups. He pursued the longer of the two, weaving in and out of the line as it snaked up the hill toward the detention center. He turned and peered back at the approaching faces before rushing forward again to examine the next group.

"Sergeant, where are you going?" Corporal Smith trailed after him. They locked eyes, and Armitage stopped, doubling over as he braced his hands on his knees. "Are you all right?"

"My son," he said. "I thought I saw him." He remained bent over for several seconds as he fought to catch his breath.

"C'mon, sarge. Let's find a little something to perk you up." Smith walked beside him as they left the prisoner compound and rounded the fence to the officer's quarters.

"Thanks," Armitage said as they entered the building. "I'm better now. I thought—"

"You need some Christmas cheer. I have some decent whiskey in my room."

Armitage begged off, reassuring him he was all right. After showering and brushing his teeth, he lay on his bed, trying to read a copy of a just-issued novel, *The Robe*. After a few pages, he gave up, laid the book aside on his nightstand, and leaned back, his hands tucked behind his neck.

Dickie. Where had that come from? His mind was playing tricks on him. His younger son was gone, as, in all likelihood, was Henry. War was senseless, a lethal game of chess in which the king and queen sacrificed pawns to protect their positions.

Pawns like him. War had cost Armitage his mobility, three years of his youth ... and his love. He'd returned to Canada in 1918 to find that Jeanne Macallum, to whom he'd been engaged when he'd left, was now Jeanne Canavan.

Lying alone on Christmas Eve, lonely and reflective, her image floated above him. Curly auburn hair, green eyes, an upturned nose, an ever-present regal smile, as though she deigned the world to gather at her feet. Not for the first time, Armitage wondered what had become of her. Was she happy? Had her marriage endured? Did she have children? Did she ever think of him and wonder what life would have been like if only she'd waited?

On hearing the news after he'd been demobilized, Armitage reacted with denial, pretending he was unaware she'd married, writing her through her parents to tell her he'd returned more or less intact and looked forward to their reunion. It was ill-advised; he knew so the moment he sent it. Her mother responded with a brief note informing him she'd wed the previous June. She offered neither an explanation nor an apology. Jeanne's father had always thought him beneath her. He doubted they'd forwarded his message. Like the war, he was history.

After a few weeks, he found her address in Ottawa and wrote. Expressed congratulations he did not feel. Said he understood, which he did not. Told her not to pity him, which he hoped she did. She didn't write back, which angered him. He had waited for her (as though he had a choice), but she had not. He deserved an acknowledgment.

None was forthcoming. Over the years, he lost track of the woman he had loved, but he didn't forget her. She came unbidden into his dreams and crept wraithlike into his waking hours. He sometimes caught himself speaking her name under his breath, like a muttered curse.

"Sarge, you have a call." Corporal Smith pounded on his door until it sprung open. He'd been so lost in his reverie that he'd not heard him rap. "It's a woman. Your wife, I think."

He'd spoken to Margaret only this morning. They'd shared a long conversation, thanking each other for the presents brought by post, sharing their plans for the holiday, wishing each other a merry Christmas.

Armitage hobbled down the hallway to the payphone at the end of the corridor.

"We've both given so much," he'd told her weeks before. An earlier war had robbed Armitage of his fiancé and, to a great extent, his dignity. But it also robbed Margie of her husband, Harold. A mortar shell decapitated him during the Battle of Amiens, the Canadian victory that brought the war to an end three months later to the day.

We've both given so much.

"Hello," he said. He heard nothing but muffled sobbing. "Margie, what's wrong?"

"He's—Henry, he's—"

"Margie, take it slowly. I have time." He waited while she gained control. "What's the news about Henry?"

"Alive. He's alive. They've taken him prisoner, but my son is alive."

6

JANUARY 9-22, 1943

AT MIDNIGHT ON SATURDAY, January 9, a steam locomotive, Southern Railway 1401, departed the underground station at the Bureau of Engraving, traveling north. It pulled just five cars, one of which was distinctive. The *Ferdinand Magellan*, officially US Train Car Number One, was one of six private sleepers built by the Pullman Company in 1929, each named after a famous explorer. Weeks before, the company had finished rebuilding the car, reducing its original six bedrooms to four, creating two suites with private bathrooms, and enlarging the observation lounge and dining area to hold a solid mahogany table.

At the direction of Secret Service agent Mike Reilly, Pullman had encased both ends and the sides of the car in armor plating, replaced the windows with bullet-proof glass, and, because the windows were sealed, installed air conditioning. The modifications doubled the car's original weight to 142 tons, making it the heaviest railcar in the United States.

As the lights of Washington yielded to the darkness of the Maryland countryside, Roosevelt settled into his suite, dictating memos and telegrams to his secretary. Two nights before, he had delivered a rousing message to the new Congress. After reviewing the military situations in both Europe and the Pacific, he concluded, "I cannot tell you when or where the United Nations are going to strike next in Europe. But we are going to strike—and strike hard." His voice rising, he brought members of both parties to their feet. "Yes, the Nazis and the Fascists have asked for it—*and they are going to get it.*"

While the address had been a triumph, the president had no time for reflection. He was on the first leg of a mission he hoped would reshape the postwar world, a trip cloaked in secrecy. In the rail yard at Baltimore, the train reversed course and headed south from Maryland and into Virginia, through the Carolinas and Georgia, and down the east coast of Florida.

At 6:00 a.m. Monday, the train reached its destination in Miami, but the president's trip was far from over. An elevator mounted at the rear of the car lowered him to the platform. A waiting limousine whisked him, Harry Hopkins, and Admiral Leahy to the harborside terminal of Pan American World Airways, where two Boeing 314 Clipper "flying boats" awaited them. The reinforced hulls and outboard sponsons of these aircraft could withstand water takeoffs and landings. A pair of 1,600 hp Wright Twin Cyclone engines were mounted on both above-fuselage wings. The clippers were the longest-ranged aircraft in service, capable of traveling five thousand miles without refueling.

Only his closest advisers knew where Roosevelt was headed. He had planned the trip since early December, telling Churchill, "The only satisfactory way to come to the vital strategic conclusions the military situation requires is for you and me to meet personally with Stalin." Days later, the Soviet leader dealt him a disappointment, declining to leave while his armies struggled to save Stalingrad. Roosevelt would have to find another time to share his postwar vision with the Soviet leader. He forged ahead with a bilateral meeting between Churchill and himself.

Rising above the crystal waters of Biscayne Bay, the twin aircraft would follow a circuitous route, hopscotching from Miami to Trinidad, south to Brazil, across the Atlantic to South Africa. From there, Roosevelt would take an Army Air Force C-54 northwest to

Morocco, becoming not only the first president to fly overseas while in office but the first since Lincoln to visit troops on a battlefield. He and Churchill would spend eleven days plotting military strategy in Anfa, a Phoenician town on the edge of Casablanca, in a conference code-named "Symbol."

***

Snowbanks lined both sides of Highway 17 as Corporal Durham Smith drove the Jeep north past Bracebridge, chatting while his passenger, Brandon Armitage, huddled into his greatcoat in silence. The Arctic heater, installed by the army on general-purpose vehicles, directed warmth at the driver's feet. Even Smith felt the sub-freezing air leaking into the vehicle from the seams and snaps around the canvas top.

"It won't be long," Smith said as he navigated the compacted snow and ice. "Who is this man you're going to see?"

"A farmer's son, wounded at Dieppe. He's reluctant to talk about it, but his father convinced him as a favor—one parent to another."

In the two weeks since learning Henry was a prisoner, Armitage had pieced together what he could about the raid. This morning, he was on a mission to learn first-hand what it had been like at Blue Beach, where his sons had landed on the French coastline.

From the father of another prisoner, Floyd Martin of Kitchener, Armitage had already learned why it had taken so long to learn of Henry's fate. Martin had forwarded a hectographic copy of a letter his son, Avery, had written from a Silesian prison camp. When he saw the return address, his mouth dropped, and his hands shook. Armitage had spent part of his own captivity at Stalag VIII-B, near Lamsdorf, before being forced to work in the coal mine. He devoured the letter, wondering whether the Germans had replaced the wooden barracks, which had done little to shut out the winter cold. He shuddered as he recalled how he and his fellow captives had clustered around the small stove at the center of the drafty building. Despite the ready availability of coal from the mines, his captors provided only a meager supply. In the early morning hours, he and the others had huddled together as the embers died.

As he read the faint purple letters, he learned why the father had sought him out. After their capture at Dieppe, he and other prisoners, Henry among them, had been taken to a makeshift hospital in Rouen. Before the Red Cross could record their names, the Germans threw them into a cattle car. Forty men shared the boxcar for eight days with little food and no sanitary facilities.

Shortly after they reached the prison camp, Avery wrote, he and Henry joined two others assigned to a nearby farm to bring in the harvest. Thus, they remained unaccounted for until their return to Lamsdorf in December. The young man had not revealed the extent of Henry's injuries, having written only to assure his parents he had survived.

South of Utterson, Corporal Smith turned off the highway and headed east. "Moose season is over, but we could return and go fox hunting."

"I don't hunt," Armitage said. "I haven't held a weapon since 1915 and intend to keep it that way."

Smith changed the subject. "I can't believe these farmers make a living. Pioneers came up sixty years ago for the promise of free farmland, but the second they stuck a shovel in the earth, they hit rock."

Armitage didn't respond, but Smith was undeterred, giving a history of the land he had known since childhood as his passenger thought about what he'd pieced together over the past several days. Despite the paucity of press reports, he had learned that his sons had been part of a force of over six thousand soldiers, five thousand of them Canadian, who had crossed the English Channel in the predawn hours of August 19 to attack the French port of Dieppe. The town lay on a gentle slope toward the sea, bounded on both sides by promontories the Germans commanded with heavy artillery and machine-gun nests inside fortified bunkers.

British planners had assigned two forces to neutralize this firepower before the main landing force was to arrive. Both failed. The South Saskatchewan Regiment arrived on Green Beach before dawn, tasked with taking out the southern batteries. In the first of several miscalculations, the landing craft dropped them at the wrong location, forcing them to cross the river Scie. Axis troops lay in wait on the opposite bank, firing into their ranks.

To the north, the Royal Regiment of Canada and the Black Watch, assigned to take out the artillery on the other cliff, landed late in the battle. German forces trapped them on the beach and mowed them down at will.

The 14th Canadian Army Tank Regiment, which was to have provided armored support to the landing force, also arrived late.

Exposed, the landing party came under fire from three directions —the flanking headlands and German batteries ahead in the town's casino. Many never made it to the beach, floundering in the surf for hours. Of those who penetrated the town, many were killed, and the lucky ones, like Henry, captured.

The corporal interrupted his thoughts. "What?" Armitage said.

"We're here."

"Oh, sorry. I was ..."

"Not looking forward to this, I'll bet." Smith parked before a narrow, two-story, white-walled farmhouse, whose paint on the exposed northwestern corner was peeling.

Armitage pivoted in his seat and stretched his right leg before stepping into the unplowed snow. "I hope you can get us out when we've finished."

With Corporal Smith trailing, he took a deep breath and raised his arm to knock, but a frail-looking, gray-haired woman with downcast eyes opened the door and stepped back without greeting them. She wore a long woolen dress with a red shawl gathered around her shoulders. "Mrs. Bartleson?" he said.

"Step in. Don't let the flies out." Armitage searched her face for any trace of humor, but she turned away as though this were her usual message of welcome. The two men entered a small living room as she closed the door behind her, kicking a roll of dirty gray fabric into place at its base.

"Sergeant Armitage, I'm Frank Bartleson." The farmer wore heavy bib overalls over a red flannel shirt. His thinning brown hair, protruding stomach, and stooped carriage suggested he was in his late sixties, though Armitage suspected he was younger.

Although he sat in an overstuffed chair before the fireplace, a third figure dominated the room. A green woolen blanket lay over him, his left leg extending out on a footstool while the fabric fell loosely around where his right leg had been.

"Theo, say hello to Sergeant Armitage," his father said. Theodore Bartleson appeared to be in his early thirties. His face was gray. He didn't smile, but raised his right hand to Armitage, his grip weak and clammy.

"Take a seat," the older man said, placing a straight-back chair at his son's left. "He's deaf in his right ear."

"I promise not to take much of your time," Armitage said.

"That's all right," the young man replied. "You've come a ways."

"I'm sorry we're meeting under these circumstances." Theo waved him away before he could express compassion. *Of course. That's all he hears.*

"Dad says you lost one of your boys and the other's a prisoner. How can I help?"

Armitage studied his hands. Now that he was here, he didn't know how to begin.

"It was a nightmare," Theo said, saving him the trouble. "I didn't make it to shore. The Germans sent up a red flare as we approached, signaling our arrival. They opened up, hitting our landing craft head-on. The shelling was unlike anything I've heard before, like being in the middle of ten thunderstorms. The guys up front—" He stopped, unable to continue. Armitage waited, his hands folded on his lap, his eyes never leaving the man's face to avoid looking at the depression in the blanket.

"I hid inside as long as I could, but when it started sinking, I had to get out. Four or five others made it with me. The rest ..."

He looked off into the distance. "Guys on the beach took direct fire. Every few minutes, one or two tried to surmount the sea wall. The Jerrys ripped them apart. Others hid as best they could. Some ran back into the surf, swimming toward the few landing craft still afloat. The krauts picked them off like they were bagging rabbits. Their bodies twitched as bullets hit them. The sea was red. The smell of blood mixing with fuel oil was something I'll never forget."

Armitage put his hand to his mouth, fighting nausea. This was how Dickie died. He imagined his son floating in the surf, perhaps alive at that point, but alone among hundreds of bodies. "How did you get away?"

"I don't know." He shook his head once, twice, and looked down. "I was farther out, so I thought I'd be safer swimming toward another lander. That's the last thing I recall. When I came to, I was aboard a destroyer."

"A destroyer?"

"Yeah. Four hospital landing craft were supposed to treat the wounded, but they pulled out—crossed back to England without us."

Knitting his hands together, Armitage looked off to one side, his sigh audible to everyone in the room.

"A medic shot me full of morphine, and I was out again. I woke up days later in an English hospital, all of me except my leg." He looked down at the blanket concealing his stump.

"It must have been rough," said Smith, who until that point had listened without speaking. "Still, you made it back. So many others—"

Armitage closed his eyes, wishing he'd left the corporal in the Jeep, but Theo appeared unbothered. "Like those still on the beach ..." His voice broke. "They pulled out and left them there to die. I saw a kraut officer shoot one boy in the head."

A mercy killing, Armitage thought. "Maybe the raid took the Germans by surprise. They lacked sufficient doctors, hospitals, or morphine to care for the wounded. The officer may have done what he felt was humane."

"No," Theo yelled. "*They knew we were coming.* We were to have launched the raid a month before, but the Brits called it off. Our guys were wandering off base telling English barmaids about Dieppe. Because it was over. We weren't going anywhere, so why not try to impress the girls with our bravery? Then our officers announced it was back on. I got a bad feeling. Too much talk going around. The Jerries had to know."

He looked up at Armitage, a pleading look in his eyes. "What am I supposed to do? Farming is all I know. Dad needs me, and this—*this thing ...*"

Although the government would do its best to rehabilitate the young man, Armitage emptied his wallet and gave the boy's father everything he had. Corporal Smith drew out a few bills.

"Bastards." Smith inched the Jeep out of the snow. "The English will fight down to the last Canadian."

MARGIE SAT IN THE DARK, gripping the handset as her husband sought to reassure her. "Our boy is all right." Sub-freezing cold seeped through the window frame Brandon had promised to caulk in the fall. That was only part of the reason she shivered as she listened. "When this is over, we'll have him back."

"And when might that be?" She tried not to make her question sound like an accusation as she leaned into the mouthpiece. No one could tell, but many made optimistic predictions; their number, like those of the dead and captured in Dieppe, grew daily.

Margie's spirits had soared on Christmas Eve when the telegram arrived, informing her that Henry had been captured. The news that her older son was alive buoyed her during Christmas Day, which she spent under the disapproving eye of her mother, and through New Year's Day.

But Margie knew how to read. She could add. She could think for herself.

On Christmas Eve, the Defence Ministry had reported the capture of forty-seven men, including Henry, who had previously been among the missing. That brought the prisoner count to 1,158.

Four days later, the ministry added a hundred more names to the prisoner list. A week later, newspapers raised the number of captured to 1,571, with 515 reported dead, 570 wounded, and another 720 still missing. Each day, the government reported more deaths, subtracting them from the list of the missing.

Newspapers quoted military officials who praised what the raid had achieved, as though this were a glorious victory. But Margie knew it was a rout, and when Brandon called her that evening to share what he'd learned from Theo Bartleson, she was ready for him.

"Why did they send Henry and Dickie there?" she said. "What were they trying to do?"

"I don't know," he said. "An English officer said today the raid showed how to penetrate Europe's coasts."

Margie gripped the handset so hard her knuckles were white. Her voice rose. "But they didn't do that. You said yourself they never got off the beach."

She heard his intake of breath, knew he was considering how much to tell her, and didn't pierce his silence. When at last he spoke, his tone reflected his own exasperation. "They call it a raid, but you don't send six thousand men and tons of equipment on a *raid*."

"What was it, then?"

"You land in enemy territory to attain one of two objectives. If you sneak ashore with a small force, do some damage, and withdraw, it's a raid. If your intent is to get and hold territory, it's an invasion. You go in with a massive force, backed by air and naval power, throwing in everything you have."

"Which was this?"

"It was neither. It was too big and noisy for a raid, too small and with too little tactical support for an invasion. I don't know what it was. I don't know what they were thinking."

"Or if they were thinking."

He hesitated, then repeated her words. "If they were thinking."

***

No military brass greeted Roosevelt when he landed in Morocco on January 14. Concerned about alerting Axis spies he was in North

Africa, his aide had urged the Joint Chiefs of Staff to dispense with a welcoming ceremony. Instead, his son Lieutenant Colonel Elliott Roosevelt awaited him on the tarmac, having flown in from his base in Gander, Newfoundland the day before. The two enjoyed each other's company during the early days of the conference.

To Elliott, as he had to Prime Minister Mackenzie King the month before, the president outlined what had been a passion bordering on obsession. "The English mean to maintain their hold on their colonies, and they mean to help the French do the same. I'll have no part of it."

The country had been dragged into this war over the heated objections of isolationists and America-Firsters. The Japanese attack on Pearl Harbor had forced the nation to enter the conflict. Even then, it took Hitler's declaration of war to bring the US into both theaters.

"The colonial system means war," the president said. "If you exploit all the resources of those countries but put nothing back into them, you're storing up the kind of trouble that leads to war."

He knew this would be a sticking point with the allies. "The look that Churchill gets on his face when you mention India ..." he told Elliott.

The issue surfaced nights later when Roosevelt hosted a dinner for the Sultan of Morocco, the first time Muhammad V had met a foreign dignitary other than those of his country's French rulers. He arrived in a flowing white robe, bearing a gold-mounted dagger for the president and gold bracelets and a tiara for the First Lady.

Along with Churchill and French Resident-General Charles Noguès, the two leaders made small talk as they nibbled on dates, apricots, and figs and sipped glasses of water and fruit juice. Churchill did not hide his displeasure over the absence of alcohol. He harrumphed through the dinner of roasted lamb, couscous, and a variety of fresh vegetables.

Roosevelt, flanked by the sultan and Churchill and with Noguès within earshot, turned to Muhammed V. "Victory for us will be a new beginning for you."

"In what way?" The sultan asked.

"Improved education and living standards. Development of your natural resources for the benefit of your people."

"We would be interested in anything that advances our country," the sultan said. "We have no trained scientists or engineers. If we discover oil and keep the income, we can provide better housing, improve agriculture, and better the lives of my subjects."

"We'll train your technicians until you've established your own universities," FDR replied.

General Noguès shifted in his chair, signaling his annoyance that a foreign leader on French soil was promising a French subject what would become of this French protectorate at war's end. Clearing his throat with a mighty roar, Churchill rose and left the table, returning minutes later, trailing the smell of gin.

As dinner concluded, the sultan said, "Thank you for your hospitality and your kind offer. I will petition the United States to aid us in developing Morocco. A new future for my country."

With that, Roosevelt showed his hand to his allies and issued a challenge. If the US was in this war, providing not just weapons and financing but men, it would have a proportionate say in the outcome. Roosevelt was determined that something good would come from this conflict—a brighter future, not only for Morocco but also for the world.

Lieutenant Neil Morrison bent over his desk, dealing with hated paperwork, when Corporal Smith tapped on his open door.

"Lieutenant, a German officer wishes to speak with you."

Morrison laid down his pen. "Is the Lagerführer with him?"

"No, sir. He's alone. A lieutenant named Schumacher."

Morrison scratched the back of his neck. It was unusual for a prisoner to approach any of the Canadian officers without his leader. They went through the Lagerführer, Major Kuno Fischer. Morrison and Lieutenant-Colonel Wallington had heard rumors a power struggle was underway among the senior officers. Was Schumacher's appearance connected to the infighting?

"Send him in." As the corporal turned, Morrison added, "But stay with us. I may need a witness." Morrison wasn't sure he should meet with a German officer without the camp commander present. The approach was—to use one of his pet phrases—most irregular.

Schumacher proved to be a good-looking young fellow with sandy hair bordering on red, a long, thin face, and bright blue eyes. Teutonic, but not ready for one of Goebbels's posters. The prisoner smiled, came to attention, and saluted. Morrison returned the acknowledgment and offered the man a seat.

"Thank you for seeing me," Schumacher said. "I am grateful." His English was good, his accent clipped, his vowels pure and round in British fashion.

"What can I do for you?"

"I am housed in the barracks with some of my fellow flyers. We are trying to improve our English and our knowledge of Canadian culture. We wish to establish a library with books about your history, geography, flora and fauna, even your novels."

Picking up a pencil, Morrison leaned back in his chair and drummed on his desktop. "We have a library in the main building. What's wrong with that?"

"True, sir, but we would like a small one of our own, so we don't have to cross through ice and snow to get at them. Just eighty or ninety volumes. Perhaps a bookcase with three shelves." Before Morrison could deny the request, the German said, "Alexander Mackenzie. Didn't he discover the route to the Pacific before—?"

"Twelve years before Lewis and Clark," Morrison, an amateur historian, said. "Mackenzie had already explored the Arctic region searching for a Northwest Passage but failed to find it. He returned in 1793 and followed the Peace River to the Great Divide, then the Bella Coola River to the coast. How did you hear of him?"

Schumacher gave an ingratiating smile. "I've asked questions of other Canadian officers, sir." He gave a gentle laugh. "I'd barely heard of Canada a year ago, and now I live here. I'm interested."

I live here. A strange way to put it.

"I suppose we could request the Gravenhurst Library to lend us some books. They may even have older volumes they're willing to donate. Perhaps they can ask residents to contribute something."

Schumacher grinned. "That would be excellent."

"But where would you put it?"

"There's a small storage room in the basement holding old mops and buckets that haven't seen much use. May I show you?"

"Corporal Smith, take a look at this space and let me know if it's suitable. If it's not used for anything else, I don't see why we can't make it work."

The prisoner thanked him. As Smith and Schumacher turned to leave, Morrison said, "Tell me, why didn't you route this request through the Lagerführer?"

"He would not approve it, *Herr Kapitan.* We are not permitted to show interest in our captors. I know not to ask."

"Thank you. Dismissed." If that was the reason, Morrison thought to himself, these men deserved their small library. He would let nothing stand in the way.

***

WHY ASK a question if you know the answer? Only later would Margie ask herself why she had agreed to her new friend Sarah's recommendation that she meet with Father Michael, the younger priest who had officiated the first evening she attended Mass at St. Johns. "He listens," Sarah had assured her. "He's thoughtful, not doctrinaire like the old priests. They just tell you what the law is and send you on your merry way."

"For confession? I haven't done anything ..."

"No, he calls it a 'listening session.'"

Before she had acted on that advice, a late evening telephone call from Ottawa had brought a Christmas present, the news that Henry was alive. In the joyous days that followed, Margie put aside the thought of visiting the priest. Henry would come home someday.

Brandon was investigating the circumstances of his capture and providing regular reports through long, newsy, hope-filled letters and twice-weekly phone calls. Everything would be fine.

And then it wasn't. A week into the New Year, the fact that some unknown general had sent her sons into a senseless slaughter overcame her. She couldn't sleep, snapped at her mother, and in a fit of rage, threw a coffee cup across the dining room, shattering the glass face of a clock her maternal grandmother had brought with her from England five decades before.

With her grief reasserting itself, she approached Father Michael after an evening Mass. He offered an appointment the next day, but no, she couldn't come during the daytime. If her mother appeared unbidden and unannounced, she would want to know why Margie was not at home, who she'd been with, and why. Since her mother never ventured out after dark, it had to be some evening. And Father Michael agreed, setting an appointment on this Thursday night.

She arrived wearing a long black dress that reached almost to her ankles. No jewelry, not even a modest string of pearls, save for a small silver cross on a thin chain. Her wool coat, which extended below the knee. A hand-knit wool cap with a suggestion of a brim. Boots, of course. Her black leather handbag, which Brandon had given her three Christmases before. And no makeup. Her reflected image in the hallway mirror was a model of domesticity.

A short, round woman greeted her at the vestry entrance without smiling and took her coat and scarf. She scowled, seemed impatient, and Margie assumed the priest had asked her to stay over to avoid any hint of impropriety. "This way," she said, leading Margie to a small office.

Father Michael rose to greet her and motioned her to a sofa, taking a seat in a stuffed leather chair that faced it. He had dark brown hair and needed a shave. He wore a black tunic and clerical collar, but no jacket. The office smelled of tobacco. A stand on the desk held five pipes. A sixth lay bowl-down in a round, orange-colored ash tray.

"Thank you for agreeing to see me at such an odd hour."

"It seemed urgent, and a priest is never off the clock." He smiled. "Tell me about yourself."

"About my problem?"

"We'll get to that. Tell me about Margaret Armitage, the person."

"There's not much to say."

"I'm sure there is. Were you born here in Toronto?"

"No. In Point Edward in 1900. My father worked in the financial department of a Sarnia shipping company. Another firm took them over and transferred him here to handle tax matters when I was still a child. I grew up here." She stopped, fearing she'd said too much.

"And attended school where?"

"At St. Anne's, and Central Catholic for high school."

And so it went for ten minutes, the priest gathering routine information from her. His voice she recognized as that of the father who had taken her confession two months before. His calm presence put her at ease.

"So what brings you here, Mrs. Armitage? I sense you are troubled. How may I help?"

She drew a long breath, hesitating as she decided how to put it. "I am in a loveless marriage, Father. I no longer love my husband. I'm not sure I ever did. And he doesn't love me."

"Is he unkind to you? Has he hurt you?"

"No, it's nothing like that. In fact, he's good to me. But I married in haste, Father."

Before he could reply, she rushed forward, dumping the problem at his feet. "I lost my first husband during the closing days of the last war. Harold and I had been together since high school. He was a year ahead of me and enlisted as soon as he graduated. Once he finished training, he came home on leave, and we got married. They sent him to England and then over to France. Two months after he arrived, he was killed."

"I'm truly sorry for your loss. War is inhumane. There is nothing fine or ennobling about it. It destroys the lives not just of young men but of widows like you, of children, of parents." He paused as she absorbed his words. "How did you come to remarry?"

"That's just it. I was pregnant when Harold died. Brandon and I met through mutual friends. They weren't trying to get us together or anything. It was a New Year's Eve Party, and Bernice—that's my friend—she and her husband invited people they knew were alone for the holiday. A dozen, maybe more. There I was, seven months gone, unwilling to dance, sitting off by myself. A young man sat nearby."

She tented her hands, holding them before her face as though in prayer, but she was reliving the night that had once seemed so magical. "We got to talking. Brandon had just returned from the war where he'd been a prisoner. He didn't go into details, didn't seem to feel sorry for himself, but he had a cane at his side. I could tell he'd had a rough time. We talked. I explained my husband had lost his life at Amiens," she said, pronouncing it "a means."

"While others danced and flirted, we spent the evening chatting. It was all very proper. At midnight, he leaned over and kissed me on the forehead. It was sweet, innocent." She halted her torrent of words, recalling the moment. "And he proposed."

The priest shook his head in surprise. "You mean, right there? Even though you had just met."

She laughed despite herself. "No one ever believes it, but that's how it happened. He said, 'Margie, you seem like a fine person, and I'm a decent fellow with a good government job. Your baby needs a father, and I need someone to care for. Will you marry me?'"

"And you said ..."

"I told him I'd have to think about it. He called on me the next day, New Year's Day, 1919. My mother didn't like him showing up unannounced, but it delighted me. We went into the parlor and talked some more. He said he feared I'd not taken him seriously, that I thought it was the punch talking, but he assured me he meant what he'd said. 'If I could get down on one knee, I would,' he said, 'but if I do, I won't be able to get up.' That's when I realized how badly he'd been hurt."

"So?"

"I said yes."

Father Michael smiled. "I've heard many beautiful stories coming out of war, but nothing like this."

"But that's the problem, don't you see? We didn't know each other and certainly didn't love each other."

The priest rose and took the pipe out of his ashtray. He filled it, tamped the tobacco, and lit it, brushing the smoke with his hand. "But you made a commitment," he said, "not just to each other, but to God."

"Like I said during my confession, I married outside the church. I wasn't—after Harold was taken from me, I turned my back on my faith. I married Brandon in a Protestant ceremony. So it doesn't count, does it?"

Father Michael sighed. "Is he seeing someone else?"

"Yes," she said, "no. I mean ... I think so. He talks about her in his sleep. Cries out loud to her. Jeanie, her name is."

"Have you asked who this woman is?" She shook her head. "It could be anyone—a nurse who cared for him, a sister ..."

"He doesn't have a sister."

"And you? You say you no longer love him."

"I never did. Perhaps I should confess that. I promised to love him, but I didn't. And I don't." She enunciated the last words, studying the ceiling for help as she dabbed her eyes with a handkerchief.

"What has brought about this decision, after all this time?"

"I've lost both my sons. *Our* son, Dickie, died at Dieppe. *My* son, Henry, is in a German prison camp. Our boys tied us together; now they're gone."

"You refer to one son as 'ours' and the other as 'yours.' Is this how your husband views it?"

"He always favored Dickie. He never said it, but a mother can tell."

"Did he mistreat Henry? Was he unkind to him?"

"No. He was good to both boys. I'll give him that."

"And he fed them and clothed them and provided a home for them?"

"Yes." The ticking of a clock cut through her silence like a scythe. "But he let them go to war. They volunteered."

The National Resources Mobilization Act of 1940 had reinstated the draft, but Mackensie King, mindful of the national schism that had followed its imposition during World War I, decreed that conscripts would serve only on Canadian soil or in Canadian waters. Only those who volunteered served overseas.

"He could have stopped them from signing up," she said, her voice breaking. "I begged him to, but he didn't. He took them from me."

The priest's pipe had gone out. He relit it, allowing the smoke to drift between them without waving it away. "Mrs. Armitage—Margaret—we are at the heart of the issue. You blame your husband for this war, perhaps even hold him responsible for the last one."

"No, it's not like that." Margie snuffled for a moment and, in a small voice that collapsed in sobbing, said, "He came back. Harold died, and Brandon lived, and he allowed my boys ..."

There it was. The awful truth. "I can't forgive him, Father."

Putting his pipe aside, the priest leaned forward. "You are mourning. You're in shock. The Lord understands that. He forgives you. Can you find it in your heart to forgive your husband?"

Margie shook her head, but no words came.

"Think of the Blessed Virgin and what she gave up, the pain she endured for us. You still have a son. He's a prisoner, but he'll return, and when he does, he'll need both of you. Your husband has cared for him as his own."

Looking into her eyes until he commanded her attention, Father Michael said, "And he *is* his own, Margaret. Your husband raised this boy as a father should; he belongs to you both. And to God."

She sobbed, waving a hand in the air as though to ward off anything further the priest might say.

"Have you considered how your husband feels? Have you talked with him? Have you told him what's in your heart, or have you held all this inside, allowing it to fester?"

Margie looked down without speaking.

"Margaret, I want you to go home, open your Bible, and read Proverbs 14:1. Let it speak to you. I pray you will think about your marriage and not act rashly."

The priest blessed her. She did not thank him as she took her leave, walking the two blocks to the bus stop, transferring to another, and arriving home well after ten o'clock, weeping all the way. She opened her Bible and read. "Every wise woman buildeth her house: but the foolish plucketh it down with her hands."

Tossing it aside, she cried herself to sleep.

7

JANUARY 23–FEBRUARY 1, 1943

ARMITAGE STOOD BEFORE THE MIRROR, rehearsing what he planned to say. He'd lain awake for hours over the past few nights, knowing it was the moment to act. For the third time that morning, he spoke the words that had formed in his mind. After inspecting himself to make sure his hair was combed and his uniform neat and free of any underarm stain, he made the painful ascent to the second floor and entered the adjutant's office. "Request permission to speak to Lieutenant Morrison," he said.

"On what subject?"

"It's a personal matter."

"Can I help?"

"It's about my son. He's a prisoner of war."

"I don't know Lieutenant Morrison can be of help. He's quite busy."

Armitage stood his ground, cap in hand.

"Let me see." The adjutant disappeared through the office door, returning a moment later. "The lieutenant can spare five minutes."

Thanking him, Armitage entered the office and saluted.

"At ease, Sergeant." Morrison motioned him into one of the two office chairs facing his desk. "I'm sorry to learn about your son. What can I do for you?"

Through the windows, Armitage saw snow blowing sideways, driven by wind off the bay. German prisoners would soon be asked to man shovels to clear the west-facing doorways. "I had a purpose in signing up for the Veterans Guard, sir. One of my two sons was killed at Dieppe. The other was missing, and I—we were certain he was also dead. I was so angry I thought that by coming here, I could avenge their deaths. That was wrong of me. I was in a German prison camp for three years. I know what it's like."

Armitage raised both hands and wiped his eyes before plunging ahead. "We've learned my older son is alive and held at Sandbostel in Lower Saxony. He was wounded but appears to be doing all right."

"I'm happy to hear that." The lieutenant affected a smile and tapped his desk with the eraser end of a pencil.

"I was wrong in treating Major Wilhelm as I did. I want to apologize to him. And I'd like to return to regular duty, interacting with the prisoners."

The lieutenant shifted in his chair, pausing the pencil mid-beat. "For what purpose?"

"My German is improving. I hadn't spoken it in a quarter-century, but it's returning. I can befriend these prisoners and—not interrogate them exactly—but learn what is going on."

Morrison merely raised his eyebrows.

"As I said last month, sir, I'm convinced Berlin is communicating with them. Some prisoners include coded messages in their letters—elliptical references to the food, the weather, and to relatives they never mention again. They're planning something."

The lieutenant's face broke into a smile as he tossed the pencil onto his desk. "Of course they are, Sergeant. They're planning to escape. It's what prisoners do."

"Yes, sir. And it's our duty to stop them." Armitage rose from his chair, pacing at an awkward gait. "Where would they go if they escaped? Not to the US. They're holding thousands of prisoners themselves. If these men are planning escapes, they have some purpose in mind. By speaking with them, I may be able to find out what they're up to and put a stop to it before they do damage."

"More likely, they're trying to keep us busy," the lieutenant said. "They escape knowing they'll be recaptured, but they enjoy seeing us chase our tails."

"Sir, the Norwegians have an airfield just north of here. If some of these flyboys reach it ..."

Morrison's right finger sawed at the base of his lip. "A new commandant is coming next week. After I get him settled, I'll take it up with him."

"Thank you, sir."

"If you were to lay a hand on any of these prisoners, we wouldn't just return you to desk duty. You would face a court-martial."

"I understand, sir. It won't happen again."

<hr>

Books lined the lower floor of the barracks. Through a combination of kindness and national pride, Gravenhurst residents had responded to an appeal by the town librarian to augment the collection of Canadiana retired from circulation.

While the commandant's staff removed items such as atlases that might be helpful to anyone planning to escape, they allowed books on Canadian history, geology, and flora and fauna; English dictionaries; biographies; medical and scientific textbooks; cookbooks; handbooks on how to build canoes, repair an engine, blow glass, and collect stamps; reference books on antiques, the law, and childcare; and Canadian poetry and fiction ranging from mysteries, romances, and an aged and tattered copy of Catherine Parr Traill's *The Backwoods of Canada*. The librarian had been reluctant to part with that, as it was a rare historical find that should have gone into her collection, but the donor insisted.

Generous citizens of Gravenhurst had also donated bookcases, ranging from four to six shelves. Leutnant Jörg Schumacher arranged these gifts, flanking a pair of four-shelf cabinets between two towering ones, placing the heaviest books in the tall cabinets and slimmer volumes in the smaller two. The Canadian doctor had told him to nurse his left arm for a few more weeks, but he disregarded the advice.

"A little light reading," he joked in English as he paid particular care to the arrangement in one of the four-shelf units. He had considered installing makeshift casters into its base but rejected it. A guard was sure to spot the alteration and guess the reason for the prisoners' sudden interest in expanding their cultural horizons. He fitted a pair of pilfered handles on either side of the top shelf to facilitate shifting the bookcase away from the wall.

Christoph Helbig picked the garden toolshed lock and scrounged a shovel, spade, two trowels, a broom, a dustpan, and work gloves. The dirt would become a problem, but for the time being, they moved a beaten-up trash can from the shed into the basement during the middle of the night, concealing it in a supply closet behind a length of canvas slung from improvised tent poles of mops and the broom.

On a Friday evening, when many of the local guards took leave to spend the weekend with wives and families, ten prisoners chipped away at the mortar between the concrete blocks behind the bookcase. They worked in shifts, five catching a few hours of sleep, two standing guard at the base of both front and rear stairways, two huddled over their work, and one cleaning up as they dug so they could shove the bookcase into place and replace the volumes at a moment's notice. Before beginning work, they had drilled the routine until they could slide back the cabinet and repopulate the shelves within thirty seconds.

While the two teams worked by night, Schumacher sketched a rudimentary map of the escape route through the town he had reconstructed from memory. Throughout the day, he listened for the sound of trains moving down the track on the east end of Gravenhurst, noting down the times of their passage and, based on the duration of the rumbling and clattering, whether they carried passengers or freight.

ON THE EVE of their departure for Morocco, Roosevelt had gathered his Joint Chiefs together for one last strategy session. "Are you all agreed that we should meet the British united in advocating a cross-Channel operation?" he asked.

The Chiefs indicated their agreement, and General Marshall said, "We are." He repeated highlights of the plan developed by Brigadier General Albert Wedemeyer for a massive invasion of the French Coast in the summer.

Roosevelt was not convinced his chiefs were ready. "The British will come well prepared with their plan and will stick to it."

His warning was prescient. As the conference opened on January 14, Chief of the British Imperial General Staff, Sir Alan Brooke, who had brought a contingent of officers and planners with him that dwarfed the US delegation, deftly pushed the US cross-Channel strategy into a vague future. The Battle of the Atlantic against U-boats still raged, he said. How were the Americans to get the needed men and equipment into England without it ending up at the bottom of the sea? They were still fighting in North Africa, and so far, American troops had not performed well. How were they to take on the Wehrmacht in France when they hadn't shown they could turn the tide in Tunisia?

Brooke enumerated every option for a cross-Channel attack and systematically dismissed each of them. Lacking adequate staff support, Marshall and the other US Chiefs argued back in a losing contest. The British had come prepared; the Americans had not.

It took two weeks of wrangling between the military staffs and their leaders to reach a compromise. They would give top priority to ending U-boat attacks on trans-Atlantic convoys. Following victory in North Africa, the Allies would invade Sicily, helping secure shipping traffic through the Mediterranean. Marshall accepted the Sicilian operation as an unavoidable next step from North Africa. An amphibious landing on the island would be "similar to an operation across the Channel," he said, preparing the Allies for what they would later encounter.

They left the steps beyond Sicily undetermined. The British wanted to conquer Italy itself. While such a move would require Germany to divert divisions to the peninsula, Marshall considered this a costly sideshow and was resolved not to get sucked in. The two sides agreed to a Combined Bomber Offensive, with the Royal Air Force attacking Germany at night and the Americans attacking by day. And last, the Combined Chiefs agreed to set up an Anglo-American team in London to plan the Allies' return to the Continent.

The latter was not quite a triumph for the American side. Churchill made clear he was banking on Allied bombing to bring the Third Reich to its knees before committing to a risky assault on the Continent. The Americans wanted a direct assault, striking into the heart of the Reich for a quick victory before shifting forces to the Pacific to defeat Japan. The Allies would leave Casablanca with the ultimate strategy for the European Theater still open to debate. And there would be plenty of it.

That evening, Roosevelt told Elliott, "Marshall is angry. He feels he's been double-crossed. But this may have been a blessing. I listened to Brooke's arguments, and I suspect he's right."

"So there will be no cross-Channel," Elliott said.

"Not yet. But when we're ready …"

THE FLIMSY YELLOW envelope bore no return address, but a postmark read *Stalag VIII-B*. A red stamp depicted Adolf Hitler's image, the number 40—whether marks or pfennigs she could not tell—and the word *Kriegsgefangenenpost* in bold letters. Beneath it a stamped mark, *Par Avion*, and, in shaky print she did not recognize, Mr. and Mrs. B. Armitage. The address block listed in order, *Empfangsort*, city; *Straße*, address; *Kreis*, province; and *Land,* after which the sender had written CANADA in defiant block letters. None of this was intrinsically meaningful, but Margie studied every line and letter as though they were part of a code.

Fishing in her sewing basket, she pulled out a seam ripper, speared an opening at a corner of the envelope, and slid the point along the top. She withdrew the thin piece of tissue, spread it out on the dining room table, and read.

24 Dec 1942

Dear Mom and Dad,

Merry Christmas. I am safe. I was wounded at Dieppe and taken prisoner. I lost two fingers of my right hand, which makes writing difficult but otherwise am fine. Do not worry about me, for others had it worse. I was lucky.

I have not heard news of Dickie, but I hope he made it through. You can write me at this address. Love to you both. Pray for this to soon be over.

Henry

Margie reread the letter. The joy at hearing from him overwhelmed her. She read it a third time and burst into tears. As drops spilled from her cheek onto the paper, blurring her son's name, she recalled the first time she had held her baby. As every new parent does, she counted fingers and toes to make sure they were all present and accounted for. She slipped her index finger into his tiny hand, and the little being closed his fist, clutching her finger and refusing to let go. Now they had destroyed that little hand. With that vision in her mind, grief overcame her. She slumped on the table, burying her head in her arms, her body quaking, her cries so loud that neighbors on either side would have run to her door if they were home to hear.

With Brandon gone, Margie faced her anger and sorrow alone, a self-isolation that compounded the pain. She shunned her friends because they did not—could not understand. She shut out her mother, whose attempts at comfort were laced with blame.

She had turned her back on one church. She now rejected another because it preached rather than listened, offered bromides instead of solutions, and counseled duty, as though losing a husband and child were obligations she owed the Crown.

It made no difference that other wives and other mothers had suffered the same pointless losses. If anyone thought she should take comfort in hundreds of other young Canadians giving their lives in a meaningless battle in a French port she'd never heard of, they were mistaken.

On the day after receiving Henry's letter and a week after meeting with the unhelpful priest, who expected a few words from the Bible to soothe her, she pulled the drapes and stayed indoors. When the phone rang at seven—their appointed hour—she did not answer her husband's call.

Sarah Tice, her new friend from St. Johns, appeared at her front door. Margie stood motionless in the hallway, watching her through the rippled glass panes until she departed.

A day later, with nothing but a tin of crackers, some potted meat, and a half stick of margarine in the house, she was forced to go out for groceries. Although the evening was warm for late January, she dressed in a long coat and boots and tied a scarf over her unbrushed hair. She wore no makeup, venturing out at the dinner hour to avoid meeting anyone she knew. Because she had ration coupons for a family of two, she could buy anything she wanted, anything the grocer had. If he had ham, she could have ham and eggs if he had eggs.

She bought a whole chicken that would last her in various forms for days, a few mealy potatoes, a winter squash, oatmeal, a block of oleo, a precious two-pound bag of flour, and a carton of milk.

And a bottle of whiskey which, since she was a dutiful, patriotic war widow, was Canadian.

FIFTY JOURNALISTS, most assigned to cover General George Patton's nearby 2nd Armored Division, crowded together in the garden of a villa, a gleaming white home overlooking the Atlantic on the outskirts of Casablanca. They'd been summoned two hours before to attend a promised "momentous announcement." None knew why they were there, but they'd passed a thousand troops, anti-aircraft emplacements, and barbed wire fencing to arrive at the location.

"This is going to be something," Dan Sullivan, the correspondent for Hearst's International News Service, said. Two white leather chairs separated by a single microphone backed up to the garden, whose red roses and Oriental lilies perfumed the air and provided a colorful backdrop that would be lost in the black and white newsreel footage.

"Say, isn't that Harry Hopkins?" Sullivan said.

"Yeah." A fellow reporter also spotted the figure darting around inside the windowed villa. "And that's his son, Robert, an army corporal. He's a combat photographer. I'll bet ..."

As though on cue, Lieutenant Colonel Elliott Roosevelt appeared from a door of the residence carrying two chairs. President Roosevelt followed him, wearing a gray suit and black tie, his chin thrust forward like the prow of a destroyer. As an aide helped him into one of the white chairs, Roosevelt smoked a cigarette in a long silver holder, casting a wily grin at the startled reporters.

Churchill followed, shuffling forward with a cigar jutting out from his mouth. Sullivan, who had never seen the man before, was surprised at his small stature. "Christ," he said. "How long have they been here?"

Completing the tableau, Free French General de Gaulle and General Henri Giraud emerged. Sullivan dropped his pencil, bending sheepishly to pick it up. How had he and his colleagues failed to discover this meeting?

Franklin Delano Roosevelt suppressed the urge to lean back in his chair and chortle. The looks on the faces of the press corps were priceless. He'd outfoxed them once again, not only traveling thousands of miles without them knowing about it, but hiding out with the other leader of the free world.

And that wasn't all. He'd scored a public relations triumph the entire world would notice. Generals de Gaulle and Giraud might appear stiff and uncomfortable, but they were there. Together. And that had been no easy feat.

Winston had tried to get the recalcitrant de Gaulle to cooperate, but failed. The arrogant French general so bristled at being hosted by foreign powers on French territory that Churchill had threatened to withdraw the financial support of His Majesty's government. Although he was on the British dole and had few options, de Gaulle still resisted.

Roosevelt had stepped in. "Surely," he said, "you can at least appear together for a photo. We're sending a message to Berlin, and I know you'll want to affix your signature."

The arrogant French general had given in. "De Gaulle said yesterday he was Jeanne d'Arc and today that he is Georges Clemenceau," Franklin told Elliott, "but one or the other will show up tomorrow." As camera shutters clattered and 16 mm film rattled through the gates of newsreel cameras, the two generals dutifully shook hands, portraying to the public something that did not exist—unity among French forces.

Basking in the moment, Roosevelt joined Churchill in revealing to the press that they were not only present this morning but had been meeting in North Africa for an entire week without the world knowing.

"These conferences have discussed the whole global picture. It isn't just one front, one ocean, or one continent—it is literally the whole world," he told reporters. "We have proceeded on the principle of pooling all the resources of the United Nations."

His words papered over substantial Anglo-American differences that had been laid bare at the conference and would continue for months. He gave no hint of any conflict, even seeming to deny it existed. Berlin—and his political opponents—would seize on any hint of disunity. The Americans, British, Russians, Chinese, and even the French were, he insisted, *united* nations.

With Churchill standing by his side, the president closed the Casablanca conference by uttering two words he had previewed to Canadian Prime Minister Mackenzie King a month before, an expression that would change the calculus of the European end game.

"The elimination of enemy war power means the *unconditional surrender* by Germany, Italy, and Japan." He watched as a few of the reporters gaped. In case the others had missed his message, he said, "Ours has been the *unconditional surrender meeting*."

AT HIS OFFICE in the *Ordenpalais* on the *Wilhemplatz*, steps away from the Reich Chancellery, Joseph Goebbels allowed himself a rare smile. His fingers traced details of the military advance on the thin sheet sent him from the press office, one floor below. The 21st Panzer Division had struck at Faid Pass, throwing French forces back on their heels.

Just as quickly as it had come, the smirk disappeared from his face, replaced by lines of worry. Despite his effort to conceal news of reverses at Stalingrad, word was leaking out. The Minister for Propaganda, ever alert to any sign of dissension among the German people, wondered how he might use the news from North Africa to offset the looming defeat in the East.

Controlling the war message at home was far from his only problem. Goebbels sought to divide the western powers by selling the story that Germany was fighting against Bolshevism. Now, with the British, French, and Americans making a show of unity in Casablanca, he feared the tacit support of English fascists and US isolationists would crumble.

Equally troubling was the Führer's refusal to appear in public and his increasingly acrimonious relationship with his generals. At his meetings with them, Hitler lashed out, blaming anyone and everyone for the setbacks. He refused to listen to advice. His hands shook. His color was sallow.

Although Goebbels was the most loyal of Hitler's acolytes, he had made an ill-considered admission to Armaments Minister Albert Speer days before. "Germany does not have a leadership crisis; it has a leader crisis."

Now, however, as he studied reports of Roosevelt's call for unconditional surrender, his spirits rose. How could this "plutocrat," as he referred to the American president, dictate the terms of peace in a war he was losing?

Unconditional surrender. What a joke! The propaganda minister recognized the power of words—and the emptiness of what often lay behind them. Two could play that game. Goebbels would supply the direction the nation so needed. He began writing the most important speech he would ever deliver, a call to arms the *Volk* longed to hear and to which they would rally. *Total war,* an all-consuming commitment to the cause that would demand sacrifice not just from the leaders and the troops but from every citizen. By waging *Totaler Krieg,* the Third Reich would triumph over the forces of Bolshevism and Plutocracy.

As he laid out the words he would deliver at the *Sportspalast*, one of Churchill's sentences at the press conference intruded itself: "This enterprise which the President has organized—and he knows I have been his active lieutenant since the start—has altered the whole strategic aspect of the war."

He considered its implications. Goebbels fired off a message to the Führer, pointing out the improbable, that Churchill "officially designates himself now as Roosevelt's adjutant. No such humiliation has probably been seen in British history."

Something else lodged in Goebbels's craw that morning. The Abwehr, which had known for days that the two were meeting somewhere, had misinterpreted the location. As they had bombed 10 Downing Street and the British Parliament, the Luftwaffe could have attacked the conference in Morocco, eliminating both leaders and most of the general staffs of both nations. The intelligence service might have assured German victory if only they had not taken literally Casablanca's English translation: *White House*.

If we lose this war, he thought to himself, it will owe much to our own stupidity.

8

MARCH 18-APRIL 1, 1943

"My God, he was right." Secretary of War Henry L. Stimson removed his steel-rimmed glasses, massaged the bridge of his nose, and uttered a loud sigh. Getting to his feet, he spun the globe while he stared out the window of his office at the newly completed Pentagon.

He had been in a rage since learning the "bad news" from the Casablanca Conference. Stimson and Marshall had agreed the US would hold firm to a cross-Channel invasion of the European Continent that summer. Instead, Britain had substituted these well-considered plans with their own, "getting away with their own theories."

Stimson had served every president since Theodore Roosevelt. His vast experience in foreign affairs and defense matters compelled him to speak when he felt he was correct. With American forces having secured Guadalcanal, Stimson was eager to bring the European Theater to a close so the nation could focus on Japan. Churchill's European power-politics long game blocked that path, and in Stimson's opinion, Roosevelt had yielded to their views as against those of his Joint Chiefs of Staff.

Events in North Africa now stilled his fury. After French troops retreated at Faïd Pass, the Wehrmacht threw allied forces back fifty miles. Seizing the opportunity, Field Marshall Rommel attacked at Kasserine Pass, destroying 220 Allied tanks and inflicting six thousand casualties.

The debacle cast a pall over Washington, and nowhere was the mood darker than at the Pentagon. The Germans were stronger than they had realized, and the US less well prepared. In one stroke, Rommel's pummeling of Allied forces showed the Americans they were unready for an amphibious assault of the scale needed to get an army ashore in France and carry the fight to Berlin.

Stimson accepted that Roosevelt's cautious approach had been providential. "The only way you can make a man trustworthy is to trust him," he told fellow Republicans in Congress.

WHEN HE SPOTTED the young man at the end of the barracks hallway, Armitage froze. "Dickie?" The name caught in his throat.

The prisoner returned his stare in confusion. "*Was?*"

"*Entschuldigung,*" Brandon said as he approached. "I thought you were someone else." He had not hallucinated on Christmas Eve. From a distance of ten feet or more, the resemblance was striking. As he drew closer, he realized this fellow was a few years older, an inch or two taller, and carried himself with an assurance that was unlike his younger son.

He sniffed at the dank, earthy smell permeating the lower level, thinking to himself that they needed to improve conditions here. "I'm Sergeant Armitage."

Drawing himself up to his full height to emphasize the differences in their ranks, the prisoner said, "Leutnant Jörg Schumacher."

Armitage grinned and reached into his shirt pocket. "*Eine Zigarette?*"

"No, thank you. I don't smoke."

Armitage pocketed the pack. Neither did he. "Where do you hail from?"

"Germany."

"Yes, but ..."

"Dortmund," Schumacher said.

"*Im Ruhrgebiet.*"

"Yes, the Ruhr," he said, "you know it?"

"I know *of* it. I spent three years in your country during the last war, involuntarily."

"*Ach*, that explains it. Your German is quite good."

"It's coming back," Armitage said. "And your English is excellent."

It was his third week back on guard duty. The new commandant, Lieutenant-Colonel James McHugh, had accepted his groveling apology, agreeing to Lieutenant Morrison's recommendation that he use his language skills to keep tabs on the prisoners.

"Who did you take me for a moment ago?"

"Someone I used to know. A young man like yourself." He considered whether to unburden himself, but changed the subject. "What branch are you in?"

Schumacher took his time before answering, and Armitage felt the prisoner was studying him. "Luftwaffe. I was a fighter pilot, shot down over southern England in 1940."

"The Battle of Britain. You're lucky to have survived."

Schumacher made a noncommittal grunt, and Armitage sensed the prisoner didn't want to discuss it. "What's news do you have from home?" How much did the Germans know? Was this man aware that Patton had taken Gafsa in Tunisia and that Montgomery's troops had broken through the Mareth Line, driving the Africa Korps north where their backs would be against the Mediterranean?

Before he could answer, a prisoner with a scarred face confronted them. "Who's this, then?"

Schumacher introduced Christoph Helbig, who greeted Armitage in German.

"Should we be speaking with him?" Helbig asked.

"I mean no harm. I'm practicing my German."

"He's all right," Schumacher assured him. "He was a prisoner himself."

Helbig still stood mutely, leading Armitage to wonder if he and

Schumacher were hiding something. Before Armitage could continue the conversation, however, Corporal Smith rushed in, out of breath. "There you are. You're wanted on the phone."

"Who is it?" It had to be someone local. No one would place a long-distance call and remain on the line while people scoured the camp for him.

"Some woman. She sounds hysterical. You'd better come."

Armitage raced out of the building, leaving the two prisoners and Corporal Smith in his wake.

"I THINK I picked up a sleeping sickness or Gambia fever or some kindred bug in that hellhole of yours," Roosevelt wrote Churchill in early March. For days he couldn't function after two o'clock. Shortly after his return from Casablanca, he'd hosted a dinner for the explorer Admiral Richard Byrd. He excused himself during the meal, wheeled to his private residence, and told Daisy Suckley, "I'm exhausted."

For a week, he struggled through morning meetings but retired to his living quarters after lunch. On February 21, he visited his doctor, Ross McIntire, complaining of a sinus infection. McIntire, an ear, nose, and throat specialist who attended to the president's every complaint, prescribed a sulfa drug.

Three days later, the White House canceled all Roosevelt's appointments. He spent the next four days in bed while a fever raged. He tried to resume work but arose late, grouped all his meetings around noon, and retired after lunch, too exhausted to continue.

On March 4, he held an afternoon cabinet meeting before decamping for Hyde Park. With Eleanor in Chicago, Daisy traveled along to care for him. The fever "left me feeling like a wet rag," he wrote Churchill.

Five days later, the fever broke. Roosevelt returned to the Executive Mansion the following morning, writing Churchill, "I feel like a fighting cock."

Those around him didn't share the assessment. Daisy phoned Eleanor about her concern, telling her, "He has a pinched look in his face, and his hands sometimes shake." Eleanor rushed home from Chicago. Confronting him while he lay in bed, she told him, "You look ghastly."

He waved away her concern. "I caught something in Morocco, but I'm better now."

"You don't look it. You're pale, and I don't like the sound of that cough. Perhaps you should see a specialist."

"There's no need," he said. "McIntire is taking good care of me."

Knowing that he would not be swayed from his dependence on the White House physician for every ailment, she gave in.

SCHUMACHER TURNED from his encounter with the strange Canadian. The man was too friendly, struggling to ingratiate himself by offering cigarettes and conversation. What did he mean by asking about news from Germany? What was he after?

Which was the question Helbig asked. "What does he want with us?"

"He was just making small talk. He took me for someone else," he said, hiding his own reservations. Schumacher recalled the guard's eager smile when he first spotted him, and his crestfallen expression when he realized his mistake.

"I don't like him nosing around," Helbig said. "If he speaks German, he may pick up clues to our project—one man grumbling about how tired he is, what to do with the dirt, any muttered complaint."

"It would help if you cleaned your fingernails," Schumacher replied. Helbig looked down at the evidence of tunneling written on his hands. "If we act like we have something to hide, we'll make him suspicious. He's trying to cultivate me. It could be innocent, or he may have some purpose in mind."

"Be careful," Helbig said. "You don't want Kretschmer coming down on you." As the Luftwaffe major had done at Bowmanville, he now had displaced the Lagerführer at Camp 20, issuing orders as though he were Field Marshal Keitel himself. He had re-instituted daily drills, organized a network of spies to keep track of prisoner activities, and meted out punishment whenever there was an infraction. One of his directives was that prisoners were not to fraternize with their guards.

While, like all German officers, obedience to the chain of command had been drilled into him, Schumacher held Kretschmer in contempt, obeying his incessant instructions only to the extent necessary. His biggest concern was concealing from him the unapproved tunneling operation. Why he kept it a secret, Schumacher couldn't say. His instincts, which had not failed him up to this point, told him to keep its existence closely held, and so he did, instructing his comrades to do the same.

With spring coming, he was about to solve the problem of the dirt from the tunnel, which now occupied two metal barrels in the supply closet. One prisoner, who had apprenticed to a tailor before escaping into the military, sewed flour bags into the lining of dungarees, one end secured to the waistband, the other open and tied with a length of twine to the belt loops. Once the prisoners planted their vegetable garden in a few weeks, they would fill the inner bags with earth, walk out to the garden, untie the straps, and let the dirt fall at their feet before working it into the soil. The scheme would work until the present barrels were empty, but as the color and quality of the garden's soil changed, he'd have to think of something else.

Leaving Helbig behind, Schumacher left the building and set off for a stroll around the enclosure. The sky was cloudless. Morning temperatures were still below freezing, even this close to spring. A fresh breeze off the bay made the early hour seem even colder. He breathed in the clean air, exhaling a cloud of vapor as he strode forward, looking to anyone watching that he was out for exercise.

As he rounded the garden, he saw a young woman staring at him through the links of the north fence. He smiled, and she returned it, batting her eyes in a coquettish display. Recognizing her from the day he'd arrived at the train station, he approached her. "My name is Jörg. What's yours?"

"Pamela," she said in a quiet voice. A moment ago, she'd seemed eager to engage him. Now she seemed shy. He slowed his pace, walking along the fence, and she kept in step. "I shouldn't be speaking to you," she said.

"Why not?"

"I don't know."

"Are you more afraid of our guards or your neighbors in town?"

"Both, I guess."

"Don't worry about the guards. They will protect you."

She giggled. "Your English is very good." She articulated it slowly, as though she feared he wouldn't understand her.

"I've been studying ever since the day I arrived and saw you at the train station. I have to practice my English, I said, for when I see that young woman again."

Did she blush, or was it the cold weather that made her face turn crimson? "That's silly."

"No, it's true." He glanced at the tower, where a lone guard watched them. This is not what Schumacher wanted. Still, he couldn't bear to turn this lovely girl away.

"I have to go now," she said.

"Come see me again. Write me. Jörg Schumacher, in care of the camp."

"I'll leave you a potato."

"What?"

"I'll toss a potato over the fence, just where it meets the road," she said, looking toward where they'd met. "I'll enclose a message, and you can write back. They feed you potatoes, don't they?"

He reared back his head and laughed. "Agreed. I look forward to it. Perhaps we can meet in town sometime."

But she had turned and walked away. Schumacher smiled, waiting for her to turn around for one more look at him, but it never came. He glanced up at the watchtower, laughed, and waved a greeting. The guard returned it. Schumacher hoped the guard didn't know the girl. He didn't want to make trouble for her. Her fears about being seen with an enemy might be justified.

He resumed his walk, circumnavigating the prison grounds twice until he was confident the guard was bored with him. He rested his back against the edge of the barracks, inhaling deep gulps as he feigned exhaustion. Satisfied that his watcher was paying him no attention, he reached in his pocket for a string, which he'd wrapped around a nail. Turning to face the building, he did a series of pushups, planting the pin in the ground midway through, then inched the rest of the cord forward with his toe.

He did some quick math. At this rate, it would be mid-June before they tunneled their way beneath the fence.

MARGIE HEARD him before she saw him. Standing at the kitchen sink in a pink woolen housecoat, she heard the front door open and a cheery, "Hello, there."

She dumped the dishtowel on the counter and padded into the hallway in her moccasins. "What are you doing here?"

Armitage dropped his duffel bag and held out his arms. "I took leave so we could spend some time together."

She stepped toward him but did not enter his embrace. "You might have let me know."

Armitage sighed. "I called. Called several times, but you didn't answer."

Margie offered no explanation. "I suppose you'll want coffee."

"Only if you can spare it. I had a small breakfast on the train."

She retreated to the kitchen, poured water into the percolator, spooned two measures of coffee, turned on the Emerson two-burner countertop stove, and folded her arms. Her husband followed her, leaning against the doorframe. "You look tired," he said.

"I'm fine."

"Are you sleeping?"

"I said I'm fine."

"You look—"

"No, I can't sleep. You?"

"I'm doing all right. They keep me busy. I'm exhausted by day's end, but it's important work."

Margie didn't answer. Liquid bubbled into the percolator's glass ball, and she reduced the heat.

"I've run into an interesting man, a prisoner. He looks so much like Dickie I called out his name when I first saw him. It was eerie."

"I don't want to talk about Dickie." They stood in silence for over a minute. Margie turned off the burner and poured a steaming cup. She set it down on the dinette and reached for the sugar bowl.

"Don't bother," he said. "It's too dear. I've learned to take my coffee black."

"Good for you."

"Sit down with me. Please." She sat, her arms folded beneath her breasts, eyes fixed on the kitchen window. "What have you been doing?"

"Doing? I get up in the morning, clean up the house, listen to the radio, take walks if the weather allows it, cook my meals, and go to bed."

"Do you get out at all? To movies or church, I mean?"

She tapped her right foot, marking time. "How long are you staying?"

"I have seven days leave."

She massaged her left arm with her right hand.

"You don't seem pleased," he said.

"What are we going to talk about all week?"

Now it was his turn to reward a question with silence. He drank his coffee, never taking his eyes off her. "Margie, what's wrong?"

"Nothing. Nothing is wrong."

"If you must know, I'm here because your mother called me. She's concerned about you. She says you don't answer her calls, keep the door locked, and don't open it when she drops by."

"So, you're here because my mother told you to come, not because you chose to."

"That's not true, I—"

"You've been home four days since you joined up, right around New Year's, and that was just so you could sleep with me. Otherwise, I haven't seen or heard from you. So now, because Mother calls, you come running."

"I've written, called, sent all the information I could gather on Henry's situation. You don't answer the phone and never write back. Please stop tapping your foot."

"It's my house and my foot. I'll do as I please."

He shoved his empty coffee cup aside. "Please tell me what's wrong, Margie."

She sprang from the table, grabbed the empty cup and saucer, and lowered them into the sink with a clatter. Turning to face him, she crossed her arms again. "What do you think is wrong? One son is dead. The other is wounded and held prisoner by the Germans. My husband is off playing soldier. My mother tries to run my life. What could be wrong?" As she spoke, her voice rose from a low, stolid recitation to a frenzied shout.

"Come sit down," he said.

"I'm not going to sit down, and I won't calm down."

Armitage got up from the table and tried to take her in his arms, but she moved away, both hands in front of her as though fending off an attack. "Don't touch me."

"Margie, I'm home because I care about you. I love you. You're all I have, all I ever wanted."

"You liar." She grabbed the tea towel from the counter and swung it at him.

He dropped his arms, looking dazed. "What do you mean?"

"Who is Jeanie?"

"Who?"

"Don't give me 'who.' Jeanie, that's who. The woman you've been seeing while you're up north."

Armitage buried his head in his hands. "Her name is Jeanne Macallum—Jeanne Canavan now. When I went overseas in 1915, we were engaged. Sit down. I'll tell you all about her."

She joined him at the table, clutching the towel in her hands. He poured out his heart, telling of his relationship with the teenaged girl he'd courted and won, his three years of longing for her, fingering her faded photograph he used as a bookmark in his Bible, the long lapses between her letters, the months of silence preceding his release, and his return to find she hadn't waited for him.

"I haven't seen her since. I don't communicate with her. I tried once after I returned, but that was before we met."

She listened to this without betraying emotion, sitting erect in the iron chair, still holding the tea towel. "Do you still love her?"

He looked at her, frowned, and turned away. "Why would you ask me that?"

"Because you call out to her in your dreams."

He took in a deep breath and stroked his chin. "It's the war, I think."

"Oh, come on."

"No, really. For my three years and—what?—two months in captivity, she was all I thought about. Particularly after this," he said, pounding his fist on his right leg. "Her memory gave me something to live for, a pot of gold at the end of the rainbow. When our boys shipped out, all the memories came flooding back—not of her, but of the battle, imprisonment, hopelessness. I spend my nights reliving those years. I suppose that's why I call her name."

"Why haven't you told me this before? Why did you hide it? I told you everything about my life."

"I didn't want to burden you. You had your own problems. You'd lost a husband and had a child on the way."

"Is that why you married me? You were mourning her loss and needed someone? Anyone?"

He reached for her hand, and this time she didn't flinch. "No, Margie. I married you because I love you. Understand? I'd lost someone, and you'd lost someone. I thought we'd be good for one another."

Again, she asked, "Do you still love her?"

"No," he repeated, "I love only you." Her flat expression told him she didn't believe him.

She banished him to the single bed in Dickie's room. Four days after his arrival, he left, telling her he'd been called back to Gravenhurst.

***

"HARRY, I want you to read this." Roosevelt summoned Harry Hopkins to join him in the White House family quarters during breakfast. Although Hopkins found the bedroom hot, the president sat in his wheelchair with an afghan draped over his legs. He looked pale, and the tremor in his hands as he thrust out two pages made it difficult for Hopkins to grasp them.

His friend's deteriorating condition concerned him, but Hopkins was in no better shape, having battled stomach cancer since 1939. Here we are, he thought, two semi-invalids trying to save the world.

The message, dated March 18, 1943, was a letter from Soviet Premier Joseph Stalin to Churchill, translated into barely readable English. Hopkins was Roosevelt's liaison to "Uncle Joe." As he read what was stated and unstated, his prominent forehead crinkled with lines of worry.

> At height of our fighting against Hitler's forces, the weight of Anglo-American offensive in North Africa has not only not increased but there has been no development of offensive at all and time limit for operations set by yourself has been extended. Meanwhile Germany succeeded in transferring 36 divisions from west against Soviet troops. It is easy to see what difficulties this created for Soviet armies and how position of Germans on Soviet-German front was alleviated.

Stalin wrote that he welcomed the plan to invade Sicily once North Africa was secure but continued,

I see main task in hastening a second front in France. As you remember you admitted possibility of such a front already in 1942 and in any case not later than in the spring of 1943. I underlined in my previous message necessity of the blow from the west not later than in the spring or in the early summer of this year.

"Soviet troops spent the whole winter in tense fighting," he wrote, and with Hitler transferring troops to the Russian front, it promised to be a bloody spring. And then came the last touch, the reason Roosevelt had interrupted his advisor's breakfast. "I deem it my duty to warn you in the strongest possible manner how dangerous would be from the viewpoint of our common cause further delay in opening second front in France."

"Dangerous to our common cause." Hopkins repeated. He looked up at Roosevelt, sighed, and reread the paragraph.

"It's a warning," Roosevelt said.

"No question. He suggests that if we don't attack through France this summer, he may sue for a separate peace." If Stalin and Hitler were to settle their differences, Germany would shift divisions westward to renew the planned invasion of Great Britain called off in 1940.

Hopkins handed back the ominous message. "I recommend you try again to meet with him. Perhaps one-on-one."

"I agree. I wish he had met with us in Morocco. This business about remaining near the front …"

"From what I gather, he has been nowhere close to it."

"Of course not. His real fear is what his enemies might do if he were to leave Moscow."

"Give it another try, Mr. President. Stalin doesn't trust Churchill. You are persuasive, and Lend-Lease provides leverage we will no longer have after the war."

"I agree. We face two issues, Harry. We have to persuade Stalin to join a post-war peace pact, and we must get Allied troops on the Continent at the earliest practical date."

For the moment, Roosevelt and his generals were as one.

9

—————

MAY 11-25, 1943

As Schumacher returned from his daily walk around the camp perimeter, Helbig grabbed him by his injured left arm with such force he winced. "They want us at the main building." He gnawed his lower lip with his upper teeth.

"Who are *they*?" Schumacher said, though he knew full well.

"The Lagerführer and Kretschmer."

Schumacher shrugged. "Let's go, then."

"Are we in trouble?"

"We've lost another army in North Africa, the Soviets are chasing us westward, and the Allies are sinking our U-boats at will. You and I are stuck here. So, ja, I'd say we're in deep shit."

They trudged up the path, the fresh breeze off the bay enveloping them. Schumacher concealed his concern with outward nonchalance. Only weeks before, the *Triumvirat* had ordered fellow officers to beat a Kriegsmariner with a rubber hose for refusing to raise his arm and yell, "Heil Hitler." It took a week before the man could walk upright.

Kretschmer had endless rules, some arbitrary but all enforced, as though the only point was compelling obedience. He and Helbig had not just bent a cardinal rule but driven a tank through it.

Inside the main detention center, the pair mounted the metal stairs to the third level, entering the prisoners' library. A reading table had been pulled to the front, three chairs placed behind it, and an open space before it. A prisoner saw them enter and scampered away without a word.

Minutes passed while the two men waited. That was part of the game, of course. Keep them in suspense. Let their imaginations whir and crank like perpetual motion machines. But while Helbig fidgeted, Schumacher smirked as he formulated a plan.

The three officers entered, Kretschmer wearing a fierce expression, the Lagerführer appearing distracted, and *Korvettenkapitan* Otto Bruchmann, the ranking Kriegsmarine officer, cocking his head with an arched eyebrow as if to say, "What can I do?"

"The prisoners will stand at attention," Kretschmer bawled. They complied. "I am sure you wonder why we summoned you."

"Before we begin, Major, we wish to share something of importance with you," Schumacher said. Before Kretschmer could interrupt, he continued, "A present."

"What sort of 'present?'"

Schumacher lowered his voice, affecting a conspiratorial tone. "We have started a tunnel."

Kretschmer frowned, Helbig jerked as though pulled by a puppet master, but Bruchmann asked, "A tunnel?"

"We found a location in the barracks near the prison wall where the soil is sufficiently soft to dig. We concealed the entry from the guards."

"You also hid it from us," Kretschmer said. "The Lagerführer must approve any escape plan."

"We do not have an escape plan. That would need your approval," Schumacher said, the picture of innocence. "That's why we're presenting it now."

"You should have brought it to our attention before you began work," the Lagerführer said.

"Perhaps, but in the past, the Canadians have planted informants among prisoners. We are separated from the main body and know all the participants from our training days. Leutnant Helbig saw this as an opportunity. 'Let's keep this to ourselves to prevent a spy from finding out and exposing us,' he said. 'When we've nearly finished, we'll notify the Triumvirat, and they will assume control.'" His smile was guileless as he turned toward his companion.

"How far have you come?" Bruchmann said.

Schumacher turned toward Helbig in deference to the "mastermind."

"We're almost to the fence." Helbig's voice trembled. "Another ten meters ..."

Together, they outlined the progress they'd made, but Kretschmer waved them away. "We must inspect it. Two officers here worked on the tunnel at Bowmanville. They know what they're doing. This project is now ours. You aren't to go near the tunnel unless ordered to do so. Dismissed."

The two turned and left without another word. As they trudged down the hill toward the barracks, Helbig asked, "Do you think that's why they ordered us here?"

"They raised nothing else, did they?"

"I'm disappointed. Will they include us in the escape?"

"How could they refuse?" Schumacher suspected they were being cut out but was unconcerned. He had an alternate plan, one he felt had a greater chance for success.

By early May, spring had fled the nation's capital. The temperature had reached ninety muggy degrees the weekend before. Residents mounted fans in their open windows, trying to create cooling breezes, to little effect. Men rode to work on the city's bus lines with their collars open, ties dangling at the front, suit coats slung across one shoulder. An army of typists and stenographers converged bare legged on the imposing office buildings lining Pennsylvania Avenue. Some had painted thin stripes down their calves to simulate silk stockings. Along the Tidal Basin, the "Oriental Cherry Trees," as they had been called since the Pearl Harbor attack, had shed their blossoms. The city wilted under the oppressive heat, fearing that this summer would be unrelenting.

At the Pentagon and the White House, however, an atmosphere of quiet optimism prevailed. In the Pacific two weeks before, a Mitsubishi G4M had slowed as it prepared to land at Ballale, off Bougainville, on the morning of April 18. The plane carried Admiral Isoroku Yamamoto, commander-in-chief of the Combined Imperial Japanese Fleet and architect of the attack on Pearl Harbor. He was beginning an inspection tour of naval bases, intended to boost morale after losing Guadalcanal. Having broken Japanese naval code JN25, US intelligence pinpointed the exact time and place of his arrival. As the bomber and a companion aircraft approached the field, eighteen Lockheed P-38G Lightnings from the 339th Fighter Squadron on Guadalcanal closed in, bringing both planes down.

The attack had followed soul-searching at the highest levels in Washington. Was it right, even in wartime, to assassinate the military leader of your enemy? The question went up the chain of command to Admiral King, who passed it to Secretary of the Navy Frank Knox, who kicked it to the president. He did not hesitate. "Get Yamamoto."

For days, Roosevelt had longed to tell the American public of the successful mission, but as long as the Japanese remained silent, he could not. As far as they knew, the American fighters had happened upon the bombers by chance. To reveal that the US knew Yamamoto was aboard would reveal the secret of "Magic," that it was reading Japanese communications.

Now, General Marshall asked Roosevelt to cross the Potomac for a briefing on North Africa. With the other military chiefs leaning forward to catch every word, Marshall said, "It's the beginning of the end. The British First Army took Tunis last night, and our troops have reached Bizerte. German forces under General von Arnim have just surrendered."

"That's it, then?"

"Not quite, Mr. President." Standing before a map of northern Tunisia, Marshall pointed to a small peninsula jutting out into the

Mediterranean, pointing northeast toward Sicily. "We've bottled up the remaining German and Italian forces here at Cap Bon. As you know, Hitler threw additional troops into the fray last month. We have them outflanked, outmanned, and outgunned. They face certain defeat. It's a matter of hours."

Amid their euphoria, Marshall said, "But now we have an additional problem."

Roosevelt looked up at his Army chief of staff, waiting for him to continue. Despite his weariness, which he fought to conceal from others, nothing engaged him more than an issue to be addressed.

"We've learned Churchill wants to follow our landings in Sicily with an invasion of the Italian Peninsula." Roosevelt was well aware of the prime minister's preference.

"This information comes from Field Marshal Dill," Marshall said. Dill was the head of the British military liaison. Like Canadian Prime Minister Mackenzie King, he often aided as an interpreter between the two sides, divided, as George Bernard Shaw had observed, by a common language. "He wants to follow that with a move on Turkey and the Balkans."

Roosevelt frowned, pushing his wheelchair back from the table with his powerful arms. "I thought we had an agreement."

The British Prime Minister had arrived in Washington two nights before with a retinue of 160 officers, clerks, and spear carriers for a two-week conference code-named "Trident," meant to determine the strategy for the war in Europe. After Casablanca, the next steps had seemed clear: first North Africa, Sicily next, then planning for a cross-Channel invasion.

"General Brooke listed that as an option," Marshall said, "but he was careful not to state it as a commitment."

"What about the Second Front?" The president's soft voice concealed his consternation. "I've promised Stalin we're moving on to Berlin. We must keep that commitment."

Marshall cleared his throat. "Churchill believes that by involving Turkey, he can draw German troops from the Russian front and satisfy Stalin."

"They're still angling for a war of attrition," Leahy warned. "The British Chiefs won't agree to a cross-Channel invasion until Germany has collapsed under pressure from Russia and our air attacks."

"If they get their way, it postpones victory in Europe until 1946 or 1947," Admiral King said. "Another year or two on the European Continent while Japan goes unpunished? The American people won't stand for it, Mr. President."

"We cannot be bulldozed this time." Marshall was mindful that his commander-in-chief did not agree that the British had gotten the better of them at Casablanca.

Roosevelt was aware he faced a united front but said nothing.

After they returned to the White House, Secretary Stimson grabbed the president's good ear, reminding him that Republican leaders were encouraging General Douglas MacArthur to run for president in 1944. "If we don't open a Second Front by the election ..."

"I know, Henry. We'll listen and see what unfolds. As you know, I don't make a decision until the last minute; only then do I have all the facts."

MARGIE STUDIED herself in the full-length mirror, modeling the royal blue felt turban hat in the "Latin America style," a dramatic sweep in front like a fighter plane taking off. Pinson's Department Store required all women who worked in its millinery department to wear hats chosen from its regular stock, paying for them out of their own pockets. Bernice Oberholzer had helped her select this one. It had cost her eighty-eight cents, two hours' wages. It was all she could afford, but Margie loved it. The blue brought out the color of her eyes and contrasted with her vivid red lipstick.

While still grieving over the death of her younger son, her spirits had begun to recover as she exchanged letters with Henry. He seemed to enjoy his work on the farm, writing, "They feed me well, and being outside all day is better than being confined to a camp."

The end of a cruel winter had further brightened her mood.

Spring brought rebirth, and news reports brought hope that this war would soon be over.

And now she had a job to occupy her time. It had been Bernie's idea. Her childhood friend had come limping back into Margie's life during the first days of spring, offering a pound cake and profuse apologies for her earlier insensitivity. Margie, who could barely recall the conversation, said, "That's all right, Bernie. No one knows what to say."

The two women, one a widow, the other who felt like one, bonded again, sharing morning coffee and local gossip, avoiding mention of Margie's sons. But not of Brandon. Margie still blamed him for allowing her boys to go off to war, and during their infrequent phone calls, he seemed more interested in his work at the camp than in her well-being.

During their kaffeeklatsches, she complained to Bernice about her husband's emotional distance. Her friend tut-tutted and supported Margie's lamentations without hesitation. "You know what you need?" she said one morning. "You need a job."

"A job?" Margie said, "I don't have to work."

"It's not just the money. It's the opportunity to meet new people, to socialize. We're a merry little group down at Pinson's. Almost all the girls are about our age, though there are a couple of pretty young things. A few widows like me, others like you whose husbands have gone off to serve king and country. We get along great and support each other."

Margie thought it over and, two days later, sat in the office of Godfrey Sperling, manager of the women's division. "We need an attractive, mature woman like you to work in the hat department," he said. "It's only part-time, Fridays and Saturdays, but it might work into something greater."

"I haven't worked in years," she said, "and never in a department store."

He smiled and looked her up and down. "We can teach you all that. What counts is how you look and how you carry yourself. When women shop for a hat, they want to see someone who makes them say, 'I could look like that.' You're not a silly young thing. Women will identify with you. And as for your looks, well ..."

He stopped as if embarrassed and waved his right hand in the air to complete his sentence. Margie felt her face grow warm. She lowered her eyes, though a smile never left her face.

He brought her down to the second floor and introduced her to Rowena Walter, the department manager. Shoppers surrounded them, trying on different hats and admiring themselves in the mirrors. Across the aisle, other groups of women pawed through racks of robes. The air was filled with the murmur of dozens of voices. Margie breathed in the smells of pressed fabric and dyes and silently thanked her friend for the idea. She could enjoy herself here.

But the department manager seemed resistant. "Mr. Sperling, we don't need additional help right now."

"It's just for weekends, the two days after we've advertised our specials in the *Daily Star*."

"And I don't have time to train another salesgirl."

"Mrs. Armitage is a fast learner. Bernice Oberholzer brought her to our attention."

"You know Bernie?" she said. Margie explained they'd been friends since childhood. "Well, in that case, welcome."

Now, at the start of her third Friday, Bernice stepped behind her as she primped in the women employees' lounge. "You look great," she said.

"You think so?"

"Don't overdo it. You're trying to impress our buyers, not Mr. Sperling."

"Oh, Bernie."

"Oh, Bernie," she repeated. "You know he has his eye on you."

"I know no such thing. And anyway, it's nice to be appreciated after all this time."

"Of course it is," she said. "Just be careful is all I'm saying."

JÖRG SCHUMACHER FINGERED the airmail letter before opening it. It bore an Oslo postmark and was printed in his father's precise hand. He wrote every two weeks, always on Friday at the end of a busy week. His message was invariable: How are you? We pray for you. Things are going well for us. I am doing important work. Your mother enjoys it here. Stay strong.

Not that his father was unfeeling. While he was a serious man and a strict disciplinarian, he could be tender when concerned about his family's welfare, shedding his militaristic cloak as though it were a costume.

No, his letters were perfunctory because his son was not the only audience. Censors on both sides studied it for evidence of disloyalty on the one hand and clues to enemy intentions on the other.

His mother wrote less frequently but conveyed more information. She told engaging stories of life in her native Norway, his sister's progress at university, visits with family and friends, and her delight at gorging herself on *lutefisk*, *smalahove*, and other Norwegian delicacies Schumacher found abominating. During *Jul*, she had been joyous, describing how she'd decorated their house with *nisser* figures and celebrated *Lille Julaften* with her extended family.

Thus, one line in her previous letter stood out: "I miss Germany. How much longer shall we remain here?" What was going on?

Sitting at the end of his cot, Schumacher opened his father's letter. The first three paragraphs were *pro forma*. He could have recited them without reading them. The fourth paragraph was different, unlike anything his father had written.

> I worry about your mother and sister. The Norwegians are giving them a difficult time. Your sister's classmates at university call her "*Tyskerjente*," German girl. She is that, but the word has bad connotations here. While she was shopping a few weeks ago, a woman shouted another name at her, one I will not repeat. I asked her for the woman's description so we can find her and deal with her, but she refuses.

If this continues, I may send them home. I have considered asking for a transfer, but the options are limited. My place is here.

Schumacher put the letter down and rose to his feet, staring out the window at the morning rain. By limited options, his father meant the Eastern Front. From his knowledge of Norwegian, Schumacher suspected the word he refused to print was *Tyskertøs*, German whore.

THE TWO SIDES met in the White House Cabinet Room for the first Trident meeting. With a copy of *The Signing of the Declaration of Independence* by Charles Édouard Armand-Dumaresq over the mantle and white busts of George Washington and Benjamin Franklin looking on, the president seized the high ground. "It was less than a year ago that we met here at the White House and set forth the steps leading to Operation Torch," Roosevelt said. "It is appropriate that we should meet again just as that operation is coming to a satisfactory conclusion."

The success of the North Africa campaign had given the Allies the experience they needed to move on to Sicily, Roosevelt said, expressing hope the invasion, Operation Husky, "will meet with similar good fortune."

The question now before them was what was to follow. "Where do we go from Husky? I have always shrunk from the thought of putting large armies into Italy," he said, pointing out that every mile won on that vast peninsula would increase the mouths the Allies would be obligated to feed and the housing they would have to provide. The US preferred to resurrect the cross-Channel invasion plan Brooke had rejected at Casablanca.

It was Churchill's turn. After heaping praise on the cooperation that was about to produce victory in North Africa, he launched on a different course. Following Husky, the Allies should defeat Italy, an opening wedge in what he called "the soft underbelly of Europe. With Italy's defeat, her troops will join the Allies. Our combined forces can establish bases in Turkey, perhaps even get the Turks to help attack the Third Reich from the south."

As Roosevelt sat impassively, Churchill thundered on. "There is no need for a cross-Channel operation unless Germany collapses from within. When that happens, we will cross the Channel to hasten the war's end."

The prime minister proposed five objectives, securing the Mediterranean first, a possible cross-Channel attack fourth, and only then, the defeat of Japan. Though Dill had alerted them to this possibility, Churchill's audacity stunned the American delegation. This is not what they'd agreed to at Casablanca.

Roosevelt fought back. "The US advocates a cross-Channel invasion as soon as possible, not later than next spring. That is what both sides have come to Washington to work out."

He did not state the obvious, though everyone at the table recognized it—everyone but Churchill: Great Britain was nearly bankrupt, forced to reduce its eighteen divisions to keep those that remained at full strength. The US held the cards.

Nor did he mention the pressure he was under from his public, the Congress, and his generals to finish the work in Europe and move on to the Pacific. General Joseph Stilwell, commander of US Forces in China, Burma, and India, had charged, "Churchill has Roosevelt in his pocket," echoing General MacArthur's charge. Roosevelt could not leave the conference without a plan to end the war in Europe.

The plenary session broke up with no agreement. For the next two weeks, Churchill and Roosevelt met every other day at the Executive Mansion while their military chiefs wrestled back and forth a few blocks away at the Federal Reserve Building. Better prepared, the US Joint Chiefs would insist on the cross-Channel invasion strategy.

As they met, German forces surrendered in Tunisia. The Allies took over 275,000 prisoners of war, more than the Russians had killed or taken at Stalingrad.

In North Africa, the war was over. But in Washington, DC, it was just beginning.

Armitage completed his call to Margie and left his quarters for a stroll around Gravenhurst. Spring was in full bloom, crocuses and daffodils replaced by lilies and lady's slippers, their perfume drifting in the evening breeze. He poked his head inside Sloan's Restaurant and waved to the cashier, who was counting the day's take before closing up. "It's nice to have extra law enforcement in town," she said. "You've ended the crime wave."

He laughed. There was no crime in Gravenhurst, not until Americans flocked north for fishing season.

"What brings you in at this hour?"

"I'm just looking for someone to talk with other than a prisoner or a fellow imprisoner." He wasn't about to tell her he was passing the time until he could launch an important nighttime mission.

"Coffee?" She poured out the rest of the evening pot, and he waited as the grounds settled. "We're seeing a lot of your boys now."

Prisoners who behaved themselves were allowed supervised daytime walks. With April's constant rain having given way to cool, sunny days, many were taking advantage of the opportunity, and townsfolk had come to know a few of them by name. "They seem like fine young men. Too bad they got caught up in all this."

"You've only met the decent fellows. Unfortunately, we also have dedicated Nazis, members of the SS who served as political officers on submarines. Nasty individuals. Dangerous. You're unlikely to encounter them."

She shivered and shook her head. Armitage thanked her and continued on his way, walking along the shore of Gull Lake, then retracing his steps past the camp. Taking a seat on a rock above Muskoka Bay, he watched copper reflections of the setting sun dance on the ripples.

The sun was hewing north, and in another month, he'd enjoy sixteen hours of daylight, ending months of winter darkness. He reveled in the long days, keeping himself company on walks through the town and the nearby forest. His perambulations were often aimless but not tonight.

Since his return from Toronto, he called Margie at least twice a week, sometimes more. She was speaking to him now. She shared news from Henry's letters. He confined himself to topics that wouldn't upset her, life in Gravenhurst and routine news of what was happening at the camp. Nothing sensitive.

She'd taken a part-time job at a department store where she sold hats to the few women able to afford a new one in these straitened times. Armitage thought it was good for her. Her voice had a lilt he hadn't heard since the previous summer. She chattered about people she'd met during the day and those she worked with. It seemed to take her mind off her sons and herself.

The few extra dollars she brought in didn't hurt, either. "My pin money," she called it. He was grateful that she'd found a diversion.

When the last ember of daylight retreated across the bay, he rose from his perch, using his right arm to push himself erect. His leg throbbed now, as it always did when he'd sat motionless for too long. He peed against a tree and hobbled back to the camp, giving the guard a languid salute as he entered the prisoner's compound. "All quiet?" he asked.

"Nary a sound," the guard replied, rolling the "r" in his Scottish burr.

Armitage stepped inside, out of the cone of light, and waited. Ten minutes later, he watched Corporal Smith pass through the gate. Armitage trilled in imitation of a sedge warbler. Smith followed the sound and joined him, panting.

"You okay?"

"Yeah," Smith said. "A little excited is all."

"Relax. They'll either show up, or they won't. If they do, we'll catch them at it; there's not much they can do."

He went down on his right knee behind the barracks, leaning against the wall, Smith behind him, huffing. They were concealed from view but could still see the pathway leading downhill from the detention center.

While touring the compound before sunrise that morning, Armitage had spotted eight men leaving the barracks and trudging up the hill. He had not confronted them. They would deny everything and alert their fellow prisoners, but he suspected what they were doing from their disheveled appearance.

"You're sure?" Smith had said.

"I am. The nights are getting shorter, so they have less time to work. They're desperate to finish."

The pair didn't have long to wait. The sky glow had nearly disappeared when a trail of men made their way downhill, disappearing from view at the rear of the barracks. The Canadians heard a door creak open, but it did not close. Armitage could imagine one standing guard, sniffing the night air for any hint they were being watched.

The Canadians waited but heard nothing more. "Through the front," Armitage whispered. "Give me a hand."

Corporal Smith helped drag him to his feet. They crept across the side and around to the front of the building, which faced the fence. Armitage slowly pushed down the thumb piece on the handle. The door didn't give. Extracting a set of keys from his pocket, he held them up to the wan light from the guard tower until he fingered what he believed was the right one.

He inserted it into the lock, turned it as slowly as possible, and depressed the thumb piece again. The hinges squeaked as he inched the door open. They hesitated a moment, but hearing no response, Armitage motioned his partner to kneel and lift the door as he swung it back. They opened it without making another sound. Armitage stepped inside while Smith braced the open door with his body.

A single bulb above the exit sign illuminated the entryway, a wooden desk and chair off to the right. Armitage wedged the chair against the frame and exhaled as the door eased silently against it.

The entry area was ten feet long. At the end, a pair of double doors led into the barracks, and a stairway headed down. Armitage whispered instructions, and they crept down the stairs. Behind a second set of double doors, a prisoner stood, his back to the door.

The two retreated into the shadows of the staircase and waited. Five minutes. Ten. At last, the prisoner moved out of sight.

"Now." Armitage moved toward the doorway as fast as his game leg would permit, jerked it open, and turned left. The guard glanced over his shoulder and shouted a warning to his companions, but he was too late. The Canadians moved past him, turned a corner to the left, and entered a small storage area.

Before them lay a hole in the concrete wall, a bookcase and stacks of books to the side, and two filthy prisoners hauling dirt out of the tunnel.

"Out." Armitage ordered. A small parade of men—two at first, then another, and finally one more—emerged, bedraggled and disappointed.

"This is over," Armitage said. They asked a few questions, but no one answered. They recognized every prisoner—*Kriegsmariners* to a man—but he took down their names. Eight in all, counting the six working the tunnel and the prisoners guarding the front and back entrances.

"Return to the detention center," he said. "We'll deal with you tomorrow." Under the Geneva Convention, he knew, the most they could get was four weeks detention; it would do little to deter future attempts.

As they shuffled out, Armitage stared at the setup, taking in the bookcase and volumes designed to conceal their work. Who had arranged all this? This was the spot where he'd encountered the prisoner, Schumacher. The smell of wet earth that day came back to him. If Schumacher was the mastermind, he wasn't present. What had happened to him?

Armitage resolved to find out.

THE FIRST WEEK of Trident negotiations passed without agreement. With the two sides at loggerheads over the next steps in the war, the military leaders authorized two studies, one to mount the invasion of

France following the fall of Sicily, the other that "accepts the elimination of Italy as a necessary preliminary."

Over the weekend, FDR tried to break the deadlock. He took the prime minister to Shangri-La to go fishing—Churchill for trout, Roosevelt for a breakthrough. They caught neither.

One incident interrupted the tension between the two. On the way through the Catoctin Mountains, *The Sunshine Special* passed through Frederick, Maryland. Spotting a sign advertising Barbara Fritchie's Candies, Churchill asked the origin of the name. Roosevelt explained Fritchie was a Civil War character, possibly legendary, of whom John Greenleaf Whittier had written,

> Shoot, if you must, this old gray head,
> But spare your country's flag, she said.

The president could remember no more of the poem, but Churchill recited it from memory. That was the last light moment of their weekend. Churchill resisted all his entreaties, and Roosevelt was uncharacteristically silent during the return trip to Washington.

On his arrival, Marshall appeared at the White House unannounced. "Did you make any progress, Mr. President?"

"No, George. He's as impassive as Gibraltar."

"Well, I may have something. Field Marshal Dill is keeping us apprised of their internal discussions. He understands the political pressure you face to bring the war to Japan. He knows Great Britain has few options, that we have the troops, the weapons, and the money. He's tried to convey to them that if we shift forces to the Pacific, Britain faces a long, lonely fight and might not prevail."

"Are they prepared to budge?"

"I think I know how to move them, Mr. President. The sticking point on their side isn't so much the chiefs; it's their staff members. You bring all those supernumeraries across the Atlantic on an ocean liner, allowing them to bring their papers and notebooks, and they feel the need for something to do. 'Well, I daresay ...' and 'But we must duly consider ...'"

Roosevelt reared back and roared at Marshall's uncharacteristic levity, accompanied by realistic approximations of the British accent. "So, what are you going to do about it?"

"I'm chairing the conference tomorrow. I'm going to throw them out. No one allowed except top brass. We shall fight on the beaches, we shall fight on the landing grounds ..."

The laughter caught in Roosevelt's throat. Marshall, he realized, wasn't being intentionally humorous. He was exasperated. "You have my blessing," he told his general. "We must break this impasse."

The following evening, Marshall reported success. Both sides had compromised. The Italian campaign would proceed but would be limited to taking Italy out of the war and establishing air bases capable of reaching Germany from the south. In return, Brooke agreed in writing to introduce twenty-nine divisions into Great Britain for a cross-Channel invasion, rechristened Operation Overlord, with a target date of May 1, 1944. Of these, seven would be combat-experienced British and American divisions to be transferred from the Mediterranean. "It's not everything we wanted, but I'm convinced it's the best we can get."

"Well done, General," the president said.

Four days later, with the military leaders having decorated their tree with ornaments, they traveled to the White House to present their final plan to Churchill and Roosevelt in what Harry Hopkins assured Roosevelt would be a *pro forma* visit.

It was anything but. "No, no, no," Churchill exploded. "You're not seeing the full picture." For an hour, he argued for a full-scale invasion of Italy followed by a push into Yugoslavia. Brooke and Marshall seethed. Roosevelt said nothing.

A celebratory dinner had been planned, and the president wanted to call it off, there being nothing to celebrate. Nor did he feel up to it. He still felt the lagging effects of whatever had felled him following his return from Casablanca.

"Go through with it," Hopkins argued. "Perhaps a few glasses of champagne will soften him up."

"I'll dine with him, Harry, but I won't enjoy it."

True to his word, Roosevelt didn't speak as he ate, barely looking at his counterpart. Hopkins and General Hastings Ismay, Churchill's chief military advisor, tried to carry on a conversation, but FDR refused to engage. As the meal concluded, however, he rolled himself back from the table. "The date is set," he said in a quiet tone. "The seven divisions must be withdrawn from the Mediterranean and sent to England by November 1 to prepare for the spring offensive."

Churchill sat in uncharacteristic silence. But the following morning, as the combined chiefs gathered at the Executive Mansion to meet with both leaders, Churchill pressed for a consolation prize. Seizing control of the meeting, he argued that they must capture not just Sicily, but Sardinia.

Roosevelt waited for a pause in the tirade. "I'm not interested in the matter," he said.

With these words, the Trident Conference ended.

"SERGEANT, YOU NEED TO SEE THIS." Armitage looked up as Lieutenant Morrison beckoned him from his doorway. He followed the adjutant downstairs to the ground floor level, taking the steps one at a time as he wondered what in hell this was all about. Morrison entered the mailroom and held out his arm. "There."

Armitage frowned as he contemplated two stacks of packages, three of which were open. "What is this?"

"Look closer."

Armitage thumbed through the first open package. Inside were a navy blue gabardine suit and a pair of denim trousers. He folded the wrapping paper over the garments to view the mailing label, "LT Kurt Ziegler" at Camp 20. The return address was Eaton's, Canada's largest department store chain.

Armitage set the package aside and examined the one beneath it, which was identical save for the addressee. The third was the same. Below it lay several other packages, alongside a larger stack. Armitage counted. "They were planning to break out thirty men," he said.

"And you stopped them."

"How can prisoners place an order—?"

"We've allowed it." Men who were lent out for farm work earned money they could spend as they pleased. Until that moment, Armitage had assumed prisoners used their pay for cigarettes, candy, sausage, and other luxuries. He didn't know prisoners could order items through the mail.

"But we're putting a stop to it," Morrison said.

"What will happen to these men, sir?" Armitage asked.

"Nothing, I'm afraid. Until today, we had no rule against ordering clothing. You, on the other hand," he said, "prevented a mass escape."

"I only did my duty, sir."

"We're putting you in for a promotion to master warrant officer."

Armitage blinked. This was the second-highest rank for a non-commissioned officer. "Thanks—thank you, sir." The promotion itself didn't matter to him; it might provide an opportunity to avenge Dicky's death in a productive way.

10

JUNE 3-30

THE PRESIDENT RETURNED from a Memorial Day weekend at Hyde Park to three days of meetings, an endless parade of ambassadors, cabinet officers, senators, congressional representatives, labor leaders, his budget director, and as always, Harry Hopkins. Despite the constant comings and goings and the need to shift attention from international to domestic affairs, from crises to the mundane, he told Leahy, "I've never felt better, Bill. There's nothing like a few days away from Washington to boost the spirits."

There were other reasons for his cheerful disposition on this Tuesday morning. In Algiers, Churchill tended to the man they called "the bride," General de Gaulle, trying to broker peace with Giraud. General Eisenhower sent encouraging reports about the launch of Operation Husky, five weeks away. And a special visitor had spent the weekend at Hyde Park, Princess Märtha of Norway and Sweden, whose presence always filled him with delight and occasioned no end of salacious rumors.

Late Thursday afternoon, however, gloom clouded his sunny spirit. Joseph Davies, who had served Roosevelt as ambassador to the Soviet Union in the 1930s, visited the White House. Davies had just deplaned from his special mission to Moscow for the president via a globe-circling route that had taken him to six countries over twenty-seven days.

"I bring mixed news, Mr. President," Davies said as he sat across from Roosevelt in the Oval Office, waving aside the acrid smoke from the president's ever-present cigarette.

While still meeting with Churchill during Trident and without telling the prime minister, Roosevelt had dispatched Davies to convey to Stalin his view of the war and invite him to meet at a mutually convenient location, without Churchill. Davies had a personal rapport with Stalin and other Russian officials. Two years before, he had published *Mission to Moscow*, an account of his time as ambassador, which depicted the Soviet Union in a favorable light and brought Davies in for heavy criticism.

Davies carried a personal letter from the president. In it, he explained why they could not invade France that year but promised intensification of the air war in Europe for "destruction of enemy industry, whittling down of German fighter plane strength, and breaking German civil morale."

Roosevelt revealed that after the Sicilian campaign, Eisenhower would "launch offensives where he saw opportunity directed toward the collapse of Italy. That will allow commencement of the air offensive against Germany from the south, will continue the attrition of their fighter strength, and will jeopardize the Axis position in the Balkans."

These steps taken, he promised, the Allies would begin concentrating ground forces in England. "There should be a sufficiently large concentration of men and materiel in the British Isles in the spring of 1944 to permit a full-scale invasion of the Continent. The great air offensive will be at its peak."

"How did he react to the letter?" Roosevelt asked.

Davies sighed. "Except for your invitation to meet with you, he doesn't accept it."

Placing his cigarette holder in the long ashtray, the president leaned back, tented his hands, and pursed his lips.

"He's suspicious of Churchill's motives. He always has been,"

Davies said, "but I'm afraid he now suspects us as well. He doesn't accept that North Africa, Sicily, and Italy will draw enough Axis forces from the Soviet Union to be meaningful. He continually mentions the number of men they have lost. And tanks and weapons.

"Throughout our meeting, he sketched. Every time, the same image." Davies waited for the president's question, but none came. "Wolves. He drew one wolf and immediately started another."

"A warning."

Davies grunted in agreement. "He wants a second front in France and wants it now, Mr. President. We made that promise last year."

"We weren't ready, Joe. Much as Marshall and the others wanted it, events in North Africa proved Winston right. It would have been another Dieppe, but on a larger scale."

Davies pressed. "We promised an invasion this summer; now we're putting that off."

"As I explained in my letter, the need to build landing craft, ship them to Great Britain, and get more than a million men on that island, let alone housed and fed, will take time."

Once more, the travel-exhausted Davies sighed. It was all he could do to stay awake. "There's a deeper problem. Stalin is convinced Churchill will consent to a cross-Channel invasion only when there is no risk to them."

A view, Roosevelt knew, shared by the Joint Chiefs and their planners. After Husky, the British had already drawn the US into Italy. His military feared that was just the beginning. Churchill would make America dance around the fringes of Europe, wasting time and resources, and postponing the eventual endgame with Hirohito.

"But he accepted my invitation?" he asked.

"Yes," the ambassador said, "he's willing to meet you in Fairbanks sometime between mid-July and mid-August. The exact date depends on the Soviet military situation."

"I *must* see him," Roosevelt said. "We have to hold our Alliance together—not just now, but after the war."

OBERLEUTNANT FRANZ MELZER WAS BLESSED—AND sometimes cursed —with an analytical mind. Whereas his fellow Abwehr officers might have noted the transfer of an Allied air squadron to a different base and handed it off to a superior without further action, Melzer puzzled over this scrap of information for hours and did not rest until he connected it to other intelligence, concluding that the Americans had increased the range of their bombers to strike deeper into the Fatherland. Because Melzer withheld his conclusions until he had triangulated them with other intelligence, he was seldom wrong. General Major Hans Oster often asked his opinion, respect he accorded few others of his rank in Abteilung Z.

Sometimes even the absence of information told a story. When Admiral Doenitz stopped trumpeting the successes of his Wolfpacks in mid-May, Melzer surmised that Allied anti-submarine warfare had gained the upper hand in the Battle of The Atlantic. Melzer was not surprised when two weeks later, Doenitz withdrew his dwindling fleet of U-boats.

Today, the intelligence officer kept his latest insight to himself. Not even the Abwehr allowed defeatism among junior officers. And defeat was what he had sensed since Russian troops had mounted a counteroffensive at Stalingrad the previous November.

Like many in the *Abwehr*, Melzer was a patriot but not a Nazi. He detested the hero worship that surrounded Hitler and the groveling that prevented his officers from speaking the truth. He was also a realist. Unless the situation changed, Germany's defeat was inevitable. The only hope was to delay it.

Much of what he knew came from intercepted telephone communications between Roosevelt and Churchill. The two gabbed as though their trans-Atlantic conversations were secure, but the Abwehr had eavesdropped on them since 1940. The cautious British prime minister spoke in elliptical terms, but not so the American president. Roosevelt was voluble, discussing troop movements, Lend-Lease shipments, and conferences.

As he sat at his desk, pushing his thin blond hair out of his eyes, Melzer projected the collapse of the Atlantic U-boat campaign to its logical conclusion. America was building a mighty army and could soon send hundreds of thousands of fresh troops to England, Italy, or wherever it pleased. Without U-boats interdicting transports, there was no way to stop them.

On the Eastern Front, Germany had one advantage. By making the Soviet Union pay for every bloody kilometer, the Axis could trade vast stretches of space for time, forestalling defeat. It had no such luxury in the west. If the Allies invaded Northwest Europe, they would be within a thousand kilometers of Berlin, and the war would be lost.

Here, his hours of listening to the two Allied leaders suggested a strategy. Roosevelt, needing a quick victory in Europe, pressed for an invasion somewhere along the coast. The British leader lobbied for a war of attrition—a thrust through Italy and the Balkans. That, Melzer knew, could produce a stalemate, giving Germany time to negotiate a truce with the West and turn its full attention toward the East.

Melzer knew Roosevelt would be unlikely to cave in to Churchill. Somehow, Germany had to tip the scales in Britain's direction. But how?

***

ARMITAGE STOOD alongside Lieutenant Morrison as he addressed the morning roll call. "The town council of Gravenhurst has asked if any of you will help with a local project."

Armitage translated. "*Der Stadtrat von Gravenhurst hat gefragt, ob einer von Ihnen bereit ist, bei einem lokalen Projekt zu helfen.*"

"They need a stairway at Gull Lake Park, similar to the one you built down to the swimming area." Again, Armitage translated as several men stepped forward.

"It's a volunteer project," Morrison continued. "There is no pay."

Most of the men retreated, but Jörg Schumacher remained in place. Five others joined him. Armitage wondered why Schumacher had made this sudden commitment to service, but he had little time to consider it.

They marched from the main gate at the west end of Lorne Street, turned south on Louise, then east toward town as shoppers and merchants gawked at them. A few smiled and waved. Armitage assumed they knew what the prisoners were there to do. When they came to a low hill overlooking the lake, they stopped.

"*Willkommen*," a man dressed in dungarees and a sleeveless sweatshirt said, "*und danke*." He had a full head of gray hair and a pronounced paunch. Armitage put him in his early sixties. Having exhausted his knowledge of the German language, the man lapsed into English, describing the work that needed to be done. Before Armitage could translate, Schumacher spoke to his fellows, gesturing toward the tiny red flags that marked the planned path to the beach and the timber stacked alongside the road.

The team began shoveling makeshift steps into the hillside. Armitage took off his hat and sat under a tree, watching an eagle soar over Dead Horse Island across the lake. The prisoners worked in silence, Schumacher directing them more by motions of his arms and hands than verbal orders. The others seemed to respect him and raised no objection to his taking charge.

With an effort, Armitage rose to his feet and approached the man who had introduced the project. "I'm Brandon Armitage." He paused, unaccustomed to his new rank. "Master warrant officer."

"Mark Stenhouse," the man responded. "I'm on the council. We're grateful you're doing this for us. With our young men off in Europe ..." He didn't finish the explanation, for none was needed.

"It's no problem. Many of the men grab at any attempt to get outside the camp." Wanting to keep the man engaged, he asked, "Do you have anyone in the service?"

Stenhouse smiled. "My son served between the wars and is too old now. All he and his wife have are daughters. That used to disappoint me, but now ..." He trailed off again. "And you?"

"One son is a POW in Germany."

"Oh." His face contorted in sympathy.

"We hear from him every month. I got a letter yesterday, written weeks ago. He says he's fine, but I was in that situation myself, so I know he's just trying to allay our anxiety."

"It's a bad time. But at last we're turning things around. Four years of this …" He shook his gray mane. "Sloan's is sending over sandwiches and drinks for your men. Do you want to come to my house for lunch?"

Armitage looked out on the six prisoners. With two guards remaining, there was no reason for him to remain, and he welcomed the opportunity to meet other townsfolk. Still, he balked, anxious to use his new position to gather what intelligence he could on the prisoners' plans. "Thanks, but some other time. I need to stay with this group. Make sure it's done right."

"Sure, and thanks again." Stenhouse wandered off, and Armitage went in search of a washroom. When he returned, a youngster in a white shirt was unloading a food container from his bicycle rack. The prisoners lined up, accepted their meals with thanks, and lounged beneath the firs while they ate. Armitage sat among them and chatted in German, answering their questions about Canada and listening to them reminisce about life in Germany.

"Canadians are kind," one said. "I think I'd like to come back after —" He interrupted himself, uncertain how to complete the thought. Did he realize Germany couldn't survive this two-front war? Did he know how many men Paulus had lost at Stalingrad and von Vaerst and Krause in Tunisia? Was he aware Doenitz had withdrawn U-boats from the Atlantic after unsupportable losses? That bombing in the Ruhr Valley was so heavy Germany was evacuating civilians?

From the letters he'd read, Armitage suspected the prisoners knew all this and more before it hit the press. He had never learned where they kept their radios, but was sure they had them.

"Perhaps you can," he told the prisoner. "This won't go on forever."

Armitage looked around, realizing that one man had left the group. Above them on the hill and almost out of sight, he spotted Schumacher's head bobbing back and forth. The German was conversing with someone while facing the water, observing his fellow prisoners and the guards while he spoke. Struggling to his feet, Armitage walked to the lakeside and turned north along the shoreline, swinging his arms as though he were out for a stroll.

The land jutted into the lake. Not quite a peninsula, but enough to conceal him. He continued around the point until he was behind the hillock and, step by painful step, climbed the bank. Finally, he stepped into the trees and returned south, pausing when the two figures came into view.

Schumacher sat with his back to him, leaning forward with his legs crossed. Sitting before him was a young woman wearing a spring frock. The sun picked up highlights in her reddish-brown hair, creating a glow. As he stepped out from the trees, the woman spotted him and looked up, her face bearing an alarmed scowl. Schumacher turned around. "Hello," he said, seeming unconcerned.

Armitage walked toward them, wearing a grin. "Beautiful day, isn't it?"

"Are you looking for me?"

"No, not at all. I was just taking a walk." He introduced himself to the young woman.

"Pamela," she said. "The lieutenant is teaching me German."

He took in her hazel-colored eyes, wide smile, and upturned nose. She reminded him of someone he had once known, and he gave an involuntary shake of recognition. "Let's hope it won't become useful."

As she uttered a forced laugh, Schumacher rose and dusted himself off. "It was good to see you again. Next time we'll discuss shopping for groceries, so study chapter six."

"I promise," she said. She cocked her head to one side and smiled as she took his hand. Again, for Armitage, this brought a stab of recognition. "Until next time."

She wandered off, swaying her hips in a display meant for only one of the two. Schumacher turned toward him, raising both eyebrows and grinning. "She approached me at the fence one day and tried to speak a few words. I'm trying to teach her."

I'll bet you are, but I doubt German is the subject. "What is her last name?"

"I don't think she's told me." They took a few steps together. "Why do you ask? To turn her in?"

"For what? There's no law against civilians speaking to prisoners. I'm just curious." Like the German, he concealed his intent.

As they approached the workgroup, Armitage stopped him. "You were behind the tunnel project, weren't you?" Apart from a slight smile, the prisoner gave no acknowledgment. "You're getting information direct from Germany. Do you have a radio?"

Schumacher faced him. "If I knew what you were talking about, do you think I'd tell you?" He snickered and returned to the group, his shoulders pushed back and chest jutted out in defiance. Armitage watched him go, convinced his suspicions were correct. This man bore watching.

"DON'T YOU LOOK NICE." Bernice gaped at Margie as she arrived at work Friday morning dressed in a navy blue full skirt dress with a polka-dot bodice and bolero jacket. "And a new hat," she said, spotting the gray Kentucky Derby hat with a bow in back and netting gathered around the brim. "Who are you dressing for?"

"Myself," Margie said, "Just me."

"Is Brandon home?"

"No, he's still at Gravenhurst."

Bernice gave her a probing look. "Where did you find the dress?"

"I spotted it on a mannequin Saturday and bought it. It's nice to have money of my own."

Bernice harrumphed.

Can I help it if Walter left her with so little she has to work? Margie was glad her friend worked in the shoe department, a floor removed from millinery, unable to keep tabs on her. Perhaps she could escape today without being seen.

For the next two hours, she attended to customers drawn into the store by the display ad in the *Toronto Daily Star* for Panama straw dome hats for summer. Margie didn't much care for the look—better for the beach than for town—but women flocked in to try them, and more than a few purchased them. At this rate, they'd sell out by closing time Saturday.

"You're doing great," Rowena Walter said. The department manager had taken her under her wing, praising her work and her way with customers. "I'm so glad Bernie brought you to us."

The job had helped her ease the loss of her younger son and her husband's prolonged absence. It kept her mind off her problems and built her self-confidence. Adding to her resiliency, yesterday's mail had brought another letter from Henry.

> I am fine. I'm helping with spring planting on a nearby farm, and they feed us well. Most of the camp guards treat us with respect. Thank you for your package. It arrived safely, though you forgot to include chocolate. I look forward to coming home soon so we can all be together again.

Brandon had warned her the guards took whatever they wanted, but she would send things anyway, hoping that at least some of it would make it to her son. It appeared the chocolate had not. This was Henry's way of telling her not to spend her money on things he would never see. What was important was that Henry was all right. He hadn't made further mention of his two missing fingers, and Margie tried not to think about it.

Brandon was getting leave more often. At first, they had gone for months without seeing each other, but now he came down at least once a month. He told her he was proud of her. He listened as she described the customers she encountered, some of whom had husbands or sons in the war, others whose complaints about scarcity of stock and other shortages made her think they were unaware a war was going on. That was the case now, as an older woman, her nose aloft, fingered one hat after another, leaving each askew so that Margie would be forced to rearrange it. "You have nothing else?" It emerged as a reproof rather than a question.

"Are you ready, Mrs. Armitage?" She looked up to see Mr. Sperling peering at her over his glasses.

"I just need to finish with this customer."

"Gladys, can you see to this lovely lady?" Then, turning to the customer, he said, "Good morning. Mrs. Duarte will be glad to help you."

The manager stepped aside and motioned for Margie to precede him. She did as directed and moved to the bank of elevators. As Sperling pushed the up button, Margie was conscious of the eyes of other saleswomen on her. The cage arrived, and he ushered her inside. Four customers were aboard, but without a word from Sperling, the operator skipped the floors and whisked them to the top. "Thank you, ladies," he said as he alighted, ushering Margie forward with a sweep of his arm.

He directed her into a small dining room and toward a table whose window afforded a view of downtown Toronto and Lake Ontario. Well-dressed men and women sat at other tables, speaking in low tones. Margie was unsure whether they were other executives or important customers.

A waitress wearing a black dress and a pristine white apron approached and handed them menus, a single sheet in a leather folder. The list was spartan, a few salads and sandwiches, and four selections for the main course. "I recommend the trout *a la meunière*," Sperling said without consulting the offerings. "Marcel gets a fresh supply every morning and knows precisely what to do with it."

Margie would have preferred the pork cutlet, but did as he suggested. It would not do to make a false step this early in their conversation.

"Would you care to start with something? A martini, perhaps?"

Margie, who had given up hard liquor after her confrontation with Brandon, said, "No, thank you. I never drink during the daytime and never while working." She bit her tongue, fearing he would take it as a reproach, but Sperling didn't seem to notice.

"A salad then. Marcel gets fresh greens in each day." She ordered the house salad, unsure what was in it, and the waitress drifted away.

"This is lovely," she said, gazing at the lake.

"I lunch here every day and never tire of the view."

She felt his eyes on her and, despite herself, was pleased at the attention. It had been a long time since she'd attracted the attention of a man.

"Tell me about yourself," he said, ending an uncomfortable silence.

"I work because I want to and because I enjoy it."

"There's time for that. But you're originally from Toronto?"

"No, Point Edward outside of Sarnia. My parents moved here while I was still in grade school." She began describing her childhood, but stopped as he seemed to lose interest.

The waitress brought a martini, which she hadn't heard him order. "And you're a married lady," he said.

"Yes, my husband—it's my second marriage, actually. Harold and I married when I was eighteen. I was just a girl and didn't know anything." She blushed and rushed on. "He died at Amiens. Another three months ..."

"That must have been difficult, you being so young and all."

"And I had a baby on the way. That's when I met my current husband." Without going into details, she sketched how she had married Brandon, what he did for a living, and the birth of her second son. "He's gone now," she said, turning away. "Killed at Dieppe. And they've taken Henry prisoner."

He reached out, covering her hand in his. She withdrew it. "I'm sorry. I didn't mean to intrude. This must be a difficult time."

She nodded and dabbed her eyes with a handkerchief.

"Your husband? Is he in the service?"

"He's with the Veteran's Guard, looking after German prisoners north of here." She brightened. "He earned a promotion. They think a lot of him."

"As do you, I'm sure."

Their meals arrived and, with them, a second martini for Sperling. "Exquisite. Doesn't this fish look delicious? They do a fine job."

She took a bite and had to admit his suggestion had been excellent. "You mentioned the possibility of a different position."

Ignoring her question, he tore into the meal, finished, drained his glass, and wiped his mouth with his handkerchief. "I have nothing specific right now, but something will come up. You have a certain elegance. I'm sure our customers identify with you, may even see you as a model of what they aspire to be. Everyone in the department speaks well of you."

"Thank you," she said, her voice lowered as she registered disappointment her own promotion was not forthcoming. "I do my best."

"Meanwhile, we can expand your hours. Mrs. Duarte is getting on a bit, and we could use a younger presence for more of the week. Perhaps adding Wednesday and Thursday to your schedule? If you have the time, of course."

"But Gladys—she's all alone. She needs the work more than I do."

He tossed his napkin over his sauce-laden plate, a signal that the luncheon was over. "Don't worry. We'll find someplace else for her. You're kind to be so concerned for her."

Sperling rose from the table, and Margie did as well, even though she hadn't finished her meal. "It has been a pleasure getting to know about you, Mrs. Armitage. I believe you have a bright future here at Pinson's." He escorted her to the elevator, but stayed behind. "Until next time, then."

LIEUTENANT MORRISON CALLED, "Warrant, you need to hear this." Armitage got to his feet and joined the lieutenant in his office. A civilian who hid his features behind a full beard sat facing the desk. He was in his late forties and wore denim pants and a flannel shirt under a heavy wool jacket. Morrison introduced him as Euan Walker but gave no hint what he was doing here. "Please repeat your complaint to my warrant officer."

"Chirping," the man said. He looked up at Armitage through

rheumy eyes. "Someone's transmitting a CW signal that chirps. It's coming from here."

Armitage understood that CW stood for continuous wave, the manner in which Morse code was transmitted, but the rest of the man's complaint meant nothing to him.

"Mr. Walker listens to shortwave radio," the lieutenant said.

"I tune it to stations throughout the world."

"And what is chirping?" Armitage asked

Walker spoke deliberately as though explaining a child. "A shift in frequency that makes the continuous wave tone warble. It's not just annoying; it interferes with other signals."

Armitage locked eyes with Morrison. "What makes you think it's coming from the camp?"

"It's strongest here. I live down in Severn Bridge but don't have a direction finder. I brought my receiver up to my brother's place last night, and there it was, right on time at 2:00 A.M., strong enough to be next door. You guys must have built it yourselves."

"And why do you say that?"

The man snorted, as though anyone with a brain would know the answer. "It's caused by poor voltage regulation of the power supply feeding the oscillator. I'd have to look at it to tell what's wrong, but if you're using a one-tube transmitter, you'll get chirp. You need at least two, one as a regulator. Three would be better."

"Perhaps that's all we could get our hands on," the lieutenant said.

"Oh, come on. You can get regulator tubes all over town, even scrounge them from old radios."

Morrison thanked the man for coming. "I promise you Mr. Armitage will fix this problem by tonight."

"WE'LL START on the top floor," Armitage told the five guards he had selected for the sweep as they gathered outside the detention center. "They need to place their antenna at the highest possible point."

At dinnertime, they took the stairs to the top floor. A prisoner lay on his cot, reading a magazine. "What are you doing here?" Armitage said. "Get down to the mess."

"I'm not feeling well."

"Report to the clinic," Armitage said.

"I'm not that sick. My stomach is just upset."

"Clinic," Armitage ordered.

The prisoner seemed to consider, perhaps wondering whether he would raise more suspicion by resisting. He arose from his bed and left the room.

"I'll bet someone always stays behind," Armitage said.

"Now that you mention it," a guard said.

With the upper floor to themselves, the guards began searching, checking the storage bins beneath every cot, raising ceiling tiles, searching behind the toilets, and pulling supplies from the storage closet. Fifteen minutes passed, twenty. Armitage grew concerned the prisoners would return before they found the device.

They'd begun shuffling back into the building when Smith had an inspiration. Armitage followed him back into the communal washroom. The corporal stood on one toilet seat after another, running his hand atop the tanks mounted above them. On the fourth try, he hollered "Eureka," the sound echoing across the tiled walls. He stepped off the commode holding a package encased in a rubber water bottle whose bottom had been sliced open.

He peeled off the tape that sealed the opening and extracted a pine board on which a single vacuum tube and several other components were mounted. Wires ran across the wooden board and, from holes drilled beneath it, into the connections at the tube's base. At one end, two wires connected to a contraption in which a spring separated the hacked-off handle of a spoon from the flat blade of a dinner knife.

"The Morse key," Armitage said. "Ingenious. This is the transmitter. Let's find the receiver." Walker had told him the units used to send and receive signals were separate. But search though they did, none of the guards were able to locate the receiver.

"Half a loaf," Armitage said.

For the second time in a month, Schumacher was hauled before the Triumvirat. While the charge this time was without foundation, it was more serious. "How did your Canadian friend discover the tunnel?" Kretschmer demanded.

"My Canadian friend?" Only one person matched that description, and he had told her nothing about what went on inside the camp.

"Herr Armitage," *Korvettenkapitan* Bruchmann said. "You were seen conversing with him three days ago."

He wondered who had reported the encounter. "I am not 'friends' with this man. He approached me as I was finishing my lunch. I'd moved to the top of the hill for a better view of the lake." He would not bring the girl into this unless they asked about her. "I was minding my business when he came up behind me. I did not start the conversation. In fact, I said nothing to him other than to talk about the stairway project."

"You have spoken with him before."

Schumacher thought for a moment. "He found Helbig and me one day down at the barracks. He spoke German to us and offered me a cigarette, which I refused. I told him nothing."

"How did he learn about the tunnel?" the Lagerführer asked.

Schumacher drew himself up. "Major, for four months, a small group of us labored in this tunnel, never leaving the building at night. We took turns guarding the entrances and practiced our concealment drill. During all that time, we went undetected. When you reassigned responsibility in May, men came down to the barracks from the officers' quarters every night. They had not rehearsed concealing the tunnel as we had. As the outside activity increased and hours of darkness waned, the risk of discovery grew."

In the silence that followed, he wondered if his response had bordered on impertinence. "I only speak the truth."

"And what about our transmitter? After you spoke with this

Armitage, he led a group that invaded our floor last night, seizing the radio we use to communicate with Berlin and other camps."

"He asked me about radios on Monday. I told him I knew nothing about them and wouldn't tell him if I did." Kretschmer glowered at him. "I had nothing to do with the detection of the tunnel. I know nothing about how we communicate with the outside. I would never betray my country or my fellow officers."

While the Lagerführer and Korvettenkapitan Bruchmann seemed satisfied, Kretschmer continued to stare at him through hooded eyes. "Yesterday in Medicine Hat, our officers dealt with a turncoat, a prisoner who had been preaching anti-Nazi propaganda. We broke into a barracks, overcame the guards, and expelled them. We dragged the traitor to the gymnasium and hanged him. The Canadians could not stop us."

How do you know this if it only happened yesterday? Armitage hadn't uncovered all the radio gear.

Kretschmer pounded the table. "When you are in this camp, you are not in Canada; you are in the Fatherland. Disobey orders, betray us, and we will deal with you."

Kretschmer wasn't finished. "Your father has a pleasant assignment in Norway. Yes, we know all about you. It would be unfortunate if you were to endanger his career. Field Marshall Keitel might be compelled to reassign him to someplace less agreeable. *Verstehst?*"

Schumacher understood. Very well. He recognized he had to escape both the Canadian camp and the prison within it, led by the Nazi. He would act, not react, planning every step of his exit. No one would stop him, not even Kretschmer, for only Schumacher had the confederate needed for his escape.

To start, he would go for an evening swim.

DAYS AFTER AGREEING TO MEET, Stalin dispatched an angry letter to Roosevelt, transmitted in code to the Russian embassy, saying that the decisions made at the Trident Conference "are in contradiction with those made by you and Mr. Churchill at the beginning of this year, regarding the terms of the opening of the second front in Western Europe."

He recounted communications he'd received after the Casablanca Conference and from Churchill a month later, promising the US and Great Britain would "divert considerable German land and air forces from the Russian front to force Germany to her knees in 1943."

He said his country had been fighting the Third Reich on its own soil for two years, while the Anglo-American response had been twice postponed. The Soviet government "does not find it possible to agree with this decision, made without its participation and without attempt to discuss jointly this most important question, which decision may result in grave consequences for the future progress of the war."

The letter seemed to foreclose Roosevelt's offer of a bilateral meeting. In the days that followed, he continued to prod the Soviet dictator, but the Kremlin did not reply.

A further problem was quick in coming. When Ambassador Averell Harriman informed Churchill of Roosevelt's invitation to Stalin, the prime minister was livid, insisting on a trilateral meeting. The Nazi Minister for Propaganda, Joseph Goebbels, he argued, would make much of any meeting that excluded Great Britain, suggesting the Allies were coming apart.

At the end of the month, Churchill relented. "If you and Uncle J can fix a meeting together, I should no longer deprecate it. On the contrary, in view of his attitude I think it important that this contact should be established."

Roosevelt tried to smooth over the differences with his ally by dissembling. "I did not suggest to Uncle Joe that we meet alone, but he told Davies he assumed we would. He agreed we should not bring staffs to what would be a preliminary meeting. I want to explore his thinking as fully as possible concerning Russia's postwar hopes and ambitions. I would want to cover much the same field with him as did Eden for you a year ago."

Hoping his reminder that the British had also held private conversations with Stalin would soften Churchill's anger, Roosevelt made another offer over the trans-Atlantic telephone link. "What would you think of coming over soon after my meeting with Uncle Joe? We can gather in the Citadel in Québec. I am sure the Canadian Government would turn it over to us, and it is a thoroughly comfortable spot, far better than Washington at this time of year."

Churchill agreed, and they gave the conference the code name *Quadrant*. "At the meeting," the president said, "we will make firm plans for the cross-Channel operation to which we agreed last month."

But the British Prime Minister still had other ideas.

11

JULY 8-22, 1943

ASIDE FROM ISLAND hopping in the Pacific and pre-invasion bombing runs in Naples and Sicily, the war was preternaturally quiet in early summer, as though the world were waiting for something to happen. FDR had twice gotten away to Hyde Park, and his White House log was often empty. Although there was a flurry of activity on June 30, when he met individually with half his cabinet and Navy brass, the president peeled away for a mid-afternoon nap on most days as Washington settled into lethargy amid the sweltering heat.

On July 5, like a pressure cooker whose steam is unleashed, all hell broke loose. In the Soviet Union, the Germans launched Operation Citadel, their summer campaign to cut off Russian forces in a pincer move three hundred miles south of Moscow near Kursk. Hitler had twice postponed the offensive, but on the first day of July, after months of dithering, he gave the go-ahead. The failure of Operation Barbarossa the previous winter had left the German army half a million men down. Hence, this offensive turned into a tank battle, with the Reich throwing everything they had at Soviet forces.

In Washington, after meeting with his War Mobilization Committee, the president bade Godspeed to Stimson as he left for Great Britain to inspect US forces. He also welcomed Free French General

Henri Giraud to the White House. After a state dinner, the two emerged from an elevator to find Daisy Suckley in a nightgown outside the family quarters. As she fled in embarrassment, Roosevelt laughed and introduced her to Giraud. "The general and I are going to have a heart-to-heart talk," he told her. "We have landed in Sicily. The word has just come."

After months of planning and waiting, Operation Husky was underway.

THE CHILL MARGIE felt as she entered the employee lounge Tuesday morning was not from the weather—it would reach eighty-five today —but from her fellow saleswomen.

No one answered her bright hello. What caused their gloom? It couldn't be the war. British and Canadian troops were pushing up the eastern half of Sicily while Americans beat back the Germans on the western half.

Something here at Pinson's? She glanced at the bulletin board, but there were no notices of concern. What then?

Bernice entered the lounge and passed without glancing at her. Margie greeted her, but her friend did not answer.

"What's wrong with everybody?"

Her friend whirled on her. "What's wrong? You have to ask?"

"Yes, for God's sake."

"You. That's what."

She turned without another word, storming out of the room and onto the floor with Margie in pursuit. "Stop. Will you just talk to me for a minute? What's going on?"

"Sperling fired Gladys Saturday night," she hissed.

Now it was Margie who grew cold. "Fired? I didn't know. Mr. Sperling said—"

"Said what?" Bernice demanded.

"Just that he would find work for her in another department." She stood in the middle of the first floor between robes and handbags, the fingers of both hands twisting around each other. "I had nothing to do with it." Two other saleswomen scowled at them.

"You flounce about like a schoolgirl whenever he comes within range. And you, a married woman."

"I have not—" Bernice turned and marched off toward the elevator, leaving Margie standing alone, sensing every eye on her. Blood rushed to her head. Her face was clammy, and she could smell her perspiration. How could Bernie think that of her? Is that what they all believed?

As Margie returned to her own department, Rowena Walter confronted her. "Exchange the turban for a tam," she said, pointing to a hat perched on a mannequin head. Her tone was imperious, lacking a semblance of her usual grace. "Something in green. Well?" She placed her hands on her hips as if Margie were balking.

Across the floor, no saleswoman met her eye. Every sound was muted, as though she were trapped in a darkened closet. Taking a deep breath and smoothing her dress down her sides, she moved toward the elevators. She asked the operator for the top floor and watched the back of the woman's head as she looked down. Did she know why Margie was headed to the executive offices?

"Is Mr. Sperling in? I need to speak with him." Her voice trembled as she addressed April Humphrey, Godfrey's gatekeeper.

"I'll see if he's in, Miss ..."

"*Mrs.* Armitage."

"Of course. Just have a seat." She directed her to a chair out of earshot and whispered into the phone, cupping her hand around the mouthpiece. "He'll be right out." She did not smile. *Does she know?*

"Mrs. Armitage, how nice to see you." Godfrey Sperling advanced on her, taking long strides, sporting a beatific smile. "What can I do for you? Come back to my office."

He swept out his arm, ushering her into the Sanctum Sanctorum. As he closed the door, she faced him, her hands folded in front of her. "Sit. Please. What seems to be the problem?"

"I—it's Mrs. Duarte. The women believe ..."

Sperling frowned, extended his right hand in a sweeping motion as though coaxing the words out. "You told me you'd find something else for Gladys, but they say you fired her, and they blame me."

"Ah," he said, leaning back in his chair, "A case of envy."

She blinked several times in succession. "I'm not sure …"

"Oh, trust me, my dear. I see so much of this." His sigh was long and drawn out as he tugged at his right eyebrow. "First, you are not responsible for Mrs. Duarte's … departure. I promised to try finding her another position, but no other department wants her. My hands are tied."

"But I displaced her."

"Not true. You played no role in her leaving. It's not right for me to discuss someone else's job performance. But there had been *problems* —a series of them. Too often, cash didn't tally with the receipts. I'm not saying she stole from us. Sometimes she was short, but just as often, she had more money in the till than she should have, so she was shortchanging customers. We'd received many complaints."

He leaned forward and lowered his voice. "It was simple carelessness, you see. Advanced age, perhaps. And there was the style issue." In answer to her perplexed expression, Sperling said, "Gladys didn't keep up with current trends. She was … *thirties*. You, on the other hand—the moment I met you, I said, Godfrey, this is an attractive, stylish woman. This is the breath of fresh air we need in millinery. Just the person for this time."

Margie felt herself blushing. "Thank you, sir, but—"

"Godfrey. When we're together like this, call me Godfrey. May I call you Margie?"

He made the g sound like a j. She politely corrected his pronunciation.

"Margie," he said. "I like the sound of that." He rested his chin on his knuckles. "Now, Margie, the women are jealous, and they're giving you a rough time. It's difficult, and I understand that. But I can't go down there and tell them we had to fire Gladys because of nonperformance issues, can I?"

"I suppose not."

"So, I'm afraid you must hold your head high and rise above it."

Gesturing with both hands. "You have to ignore these things. That's the downside of management."

"Management?"

"Yes, didn't I make that clear? I'm grooming you to lead a department. I thought you understood that."

"No, I—well, thank you."

"Margie, you're in a difficult position, and I feel somehow responsible. I'd like to make it up to you. Do you have dinner plans?"

"Tonight, you mean?"

"Yes, if you're free."

"I don't have any plans, but should we—?"

"That's settled then." He rose, extending his hand. "I'll let you go home and change after your shift and call for you at seven o'clock. And, again, welcome to Pinson's. I'm so happy we've found each other."

ROOSEVELT WHEELED himself to his desk, grabbed a piece of stationery and a pen, and began a message to Joseph Stalin. Although the State Department would encrypt his message into a series of dots and dashes for transmission to the American Embassy in Moscow, the president wanted to get his words just right.

"I am deeply sorry for the sinking of one of your ships in the North Pacific," he wrote. A US submarine in the Aleutian Islands had mistaken a Soviet trawler for an enemy ship, opening fire, and sinking it, killing two merchant seamen.

He reread what he'd written and inserted a single word into the sentence so it read "the *unfortunate* sinking."

The president wrote another line, promising that the incident would not be repeated but crossed it out, knowing he could not guarantee that. "I have directed every possible future precaution," he wrote.

He reread the two sentences and, nodding his head in satisfaction, continued. "Although I have no detailed news, I think I can safely congratulate you on the splendid showing your armies are making against the German offensive."

Finally he got to the reason for this personal message. "I hope to hear from you soon about the other matter which I still feel to be of great importance to you and me." This "other matter" was his invitation to meet one-on-one with the Soviet leader to ease his anger at the postponement of the cross-Channel assault.

As the weather warmed, most prisoners took advantage of the opportunity to swim in the fenced enclosure outside the camp. Guards marched them in ranks of five out the front gate on Lorne Street and left toward the inlet. They had fashioned sandals from discarded rubber tires to protect their feet against splinters in the stairway they had built. A guard tower overlooked the site, although, with the fencing secured to the inlet's bed and topped with barbed wire, no one was likely to go anywhere.

Schumacher seldom missed his chance for the daytime communal swim and, along with other prisoners, took another dip in the evening. While the cooler nighttime air and cold water of the bay often set their teeth chattering, the swim held special attractions—boatloads of them. Teenaged girls from the camp across the inlet paddled across in canoes, clinging to the fence to gawk and talk.

Where are you from? Do you have a girl back home? Do they ever let you out? Will you take me dancing?

Ja, ja. Wir werden tanzen gehen. Yes, We'll go dancing.

Wie heißen Sie? What's your name?

Du bist sehr schön. You are very beautiful.

Back and forth it went. Counselors from the girls' camp failed to put a stop to it. The Canadian guards didn't bother. It seemed innocent enough. Nothing could come of it. The prisoners welcomed the attention, and since their captors could withdraw swimming privileges at any time, the visits served as a reward for good behavior.

Six canoes, each carrying two girls. But on this night, a seventh with only one person at the paddles. Not a girl but a young woman who had come not from the camp but from Gravenhurst and who gripped the fence at the south end of the boom, speaking to a single prisoner.

"You have everything?" Schumacher asked.

She nodded. "I hope it fits. I had to estimate, and Canadian sizes are different."

"It will be fine."

"And soon we'll be together."

"Ja, for all time."

She reached out and touched his fingers through the mesh. "Have you picked a date?"

"No, but it won't be long. Near the end of the month. I need help, a—" He searched for the right word. "*Eine Ablenkung. I* need to draw the guards' attention."

"A diversion."

"Ja, ein diversion." To get that, he required Kretschmer's approval. Since Pamela was essential to the escape and would help no one but him, Schumacher felt confident he could persuade the Nazi to allow it. He needed the right moment to broach the subject.

"Until Friday then," she said. "I love you."

"*Ich liebe dich.*" They touched fingers again, and he turned and swam to shore.

WITH PARANOIA INTENSIFYING within Hitler's inner circle, Joseph Goebbels found it impossible to confide in any of his colleagues, not even Albert Speer, to whom he'd once uttered many an indiscreet thought. One wrong word, and you could be out. Or worse.

Therefore, the propaganda minister increasingly spoke only to himself through his diary. On this evening in mid-July, he wrote, "How are we supposed to cope with a two-front war?"

Operation Citadel, the long-delayed summer offensive against the Soviet army, had failed. Part of the blame lay at the feet of the Führer, who had delayed the attack until, as his generals warned, Soviet forces were well aware they were coming.

In the Battle of Prokhorovka, the German Second SS Panzer Corps and the Soviet Fifth Guards Army fought a prolonged battle that destroyed hundreds of tanks in a single day. Over four hundred German and six hundred Soviet tanks battled over the next forty-six hours, one of the largest armored battles in history. Russian strength was far greater than Hitler's military leaders predicted, and Citadel became a costly disaster.

The other factor leading to the collapse was beyond their control. After a shaky start, Anglo-American forces were now advancing north in Sicily, almost unimpeded. Their success forced Hitler to call off the tank battle to rush troops south to Italy. Their summer offensive, vital to defeating the Red Army, had been a colossal waste.

"We now have no choice but to find a political solution," Goebbels wrote to himself. "Operation Citadel was a second Stalingrad. Our generals now doubt they can beat the Soviet Union militarily."

It was the first time he had countenanced the possibility that the two-front war that, in Goebbels's view "has always been Germany's misfortune" might be lost.

ARMITAGE ASCENDED the guard tower overlooking the bay, taking the steps one at a time, grasping the railing with his right hand to maintain his balance.

"Beautiful evening," Corporal Smith said.

"Stunning, and it's great to catch the breeze after this hellish day." Armitage looked north, holding a monocular to his right eye as he tracked the course of an eagle over Percy Island.

"Isn't that terrific news from Europe?" Smith said. "Maybe the war will be over soon." In Sicily, Enna had fallen to the Allies. Since it was the center of Italian defenses, Eisenhower expressed confidence in complete victory. In the East, the Red Army was driving the Axis back along a four-hundred-mile front.

Everyone Armitage encountered that day seemed to share this optimism. His fellow officers laughed as they passed each other in hallways, and during his morning walk, Gravenhurst shop owners smiled and waved.

Even Margie was caught up in the spirit, sounding happier during their call this evening than she had been since their sons had shipped out. "I'm up for a promotion," she said.

"So soon? That's wonderful."

"Nothing is certain yet, but my supervisor says he's training me for a management position."

Armitage didn't know many women in management, but wartime manpower shortages were changing every aspect of life. "I'm proud of you," he said, offering to come down for the weekend. Margie begged off, saying the new job kept her busy.

Only the German prisoners were immune to the joyous spirit. Despite capturing the transmitter two weeks before, Armitage had not found their receiver. Recalling his days building a crystal radio, he knew such devices were small and could be assembled from spare parts. Concerned that kriegsmariner radio operators might be constructing a new transmitter, he suggested that Morrison request a signal tracking unit from Ottawa; the lieutenant doubted they could spare it. "After all, why do we care? We have no great secrets here, and the prisoners aren't going anywhere."

That was always the answer: They're not going anywhere. But the volume and accuracy of their information concerned him. However they were getting their news, the prisoners were well informed about Axis setbacks. You could see it on their faces.

The lone exception was this fellow Schumacher. He always wore a grin, joking and backslapping with his fellows. Was this just his nature, or did he know something the others did not?

Armitage focused on him because he reminded him of his late son. The German always returned his "*Wie gehts*?" with assurances of his good health, asking the Canadian how he was doing. For a while, he had thought they were forming a bond. Schumacher passed him a few slices of venison sausage the prisoners made. In return, Armitage brought in an occasional bottle of local beer, always with the lieutenant's permission.

Several days ago, however, the German had shut him out, refusing to banter in German or English. "What's wrong?" Armitage asked, "I thought we were friends."

The prisoner glanced over his shoulder. "We are not friends. I am a captive, and you are my captor. That is all."

Something had happened, but when Armitage questioned his fellow guards, they assured him Schumacher had done nothing to merit any discipline, nor had they given him any. Whatever had come between the two men, he decided, had not originated on the Canadian side.

Now, as Armitage tracked his eagle, Corporal Smith grabbed his arm. "Here come the girls."

Armitage grunted in response. Six canoes were making their way across the inlet from Mounts Bay. "Foolish kids."

"Ah, they're just having a spot of fun. No harm in it, is there?"

"I suppose not."

The eagle dived toward the water and came up clutching a bass in its talons. "What a beautiful sight," Armitage said. Smith trained his binoculars on the bay but was too late. The eagle disappeared in the low-hanging sun, forcing Armitage to look away. "Hello, what's this?"

Smith aimed his field glasses in the direction he was looking. "That's a *Luftwaffe* officer. We've met him. I don't recall his name."

"I do. Who's the girl?"

"I don't know. I've seen her around town. She paddles up twice a week, Fridays and Tuesdays, and they meet at the fence. Look. They're touching hands. She really has a thing for him. Sir?"

As the woman lowered her paddle into the water and pulled away, Armitage began his painful journey down the tower two steps at a time. He slipped but was fortunate to fall just above a landing. He steadied himself and continued down, grimacing in pain.

Walking as quickly as he could, he retraced his way through the compound and out onto Lorne Street, turned right on Austin, and headed south. Trees blocked his view of the bay, but he lumbered on, leaving the road as it angled away from the water and cutting through the conifers. The monocular banged against his chest as he rushed forward. He hadn't taken the time to cap it.

Darkness crept in as he left the woods. He glimpsed the retreating canoe to the south. The girl was making for shore. He'd never catch up.

Armitage blundered through the brush onto Hotchkiss Street and turned toward the bay. Seeing no one, he reversed course and spotted her walking toward town, two blocks from him. He limped after her. As she neared the corner of John Street, she broke into a trot and turned south.

He made up the distance in what, for him, was record time, turned right but saw no one. He hobbled between cross streets for fifteen minutes, but as darkness closed in, he gave up and returned to his quarters.

Tomorrow, he thought. Tomorrow I will find that girl.

HENRY LOUIS STIMSON, graduate of Yale University and Harvard Law School, World War I colonel, Wall Street lawyer turned US attorney, and lifelong Republican who had served three presidents, was pissed.

Since his arrival in England on July 9 for an inspection visit to US commanders, Prime Minister Churchill and Foreign Secretary Anthony Eden had nagged him about the viability of the cross-Channel operation.

"I continue to have doubts it can succeed," Churchill said over a welcoming dinner at 10 Downing Street. "If Dieppe taught us anything, it's about the danger inherent in a seaborne invasion of the Continent."

"Our troops have just landed on Sicily," the secretary of war replied. "We're moving inland at this very moment."

"But only with tremendous loss of life. Bad weather blew paratroopers off course, making the landings a deadly affair. Weather across the Channel is even more unpredictable."

"But the invasion is a success," Stimson said. "Yes, we lost men during the landings. It's the nature of war. The important thing is, we came by sea, and we're winning by land."

Eden broke in. "Now that we're there, it would be more sensible to move on to Italy and proceed to the Balkans and Greece to stimulate trouble."

Stimson pushed his half-eaten plate away. "Gentlemen, only by an intellectual effort has the president been able to convince the American people Berlin should be disposed of before Tokyo. Their anger at Japan has always competed with our 'Europe first' strategy. Any delay in defeating the Nazis poses a danger to the president's authority, with immense consequence to our common cause."

As the pair fell silent, Stimson pressed his advantage. "Lose the American public, and you could well find yourselves fighting alone. Congress could compel us to shift resources from Hitler to Hirohito."

While he seemed to have won the round, Stimson kept in touch with Churchill and his ministers as he visited commanders in Great Britain, alert for further signs of back-pedaling on the agreements reached at the Trident Conference weeks before.

His spirits soared when he met with the Chief of Staff to the Supreme Allied Commander (COSSAC). The enthusiastic Anglo-American group, led by British Lieutenant-General Frederick Morgan, had nearly completed an "Overlord Outline Plan" and was preparing to submit it to the military chiefs on both sides at their forthcoming conference in Québec. The plan would set in motion the Second Front, a cross-Channel invasion into Normandy, France, leading to the liberation of Europe. Once COSSAC's plan was in place, Stimson believed, there was no way Churchill could reverse course.

His optimism was short-lived. On July 17, the prime minister invited Stimson to join him in inspecting Britain's coastal defenses. As they traveled by train to Dover, Churchill again coaxed him to consider alternatives to the cross-Channel operation. "General

Marshall agrees with me, you know. He's requested a study of landing on the Italian mainland at Salerno."

"His aim isn't to mount the operation *instead* of Overlord," Stimson said. "It's to accelerate the capture of Rome so we can shift men and material *here* for the invasion."

"We encountered strong German resistance on Sicily," Churchill said. "If we had fifty thousand men ashore in France right now, I would not have an easy moment. The Germans could rush in with sufficient force to drive them back."

Stimson exploded. "We've been over this time and again. This continued waffling is like poking us in the eye."

Churchill seemed to relent. "I would not have Overlord if the choice were mine, but the decision has been made, and I will loyally implement it."

That night, via radio-telephone, Stimson told Harry Hopkins, "Winston is like a dog with a bone. A stubborn English bulldog. He will continue to meddle. He will use every setback as justification to abandon Overlord and seize on every opportunity to advance his interests in the Mediterranean."

"I agree," Hopkins said.

"Overlord cannot succeed under a British commander. Churchill will undermine him at every turn. The president must insist on an American commander-in-chief."

"I'll work on it, and you can reinforce the message when you get home," Hopkins said. "Meanwhile, there's an additional complication. Churchill now plans to arrive early for the Québec Conference. I'm sure he means to lean on the president to abandon the invasion."

"We mustn't allow that."

"I have an idea. A year ago, an old friend of the president's, E.F. McDonald, invited him to go fishing on McGregor Bay in Ontario. We should encourage the trip now."

"Just the thing, Harry. We can't prevent Churchill from seeing him prior to Quadrant, but we can keep them apart for as long as possible while we shore up our commitment. The president has earned a calm, relaxing vacation. So let's get him out of town."

12

———

JULY 23-30, 1943

Schumacher stood at attention and saluted Kretschmer and the Lagerführer, Major Fischer. "Tell us what you have in mind," Fischer said.

He had approached Fischer the afternoon before with his request to attempt another escape. The Lagerführer, who was nominally in charge of every aspect of camp life not dictated by their captors, had deferred to Kretschmer.

"I will escape during one of our evening swims."

Lightning from a summer storm illuminated the room. The thunder made it so difficult to hear Fischer asked him to repeat himself.

"How do you propose to accomplish it?" Kretschmer demanded. "Are you going to climb the fence like *ein Affe* or dive like *ein Wal*?" A giraffe or a whale?

"Neither. I plan to drown."

"What do you mean?" Major Fischer said.

"I will leave the compound with my fellow officers, but when they come up the stairway at dusk, I will not be among them. Since it will be dark by then, the Canadians will have to wait until morning to sweep the area. When they don't find my body, they will assume I have drowned, swept under the fence by the current."

They peppered him with questions. Schumacher walked them through his plan, including the pivotal role an unnamed Canadian confederate would play.

"It's too risky," Kretschmer said. A lightning bolt struck something nearby, filling the air with a chemical smell. The thunderclap stamped an exclamation mark on his statement. "This friend of yours, can you trust her?"

Schumacher smirked. "She loves me. We've been meeting ever since I arrived. She thinks I'm going to marry her once Germany achieves its glorious victory." He no longer believed Germany could win the war, nor did any of the other prisoners he knew, but he had to maintain appearances.

"Women are fickle," Kretschmer said. "What if her patriotism overrules her passion, and she betrays you?"

He shrugged. "What harm would it do? The Canadians will give me twenty-eight days of detention and release me. They'll tighten up security for future swims, but if it fails, no one else will attempt this means of escape. We lose nothing by trying."

Kretschmer inclined his head, indicating agreement. "Suppose this works," he said, "what will you do? Do you expect this girl to hide you? They'll be on to her within hours. The Americans have tightened up border security, so you can't make it to the US. Even if you do, they will capture you and won't treat you as kindly as the Canadians."

"I won't cross the border. I'm going west to Vancouver. Once there, I'll sign on to a merchant vessel and stay aboard until I reach a friendly country."

"How will you get that far?" Major Fischer said.

"By rail. The local lines and transcontinental routes intersect just south of here." He launched into a detailed description of the Canadian National and Canadian Pacific routes, which he'd gleaned by studying pilfered system maps.

"They'll expect me to go south or east; they won't look toward the west. The only problem will be if another prisoner escapes from Medicine Hat. They will search from Alberta to the Pacific."

"We can get a message to the camp," Kretschmer said, without explaining how he planned to do so. "But your chance of success seems slender. What is it, four thousand kilometers to Vancouver? A lot can go wrong."

Major Fischer allowed himself an uncharacteristic smile. "Think of the turmoil it will create, civilian and military police looking for this one man throughout the country. Even if he doesn't get far, they'll spend valuable man-hours trying to catch him."

"And it is my duty to escape, sir. It is all I've been thinking about since I was taken prisoner, in England, at Bowmanville, and here." Rain beat against the windows. Schumacher waited, hoping the downpour wasn't drowning his proposal.

Fischer leaned forward, twisting a pen between his fingers. "We can put a hold on all escapes in the west."

Now even Kretschmer smiled. "What do you need from us?"

Pamela had provided the clothing and disguises that were prerequisites to any escape attempt. He required forged documents and a way to distract the guards during his getaway. The former would take time. They spent another half hour considering the latter. The plan they produced was clumsy and, Schumacher felt, the weakest link in the chain. The diversion depended on others, which made him uncomfortable. But it would have to do.

On Saturday, July 24, Roosevelt motored to Shangri-La, accompanied by his speechwriters and his secretary. He hoped to spend a working weekend planning his twenty-fifth fireside chat, a term coined by a CBS News reporter, scheduled four days from then.

General Marshall arrived the following morning with news that forced him to delay the agenda. Italy's fascist Grand Council had voted Benito Mussolini out of power. As the duce left a meeting with

King Vittorio Emanuel, during which the king had told him the war was lost, he was arrested.

FDR and Marshall sat in the mountain air, a release from the humid sinkhole that was the nation's capital. With the jays chattering around them, Marshall said, "King Emmanuel has appointed General Pietro Badoglio to head the government. We're trying to get in touch to see what his intentions are."

Roosevelt brightened, sensing an opportunity for the Allies. "Perhaps we can avoid having to invade."

"Germany has thousands of troops stationed there," Marshall replied. "I doubt Hitler will stand idly by."

Roosevelt sighed, drumming his fingers on the push rims of his wheelchair. "I'm sure not."

Marshall had brought even more disturbing news as he raced north from Washington that morning. "The British issued a standfast order yesterday, barring further redeployment of troops from the Mediterranean to Great Britain. They have asked us to do the same."

"But we agreed to the transfer at Trident. What are they up to?"

"The prime minister has been leaning on Stimson to postpone or abandon the cross-Channel invasion."

"So Churchill has given orders to hold their troops in place." It was a statement, not a question.

"Mr. President, the Quadrant Conference is a month away. The British are looking for any sign of weakness or uncertainty from us."

FDR listened but did not respond, as was his custom, leaving Marshall to forge ahead. "We don't know whether the proposals they advance are those of the prime minister or his military advisors."

Marshall sat up straight in his chair as though coming to attention. He cleared his throat. FDR, an avid poker player, knew Marshall was about to show his cards. "Anything to which you and Churchill agree prior to Quadrant could tie the hands of both military delegations. What we both want from Quadrant is a firm decision to cross the Channel at the time and place of our choosing, even if we face resistance."

Marshall reminded him Churchill believed the bombing

campaign would weaken Germany to the point of internal collapse, as had happened in 1918. So far, he said, the aerial campaign seemed only to have pulled the country together. "If Mr. Churchill approaches you before the conference, I hope you will seek our advice before committing yourself."

Although these words were tantamount to insubordination, the president smiled and thanked him. While Marshall wanted his firm commitment, Roosevelt would hold his counsel until he heard what Churchill proposed.

BRANDON ARMITAGE ROSE EARLY. He was to supervise the guards at the breakfast shift but begged off once the prisoners had eaten. He walked into Gravenhurst, enjoying the cool morning air. The heat would be brutal by mid-afternoon.

Mark Stenhouse owned the town's one hardware store. As Armitage entered, he grinned, his customer turning and looking the Veterans Guard officer up and down. "That'll be three-ten," Stenhouse said.

The customer grunted and pulled a wad of cash out of the hip pocket of his denim pants, removing the rubber band and peeling off three bills. He fished in his front pocket and pulled out two V-coins. "It's a lot for an axe," he said. "And the quality's not what it used to be."

"It's the war," Stenhouse said. "They save the best steel for tanks."

"Aye." The customer turned, giving Armitage another head-to-toe examination before leaving the store.

"What can I do for the warrant officer this morning?" Stenhouse said. "We have a great deal on low-quality axes. Have you noticed how many people think the war effort is someone else's business?"

"Unfortunately, I have. Much as I'd like to take an axe off your hands, there's something else I need today." Stenhouse spread both arms in an open invitation. "There's a girl—a young woman I'm trying to find. She's eighteen or nineteen. No more, I think. Reddish-brown hair, green eyes, lovely figure. She paddles her canoe around the bay in the evening."

"That's Pam. You could have stopped with the green eyes."

"Pam ...?"

Stenhouse wrinkled his brow and scratched his cheek. "Can't recall, I'm afraid. What do you want her for? Has she done something wrong?"

"Not that I know of." He cursed himself for not having concocted an excuse. "She may have observed one of our prisoners breaking a rule. Where can I find her?"

The explanation appeared to satisfy him. "She works for the local MP, James Francis Kelly, handling constituent business. She has a desk in the offices of Tim McQuire, the attorney."

"I didn't know MP's had local offices. I've never heard of that."

"Yeah, well, I hear her father is some sort of muckety-muck in Ottawa. It may be a—what do you call it?"

"Sinecure," Armitage supplied. "A job without real responsibility."

"Something like that. 'Patronage' is what I was thinking."

"It amounts to the same thing. Do you know anything else about her?"

"Afraid not. She turned up last fall. She keeps herself to herself but seems friendly enough when you say hello. I've seen her at council meetings. She never comes in here."

"Maybe she doesn't need an axe," Armitage said. He thanked the man and left, heading down Muskoka Avenue and turning onto George Street.

The law office was in a turn-of-the-century house that might once have been Gravenhurst's version of a mansion. White paint, a side porch, a stained-glass window in front, and a modest sign held to a post by two chains. Armitage stood across the street, debating whether to step inside. What would he say? How would he explain himself? One of the CO's top priorities was maintaining good relations with the populace. Would the lawyer see his interest as an invasion of privacy?

Standing in uniform while staring at the structure was almost worse than risking a confrontation. He crossed and mounted the porch, left foot first, then the right, and rang the bell. A small sign beneath it instructed him to enter, so after waiting for a moment to see if anyone would come to the door, he opened it and walked in.

The door to the living room on his right was closed. To the left was a parlor serving as a reception area. There was no one at the desk. He took a seat and waited.

A minute passed, then two. A middle-aged woman entered, carrying several folders. "Hello," she said. "I'm sorry. I was pulling the files for the day. Do you have an appointment, Mr. …?"

"Armitage," he said. "Brandon Armitage. I'm a warrant officer at the camp."

"I can see that. Did you wish to see Mr. McQuire?"

"No. I believe the MP has an aide working here, Pam …"

"Pamela. She's not in at the moment. I don't know when to expect her. She comes and goes as she pleases." She sniffed and raised her head, signaling her disapproval. "It's not a full-time job, you see."

"Can you tell me where I might find her?"

"What's this about?"

"I'm not authorized to discuss this business with anyone other than the MP or his staff. She's done nothing wrong, if that's your concern."

"I'm not sure I should give out personal information."

To press the matter or not? "It's a district matter. I'll come back at another time."

"Very well. Shall I tell Pamela you called?"

She would anyway. "Of course. Just tell her that there's a matter I need to share with Mr. Kelly. Nothing urgent.

"Oh," he said, as though it were an afterthought. "Her last name. Pamela …?"

"Canavan," she said. "Pamela Canavan."

Armitage stepped back. His mouth fell open, and his heart raced.

ON THE EVENING of July 28, FDR discussed Mussolini's removal during his fireside chat. There was no fireplace on this humid summer night. That existed only in official White House photos. Instead, as he always did, Roosevelt sat at a cloth-covered desk, speaking into a nest of microphones bearing the flags of all the radio networks.

"Hitler refused to send sufficient help to save Mussolini," he told the American people. "Once again, the Germans betrayed their Italian allies."

Leaning into the microphones and lowering his voice, he said, "Mussolini and his Fascist gang will be brought to book and punished for their crimes against humanity. No criminal will be allowed to escape through the expedient of resignation. So our terms to Italy remain the same as our terms to Germany and Japan: unconditional surrender."

The Allies had brought about this development, he said, praising military leaders on both sides of the Atlantic. "You have heard some people say that the British and the Americans can never get along well together—that real cooperation between them is impossible. Tunisia and Sicily have given the lie, once and for all, to these narrow-minded prejudices."

This was far from the truth. At the Pentagon, uncertainty over the wisdom of a cross-Channel invasion had infected the US planning group. Even as Roosevelt spoke, the Joint Chiefs of Staff grappled with insurrection within their team. British military chiefs had asked their American counterparts to arrive at Québec early for talks, but the JCS were unwilling to comply before extinguishing the blaze.

The British submitted a proposed agenda suggesting that the invasion, agreed to only weeks before at Trident, was still an open question, listing "Operations from the UK" as the last item for discussion at Quadrant. The JCS responded by moving it to the top of the list.

Roosevelt knew some of this back-and-forth but concealed it from the public. "Ahead of us are bigger fights," he told the nation. "We and our Allies will go into them as we went into Sicily—together. And we shall carry on together."

Turning to domestic issues, he outlined a proposal that would become known as the GI bill, a program of pay, unemployment insurance, education, and health care that would transform American life for two decades.

He concluded by urging his fellow citizens to do everything possible to support the war effort. "We are a great nation—a rich nation—but we are not so great or so rich that we can afford to waste our substance or the lives of our men by relaxing along the way. We shall not settle for less than total victory. That is the determination of every American on the fighting fronts. That must be, and will be, the determination of every American here at home."

The red light over the desk went out. The president leaned back and smiled at Hopkins and Leahy. "One of my best, I thought."

"I agree, Mr. President."

Roosevelt shared with Leahy something Hopkins already knew. "I've invited Prime Minister and Lady Churchill to visit Hyde Park before leaving for Quadrant. He's arriving in Halifax on August 9, but I told him this morning I won't be home until August 12."

"Did you explain why?"

"I told him I'm going fishing but nothing more." The trip was top secret. Few in Washington knew Roosevelt was absenting himself before the conference. Fewer still knew his destination, the north shore of Lake Huron in Ontario.

Stalin still had not responded to his repeated requests for a two-way meeting, but should he agree, Roosevelt would drop everything and fly to Fairbanks from a Canadian airbase.

He lit a cigarette and blew out a perfect smoke ring, a halo to mark the evening. "Now, to get out of town for a few days. Time to hide out, boys."

MARGIE ARRIVED EARLY at the restaurant in Scarborough, but Godfrey Sperling was already there, camped on the outdoor patio. He rose as she stepped onto the polished wooden surface. "My dear, you look lovely tonight."

She batted away the compliment with a smile. "And so do you, Mr. Sperling. Not lovely, of course, but you look … distinguished."

"Please call me Godfrey."

"I'm sorry. I forgot."

"Not at work, mind you, but when we're visiting together like this, we can be less formal."

This was the third such "visit," always at a different restaurant and always on Wednesday evening. "Things pick up on Thursday through the weekend, and we're both much too busy then."

His attention flattered her, and his proper behavior allayed her misgivings. For all his attributes, Brandon seldom asked how she was doing, but Mr. Sperling—Godfrey—never ceased to inquire. Her husband rarely took her out. When he did, it followed church on Sunday at a nearby family restaurant that emphasized quantity over quality.

Yet here she was, being treated to a dinner in one of Toronto's finer restaurants three weeks in a row. She gazed out at Lake Ontario, shimmering in the early evening sunshine, and breathed in the fresh air.

"What is going on in your life?" Sperling asked.

"Nothing much. I lead a rather dull existence."

"Your husband? Was he home this weekend?"

She averted her eyes. "No." She hadn't encouraged him to return, reveling in being Margie Armitage rather than Brandon's wife. She had her own life now, happier than she'd been in years. Her drinking was under control, and while she mourned both her dead and missing sons, she had found—if not acceptance—perspective.

"And you?" she said. "I never ask about you. How selfish of me."

"Not at all," he said, turning to the menu. "The lamb is excellent here."

"I don't much care for—"

"Of course not. It's an acquired taste, I think. They get fresh halibut this time of year."

She grinned. "Halibut it is, then."

He ordered for them. He asked if she cared for a martini—not a drink but specifically a martini—and Margie, though she found them too strong, agreed. They sipped in silence, taking in the cool breeze off the lake. "Another?" he said.

"No, thank you. One is enough."

"You're quite certain?"

"I am."

It being wartime, no wine was available, and liquor was watered down—"Mackenzie King whiskey," they called it. The prime minister, who had sworn off alcohol for the duration of the war, had failed in his attempt to reimpose prohibition, but liquor remained scarce. Somehow Mr. Sperling found gin for his martinis.

Their dinners arrived, and Margie picked delicately at the fish as he dived into a rack of lamb. "This is excellent," he said. "You really should try a bite." He sliced off a chunk and dangled it before her on his fork.

"Just put it here," she said, indicating her plate.

"I don't have any germs." She did as she was told, letting him extend the fork into her mouth.

She agreed it was delicious, none of the gamey quality she abhorred. "Do tell me about yourself," she said. "Whenever we meet, we only discuss my problems."

"Oh, my dear, you don't want to hear about me."

She giggled. "Yes, I do. Unless it's too personal."

He took his last bite, put down his knife and fork, and tented his hands. "All right. It's nothing I like to talk about, but you've been so open with me. I'm married. You've probably guessed that."

Sperling looked her in the eye as though to gauge her reaction. "My wife is ..." He peered off at some distant place, removed his horn-rimmed glasses, stroked his chin. "She's quite ill, you see."

"Is it physical? A disease of some sort? I don't mean to pry."

"No, no. That's perfectly all right. She is not of sound mind. She imagines things, hallucinates. We've been to several doctors, but they're unable to do anything for her."

He had returned his glasses to his face during these few sentences; he now removed them again and wiped his eyes with his napkin. "We're not—I'm quite lonely. But I'm married. If I weren't, I would seek a different sort of relationship. There. I've said it. Made a damned fool of myself."

She reached out for his hand and took it in hers. "No, Godfrey, you haven't. I know exactly how you feel. Exactly," she repeated, no longer speaking to him but to herself.

"So I confess," his voice cracked as he spoke, "that I have invited you out not just for business reasons but for companionship. Just that. Nothing more. Just the friendship of another human being. I hope you aren't offended."

"Of course not."

"Or feel used."

"Not at all."

"And I know I can rely on your discretion."

"Absolutely."

"Because no one else knows this. I don't share my personal affairs with anyone. But with you …"

"I understand, Godfrey. My lips are sealed."

He smiled, exhaling as though he'd spent the last hour holding his breath. "Dessert?"

"No, thank you. I'm full. And we must preserve our sugar supplies for the boys." A lighthearted laugh. This time he did not press her.

"Godfrey, is there anything new about the management training? I'm really looking forward to it."

He wiped his lips with his napkin. "All in good time, Margie. Things are slow right now because of the summer. But come fall, as we look toward the holiday season, I'm going to need you." He nodded in agreement with himself. "Yes, Pinson's is going to need you very much."

He paid the bill, laying out two ten-dollar bills and waving away the change. "Let me drive you home."

"I don't want to put you out. If you take me to the bus stop, I'll be fine."

"I won't hear of it. Not at this hour. I insist."

ON JULY 28, *Oberleutnant* Franz Melzer hunched over the transcript of a conversation the Abwehr had intercepted hours before between Prime Minister Churchill and President Roosevelt. The two leaders had spoken via trans-Atlantic radiotelephone, discussing their approach to an expected peace proposal from the new Italian government. As he read the text, his pulse quickened, and he requested the Magnetophon recordings so that he could listen for any nuances. Cupping the headphones to his ears, Melzer heard Churchill say, "We do not wish to present any specific armistice terms before we are asked in so many words."

"That is right," Roosevelt replied.

"We can wait one or two days," the prime minister said. Roosevelt again agreed.

Churchill speculated how they might free British prisoners held in Italy before their transfer to "the land of the Hun," saying he would contact King Victor Emmanuel for help. Roosevelt promised to do the same.

Changing the subject, the American president said, "I'm sorry I won't see you until August 12. I'm going fishing."

Churchill answered with a perfunctory, "Oh." Something in his tone alerted Melzer, who combed through records of past interceptions. He found a year-old reference Roosevelt had made to an invitation from a Chicago entrepreneur, E. F. McDonald, for a fishing trip the following summer.

Melzer knew of the forthcoming conference in Québec and was aware Roosevelt sought a meeting with Stalin beforehand. Now, less than a month before the conference, the president had made this curious allusion to a fishing trip. Was this some sort of code about the Soviet dictator, or was he referring to something more mundane?

He found McDonald's name in Section Z's files and learned that, before the war, the industrialist had hosted a German friend, Count Felix von Luckner, at his summer home on Ontario's Birch Island. The count, known as the Sea Devil for his Naval exploits during the Great War, was a Nazi, though he had lost favor with Hitler by refusing to renounce his membership in the Freemasons. The Abwehr also knew he was helping a Jewish woman escape from Germany, but its commander, Admiral Wilhelm Canaris, had withheld this tidbit from the Nazi hierarchy. Now the information proved useful. When an agent reached the Sea Devil at his home in Halle, he had no difficulty persuading him to divulge everything he knew about McDonald and his much-loved McGregor Bay.

Continuing his search, Melzer unearthed a report made two days before by an Abwehr agent named Bruno Auer, who owned a cabin near Whitefish Falls, just north of Birch Island. Auer was a naturalized Canadian citizen, Austrian by birth, a retired railway engineer who provided the Axis with routine information about everything from train and troop movements to the availability of staples on grocery shelves.

Auer reported that, having heard of unusual activity on the island, he had motored south and watched carpenters constructing a ramp from the Birch Island railway station to the water's edge. A local woman told him seventeen Royal Canadian Mounted Police had arrived the day before, along with official-looking men dressed in civilian clothing. None appeared to be there to fish. She had also spotted two civilians out boating with a summer resident, an American named E. F. McDonald.

Auer did not know what these comings and goings meant, but he radioed them to Abwehr headquarters in Berlin, convinced they might be significant.

It was after seven o'clock when Melzer put the pieces together. He raced up the stairs to the office of General Hans Oster. The head of Department Z listened and thanked his young agent without commenting on his discovery. After Melzer left, Oster sat at his desk, considering how to handle the news.

At that moment, Oster was being investigated by Judge Advocate Dr. Manfred Roeder for helping Jews to escape Germany. If Roeder continued digging, he might discover Oster's central role in a plan to assassinate the Führer. He could not keep this to himself. Tapping the report against his hand, he walked the few steps to the office of his chief, Admiral Canaris.

Canaris acknowledged him by merely turning his head and raising his eyebrows. "An officer in the radio monitoring service has discovered something that may be significant," Oster said. "Roosevelt appears to be leaving Washington for a week's fishing in Canada."

The admiral frowned. Roeder was also investigating his role in the affair and had already arrested Oster's assistant, Hans von Dohnanyi who was even more involved in the Hitler plot than Oster. Canaris, one of National Socialism's earliest devotees, had come to detest the party so much that he had passed military secrets to the British and the Vatican. He was tempted to withhold this.

"What would you like me to do?" Oster said.

The admiral gave the general a blank look while he pondered. As the walls had closed in on him in recent months, his physical appearance had deteriorated. His officers found him lackluster and lethargic. While his conscience told him to withhold the information, he knew that, if discovered, his failure to advise Heinrich Himmler of this opportunity would not only cost Canaris his position but would make the Abwehr itself a casualty.

"I'll handle it," Canaris said.

Oster saluted and left without any sense of what his superior would do with this information.

Canaris sat at his desk for another ten minutes, stroking the fur of his beloved dachshunds, Kasper and Sabine, as he thought. Finally, he picked up the telephone, having made his decision.

Thus, Himmler got the news at 8 p.m. Minutes later, so did the Führer, who immediately summoned his top aides to the Wolf's Lair. As Himmler sent his minions scurrying to find a potential assassin among the thousands of German prisoners held captive in Canada, the tight ship that was FDR's planned getaway sprang a leak.

WAS IST FALSCH? What's wrong, Schumacher thought as, responding to the summons, he climbed to the top floor of the main detention center. *Alles ist in Ordnung?* Is everything all right?

He was only a day from his escape attempt. Pamela had everything ready. The camp forger was preparing false papers. The prisoners had rehearsed their roles—too well, in fact. It looked like a play, and he had asked them to loosen up. "*Lässig handeln,* as the English say." Act nonchalant.

And now this. "Leutnant Schumacher reporting, sir."

Today there was no *Triumvirat*, no *Lagerführer*, only Kretschmer. Instead of sitting behind the oak table in the library, he threw his arm around the lieutenant, drawing him close.

"Let's take a walk," he said.

"Is there a problem?"

"No. Not at all. Come." He took the stairs two at a time, left the building, and moved about the compound as though someone might overhear their conversation. "You have new orders from Berlin."

Schumacher grunted an affirmation but didn't ask.

"This girl. Can she get you a radio?"

"I don't know. I suppose she—you don't mean *die Mittelfrequenz,* do you? We're not talking about civilian stations?"

"No. Zenith makes a radio that receives *Kurzwellenradio.* Not as good as Telefunken, but it will do. You must be able to hear Berlin. Will she get one for you?"

"I'm sure she can," he said, although he had no idea how she might go about it.

"You are committed to the Fatherland, are you not? We have had our differences, you and I, but you are a resourceful officer."

"Thank you, sir."

"I saw how you fought the Canadian guards at Bowmanville. You have the makings of a true leader."

Kretschmer had never spoken to him this way and would not be doing so now if he didn't want something.

"The US killed the Japanese Admiral, Yamamoto. They shot down his plane, not in open combat, but while he was landing. A cowardly approach. We would not murder a country's leader, but the Americans have no hesitancy about such an action. They have changed the rules." Kretschmer stared at him, studying his reaction.

"We must be strong in these times. Resolute."

"*Ja*," Schumacher said, as though he understood.

They reached a bench near the vegetable garden, the air redolent with warm pig manure. Kretschmer indicated that he was to sit across from him. He waved the prisoners working the plot away, and with the afternoon heat at its most intense, they didn't object. "We have selected you to carry out a special mission, one you alone can perform. If you succeed, you will change the course of the war."

Kretschmer laced his fingers together and studied him. "Roosevelt is coming our way to fish at a place called Birch Island. It is three hundred kilometers northwest of here, above Lake Huron, near Sudbury."

"Ja, ja." Sudbury was on his planned escape route.

"You are to go there, find Roosevelt, and kill him."

Schumacher jerked backward as though shot. "Assassinate the American president? How am I to do that?"

"It is up to you. He will be there for a week, time for you to reconnoiter, devise a plan, find a weapon, and end his life."

Schumacher shook his head. "I am a pilot, not an assassin. I've never done such a thing."

"You've hunted with your father, haven't you? Instead of game, your prey is Germany's mortal enemy. With Roosevelt removed, England will crumple like a leaf in autumn." He clenched his fist, held it aloft, and released it.

"Where does this order come from?"

"Who are you to ask? It comes from the highest level of the SS. That is all you need to know."

Which meant Himmler, Schumacher thought, and that meant from the Führer himself. Schumacher rested his forehead on his

upraised palm. How could he worm his way out of this? "There must
be others better qualified."

"The SS issued the call only yesterday afternoon. I volunteered
you, explaining your escape plan. Your orders have just come back.
They are unequivocal."

"There is no time to plan. This is too sudden."

"We have no choice. We learned of this opportunity only twenty-
four hours ago."

As though reading his thoughts, Kretschmer said, "Your father is
counting on you. We visited him this morning in Oslo and explained
the importance of this assignment. He is quite proud of his *Bärli*."

Little bear, what his father had called him for as long as he could
recall.

"*Hauptmann* Schumacher is privileged to serve in Norway. It's a
comfortable position, don't you agree? I believe your mother is with
him. She's Norwegian, isn't she?"

What did his parents have to do with this?

"Such a lovely country," Kretschmer continued. "Cold in winter
but far better than the Eastern Front."

So there it was. Do this for the SS, and we won't send your father
to a likely death in Russia.

"He will be very proud of his son when he has changed
Germany's destiny."

Schumacher knew when he was defeated. "When must I do this?"

"Roosevelt's train arrives Sunday afternoon. He's to stay a week."

Schumacher's escape was to take place tomorrow evening. The
Canadians wouldn't discover he was missing until Saturday morning.
That gave him a bit of time, but how was he to get there? By train to
Sudbury, then ...

"Security will be tight," Schumacher said.

"I'm sure. US and Canadian, military and civilian. But I suspect
there are miles of wilderness and coastline, many islands and coves.
You are resourceful, as I said. You'll think of something."

13

JULY 31, 1943

In the early hours of July 31, a locomotive left the siding beneath the Bureau of Engraving Building on 14th Street, SW, near the National Mall. It pulled nine cars, including the 142-ton presidential railcar, the armor-plated *Ferdinand Magellan*.

Riding with President Roosevelt were Admiral Leahy; Jimmy Byrnes; Rear Admiral William Brown; Major General Edwin Watson; Roosevelt's physician, Ross McIntire; and Falla, the president's dog.

Ten Army radio operators and a secret service detail were also on board. Their number would grow to thirty before the president reached Birch Island. This morning, the train was bound for Hyde Park, where FDR would spend Saturday before continuing on to Canada for a fishing trip in Lake Huron on a siding that had once served as a lumber camp.

At the end of his week-long getaway, FDR planned to travel east from Sudbury to join the scenic Ottawa River, separating Ontario and Quebec. In Ottawa, he would spend an afternoon with Prime Minister Mackenzie King.

The train passed through Anacostia Junction in Maryland and picked up speed on its northward journey on tracks owned by the B&O Railroad. Members of his party gathered in the president's car, shedding their wartime pressures. Porter Henry Lucas, who would lose his job only days later after pocketing tips intended for all the porters, pulled the shades and served orangeade and lemonade. As the train left the rail yard at Baltimore, the president turned in for the night, treasuring nine days of fishing and companionship and what he imagined would be a peaceful and relaxing time away from Washington.

He left two pieces of unfinished business. Henry Stimson's return from Great Britain had been delayed, causing him to miss a planned meeting with the president. The visit with Stalin was still up in the air.

Apart from these two issues, nothing was to disturb his tranquility for a week.

MARGIE ARMITAGE WAS AWAKENED Saturday morning by a neighbor gunning his motorcycle. "Damn," she thought. "I've overslept."

She had no time for breakfast. She stepped into the shower, washing the smell of him away. It had been their third night together. Sperling had taken his time after bringing her home Wednesday, sitting alongside her on the sofa as they talked, reaching for her hand once or twice and giving it a little squeeze, rising as though to leave and planting a chaste kiss on her forehead. They locked eyes, she granting him permission. He sat down again, closer now, leaning toward her, kissing her on the lips, and, when she responded, embracing her.

They cuddled for a few minutes. His hand found her breast. Without a word, she unbuttoned her blouse. He slipped his hand inside her brassiere, fondling her as he explored her mouth with his tongue, pulling the bra down and lowering his mouth to her nipple. She guided his hand to her inner thigh. His fingers probed higher, and as she moaned, he laid her gently back, pulled down her panties, and entered her.

"Thank you," he said as he took his leave. "It has been so long. You are precious to me, Margie."

"Come again," she said, and they both laughed at the implication.

And so he had, parking around the corner Thursday night as she'd asked, creeping up the alley at nightfall, and entering through the back door. She'd prepared a light dinner, after which they'd listened to a program of dance music on the CBC and gone to bed.

When he returned last night, their meeting was hurried. "Dorothy is in a bad way, I'm afraid. I can't stay long."

But he stayed long enough. They made love on her double bed, she completely undressing and lying on her back with her legs slightly spread, inviting him in. "I am shameless."

"You are wonderful."

After they had locked in an embrace for fifteen minutes, he tried again but could not achieve an erection. Instead, he stroked between her legs while licking her breasts until she reached orgasm. She returned the favor, taking him in her hand until he climaxed.

They lay together for a few minutes, but the sheets were stained and uncomfortable. He rinsed his body while standing at the washroom sink and made his way downstairs to the kitchen, where she waited. As he had the first night, he thanked her as though she had done him a great favor. "I've never felt—"

Margie placed a finger over his lips. He smiled, kissed her, and returned the way he'd come.

She spent the night in Henry's room, folding the comforter atop the dresser and pulling the light blanket over her against the cool evening air. Eyeing the photo of Syl Apps lifting the Stanley Cup after the seventh game of last year's championship win over Detroit, she whispered, "I shouldn't stay in here." It was her last conscious thought. For the third night in a row, Margie slept soundly—too soundly.

It was too late to change the sheets. She would take care of that tonight. As she dressed, she hummed a song that had been on her mind from the moment she awakened, "Taking a Chance on Love."

She laughed at herself as she studied her image in the mirror. "What have you done, Margie?"

She put the thought away. *I've done something for myself. And for Godfrey. We are lonely and unloved. We deserve a bit of happiness.*

And Brandon? She gave him no thought at all.

SCHUMACHER LINED up with the other prisoners as they prepared for their evening swim. Each carried a towel, most draped around their necks, but a few slung over an arm on this warm night. They arrayed themselves in groups of five, standing at the camp entrance on Lorne Street, awaiting the command.

"All right, men, move out." The lead guard walked backward as they turned left toward the bay. Two more guards took up the rear.

Schumacher had placed himself to the right of his row halfway back. As the men neared the top of the stairway, Helbig, positioned just ahead of him, handed out pieces of candy to those around him. The others broke ranks to make a grab. The bag flew from his hand. "*Scheisse,*" he shouted as hard candies scattered in every direction.

Two prisoners slipped wrapped packages from beneath their folded towels and handed them to Schumacher. Securing them beneath his own towel, he scurried to pick up a few of the sweets that had rolled into the foliage. Two others followed him. The guards at the rear, viewing the commotion against the low-hanging sun, shouted at them. They arose and rejoined the group as the ranks of five funneled into a single stream and passed down the stairway without further incident.

Most of the men plunged into the cold water. Some swam out to the fence as the first canoes from the girl's camp approached. Others ignored the young ladies and swam laps. A few rested on the beach, enjoying the setting sun and sharing a pack of cigarettes another prisoner had brought along.

As the sun disappeared below the horizon and the guards organized the return to the camp, a voice cried, "Help! We have to save him!"

Every man, guards and prisoner alike, turned in Helbig's direction. "It's Schumacher. He dived in and hasn't come up. Help me find him."

The water erupted in a flurry of activity as one man after another dived to the bottom along the fence line. As one surfaced, another would take his place. "It's too dark down here. I can't see a fucking thing. Train the searchlights here."

Guards yelled to Corporal Smith in the tower to direct the spotlight on the water, but all he achieved was to blind those looking toward it. The search went on for another fifteen minutes until the guards demanded the prisoners give it up. "We'll search for him tomorrow."

"It will be too late then. He's trapped down there. The fence is ragged in this section."

"C'mon, Helbig. There's nothing we can do at this hour."

The distraught man kept diving until he was exhausted. His fellow prisoners pulled him into shore, shivering and sobbing. "You have to find him. He's my best friend."

"I'm sorry," the sergeant said.

Others put their arms around Helbig in solidarity. "You let it happen," one prisoner screamed at the sergeant. The officer didn't answer, urging the men, now united in their mourning, up the stairs and into the compound.

***

ARMITAGE HITCHED a ride with a supply truck on its return run and entered the house before five, dripping wet from two hours spent in the cab in blazing heat. He dropped his duffel bag at the entrance and wandered into the kitchen, opening the refrigerator door and staring into it. Finding nothing, he took a drinking glass from the cupboard above the sink, filled it with tap water, and drank in a series of greedy gulps.

Margie would be home soon. He had three days of leave and looked forward to surprising her. After church on Sunday, he'd treat her to dinner. They hadn't gone out together in a long time. He'd mow the lawn and do odd jobs around the house.

He checked the table at the entrance to see if Henry had sent another letter and riffled through those that lay below the mail slot in the door. Nothing.

Taking his duffel bag with him, he mounted the stairs and dropped it at the foot of the bed. How unlike Margie to leave it unmade; how busy she must be. He stripped and showered, ignoring the washcloth wadded up along the sink. His towel was askew on the rack, but he dried himself and hung it up straight, put on a clean pair of boxer shorts and a T-shirt, and prepared to grab a quick nap before she returned.

As he pulled the sheet back, his hand brushed a stiff patch. He stood and stared at it. Leaned down and sniffed. Arose and stared wordlessly at what he'd found.

His right leg throbbed. He needed to sit down. But not here. Not on this bed. He walked into Dickie's room but couldn't stay. Entered Henry's room and sat on the end, running his hand across the light summer blanket. The comforter was folded on the bureau. Had she slept here? He thought so but couldn't be sure.

As his mind rewound everything he'd seen, smelled, and sensed in the past twenty minutes, the general outline of what had occurred became clear. He rubbed his leg, considering what course to take. Should he stay and confront her or leave and find a way back to camp?

Margie decided for him. He heard the front door open. No one on Langford Avenue locked their doors; there was no need. From below, a song reached his ears. What was it? Something Benny Goodman had recorded. He placed it. "Taking a Chance on Love." He sat transfixed as she banged around downstairs.

Five minutes passed, ten, as Armitage sat at the foot of his son's bed, waiting for whatever was about to happen.

He tried to analyze his emotions but felt nothing. Cold and

empty, he felt neither anger nor rage. The tune she was half humming, half singing grew words. "Here I go again, taking a chance on love."

Her footsteps on the stairway, still singing. Entering the bedroom at the top of the stairs. Her song ceasing as if she'd lifted the tonearm from the record. He pictured her as she spotted his bag at the end of the bed—their bed.

"Brandon?" A small, quiet voice. Again, a bit louder this time. "Brandon, are you here?"

He remained quiet. Her steps grew louder as she approached. He heard her pass Dickie's room, then she appeared in the doorframe. "You're home."

"Who is he?"

"What?" The slight hesitation before she spoke confirmed his suspicions.

"Who is he?" Spoken deliberately but without raising his voice.

"Who is who?"

"A man slept here last night. He stained the sheet. The smell of him is in our bed, Margie."

"A couple of friends stayed overnight. I fell asleep in here."

"Who are they?"

"You don't know them."

He pushed himself upright. She stepped back as though he were about to strike her, something he would never consider. "Tell me the truth."

She lowered her head, her first sign of contrition. "It's no one you know."

"Someone from Pinson's, I take it. I thought your spirits had improved because of your job. But there's more to it, isn't there?"

Margie brought her hands to her face, embracing her temples. "It was a one-time thing. A mistake."

"A closet full of new dresses and a payroll check for $12.40—is that what you're worth?"

"It's not like that. How can you think that?" She covered her eyes and wept while he waited. "He's kind, and he's lonely. His wife has mental problems."

"No doubt." When she didn't take the bait, he added, "And what about me? What excuse do you give him?"

"Stop it!" Her scream cut a path between them. "You're not here. You're off playing soldier, trying to redeem yourself."

"What the hell do you—"

"Even when you are here, you're not present. But he is and was. We had a fling—a stupid thing, I see that now—and it's over. I'm sorry."

He walked past her into their bedroom, picked up his duffel bag, and took the stairs, leading with his left as he always did.

"What are you doing? Where are you going?"

He turned on the landing. "In order, I have no idea, and back to camp."

"That's right. Just walk away, like you always do."

He closed the door and left the house. Their house.

———

SCHUMACHER HAD PLANNED to take Pamela only as far as Toronto and give her the slip. By the time the guards discovered he was alive, he would be hundreds of miles from the camp. If they connected him to the girl who worked for the member of parliament, they would first have to find her. When they did, she could only reveal what he'd told her, that he was headed toward Halifax.

Kretschmer's abrupt order had forced him to change his plan. Now he needed her. Pamela had connections—a father in Ottawa, a mother in Toronto, and an uncle in Sudbury.

They had a signal, an isosceles-shaped rock close to the northern fence. If he pointed it north, the escape was on; south, it was off for the night; and east, they needed to meet. Pamela had seen the warning during her early morning walk and returned at ten o'clock to stroll along the fence as he kept pace with her.

"We need to travel to Sudbury tonight. Will your uncle take us in?"

"I'm sure he will, but why Sudbury? It's in the wrong direction."

"I'll explain tonight. How do we get there?"

"I'll check the train schedules. It may be best to head into Toronto on the local line and take the trans-Continental route north. I'll find out."

This would double his risk of exposure, but it was better than spending the night in Gravenhurst and trying to creep away in daylight. "Good girl. Have you found a radio?"

"No luck, I'm afraid, but Uncle George may have one."

"And the dictionary?"

"I told you two days ago. I found one at the library and walked away with it. I don't understand why you need one. I'll be along to handle any language problem. And why did it have to be a Winston Dictionary?"

He ignored the question, having no answer he could share. "Tonight, then. I love you."

"You too." She turned toward the fence, hoping he would touch her fingers, but he'd started back toward the barracks.

Now, only two hours after his escape, they stood together on the train platform. Pamela peered north while Schumacher stood in the shadows, keeping his distance from the crowd of airmen on leave from Camp Norway, off to the big city for the weekend.

He carried a Norwegian passport, papers identifying him as an airman on leave, and a role of currency, all provided by members of the escape committee. The clothes Pamela had found were Muskoka fishing togs, helping him blend in.

The 11:06 train from Toronto was four minutes late. Through the windows of the carriages, they could see a small number of passengers, most of them civilians, alight on the opposite platform. As the locomotive pulled out, heading north, they were exposed to the group waiting to cross the tracks. The German drew further into the shadows, pulling the brim of his flat cap lower over his eyes. Spotting a figure he knew, he turned his back, raising the collar of his jacket to conceal his blondish hair from the man's view. The guard—what was his name?—Armitage, dressed in civvies, the strap of his duffel bag over his left shoulder. He'd seen him in the mess hall during lunch. Where had he gone, and why was he returning so soon?

He waited until he was sure the Canadian had disappeared behind the terminal building before turning forward again. After a minute, he glanced around once more. Pamela understood his need for concealment, but if she noticed his heightened precaution now, she didn't show it.

Ten minutes later, the last train to Toronto arrived. The pair hung back until all the Norwegian airmen had boarded. When they turned left into the railcar, Schumacher led Pamela in the opposite direction. He traveled through two cars before finding an empty row. He took the window seat, his hat turned down. He need not have worried. Most of their fellow passengers were asleep.

Pamela said nothing for more than a quarter-hour. She leaned into him and whispered, "I still don't see why we're going to Sudbury tomorrow. What is so important there?"

Schumacher, who'd been thinking about elements of his cover story as he cobbled together a revised plan, said, "My father has a friend who lives nearby. They served in the Great War, after which he moved to Canada. I hope he'll be able to help us."

She frowned. "Are you sure he won't—you know ...?"

"My father saved his life."

She closed her eyes and leaned against his shoulder while Schumacher worried it was a mistake to bring her along. Whoever gave the order in Berlin hadn't thought this through. After his weeks of planning, they were forcing him to improvise. He didn't like it.

ARMITAGE WALKED FROM THE STATION, his thoughts on Margie. His initial shock at her betrayal had hardened to anger. How could she have done this to him—to them?

And to turn it around and make it his fault! What had she meant by "playing soldier?" Did she think this was some sort of game? To 'redeem' himself? Did she think he was doing this to erase the stain of his spending the last war as a prisoner?

Her spirits had soared when she'd taken the job. He supported her, reveling in her news that she, too, was in line for a promotion. She had proved herself, he thought. Now he knew the truth, and it disgusted him.

Lying on his cot, he studied the ceiling as he considered his options. What were the four options Lieutenant Morrison had taught him about decision-making? *Do, delay, delegate, or drop.* The last two didn't apply. He couldn't turn the matter over to anyone else or pretend nothing had happened. By leaving, he delayed a resolution, but that wouldn't suffice for long.

He would have to take some action, but what? Forgive her and hope for reconciliation? Divorce her? What did he want? At the moment, he couldn't decide.

A knock at the door interrupted his internal debate. Corporal Smith entered, his face flushed. "You've heard, then?"

"Heard what?" he said, sitting up.

"I figured that's why you've returned. A prisoner drowned tonight. We had to suspend the search when the light faded. We're sending down divers in the morning, but no one's optimistic."

"Who was it?"

"Lieutenant Schumacher."

"Schumacher?" Armitage stood up.

"He was diving toward the bottom of the fence and must have gotten entangled."

Armitage massaged his forehead, the image of Dickie's near-doppelgänger hovering over him. "Poor bastard. I rather liked him. How did it happen?"

"The prisoners went down to the beach, as they always do. Most were swimming, some were lying around talking or smoking. You know the drill. His partner, that guy Helbig, put up a cry. He kept diving, trying to save him. Others joined in. I was up in the guard tower, but I couldn't see much at that hour. After sunset, we had to call it off. Helbig was distraught."

"Was the girl there?"

Smith shook his head in bewilderment.

"The one that paddled up from Gravenhurst two weeks ago and spoke to him through the fence. She works for the local MP. "

"A few girls came over from the camp, but I didn't notice anyone from town."

Armitage left his room and corralled two other guards who had been present. No one had seen a woman at the south end of the boom fence. The few who had crossed the inlet were camp girls.

He turned in, but sleep wouldn't come. Something about this incident didn't add up. Lying awake in bed and staring at the patterns the moonlight traced on the ceiling, he thought about Schumacher's past escape attempts and his certainty that the prisoner had been behind the tunnel operation. He could do nothing tonight, but dawn might cast more light on his suspicions.

14

AUGUST 1, 1943

"Mother, this is Roald Forren, a Norwegian pilot."

Jörg Schumacher stood erect, displaying his perfect white teeth as Pamela introduced him to her mother. It was almost two in the morning as Jeanne Canavan, her robe belted around her, extended a hand to greet him. "Welcome. Pamela has told me a great deal about you. Your unit is training north of here, is that right?"

"Yes, madam," Schumacher said, bowing, trying to hide his admiration at her appearance. Even without makeup and hair undone, she was a beautiful woman. It struck him that this is the way her daughter would age, and he wished he could remain a part of their lives.

"I escaped to England with two dozen other pilots after the Germans invaded in April 1940. The government-in-exile transferred us to Canada to set up a training base at Muskoka Airport."

"That's where we met," Pamela said. "Roald trains other flyers for the coming invasion."

"And how much longer will that be?" Jeanne suppressed a sigh.

"By next spring, I think. After the war, I hope—Pamela and I, that is—"

"He's going to stay and apply for Canadian citizenship, Mother. He plans to go into commercial aviation."

"Once we've won, the entire civilian economy will change," Schumacher said. "We've developed new classes of engines that allow planes to fly higher and longer. Within a few years, most long-distance travel will be by air."

Jeanne gave a dismissive laugh. "Not this lady. I've never been in one of those things and don't intend to. The CNR and Canadian Pacific can get me from here to Vancouver in complete safety."

Pamela nudged him before he could protest.

"Well, young man, make yourself at home. I have a spare bedroom. Unpack your bag and get settled."

"We won't be staying long, Mother. We're headed up to Sudbury tonight. Do you think Uncle George will let us stay with him for a day or two?"

"I'm sure he won't mind. I'll call him. But why Sudbury?"

"Roald has business there. He's asking a fellow countryman to finance the purchase of more training aircraft."

"That's a noble thought. We must all do our part. Still, Pamela, show him the guest room; come talk to me before you turn in."

The young woman led Schumacher up the stairs and into the bedroom to the right. "She wants to question me," she whispered to him. "She wants to know your intentions. And mine." Giggling, she kissed him on the cheek and closed the door behind her as she made her way down the hall.

Schumacher collapsed on the single bed without changing out of his clothes, enveloped by the sweet smell of roses in a small vase on the nightstand. Though exhausted, sleep would not come. His Canadian captors were no fools. Within hours they would search the enclosure and, not finding a body, realize he couldn't have just floated beneath the fence.

As for the girl, his hastily concocted cover story was as thin as his plan for ending Roosevelt's life. Even as the woman spoke with her daughter two doors away, he wondered whether she had seen through it.

At first light, he crept back downstairs, through the living room, and into a small den that seemed to serve as an office. *"Jesus Christus,"* he whispered. A Zenith Trans-oceanic Clipper sat atop the bookcase, its grill cloth emblazoned with the image of a sailboat. He checked his watch. Three hours until Berlin would broadcast messages.

He returned to the bedroom and waited, staring at the ceiling, fidgeting, glancing at his watch every few minutes. At 8:55, he returned to the lower level. "Pamela is sleeping," her mother said. "What would you like for breakfast? French toast, perhaps?"

"I'll wait a few minutes. I must write my mother. May I use your office?"

"Of course." She smiled as she passed through the open door of the kitchen and into her garden, leaving him alone. Plugging in the set of headphones, he turned on the radio and tuned to the top end of the 31-meter band. He took a sheet of writing paper from the desk and, with a pencil poised in his hand, waited until he heard the series he'd been awaiting: *190a22, 1162b6, 1026a14 ...*

Upstairs, he opened the dictionary Pamela had stolen from the library, turned to page 190, and counted to the twenty-second entry in the first column. *Coal.*

He flipped to page 1,162, his finger finding the sixth entry in the second column. *Train.*

It took fifteen minutes to decode the entire message. He committed it to memory, tore the paper into small bits, and flushed them down the commode. A book cipher was crude. A cryptologist had only to glance at the numbers to see what they represented. The only problem was matching it with the right source book. Using a dictionary was so obvious it was almost no code at all, but there had been no time for anything more sophisticated. It only had to work for a few days.

"When the war ends," Pamela had said, "I suppose it will be some months before they allow you to return." He doubted he would ever see his home again. He would get nowhere close to the American president before security officers intercepted him. Even if he carried out the assassination, every police force in the US and Canada would hunt him down like an eagle eyeing a silver salmon.

His mission was not just impossible to carry out. It was a death sentence.

———

ALONG WITH THREE other guards and Lieutenant Morrison, Armitage stood on the shore of the bay, watching a pair of divers launch themselves from the raft in the middle of the swimming area. The water was crystalline; no breeze disturbed its surface on this warm August morning. One diver would fling himself off the edge, disappear for a minute at a time, and resurface, only to be replaced by the other. The guards observed this slow-moving operation for a half hour, after which the divers conferred and swam to shore.

"Nothing down there," one said, panting after his exertions. "There is a small gap between the fencing and the bottom near the second buoy, but it's only a foot high,"

"Big enough for him to escape?" the lieutenant asked.

The diver sat down on a rock and thought it through. "The depth there is about ten feet. He'd have to dive and worm beneath the wire while holding his breath. Buoyancy wouldn't be a problem if he clung to the fence. An accomplished swimmer might make it."

His fellow diver ran his hands through his jet-black hair and shook his head. "I wouldn't try it. I'll say that."

"Suppose he tried to make it through but caught himself on the fencing. Might he have surfaced outside it?"

"A body sinks until it decomposes; gases bring it to the surface. If the current's right, it's possible."

"Sir," Armitage said, "wouldn't his body have floated south to Steamship Bay? No one has reported a sighting." The camp had alerted every resident and business along both shores of the inlet.

Morrison thanked the divers and dismissed them. As Armitage followed him up the stairs, he had a sudden thought. "I wonder if he escaped before he came down to the beach." He had questioned two of the three guards during the early morning hours. Both said they had counted the men as they left the compound.

"I doubt it. The Germans are taking this hard. They're holding a memorial service this afternoon."

"Did we question everyone? Who was in charge?"

"Sergeant Phillips was in command. He's at church this morning. I'll meet with him when he returns."

Armitage returned to his desk to censor a backlog of outgoing mail. Corporal Smith interrupted him an hour later. "Lieutenant wants to see you."

As he entered his superior's office, Morrison sat beating time with the eraser end of his pencil. Sergeant Phillips stood before him, kneading his cap between his hands. "I want you to repeat what you've just told me," Morrison said.

"It was like I said to the lieutenant. There was some sort of disturbance as the men started down the stairs. Someone spilled something, and the prisoners broke ranks and went after whatever it was. It only took a few seconds—thirty at most."

"Time enough, sir."

Morrison muttered in agreement.

"I was trying to get everyone back in line, but a guard at the rear stooped to help pick up whatever was rolling around."

Armitage turned toward Morrison. "Sir, I ask permission—"

"Go ahead."

"There's a young woman in town who visits Schumacher during evening swims. They talk to each other and sometimes touch hands through the fence. They even met during a work project a month ago. If he escaped last night, she may have helped him."

"Who is she?"

"Pamela Canavan. She works for Mr. Kelly, the local MP." The lieutenant winced at the mention of a member of parliament. "I don't know where she lives, but I request permission to find her."

Morrison considered for a moment, halting his incessant drum beating. "Just to talk with her? I have no objection."

"If I'm right, she's left with him. I intend to speak with her friends, the MP, and her relatives."

"*If* she's gone," the lieutenant said, making no attempt to conceal his doubt. "All right, try to find her, but if she's missing, report back to me before proceeding. Lieutenant-Colonel McHugh must approve."

"All right, sir. Thank you."

"On second thought," Morrison said, stopping Armitage in his tracks, "the commandant will want to handle any direct contact with the MP if it comes to that."

"I understand, sir." Armitage limped off to follow his instinct.

⁎

Bernice Oberholzer stepped back from her door, gasping in surprise. "Margie, what are you doing here? You might have called."

"I did, but you didn't answer."

"I was at church." She studied her erstwhile friend and confidante. "You look ghastly. Come in. It's hot out there. What's wrong?"

Margie took a seat in an upholstered armchair whose colors had faded in the sunlight pouring through the window. Twisting a handkerchief in her hands, she stared at Bernice and burst into tears.

"Let me get some water," her companion said, charging from the room as though pursued by a mad dog. Not until Margie's sobs subsided did she reenter, carrying two glasses in one hand, and a pitcher of iced water in the other. She poured each of them a drink, set the pitcher on a doily on the coffee table, and sat on the sofa across from her, folding her hands in her lap. "Tell me what's bothering you."

"I can't. I shouldn't have come."

"Of course you should have. Where else could you go?"

What was meant to be comforting hit Margie like sticking a fork into an electrical outlet. Where indeed? That was the problem. She couldn't confide in her mother, for she'd do nothing but blame her. She had no other close friends except for the younger woman, Sarah. Would she understand?

And Bernie—if Margie unburdened herself, she would have it all over Pinson's before the doors opened tomorrow.

"Be honest. What do the other women think of me?"

Bernice studied her for several seconds before responding. "Do you really want to know?"

"Yes. No. I'm not sure." She twisted the handkerchief between her fingers. "I suppose the fact you asked me that is all the answer I need. They think I cost Gladys her job."

"Didn't you?"

"No, I did not."

"Anyway, she's found herself a new job at the Vogue Shop at better pay. Jobs aren't going begging, in case you hadn't noticed. No, it's about more than Gladys. Much more."

"I'd better go." She rose from the chair.

"Margie, I've always loved you. I'd do anything for you. Let me help you now."

"I'm sorry for taking up your time."

As she reached the door, her friend said, "You're not the first, you know. You won't be the last."

Margie turned to her, tears glistening in her eyes.

"Margie, come back inside. I'll pour you something stronger, and you can pour your heart out."

"No, I can't do that. Thank you, Bernie, but I just can't talk about it now." She left the duplex and walked toward the trolley stop.

Since it was Sunday, the attorney's office was closed, as was everything else. Armitage stood in the middle of Gravenhurst, looking up and down the street, shared only by tourist fishermen returning to their rented cottages with their day's catches. The temperature was near ninety, and the air reeked of asphalt and dead fish. He felt like an idiot standing around in his sweat-stained uniform.

Minutes passed before he thought of a solution. He entered the train station, opened the phone directory, and found a listing for Mark Stenhouse. Ten minutes later, he stepped onto the councilman's porch and rang the doorbell. He appeared at the screen door, clearly displeased. "It's Sunday afternoon."

"Yes, and I apologize, but this is vitally important."

Stenhouse stepped outside rather than inviting him in. "I don't mean to be rude, but Tammy's mother is unwell. She takes a nap every afternoon."

"I understand. I'm looking for either the attorney, Timothy McQuire, or the woman who guards the palace for him. Her name is Harrington."

"Janice," he said, emphasizing the second syllable. "You won't find Tim around on a summer weekend, but she may be home. Why do you need her?"

"I must locate Pamela Canavan, the girl who works for the MP."

"Why?"

"I can't explain, but it's urgent that I find her."

Stenhouse didn't recall the woman's address but gave her location, "on David past Raynor, third house on the right from the corner."

He found the woman's home, knocked, and received a frosty greeting. "What are *you* doing here?"

"Pardon the intrusion, Mrs. Harrington—"

"It's Miss."

"Pardon me. Miss Harrington. I need to find Pamela Canavan."

She sniffed. "I told you before, I can't give out that information."

Armitage took a chance. "A prisoner has escaped, and Miss Canavan may know where he is. I need your help to find her."

"Escaped? Is he dangerous?"

"He's a German officer—a pilot. He's escaped before. We are treating this with utmost caution."

"I really shouldn't—"

"We can contact Mr. Kelly, of course, but I hate to bother him."

"He's on vacation up north. You can't reach him right now."

"That means involving the RCMP. A lot of bother when you could help. I doubt he'll be pleased." He turned as though to leave.

"Of course I'll help. It's just that I shouldn't. I'll trust you not to tell where you got her address."

"And I'll trust you not to spread the word about our escaped prisoner. We don't want to alarm townsfolk. We just want him back."

"Of course," she said. "We'll have to go to the office."

She rode her bicycle while he struggled to keep up. Five minutes later, sitting at her desk, she flipped through an index file and gave him an address on John Street near where he'd lost Pamela the week before. He thanked her and walked the few blocks to the dry goods store, above which was Pamela Canavan's apartment.

He made his painful climb up the wooden stairway outside the building and rapped on the blue door. A woman's voice told him to wait a minute. He took a step down the stairs in case Schumacher was armed. Instead, a young woman opened the door and spotted him on the stairs. She wrinkled her nose as though she'd detected a foul smell.

He introduced himself. "Is Pamela here?"

"No. Come in, please. Let me put on my glasses so I can see you."

He stepped into a small living area with a sofa against one wall, a chair against the other, and a breakfast table with two chairs at the far end alongside the kitchenette. Posters of Canadian national parks, Banff, Jasper, and Cape Breton Highlands, adorned the walls.

"I'm Shelley Owen," she said, shoving her hand in his direction. She was short but slender, hair a dirty blonde, wearing tight dungarees and a plaid, long-sleeve shirt open to a point between her small breasts. "What do you want with Pam?"

"How well do you know her?"

"As well as anyone you've roomed with for almost a year. I'm a grade school teacher, about to start my second term here. She works for the member of parliament for this riding."

"I see," Armitage said, as though this were news to him. "Where is she today?"

The young teacher frowned. "What's she done?"

"Nothing, but she may have information on the location of one of our prisoners. I can't be more specific."

"I don't see how she could. She doesn't know any of them. She spends all her time with her boyfriend. They've gone to Toronto, I think. Her mother lives there."

"This boyfriend, is he local?"

"No, he's a pilot up at Little Norway. I've never met the guy, but she's crazy about him."

Armitage swallowed, his mouth dry. "Miss Owen, do you have her mother's address?"

"Is it that important?"

"It is extremely so. Miss Canavan can be of great help to us. I need to speak with her as soon as possible."

"Her mother writes every week." She retreated to a room to her left, evidently a shared bedroom, and returned with an envelope. "She's in Lawrence Park. Nice neighborhood."

"Indeed," he said. He gazed at the return address and at the name written above it, Jeanne Canavan.

THE PRESIDENTIAL TRAIN crossed from Buffalo into Canada during the night, stopping at Hamilton for security officers of the Royal Canadian Mounted Police to board. They would join other Mounties and US Navy and Secret Service agents who had already arrived at Birch Island.

At Romford, east of Sudbury, the locomotive that had pulled the nine-car train from the border decoupled, and a freight engine, suited for the winding, single-track lane they would follow south on the last leg of the journey, took over. The Canadian Pacific had chosen its engineer for his familiarity with the route. No one had told him who was aboard this special train, only that it was "the most important that had ever crossed Canada." An air patrol scouted the track, giving an all-clear signal before the engine got underway.

As the presidential party watched through the windows of the

Ferdinand Magellan, the cars snaked through the La Cloche Mountains, from Espanola on the Spanish River to West River, Whitefish Falls, and on to Birch Island. Puffy white clouds dotted the azure sky.

FDR, who loved rail travel, pressed his face to the window like a small child, remarking at the lakes and streams as they slipped by. "I wish we could open the windows and smell the forest," he told Leahy. He felt like a caged animal inside the sealed rail car.

Instead of stopping at Birch Island, the train continued south, past the McGregor Bay station and across the Goat Island bridge. Secret Service Agent Mike Reilly joined Roosevelt in his rail car to explain what was happening.

"I'm sorry, Mr. President, but this track dead-ends at Little Current, and we need to turn it around so we're heading in the right direction when we leave." Roosevelt, all too familiar with such security requirements, did not need to be told that the precaution was necessary if they needed to make a quick getaway.

Eleven miles to the south, the train slowed, "Off to our left," Reilly said, "you can see a single track heading east. We're passing over two switches and halting. The brakeman will throw a switch, and we'll back onto this spur. Once he throws a second switch, we'll move forward again, heading back the way we came."

"A wye," Roosevelt said, a twinkle in his eye. No one needed to explain to him the section of tracks, shaped like the letter Y, that branched off the spur and allowed the train to execute a two-way turn.

As the train came to a stop, Roosevelt watched the brakeman pass below his window as he walked to the rear of the train to unlock the switch stand with his key and change the "points," the direction in which the rails at the switch pointed. The train backed onto the left arm of the wye and onto its stem, the eastbound, dead-end track. Several minutes passed while the president pictured the brakeman switching the track at the stem of the wye to direct the points toward the right arm and another at the junction where the wye rejoined the main track. The train crept forward, halting as the brakeman returned all the switches to their original positions and climbed aboard.

A few minutes before 4:00 p.m., the engine slowed to a stop at the Birch Island station, a long, single-story building painted Tuscan red with cream trim, brown windows and doors. The north end of the structure held the station agent's office, the baggage and freight room were to the south, and the waiting room lay in the center. For the coming week, these rooms would house the security operation while the presidential train remained in place, the president's car at the rear serving as his living quarters.

Roosevelt knew Reilly had made all these arrangements on short notice. Workmen had rerouted coal trains to a passing siding, driving spikes into the ties at both switches to make it impossible for another locomotive to enter the track on which FDR's train rested.

Naval command in Chicago had dispatched the 300-foot USS Wilmette through the Straits of Mackinac, carrying motorized whale-boats and speedboats. The RCMP stationed officers at either end of the train, and an armed US Navy shore party patrolled the woods east of the site.

Floatplanes would bring the mail in daily. Bell Telephone had installed special circuits connecting the communications car to the White House.

Two vessels would take the presidential party fishing each day. One was a thirty-eight-foot Williams cabin cruiser, the *Anna H*. The admiral at Great Lakes Naval Training Station had requisitioned it from a civilian to give the president something classier than a navy whaleboat. A companion vessel, the *Mizpah*, belonged to Roosevelt's host, E. F. McDonald, who would serve as its captain during the visit.

The train station lay on an isthmus, a half-mile wide. To the west lay the Bay of Islands off Lake Huron; to the east, McGregor Bay. The two cruisers could fish the Bay of Islands one day, then, after discharging their passengers, sail through a channel between Birch and Little LaCloche Island to board the party on McGregor Bay the following morning. McDonald had supplied a map marking the best fishing spots for bass, wall-eyed pike, and lake trout. Roosevelt hoped to explore them all.

When the president was on land, Navy ships would patrol close to shore. When he was out on the water, he was shadowed by three fully equipped escort boats with eight Secret Service agents and three Royal Canadian Mounted Police. They were to remain near the President's craft at all times. An air patrol combed the contemplated fishing area each morning.

The White House had given Reilly little time to arrange all this, but Roosevelt was confident he had planned for every conceivable contingency. Though he hated the fuss that accompanied him wherever he went, FDR expressed his gratitude to his most trusted Secret Service agent. "You've done splendid work, Mike. We'll have no interruptions. No one knows where I am or what I'm doing. Peace. It's just what I need."

15

AUGUST 2, 1943

ARMITAGE PAID off the cabbie and stood before the narrow, two-story stone house off Weybridge Crescent in Lawrence Park. By the time the commandant had approved his travel, the last train had left for Toronto. He'd lost precious hours, having to wait until Monday morning to hitch a ride with a truck that had delivered the week's provisions.

Neither the commandant nor his adjutant was convinced Schumacher had escaped. A call to the Norwegian airbase further confused matters. Several dozen airmen were on leave that weekend. A number were known to be dating local girls, although the Norwegian brass didn't keep track of the liaisons. Pamela's Norwegian flyboy might be just that, they believed, and the solemnity of the prisoners' memorial service only reinforced their doubts.

Armitage crossed to the flower garden on St. Edmund's Drive and studied the house, looking for any sign of life inside. After several minutes, he shouldered his duffel bag, recrossed the street, and rang the doorbell. Hearing no answer, he knocked, then took the narrow cobbled sidewalk around to the side, peering through the window as he went.

At the rear, he encountered a well-tended rose garden. Pathways formed a cross at the center, in which four concrete benches faced each other. At one of them, her back to him, sat a woman with long auburn hair flecked with streaks of gray. She wore a knee-length dress, blue with white polka-dots, sleeves reaching her elbows.

Armitage stood watching her. She sensed his presence and turned, a concerned look on her face.

"Hello, Jeanne," he said.

"Hello?" Raising her arm, she shielded her eyes from the sunlight. "I'm sorry. Have we met?"

He took a few steps toward her. "It's been thirty years. You don't recognize me?"

"Brandon," she said. "It's your voice I remember. You've changed a bit." She stared at his twisted gait as he approached her.

"You haven't changed at all. Do you mind if I sit down?"

She hesitated. "Of course, but what brings you here?"

"It's not a social call, I'm afraid. Is your daughter here?"

"Pamela? No, she left late last night. What do you want with her?"

"Where is she? Is she traveling with someone?"

"What's this about?" she said, a cloud of anger crossing her face. "You can't just show up and demand information about my daughter."

She was an older, more mature version of Pamela, whose resemblance to the girl he'd loved years before had struck him the moment he encountered her. The perfume of roses filled the air, and finches chattered from among the flowers.

"I'm a guard at the German POW camp in Gravenhurst."

She scowled. "What does this have to do with Pamela?"

"She came here two nights ago, didn't she? Did she have someone with her?"

"Her fiancé, Roald."

"Roald."

"A Norwegian fighter pilot. He's training at the airport up there."

"Describe him."

"Why? What's going on?"

He leaned toward her, staring into her eyes. "Jeanne, this is important. Please describe him for me." When she didn't respond, he said, "Tall, slender, sandy hair, handsome in a Teutonic way, pointed chin."

She stiffened, her face wrinkled in concern.

"He spoke to you, I'm sure. Did his accent sound Norwegian? Somewhat sing-song? Sentence raised at the end? Clipped consonants?"

Her eyes widened as he spoke, but she said nothing.

"Swallowed *r* sound, almost like *d*?" He demonstrated. "'Th' pronounced like a *z*? 'Ziss moment?'"

She drew a deep breath. "He's German, isn't he?"

Leaning back, Armitage crossed his arms, relaxing a bit. "I think you knew that."

"Something didn't seem quite right. I couldn't put my finger on it. What's he done?"

"He's an escaped prisoner, a Luftwaffe pilot, quite a clever fellow. This isn't his first escape. Last year, he made it almost to Mexico."

She kneaded her hands together. "Does Pam know?"

His momentary silence answered her question. "She helped him. Just how we don't yet know, but they'd been planning this for some time." He described their evening meetings at the swimming area and their encounter at the Gravenhurst work site.

"What will happen to her?"

"It's not for me to say. The quicker we recapture him, the easier it will be for her."

Leaning forward, she rested her forehead against her balled fists. "Whatever is she thinking?"

"I suppose she's in love," he said, pausing several seconds before continuing. "People in love do crazy things, as you might recall."

She raised her head and looked at him, tears in her eyes. "I didn't think you were coming back. I met David. We—I got pregnant. Martin, my son, is in England now." She averted his gaze and scanned the garden. Armitage suspected why her son was in England and what he might have to face. *This fucking war.*

"So we had to marry. My mother—" She leaned toward him. "Brandon, I know what I must have done to you."

"I got over it, married a war widow. We have ... we *had* two sons. One died at Dieppe; the other is in a prison camp."

"I'm so sorry."

He had no time to dwell on it. He turned and looked around, taking in the sculpted garden and the luxurious two-story house. "You've made a good life for yourself."

She grimaced. "We're separated, Brandon. Not divorced—that isn't done—but we live apart. His work is his life, and I play no role in it except to smile, nod, and obey. Always obey. That's why I'm here while he remains in Ottawa."

The Germans had a word for the sense of satisfaction he felt, *schadenfreude*, but he dared not show it. "Where is Pamela? I must find her before she makes a bad situation worse."

She studied her hands. "They took the night train to Sudbury."

"Why Sudbury?"

"George lives there. My brother. You remember him? They hoped to stay with him for a couple days, but when we called last night, there was no answer."

"And still they went. Why?"

"She told me Roald is trying to raise money to buy training planes for the Norwegian airmen, but that makes no sense, does it?"

"His name is Jörg, for the record. Schumacher. Did you get any hint what his real purpose might be?"

She shook her head as her hands wrestled one another.

What kind of business could it be? Sudbury was to the north and west, far from any border and more distant from the eastern seaboard than Toronto. To Sault Ste. Marie, perhaps, and down to Detroit? But entering the US seemed risky. It made no sense, but he had no choice but to believe her.

At his request, she provided her brother's address. "I have to use your phone," he said.

She took him inside through the kitchen and left as he placed a collect call to the camp. "You're certain it's him?" Lieutenant Morrison asked.

"He matches the description and speaks with a German accent. The girl is traveling with him."

"All right, I'll alert the Ontario Provincial Police. Are you coming back here?"

"With your permission, sir, I'd like to head to Sudbury." When Morrison replied the OPP could handle it, he said, "I can identify him, sir, and I should bring the girl back."

The lieutenant gave his grudging consent and rang off to alert Sudbury authorities. Armitage couldn't wait for the overnight train. He booked a ticket on the afternoon bus and called for a taxi.

When he returned to the garden, she said, "Can you stay a while and visit?"

"Thank you, Jeanne, but I'm heading north in a few hours. We're arresting him in Sudbury."

"Lunch, then? At least I can do that much for you."

He considered it for a moment. "I don't think that's wise. Thank you, but no."

She reached out, placing a cool hand on his arm. "Your wife ... you do love her, don't you?"

"Of course. Why would you ask that?"

"When I heard you'd married so suddenly, I worried you'd done it to spite me."

So she'd kept up with him. "Nothing of the sort."

"That's good to hear. She must be a remarkable woman." Seeing his raised eyebrows, she said, "You're not the most communicative man I've ever met, Brandon. You never were. Secretive, always keeping to yourself. I could never fathom you. I'm not sure things would have worked out between us. I sense she's a special person."

"She is, Jeanne. It took me a while to get over you, but I did. I regret what's happening to your daughter, but I'll do what I can for her."

Tears clouded her eyes. "Thank you."

She walked him out front, and they stood in awkward silence. As the taxi pulled to the curb, she said, "I almost forgot. He took our son's radio."

"What sort of radio?"

"A shortwave receiver. Big, bulky thing, but he asked to borrow it. I don't suppose I'll see it again."

"Probably not. Goodbye, then."

Later, he could not recall the trip to the bus station. Her words—a rebuke of sorts—kept repeating in his mind like a broken record. *Secretive? Uncommunicative? Is that how he'd seemed to her?* He was traveling without physical baggage, but he had plenty to carry as he boarded the bus north.

Canadian Pacific Railway's Train Number 3, The Dominion, reached Sudbury at 6:50 A.M. CPR's premier transcontinental line would continue west, arriving in Vancouver days later. Over a dozen people alighted here, among them a young couple, he with light, sandy hair and Nordic features, she with copper-colored tresses and hazel eyes.

CPR had built the station during the first decade of the century. It was then one of the community's most impressive structures, a one-and-a-half story, long, rectangular building in rock-faced stone, capped by a hip roof, at the southeast corner of the downtown business district. A wooden platform separated east- and westbound tracks, both of which were open to the elements.

The couple passed through the high-ceilinged waiting room without pausing. They joined the taxi queue, which was short, most of the passengers having walked north to nearby hotels. Neither spoke. While the man seemed nervous, his eyes darting from one side to the other, the young woman was relaxed, settling into the crook of his arm as they waited. She smiled up at him, but he did not return it.

A yellow pall hung over the city. The air was acrid, the price

Sudbury paid for the factories and smelters operating throughout the day to support the war effort.

A pre-war model, unmarked "plain car," providing the illusion of traveling in a private limousine, pulled to the stand. The couple got in, the woman whispering her destination to the driver in such a quiet voice that he twice asked her to repeat it.

"Are you two from out of town?" he said.

"Toronto."

"Newlyweds?"

The woman giggled. "Not yet. We're engaged." Then, to reassure him they had not traveled to Sudbury to spend an illicit week together, she said, "My uncle lives here. We've come so he can meet Roald."

The driver grunted as though that settled it. "Roald" did not utter a word during this exchange, nor for the rest of the quick trip. The taxi halted before a single-story, shake-shingled house overlooking a lake that sparkled in the morning sun, the sky clear now that they were out of the city. The woman reached into her purse and paid the fare, her companion making no move to contribute.

Only after the driver left did the man speak. "This is beautiful," he said. "It reminds me of Neubrandenburg."

This meant nothing to the woman, so she didn't comment, advancing toward the front door of the house as the man carried their bags and the dark leather case containing the radio. She tried the buzzer, waited, rang again, then knocked. She turned the handle, but the door was locked. "Perhaps he's in back," she said.

Leaving their bags, the pair rounded the house, peeking in windows as they went. They stepped onto a rear deck that projected out to the lake and knocked at the back door. Again, nothing. The door had no exterior lock, secured from the inside by a deadbolt.

"He must be away. We shouldn't have come."

Schumacher ignored her, peering under the doormat and raising each flower pot from its saucer. "He must hide a key somewhere."

"What should we do? We can't just stand here."

He made for a wooden shed near the boat dock and stepped

inside, leaving the door ajar to admit sunlight. After a few minutes, he emerged, holding a length of wire. He walked to the side of the house, looped the wire, eased it through the seam between the upper and lower windows, and maneuvered it until it engaged the handle sash lock. He nursed it open from the cam, raised the window, and hoisted himself across the casement.

Schumacher opened the back door to let Pamela in. She embraced him. "My hero," she said. "You're a genius."

For the first time that morning, he smiled. "*Jawohl. Ich bin genial.*"

"Either speak English or Norwegian," she cautioned.

"*Jeg er strålende,*" he said, repeating in Norwegian his agreement that he was a genius.

The doorbell rang, and the pair froze. "Stay here." She advanced into the living room and stole a look out the front window. The face of an older man met hers, and she jumped back. He said something she couldn't make out.

Trembling, she unlocked the door and opened it. "What do you want?"

"I might ask you the same thing. What are you doing here? The owner is away."

"George Macallum is my uncle. He said we could use his house until he returns."

The man peered past her. "Where's the guy who broke in?"

She forced a laugh. "Roald is in the washroom, if you must know. What is the problem?"

The man scowled. "If he's your uncle, what does he look like?"

"He's in his late fifties, about your height but husky. He's going bald, has a full beard, and always wears boots. He tells bad jokes but can be quite stern when he gets riled."

Still dissatisfied, the man said, "If he gave you permission to use the house, he must have told you I have a key. Arthur Larsen?"

Pamela sighed, as though this were all a bit too much. "My mother thought she had her own key but couldn't find it last night. We called Uncle George but got no answer."

"All right," he said, relenting. "But if you go anywhere, come see me for the key so you can lock up. I'm the red house over there."

She thanked him, closed the door, and leaned against it, catching her breath. Schumacher came out from the back room. "Does he believe you?"

"Of course. Why not?"

"If he calls the police—"

"I'll tell them the same thing while you stay out of sight."

Schumacher snorted. "And you think they won't insist on searching the place while they're here? This is too dangerous. I must leave."

"But we just got here."

"*Liebchen*, I can't afford to be captured. We can't risk it. They'll transfer me to another camp, and we'll never see each other again."

Pamela raised her hand to her mouth. "Where will you go? What will you do?"

"I have business here. I'll take care of it and send for you when I've finished. We'll meet at the train station and head east."

"Send for me? How will you do that?"

He ignored her question. "I'm headed into the woods far north of here. I may encounter some animals. I need to borrow something of your uncle's."

I must get word to Godfrey, Margie told herself. She needed to warn him that Brandon had discovered their affair and connected it to someone at the store. He could cause trouble. But it was a civic holiday—the day before parliamentary elections—and Pinson's was closed.

Once more, she debated calling her mother, but dismissed the idea. The woman would ladle on the blame like gravy on mashed potatoes and side with Brandon, whom she otherwise reviled.

Prowling the house, she cleaned spotless surfaces and changed sheets she'd washed two nights before. The *Daily Star* predicted it would be a warm, cloudless day, so she opened all the windows to air out the house, even though she'd done the same for days.

After a lunch of cucumber sandwiches on coarse bread, Margie could no longer delay. Despite the heat, she donned an ankle-length print dress with long sleeves and a collar, placed a pair of gloves in her purse, and headed south to catch the Strathmore Avenue bus. She transferred at Main Street, traveled as far as Kingston Road, then walked the few blocks to St. Johns.

On entering, she dipped her fingers in holy water, advanced halfway through the sanctuary, crossed herself, and entered a pew. She knelt on the bench, clasped her hands, and prayed. After a few moments, she arose and sat in quiet contemplation, studying the vault above the tabernacle.

She wept, not bothering to conceal her distress. "Oh, Lord, what have I done?"

It took five minutes to regain control. She dabbed her eyes with a handkerchief and mopped at the tears trickling down both cheeks.

She sat for another quarter hour before entering the confession booth to the left of the tabernacle. The minutes she waited for the priest to enter his side of the box felt like hours. "I confess to Almighty God and to you, Father, that I have sinned," she said. "I last confessed in January."

She paused, uncertain how to broach the subject that had drawn her here. "Yes, my child," came a voice from the other side.

"Father Michael?"

An unfamiliar voice answered. "I am ready to hear your confession."

Margie hesitated for several seconds. "I'm sorry. I shouldn't have come."

The priest said something she didn't catch as she fled the booth. She tore through the church as though it were on fire. She boarded a bus for downtown and wandered among the movie theaters, rejecting a war film and a new Abbott and Costello comedy before buying a ticket to see the Andrews Sisters in "How's About It?" featuring drummer Buddy Rich and his orchestra. Upbeat. Mindless. Just what she needed.

* * *

PAMELA HEARD them before she saw them. Alerted by the slamming of car doors, she ventured to the front window and peeked around the edge of the tea-colored muslin curtain. Four officers of the Ontario Provincial Police, clad in dark-gray uniforms, emerged from a pair of Chevrolet Coupes and advanced on the house. They rang the doorbell and simultaneously knocked—a commanding summons that shook the doorframe.

She opened the door and stepped back.

"I am Sergeant-Major Derrick Gibney of the OPP," the lead officer said. "We have orders to search this house."

She retreated into the living room.

"What is your name?"

"Pamela Canavan. This is my uncle's home."

"Is anyone with you?"

She gulped and choked out a soft denial.

"No one? A man, perhaps?"

"I'm here alone. What do you—?"

"Remain here." Along with his fellow officers, he searched the two bedrooms, den, washroom, and kitchen. Pamela, taking his admonition literally, stood rooted to the spot.

"Look out back," Gibney ordered when the search proved fruit-less. Turning to her, he said, "Where is he?"

"Where is who?"

His stare bore into her.

"Hello?" Arthur Larsen poked his head through the doorway.

"And who might you be?" the sergeant-major demanded.

He introduced himself and explained he was a neighbor. "This woman and her boyfriend broke into the house. She claims she's George's niece, but why did she have to break in?"

"How about that?" the officer said. "Let me see some identification."

Pamela groped in her cloth handbag. "I have nothing on me. I don't drive ..."

"I need to establish your right to be in this house."

She repeated the story of her mother losing her key, which evoked a flurry of questions. Who was her mother? Where did she live? How could he contact her? Gibney dispatched one of his officers to radio Sudbury headquarters to confirm her story.

"Mr. Larsen says a man was with you. Where is he?"

"No one else is here."

"I saw him crawl through the side window," Larsen said.

"Where is he?" Gibney repeated. When Pamela didn't answer, he said, "He is an escaped German prisoner. You helped him get away, which makes you an accomplice. You're in serious trouble, young lady."

"Good God," Larsen said.

The officer turned on him. "You can go now. We'll come to you when we need you. You'll need to make a formal statement. "

"Sure. Anything to help. An escaped prisoner. Lord."

Gibney waited until he left. "I'm asking you one more time. Then we're taking you in. Where is this man, Schumacher?"

Pamela collapsed onto a sofa, dust flying off it and dancing in the sunlight. "He's gone."

"Gone where?"

"I don't know. He didn't say. He has business somewhere. That's all he told me."

"What sort of business? Where?"

"Up north is all he said. He promised to return in a couple days. I'm to stay here."

Gibney, who was old enough to be her father, folded his arms and looked down at her. "You are under arrest. I'm holding you until the crown counsel decides on charges. The more you conceal, the more serious the consequences. This is your last chance—where is he, and what is he doing here?"

"I told you," she said, trembling with a mixture of anger and terror, "I don't know."

———

E. D. WATKINS glared skyward and shook his fist at the airplanes circling low over McGregor Bay. The sound of their engines filled the morning air; Watkins was sure they frightened the fish. For days he had seen planes crisscrossing the horizon, unfamiliar boats arriving, and, to his consternation, armed strangers patrolling the shoreline. He had come to Birch Island to get away from it all, and they were bringing it all to him. Why couldn't they leave him in peace?

Two cabin cruisers approached. Both carried a group of men whose loud voices could be heard over the throbbing of their motors and the roar of the circling aircraft. In the stern of the lead boat, a man wearing a rumpled canvas hat raised his arm in greeting. "What luck are you having?" he called.

Watkins was dumbstruck. The man was the spitting image of the US president. And that voice. In mute reply, he raised his stringer, displaying two bass.

"We're going after some just like that," the man shouted.

Suddenly it all made sense—the planes, the cruisers, the security detail. Franklin D. Roosevelt was his neighbor, for how long he didn't know. Watkins waved at the retreating boat and turned his eyes skyward at the patrolling aircraft.

———

BRANDON STEPPED off the bus at dusk.

"Armitage, I presume." Gibney stepped forward and introduced himself. "Welcome to Sudbury."

"I didn't expect a welcoming committee."

"Your CO asked us to meet you. I understand you provided the tip on the escapee."

"You have him, then?"

"I'm afraid not. We missed him by an hour." Gibney hustled him into the Chevy cruiser and brought him up to date. Armitage reached for a handkerchief and wiped his eyes. What was that noxious odor assailing him? The southwestern sky was alight with an orange glow, but not from the setting sun.

"We're holding his girlfriend in the city jail," the officer said. "The crown prosecutor wants her back in Toronto. I understand you're taking her."

"Is she cooperating?"

"Only to the extent she must. More insolent than intimidated. She insists your man has done nothing wrong other than escape."

"He hasn't ... yet." Gibney turned onto Route 67, skirting the south end of the business district. "Aren't we going to your headquarters?"

"The girl's uncle is making his way back. We're to meet him at the house. Unless you want me to drop you off at a hotel."

"No, let's hear what he has to say." Though what he thought he could gain from the man was unclear.

"Why did you join up? You didn't have to." Armitage assumed Gibney had noticed his limp.

"To do my part. And to stay busy."

"I get that," Gibney replied. "They captured my son at Dieppe. I need to keep my mind off it."

"That's my story. Our older boy captured, and his younger brother killed."

"Sorry. This war."

"Where's your boy held?"

"A camp near Lamsdorf."

"Mine too. That's where I spent the first war—the war to end all wars." He spat it as a curse.

"Is that where you got ...?"

"Yes."

They rode in silence for a few minutes, Gibney beating time with his fingers on the steering wheel. "We're almost there. It's a beautiful spot. I expect someone will develop it soon." He sighed at the inevitable. "You married? How is your wife taking this?"

Armitage felt as though he was being interrogated but chose not to make an issue of it. "Hard," he said.

The stab wound of Margie's betrayal was raw and bleeding, but he had spent the six-hour bus trip reliving his conversation with Jeanne Canavan. Peering out the window at the rolling landscape, he mulled over her assessment of Margie as remarkable and him as uncommunicative. She'd even cast doubt on how long their own marriage would have lasted. Her insight led to a gloomy hour of introspection that was foreign to his nature. He didn't like what he saw.

Perhaps he had given too little thought to Margie's state of mind. He had his work guarding prisoners to keep him occupied. She had nothing until she'd taken that job.

He weighed her accusation that his service in the Veterans Guard was an effort to redeem himself. Armitage wasn't the type to spend time reflecting on the course of his life, and he'd done enough of that on the long trip north, but Gibney's innocent question about his wife had brought it all back. He tried to set that all aside for now and concentrate on the mission at hand.

The cruiser came to a merciful stop before a one-story clapboard cottage. Behind it, a lake shimmered as ripples caught the reflection of the retreating sunset. A light glowed inside, and the front door was ajar, the screen door guarding against the swarming insects. Gibney tapped on its frame, and a man's voice called them to come in.

George Macallum was over six feet tall, beefy and substantial without showing an ounce of fat. He had a full beard that, like his thinning hair, was turning gray. Deep crevices lined his face, but they were the marks of an outdoorsman rather than age. Gibney introduced the two of them, and the man nodded.

"Did you know your niece was headed here?" the officer said.

"I had no idea. I was up north fishing and had to come all the way back for this. What the hell's gotten into her?"

"I've watched their friendship develop," Armitage said. "She showed an interest, as any young woman might when meeting a handsome man. He spotted a chance and took advantage of it."

"Why the hell do you let them mix with civilians?" He did not shout but spoke with the authority of a man used to giving orders and having them obeyed.

"We discourage it, but there are four hundred of them and fewer than two dozen of us. We can't be all places at all times."

"You had enough time to observe them. You should have done something."

Gibney stepped in. "Have you inspected the place?"

"Yes. They don't seem to have done any damage. I don't know how the hell they got in, but they didn't force the locks. That's not the issue."

Gibney waited, but when Macallum volunteered nothing more, he said, "What is the issue?"

"They took my deer rifle."

Both men stiffened. "What sort of rifle?"

"A Ross .303 Mark II."

"That's harmless," Armitage said, recalling the weapon's unreliable performance during the Great War.

Macallum turned on him. "What the hell are you talking about? The Ross is a great sporting rifle, thirty-inch barrel and sight bridge mounted on the receiver. Keep the ammo dry and away from dirt and it's accurate up to 600 yards."

Armitage, who hadn't touched a weapon since his capture, listened to the recitation with growing alarm. "Could a sniper use it?"

"Could? Apart from hunting, that's its primary purpose."

"Let's not get ahead of ourselves," Gibney said. "The prisoner is making a run for it. Chances are he just took it for protection in the wilderness."

Armitage shook his head. All this planning, maneuvering Pamela into helping him, taking the shortwave radio from Jeanne's house, and now a rifle. "He's up to something."

"He'll turn up," the sergeant-major replied. "There's been a flurry of breakouts over the past few days. Only yesterday, a prisoner escaped from a playing field behind the new prison camp in Hull. They caught him in a ditch a few hours later. They've rounded up most of the other escapees too. Your man won't get far."

Armitage was silent for much of the trip back to Sudbury. "We have to find him," he said with a vehemence that surprised him. "I need every man you can spare."

"I can't spare anyone. We have a major security detail south of here, below the Whitefish Reservation. RCMP, OPP, and military."

"What's going on?"

"I can't say."

"Is it a practice maneuver of some sort?"

"Like I said, it's a large security operation. I've told you too much already."

"Major, that's where he's headed."

Gibney laughed. "It's top-secret. There's no way he could know about it. No one does."

"It's not a secret to him. I'm telling you, that's why he's come here. We need to stop him. You must help me."

16

AUGUST 3, 1943

THE CPR RAILWAY spur transported coal offloaded from lake freighters at Little Current and nickel ore to smelters at Creighton, outside Sudbury. On the return trip, it carried freight that supported people on one-hundred-mile-long Manitoulin Island.

Schumacher knew none of these details. All Berlin had told him in its coded message was to take the train as far as Whitefish Falls, north of the Ojibwe reservation, and meet a man named Bruno Auer.

After leaving Pamela, he took to the woods, walking west for two hours until the forest gave way to neighborhoods on the outskirts of Sudbury. He retreated into the canopy and hid out until nightfall, carrying a rucksack on his back and the rifle case over his right shoulder. He'd left the bulky radio behind since he'd be able to receive once he linked-up with Auer.

At dusk, he began the long trek southwest from Ramsey Lake southwest to the Creighton smelter. He'd taken venison sausage and cheese from Macallum's and replenished water from the lake and streams as he passed.

At 3:00 a.m., Schumacher reached the marshaling yard outside the factory, bathed in feeble yellow lights. Hundreds of cars filled the yard, many loaded with ore and coal, ready to be offloaded. He needed to find a train heading south.

He slunk between the shadows at the western end of the yard, crawling beneath cars to get from one track to another. As he peered from underneath a flatcar, he faced a caboose sporting a red lantern. He crept forward, passing a long line of open-top hopper cars. When he felt he was sufficiently far forward, he mounted the ladder of one car and peered inside. Its hopper was empty, meaning the train was most likely headed south to Little Current.

Hiding inside the hopper seemed impossible. Its sides were vertical, and the slope sheets at either end were smooth and steep, providing nothing to grab onto. He'd have to cling to the top of the slope sheet and risk sliding to the bottom, where he might never make it out.

Climbing down, he advanced forward, looking for a better solution. As he approached the locomotive, he came upon a freight car. The door was closed, giving him no chance to hide inside. He could cling to an exterior ladder, but the engineer or fireman was certain to spot the figure when the train rounded a curve. He could lie on the top, but if the train passed through a tunnel, he could be scraped off.

Schumacher heard the locomotive building steam. He had to decide. He retreated to the first hopper car and studied the exterior. The cavities under either end of the slope sheet presented his only option. One end contained the brake gear, but the other was open. Too open. The spaces had no floor. He would have to brace himself and hang on.

The next problem was to pick the right car. Too near the front end and he'd risk being seen by the engineer or fireman. Too close to the caboose, and he risked detection by the brakeman. He crept to the middle of the train and climbed beneath a slope sheet, bracing himself against the extension supporting the top of the hopper.

The German breathed in coal dust and stifled a cough, fearing patrols in the yard would hear him, but the steady whine from the smelter masked the sound. Two minutes beneath the hopper and he was filthy, and his limbs ached with the effort of bracing himself.

There was nothing he could do about it. He could only hope that he'd guessed right and that this train was headed south. If not, he'd have to risk throwing himself off to the side and try again.

Henry Stimson fumed. "Is the entire government on vacation?" The president was off fishing, and Harry Hopkins, the palace guard, was off in Maine, though no one seemed to know where. Only Marshall and the Joint Chiefs joined him in suffering through the August heat, which that day would reach ninety-four degrees with a dew point of seventy.

Stimson, a New Yorker, often wondered if George Washington had realized the site he'd chosen for the nation's capital was not on a high hill, where it could catch a summer breeze but in a bowl, where heat and humidity settled and lingered well past its welcome.

His delayed return from England had cost him a chance to brief Roosevelt. He needed someone to confide in; there was no one better than Army Chief of Staff George Marshall. Easing himself into the general's armchair, he spat out the news. "Churchill is waffling again, and Eden is urging him on. They're coming to Québec to re-prosecute the entire war plan."

Marshall, who harbored no illusions about British machinations, had his own concerns, "The president continues to question our readiness for a cross-Channel attack, just as he did prior to Casablanca. I'm not certain he's fully on board."

"What position will he take at Quadrant?"

"That's the difficulty," Marshall said. "He takes all this information in but doesn't reveal his conclusions. He has a tête-à-tête with Churchill but doesn't divulge what was said. We learn things later."

"We have to get on the same page now, or the British will back out of the commitments they made here in May," Stimson said. "I vote we hold a war council this afternoon with all parties and create a combined strategy for ending this constant backtracking before we get to Québec."

Marshall shook his head. "Not with the president absent. If he returns to discover we've gone behind his back, he will dig in his heels."

Stimson gripped both sides of the armchair in frustration. "At least we're keeping him away from Churchill's influence for a few days."

The two men shared a wry smile. "What do you think of the COSSAC plan?" the secretary said.

Marshall spread his arms in a gesture of ignorance.

"COSSAC has submitted its cross-Channel plan to the British chiefs. You haven't seen it?"

Though seated, Marshall seemed to draw himself up to his full height. The clock behind him ticked as though counting down to an explosion. "We have not."

Stimson was speechless. Why were the British hiding details of the plan—a joint initiative—from their allies? While the US had shut Great Britain out of atomic research, the irony that both sides were concealing strategic information from each other was lost on him.

THE SECRETARY STRODE back to his office, red in the face, his hands shaking with anger. He had been away for three weeks and raced to catch up, attending to business that had come up during his absence. But as he sped through the day, his thoughts returned to how he could best convey his concerns about the uncertainty of British commitment with FDR.

Tuesday morning, he hit on an approach. He put the White House switchboard onto the Hopkins hunt. Shortly after ten, the efficient operators found him at a friend's home in Desert Island, Maine. "Welcome home," Hopkins said, sounding as though he were speaking through the opposite end of a drainpipe.

Stimson had no time for pleasantries. "Harry, I hear you're flying to Ontario tomorrow to see the president. I need to bring him up to date on our British problem. Churchill continues to meddle. He's obsessed with his Mediterranean strategy. He sends his chiefs in every direction but the one we need to end the war in Europe. At Trident, he promised to support the cross-Channel decision. Next he hedged, saying he was for it unless his advisers came up with a better strategy. Now he's after them to produce that strategy. I'm concerned they're going to spring it on us at Quadrant."

"If they do, we'll have to turn it back."

"When he arrives at Hyde Park, the prime minister will use all his wiles to get the president to see things his way. We can't afford that." Stimson, a lifelong Republican in a Democratic administration, put it in terms Hopkins would understand. "Think of the political consequences if we don't deal with Hitler so we can finish our business with Hirohito."

Even coming down the electronic drainpipe, Stimson heard his intake of breath.

"Harry, I'm not allowed to communicate with the president myself right now. I need you to intercede for me."

"You're right," Hopkins said. "I will take it up with him when I join him tomorrow."

Stimson thanked him and rang off. He lit a cigarette, leaned back in his swivel chair, and thought. After a moment, he ground the butt out in the ashtray and pulled out the trip report he had been working on since leaving London. On a legal pad, he made a series of notes, his lawyer's mind arranging his arguments sequentially and logically, tending toward the closing argument he intended to deliver in person to his jury of one.

MARGIE COCKED her head and examined the mannequin. She reached out and tilted the cloche hat to one side.

"What are you doing?" Rowena Walter readjusted the hat.

"I'm sorry. I thought the cloche would look better if it were at a jaunty angle."

"Well, don't," Rowena said. "I've managed the displays since before you arrived, and I'll do so after you leave."

"I'm sorry," she repeated, but the woman had walked away.

Margie put both hands to her temples, bowed her head, and breathed in short gasps. *I'm hyperventilating. Have to stop.* Taking a deep gulp, she held her breath until she regained control. All morning she had felt the resentment of the other women expressed in sighs and sidelong glances. Was she imagining things? No, their contempt was transparent. Did they still blame her for Gladys's departure? Did they know of her coming advancement? Had they guessed about her relationship with Godfrey? Bernice had. Had she blabbed to the others?

If it weren't for the promotion, I'd leave. When that comes, I'll show them. I'll—No, I won't. I'm not that sort of person. I'll act as though nothing has happened. They'll have to treat me with respect.

The snubs of her fellow workers were not the only thing on her mind this morning. When her break came, she took the elevator to the top floor and stepped into the management offices. "I'd like to speak to Mr. Sperling."

"What is this about?" April Humphrey said.

"It concerns an inventory issue."

"Have you spoken with your supervisor?"

Why was she so mulish? "It's a matter he asked me to look into personally."

The woman sighed and picked up a handset. "What did you say your name is?" She pushed a button and waited until Sperling's voice answered. "Mrs. Armitage to see you."

She endured a long pause until Sperling motioned to her from the end of the hall. "Ah, Mrs. Armitage," he called out. Once the door closed behind her, however, he said. "Margie, what are you doing here? This isn't a good idea."

"What isn't?"

"Coming up unannounced. I don't normally meet one-on-one with line employees."

"I told her you had me looking into an inventory issue." *Why am I on the defensive?* "I'm sorry, Godfrey." *And how many damned times have I said that this morning?*

"Something's come up." She waited a moment to make sure she had his attention. "My husband knows."

Sperling reared back in his chair as though struck. "What does he know? How?" He spluttered more than spoke.

"I'm sorry," Damn! "He doesn't know your name, but he knows I'm seeing someone here at work."

"How did he find out?"

"I got careless, that's all. I'm concerned Brandon might make trouble for you."

He smirked as he shook his head. "Don't let that concern you, my dear."

She wrinkled her brow, his reaction not what she'd expected. "I think we should break things off. At least for a while."

Sperling drummed his fingers on the desk. "Is he back in town, then?"

"I'm not sure where he is. His lieutenant called to tell me he's on an assignment somewhere."

"I don't see why we can't go on as we have been. We'll just have to be more cautious."

"Godfrey, I'm not sure—"

"And I've been meaning to tell you. I'm transferring you into lingerie next week. Therese Baillieu will train you to take over in—in a different department come fall. It's time we moved you up."

Before she could thank him, Sperling rose, moved around his desk, and embraced her. She felt his hands draw her close, felt the warmth of his body, smelled his cologne, something she'd never noticed before. "I'll see you tomorrow night. Don't prepare anything. I'm bringing dinner. It's my turn."

Opening the door, he said, "And thank you, Mrs. Armitage, for this most valuable information. We are privileged to have you working with us."

SERGEANT-MAJOR GIBNEY STOOD HIS GROUND, insisting he lacked the men or authority to support a search for the escaped prisoner. Armitage spent his entire morning and half the afternoon begging, cajoling, and even threatening every agency he could think of for a ride south. Finally, Lieutenant Morrison solved the problem.

"You're certain about this?" he said when Armitage reached him by telephone.

He reviewed what he'd put together. "Schumacher arrived here yesterday. There is no reason he would come west and less reason to bring Pamela along. Sudbury isn't a way station. He's here for some specific purpose. He's stolen a high-powered hunting rifle and left the girl behind. I don't know where he is headed, but there's a top-secret security operation south of Espanola."

Morrison thought for a moment. "You don't know where you're going or what you're looking for?"

"No, but below Whitefish Falls is a cluster of small islands reaching down to Manitoulin. Beyond that, there's nothing but Lake Huron. I plan to head south and keep my eyes open for activity."

"All right. Stay in your hotel room while I try to work something out." Armitage did as he was told, taking the time to begin a letter to Margie.

An hour later, the lieutenant called back. "You're in luck. We're closing a prison camp at Espanola, just above the Whitefish Reservation, and transporting the prisoners to a logging camp up north. A truck is headed down there this afternoon. One will meet you at the OPP headquarters at three."

Armitage thanked him and packed his duffel bag, stowing the Government Colt he had never fired in the end pocket. Before checking out, he had a lunch of overcooked pork chops at the hotel restaurant, sawing through the meat as though it were a brick. He returned to his room, finished his two-page letter to Margie, bought a stamp at the front desk, and left the envelope for the next day's post. He walked the four blocks to the OPP office on South Young and asked for Gibney.

"Still here?" The look on the officer's face suggested he was not pleased to see him.

"A Veterans Guard truck is picking me up in a half hour. Is there any word on my prisoner?"

"Nothing. I thought you were bringing the girl back with you."

"I'll return for her in a few days." He thought quickly, not wanting to let Gibney know what he was planning. "This truck is from our camp at Monteith. We're transferring prisoners there."

Gibney seemed to accept the white lie. And why not?

"Have you learned anything more about that operation to the south?" Armitage asked.

The sergeant-major stiffened and moved closer to him. "No, and it's something I shouldn't have shared. Do you understand, Warrant Officer?"

Armitage knew Gibney feared he'd said too much, which only served to increase his suspicions. A graying member of the Veterans Guard burst through the door and called out his name. His flat accent suggested he was from Manitoba or Saskatchewan, and his informal manner confirmed it.

Armitage followed the man out to a Ford F60L idling at the curb. "No need to sit under the canvas. Climb up front with us." The driver introduced himself as Fred Nash—no rank—and his partner only as Jerry. Nash careened out of town and headed west on King's Highway 17, the Trans-Canada Highway.

As they crept along at thirty-five miles per hour, Nash regaled him with tales of their efforts to ferry the men between the two camps. "We haven't had many escape attempts. Where in tarnation are they gonna go? But on our way up last night, two of them made a run for it, taking off in separate directions. One stuck to the road; I tracked him down in no time. A guard in back pursued the other and recaptured him after a half hour of chasing him through the bush."

He spat out the window and wiped his mouth on his sleeve. "I can't figure what got into them. They were in the middle of nowhere, nothing but bogs and deer flies and mosquitoes for company. It was almost like it wasn't a serious attempt, like they were playing with us."

Armitage absorbed the information, adding it to what he already knew. Was this just about an escaped prisoner, or was something bigger going on?

"So what are you doing up here?" Nash asked.

He recounted everything he knew and suspected about Schumacher's escape. "Your escapees were a diversion, one of many going on across Canada. They're sowing confusion. Have you heard of a security operation south of Whitefish?"

"Big doings." They were the first words Nash's companion had spoken during the trip. "Some bigwig is down there fishing. An Indian guide told me about it. They have planes, motorboats, and armed men on patrol. No trains are allowed to stop at Birch Island."

"Will you take me?" Armitage asked. "It's important. My CO has sent me to track down this prisoner, and I think he's headed for this Birch Island."

As Nash turned onto Highway 6, he said, "I don't know. Our orders are to go only as far as Camp 21."

"Private Nash," Armitage said, "I'm changing your orders. Get me to Birch Island or as close as you can."

"Yes, sir," came the reply, and Armitage couldn't help but notice his companion's eager grin.

US Navy Reserve Lieutenant John Manley eased the *Anna H* into her berth. The captain of the president's launch had spent his second day ferrying FDR around McGregor Bay, and today he had received a glimpse of the great man's humanity and humility.

"Lieutenant," Roosevelt had said, "you've had nothing to eat."

"That's all right, sir. I have an apple here. I'll get something more when we return."

"No, you need to eat." FDR beckoned him closer and opened his lunch box, extracted a ham sandwich, and handed half to him.

"Mr. President, I'm fine."

"Eat your lunch, Lieutenant. That's an order. And shut off the engines for fifteen minutes to let your men rest." As they floated in the bay, the president spoke to the crew, asking each man where he was from, how long he had served, and what he had done in civilian life.

He waved to each passing boat, taking particular notice of a mahogany cruiser. "Ahoy," he called out. "That's a beautiful craft. What is she?"

Two men waved back, the one at the wheel an older, dark-haired man, his companion a younger fellow with sandy-colored hair. "She's a twenty-foot Seabird," the older man called out.

"She's a beauty," FDR shouted. "Good luck."

Now, as enlisted men helped wheel the president down the ramp, Manley watched the Navy commisaryman and his assistants carry the day's catch to the dining car. The presidential party would have its fill of fresh bass tonight.

And there was more. "Mr. President," the cook shouted, "Two local ladies brought blueberry pies."

"That's capital. C'mon boys," he said to his friends, "it's cocktail time. You'll have to do better tomorrow, or I'll win the pot."

All day long, the men had talked of little more than a private bet they had on who could catch the most fish during the week. Manley suspected not only was the president in competition with his fellow anglers, the two boats were locked in piscatorial combat.

FDR laughed and waved as they lifted him into the Jeep for the half-mile trip across the isthmus to his rail car. Manley smiled and gave Roosevelt an informal salute as they elevated him onto the back of the platform, but he worried about how the women had slipped through security to deliver dessert. How had they gotten there? Security was supposed to be tight.

Bruno Auer was not what Schumacher had expected. Instead of a vigorous young man, he found an older gentleman with a florid complexion who puttered around his cabin, wheezing as he moved, talking incessantly. The man would be of little use.

Railroad memorabilia were everywhere, from the ring of keys on a hook next to the front door to the timetable and railway guide on a small table along a wall. "After I emigrated, I spent two decades with the Canadian Pacific," he had said. "Retired three years ago and bought this place. I spend winter up in Sudbury with my son and his wife. She doesn't much like me, so as soon as the snow melts, I'm back here."

Schumacher had grunted an acknowledgment, but his mind was elsewhere. "I need you to drive me to Birch Island."

"Drive? You can't get past the sentries. Didn't they tell you that?"

They hadn't told him a damned thing. "How close can we get?"

"Right up to the checkpoint, but what's the use? They've sealed off the island. Armed patrols are everywhere."

Schumacher had debated the problem and settled on reconnoitering by boat. The Austrian's neighbor owned a Seabird cruiser docked on McGregor Bay, and Auer prevailed on him to loan it to him for the afternoon. "The railway station is on the other side of the island, but whoever they have down there is fishing on both bays."

Whoever they have. So the old man didn't even know what this was about. And when Schumacher tried to take his rifle along, Auer resisted. "Whatever you're doing, I want no part of it. I have to live here."

Schumacher relented. He would come at the president on land. This reconnaissance trip would help him find the best way to get there.

They launched from a marina south of the Indian reservation. Auer turned the Seabird toward the dock local carpenters had built only the week before. It teemed with activity. The Austrian explained how the dignitary, whoever he was, could fish in either of the two bays. "They call them islands," he said, "but it's really a peninsula. The LaCloche Mountains give way to Lake Huron as you travel south."

The German snorted. They called these hills mountains? What a delusion.

"Now this spur," Auer said, "Algoma Eastern Railway built it at the turn of the century to link Sudbury with Little Current on Manitoulin Island." Schumacher tried to shush him as he scanned the horizon with the man's field glasses. "Algoma went bankrupt during the depression, and the CPR took it over."

"Let's be quiet for a moment and listen."

Auer wasn't silent for long, whining that he'd only agreed to supply information, telling the German what he was and was not prepared to do. Schumacher was tired of it and wished his mission didn't depend on the man.

"*Stille.*" he ordered as a flotilla came into view. Two cruisers and three Navy gunboats closed on them as a floatplane circled overhead.

As the lead cruiser passed before them, a man waved and called out to them, asking them what type of craft it was. Auer, awestruck, choked out a response. "She's a 20-foot Seabird."

The man wished them luck. The Austrian turned to his companion, his face red as he gasped for breath. "That's President Roosevelt."

"Who did you think it was? I wish you'd let me bring my rifle. He was so close, I could have finished this today."

His hands shaking, Auer nosed the Seabird's prow out into the bay. "Is that what you're doing here? They didn't tell me that. I won't be a part of this."

"You are a part of it."

His voice trembled. "I just pass information. I didn't sign up for anything like this."

Nor did I, Schumacher thought, but he had a job to do and would do it. "We do not control the course of events. This war was thrust upon us. We have no choice but to serve our country."

As Auer continued his protestations, Schumacher ignored him. Whereas he was a prisoner, guilty of nothing more than serving his country, Auer was free, born under a flag that no longer existed, enjoying the hospitality of a nation at war with his own. He wanted to hear no more from the man.

Now that he was at Birch Island, he couldn't believe how easy his task might be. The problem wasn't killing Roosevelt. He could have done that an hour before. The challenge was how to get away once he'd done so. The Seabird was a sturdy craft, but its engine wasn't powerful enough to outrun the security boats or outdistance the patrol planes. His instinct was correct. He would attack by land.

"They've seen you with me now," Auer said. "I wish you'd kept your head down."

"You're serving the Fatherland." Schumacher was now exasperated. "You will do as you're told."

And if you don't, you won't be around to serve it.

"HE'S USING YOU." For close to an hour, Sarah Tice had listened to Margie's story, peppering her with questions, drawing her out whenever she balked. Now, leaning forward across the dining room table and gripping her hand, she delivered her verdict.

"He's taking advantage of your loneliness and grief. He wines and dines you, probably at Pinson's expense." The window fan roared in their ears, pulling hot air out of the house and ruffling the younger woman's wavy hair. "Whenever you waver, he offers your advancement that doesn't come. You see that, don't you?"

Margie hung her head, blinking back tears.

"Decide what you want. What's best for Margie? Do you want to live alone and spend your life chasing after a married man, or do you want to save your marriage? Which is it to be?"

Margie sat in silence for several minutes, resting her forehead on her fists. She raised her head, stifling a sob as she studied the brocade pattern on the ceiling. "Brandon," she said, her voice nearly drowned out by the fan.

"Then you must end it. You've made a mistake. We all do."

"But not like this."

The younger woman drew in her breath and fingered her empty teacup. Margie refilled it from the pot, but Sarah ignored it, studying the row of ivy painted on the rim. Silence lay between them like a lake.

In a quiet voice, Sarah said, "I've never told anyone this." She cleared her throat, choking back her own tears. "I am single because I cheated on my fiancé. He was a wonderful—*is* a wonderful man, but I had an affair with his best friend. He couldn't forgive that."

Margie took both her hands in hers. "Perhaps he wasn't so wonderful."

Sarah seemed to consider the matter. "The point is, if you permit this man to see you again, you'll compound your mistake. If you want your husband back, put an end to this."

Margie straightened her shoulders and sat back in her chair as tension ebbed from her body. "I wish I'd talked to you days ago."

Her friend smiled. "You've talked to me now. We girls have to stick together. Promise me, Margie, I want your assurance that you'll break things off. Can you do that for me? For yourself?"

"I will. Thank you. I'm so grateful."

"That's what friends are for."

NASH AND JERRY, whose surname Armitage had not learned, dropped him off at the Highway 6 roadblock at half past five. One of the two guards at the checkpoint asked for his name, identification, and business. "I need to speak with the senior RCMP officer," Armitage said.

"On what matter?"

"An escaped German prisoner is headed this way. He is armed and dangerous and escaped an OPP noose in Sudbury. My CO and I are convinced he's on his way here—may already be in the area."

"Wait here." He disappeared into the guardhouse while Armitage rested his weight on his good leg. What struck him was the silence. Here he was in wilderness, and there was not a sign of wildlife, not a sound from the surrounding woods. It was as though all the birds and creatures of the forest had decided to keep their distance.

The guard returned. "They'll be out to get you in a few minutes."

It was more than a quarter-hour before a Jeep executed a U-turn, and the driver motioned him into the passenger seat. Armitage had barely settled in before the driver hit the gas, throwing him back. He drove without saying a word, braking to a stop before the train station. Another armed guard ushered him inside. "I'm Inspector Martin," an unsmiling officer said. "What do you want with the chief superintendent?" That was the fourth-highest rank in the RCMP. This was a big deal.

Armitage explained his mission for what seemed like the eighteenth time that day. The inspector asked a series of questions, most concerning Schumacher's habits and appearance.

"What makes you think he's coming to Birch Island?"

"Everything points in this direction. I don't even know why you're here, but it's not for the fishing."

The inspector's eyes clouded over. "And neither does he. That's the point. Few people know we're here, let alone why. It's top-secret, so the Germans don't know. There's no reason for him to come here."

"But he is," Armitage insisted.

"We'll be on the lookout for him. Thank you for your information."

"I'd like to help. I know the man. I've been with him every day for the past eight months. If he were in a group of a hundred others, I'd pick him out in an instant."

"That won't be necessary. There's no way he can get through this security."

Another officer tapped the inspector on the shoulder, wearing not an RCMP uniform but that of the US Navy. Behind him stood a man with a military bearing but dressed in denim, a plaid shirt, and a fishing vest.

Pieces clicked into place. US Navy personnel, a civilian in charge, an island closed off to the public. This security was meant to protect an American, not a Canadian. Someone who mattered. Despite the RCMP inspector's hubris, Armitage was convinced Schumacher had been sent to assassinate a high-ranking US official.

As the Jeep returned him to the checkpoint, Armitage cursed the man for his short-sightedness. No one would listen. He would have to act on his own.

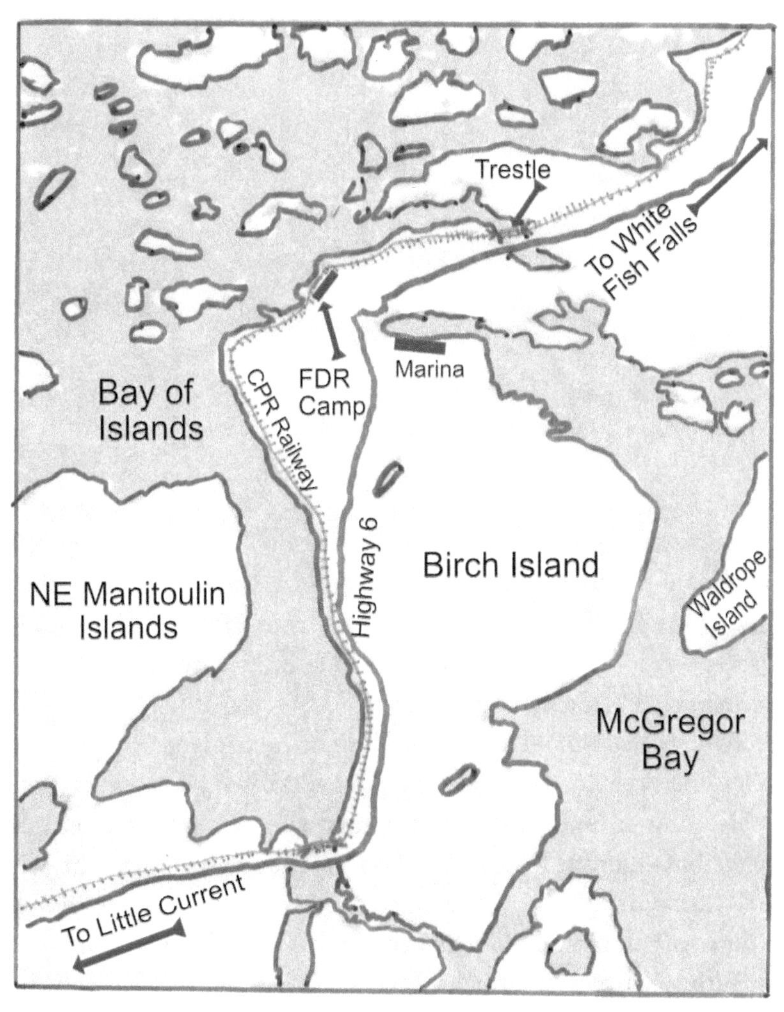

Birch Island, 1943

17

——————

AUGUST 4, 1943

JÖRG SCHUMACHER LEFT Auer's cottage at dusk, found his way to the rail bed, and walked south. He had eight miles to cover, illuminated only by the feeble light of a waxing crescent. He carried a backpack with water, food, and a bedroll, the rifle in its case, and a flashlight dimmed by fabric torn from a sheet.

The rails stretched out before him as he trudged between them, stumbling over the ties. Twice he pitched forward, losing his footing. A third time he sprawled onto the roadbed, missing the steel rail by inches but skinning his forehead on the gravel. His flashlight, which he'd extinguished to save battery life, skittered away. It took two minutes of fumbling before he brought his knee down over it.

Sitting between the tracks, he rubbed his leg with his right hand while touching his forehead with his left. He cursed to himself.

Schumacher had never encountered such rocky terrain. Everything he touched was solid granite. At the makeshift library he had assembled at Gravenhurst, he had read about the Canadian Shield. Here it was, glacier-smoothed, unrelieved rock with sparse vegetation. He trained his flashlight ahead and saw the track disappeared through a narrow path that railway workers had blasted through the granite.

I would have been better off sticking to the highway and risking the military traffic. Now it was too late. He didn't know how far he was from the road. He wished Auer had been able to drive him at least halfway.

He placed a hand on a rail to help him to his feet and detected a slight vibration. Turning the flashlight to his right, he studied the drop. It descended into the waters of the Bay of Islands. One false step and he would tumble down the embankment, landing in the water and soaking his ammunition. If, that is, he didn't dash his brains against the rock.

He swung the muted beam in the opposite direction and found a clump of brush that would provide cover. It wouldn't do him much good if he fell, however. The track was on a stone grade built from rocks mined when they blasted through the granite. He inched his way down the roadbed, dragging his backpack, bedroll, and rifle after him, and sheltered behind the sparse vegetation as a northbound locomotive emerged from the cut. The ground heaved as the train passed. The smell of creosote filled his nose, and coal ash clogged his lungs.

He waited until the lights from the caboose disappeared, then crawled up the embankment and resumed his walk. He continued his slow pace another mile until he came to a steel bridge that spanned an inlet or stream; in the near darkness, he couldn't tell which.

Had Auer warned him about this? For the first time, he wished he had paid more attention to the man's maundering. Schumacher stood at the north end of the structure and weighed his options. Highway 6 lay to his left but how far he didn't know. Finding it would require passing through a forest in almost total darkness. He could use the moon to avoid wandering in a circle but feared he might encounter cabins and set dogs to raising an alarm.

The most direct route was the railway bridge, but even with the light from his flashlight, crossing the narrow span in darkness was risky. He wished he had explored this during daylight.

Seeing no way around it, Schumacher felt his way across the two-hundred-yard span, stumbling between ties and chunks of rock. He was three-quarters along when he felt the telltale tremble in the rail. An orange glow snaked through the trees behind him.

He didn't think. He moved forward, balancing on one foot while he probed with the next. Now he could hear the locomotive. He didn't take time to look behind him, picking up his pace and moving faster. The bridge trembled as the train began to cross. Its headlight painted the forest ahead, and his shadow danced before him on the track.

The illumination allowed him to take wider steps, planting each foot squarely on a tie.

The whistle blew a warning. The headlamp loomed brighter. He broke into a run.

The blast from the whistle grew louder and more insistent.

The brakes squealed as the engineer fought to halt the train. Faster he ran, leaping between ties. The locomotive grew closer, its roar filling his ears and its heat warming the night air.

He caught his right foot between two ties and pitched forward. Pain seared up his leg.

He half twisted to his left and, reaching down, wrenched his foot from between the ties. He reached the end and, with one mighty effort, launched himself into space, not knowing whether he would hit rock or water.

Nick Cadotte removed sizzling bacon from the pan and cracked four eggs into the grease, whipping them with a fork. "You are up early, my friend."

Armitage ran both hands through his hair. "You expect me to sleep with that delicious smell filling your home?"

"If I'm to help you, we need to get moving." He divided the eggs and bacon between two plates, poured more grease into the pan, and threw in two slices of *zaasakokwaan*. Only after he had fried the bread on both sides did he shove them onto the plates, sliding one across the table to Armitage. "Tell me about this German of yours."

After being banished from the security zone on Birch Island,

Armitage had trudged north along the highway in search of a place to stay. A native fisherman in a pickup truck had picked him up, suggesting he might find shelter at Whitefish Bay.

"Isn't that an Anishinaabe village?"

"One of many, but yes."

Brandon gulped. "Do you happen to know of a man named Cadotte?"

The fisherman laughed. "Which one? We have dozens of families by that name."

"Nick. Nick Cadotte. He's about my age ..."

"*Niigaanii*," the man said. "He's my second cousin."

Armitage felt his pulse racing. "Take me to him. Please."

The fisherman wheeled to a stop in front of Cadotte's cabin. He called out to him before approaching his front doorstep, which Armitage gathered was the custom. His old friend appeared at the door, long black pigtails framing a narrow, brown face that lit up when he spotted the white man alongside his cousin.

"Brandon," he said, "what are you doing here?"

They embraced, pulled away, and stared at each other, laughing.

"*Miigwech*," he said to the cousin, and Brandon added his own thank you. Cadotte took him into his home, insisting that Armitage take his bed while he slept on the sofa.

The men had talked until late into the night, Cadotte smoking one cigarette after another and drinking cup after cup of coffee. "Tell me," he said as the clock neared midnight, "what have you done with yourself? How are your wife and boys?"

Without mentioning Margie, he told his friend of David's death and Henry's capture. "All my life, all I've known is war and its consequences. It's all so pointless."

He asked about Cadotte's life. His son worked in a mill in Sudbury and one of his daughters worked for the tribal council. He avoided mention of the other daughter, just as Armitage had done with Margie. "Daisy, my wife, passed away three years ago. Cancer." He frowned, stared at the cigarette in his hand, and ground it out, the smoldering ashes telling Armitage what had taken her.

Armitage had slept fitfully, waking at odd intervals, his thoughts drifting from Schumacher to Margie and back again.

Now, as he mopped up that last bit of egg with the fried bread, he expanded on the story he'd told his friend the night before. "I hesitate to call it arrogance, but the security force thinks they have Birch Island locked down. They underestimate Schumacher. He's cunning yet disarming, placid on the surface but wily underneath. If there's a way to get at Roosevelt, he'll do it."

The previous evening, as they'd sat together recalling their days working the Silesian mines, Cadotte revealed that the object of all the security on Birch Island was the American president. "I have not seen him," he said, "but others have. He goes fishing with a large group. They've seen him on the water."

Armitage was not surprised, having already guessed as much. "From what you know of this area, how do you think he'll come at him?"

Cadotte lit a cigarette and stared off into an imagined distance. "Not by land. They've blocked the highway, as you learned for yourself. Their security ring extends two hundred yards out from the train station. The coal trains have to take the passing siding and aren't permitted to stop.

"Incidentally," he said, "a man was killed on a railway bridge over Big Inlet this morning."

"What was he doing there?"

"Some damned fool who had too much to drink. The young men here risk it all the time. But it wasn't one of ours this time."

"Who was it?"

"No one knows. The locomotive hit him, and he went into the water. They haven't found the body yet."

Armitage leaned forward, nearly toppling his mug of coffee. "That was Schumacher. He was following the tracks from the north."

Cadotte spread his hands wide. "That's it, then. He's gone."

"Is the engineer certain he hit him? Could he have laid down on the roadbed?"

"He wouldn't have survived. The locomotives traveling that line have low pilots mounted in front," he said, using the technical term for cow-catchers.

"Could he have dived off the side?"

"If he did, he'd either go into the water, where he'd be carried out into the lake, or hit the granite slope. If he landed on the rock, he wouldn't have survived. I'm sure they're searching, but ..."

Armitage tented his hands and leaned into them as though in prayer. "He's a Luftwaffe pilot, so he knows how to land. But he is a strong swimmer."

"The current is strong there. We've lost many boys playing in that water."

"I can't take the chance, Nick. If it was Schumacher on the track, and if he survived, he'll keep trying. I doubt he'll try a ground attack. He knows they'll be combing the tracks for any sign of him. Security at the highway checkpoint is too tight. He'll come at him from the water."

"He's vulnerable there. The RCAF is patrolling with planes and the US Navy and RCMP with boats." Cadotte lit a cigarette and studied the smoke. "Roosevelt is also exposed. He hails those aboard other craft as he heads out fishing. The greatest security in the world is meaningless if the target gets careless."

"I need a boat."

"Brandon, my friend, what can you do that the US Navy can't?"

Armitage repeated a justification he had used before. "I know this guy. He looks like my son. In a sense, I've known him all my life. If he's out there, I'll recognize him before they do."

"*We* need a boat."

Stimson's memo to the president ran fourteen pages, a lengthy missive considering that his colleague, Marshall, confined complex messages to only one. After outlining his concerns that Churchill was backtracking on his Trident commitment, he recounted his warning that Roosevelt's opponents would portray further delay in the cross-

Channel invasion as a capitulation to British political interests at the expense of America's.

He wrote that COSSAC, the Allied planning team, had informed him of their conclusion an invasion of the Continent by the following spring was not only possible but likely to succeed. They warned diverting resources to the sorts of sideshows Churchill envisioned in the Mediterranean could undermine the chances for success. And now, the British were withholding that very report from American planners.

He described his contentious meeting with Churchill and Eden during which the prime minister had warned of "the disastrous effect of having the Channel full of corpses of defeated Allied soldiers." He wrote that he had told Churchill in response, "We could never win any battle by talking about corpses."

On the morning of August 4, he took his missive to Marshall who read it through before rendering his verdict. "I agree with everything you've written. On the subject of COSSAC, you'll be pleased to hear Major General Barker arrived from London last night carrying a bootleg copy of the plan." Barker was the senior American officer on the Allied planning team, second only to British Lieutenant-General Frederick Morgan.

"'Bootleg,' you say?"

"The British refused permission for Morgan to share it. Morgan and Barker decided to go around them."

"When they find out …"

"Yes," Marshall said. "Not every fight takes place on the battle-field, and not every hero is made in combat."

Stimson gave a conspiratorial chuckle. "Harry Hopkins is going to present my trip report to FDR tomorrow. I'm flying up tonight to discuss it with the president."

Marshall held up both hands. "Don't do that. It's the wrong approach."

"General, the president has to see this. He must be prepared when Churchill arrives at Hyde Park to twist his arm."

"I don't suggest you not share it, just not to confront him in person. In fact, I won't permit it."

Won't permit it? Marshall controlled the army's air force. Was the general grounding him?

"I've seen this before. If Roosevelt feels he's being accosted, he'll fight back. Once you intrigue his interest, it knows no limit. This memo," he said, fingering the fourteen pages, "is excellent. Let Hopkins present it as a neutral party. The president will study it, he'll consider it, and he'll reach the same conclusion as we have, almost as though it's his own idea."

Despite his disappointment, Stimson acquiesced. Marshall knew Roosevelt far better than he did.

Back in his office, Stimson penned a cover letter that would accompany his conclusions. "If you care to talk them over with me before Quadrant, I shall be happy to fly up to you at such time as you may suggest."

Stimson's letter and memorandum left the Pentagon at five o'clock, traveling by air to Birch Island, where Hopkins would hand-deliver it to the president.

***

MARGIE WAS DISTRACTED. She made incorrect change for one customer and boxed the wrong hat for another. She longed to confront Sperling, but he'd been clear she wasn't to come to his office unless summoned. On her break, she locked herself in a washroom stall and wept. She knew what she had to do, but didn't know how to accomplish it.

By midafternoon, it was apparent women were unwilling to brave the heat to go shopping. Margie pleaded illness and asked if she could take the day off. Rowena seemed happy to be rid of her.

She busied herself around the house, running the carpet sweeper across the rug, dusting furniture that had no dust on it, and wishing she were back at work where she would be occupied.

She lay down on the bed and tried to nap. Unable to shake the dilemma, she got up and made herself a cup of tea. *I need to call him and beg off*, she thought, *feign illness*. But to reach him, she had to go through April Humphrey, who would ask for her name and her business even if she recognized her voice. She was trapped. At six o'clock, she heard him knock. She considered ignoring it but didn't like the idea of Sperling standing at her rear door where neighbors across the alley might notice.

She opened the kitchen door, turned, and walked away. Sperling closed it behind him and followed her into the dining room.

"What's wrong, my dear? You look terrible."

She turned and faced him. "I've had a bad day. Did you bring dinner?"

"No. Did you want me to?"

"You told me you would, Godfrey. You said it was your turn."

"Did I? I don't recall. I'm sorry. Do you want to go out somewhere, or can you rustle up—?"

"I'm not hungry." She crossed her arms over her breasts, hugging herself as though cold while she summoned up the courage. "I can't go on like this. We have to end it."

"Margie. Darling." He took a step toward her, and she backed away. "You are precious to me. Before we met, I was so lonely. And so were you. Let's not lose each other."

"I can't do this to my husband, Godfrey." *I can't do it to myself.*

"Don't you have feelings for me anymore? I do for you. Margie, I care about you."

"Don't." She waved her arm before her like a windshield wiper. "Please don't."

He stepped forward and wrapped his arms around her. Her resolve shattered, and she wept into his shoulder. "Careful now," he said. "I mustn't get lipstick on my shirt."

She pulled away and looked at him.

"Margie—"

"Not tonight, please. I'm not feeling well. I need some space. Let me think this over ..."

"Of course, dear. Whatever you say. Just know that I care for you and want to give you the love you *deserve*. You owe it to yourself to be happy."

She nodded through her tears.

"We'll see each other tomorrow then. I'll stop down and say hello. And next week, you'll move over to the dress department, and we can discuss how to move forward."

Dress department? I thought you were moving me to lingerie.

"All right, Godfrey. And thank you. This is difficult for me."

"I understand, dear. Things will get better. I promise."

THE CRAFT CADOTTE found was a Canadian Canoe wooden rowboat equipped with an Evinrude Zephyr 4 outboard motor. "It belongs to my cousin. He's not going out again until Saturday, so it's ours until then."

"Not very speedy." Armitage looked at it with undisguised doubt. Seeing a cloud pass over his friend's face, he said, "I'm sorry. This man has made me a bit crazy." He was ashamed of his lack of gratitude.

Cadotte waved the apology away. "This is the peak of the season. It's the best I could do. She's not fast, but she is solid."

"We'll be fine." The pair shoved off and motored out into the Bay of Islands, the small engine putt-putting, spewing gasoline fumes in their wake.

"They spend most of their time on McGregor Bay. The fishing's better on that side. If they do so tomorrow, we'll pull the boat in and launch from there."

They cruised south toward the Birch Island launch area, their fishing poles displayed to avoid alerting Navy patrols. As they traveled, the Ojibwe gave Armitage a history of the Whitefish River First Nation. He described how, in the early nineteenth century, Lieutenant-Governor Sir Francis Bond Head abandoned efforts to impose Christianity on the Anishinaabeg, allowing them to continue their traditional native practices.

"We signed a treaty with him in 1836, reserving Manitoulin Island for us. Many of our brothers refused to move, but my people did."

The treaty seemed only to have spurred white encroachment. "They forced us to give up the northern part of the island in the 1870s," he said. "In 1881, we sold nearby LaCloche Island to the government. My people's settlement was on Birch Island until 1906. When they put the railroad through, they moved us north to the mainland. And here we are."

He presented this as nothing more than a history lesson, without apparent rancor. Armitage turned in his seat to face him. "Why are you willing to help me after all this?"

Cadotte narrowed his eyes and sat back as though struck. "This is my country. The Germans imprisoned me, just as they did you. What else am I to do?"

Armitage searched for an appropriate response but couldn't find the words. Nick saved him the trouble. "Look at the planes circling. They can't be far." Both men raised field glasses and scanned the horizon as the drone of propellers filled the air.

"There she is," Cadotte said after a few minutes. Ahead lay the shapes of two cabin cruisers making for the anchorage at Birch Island. The pair studied the men sitting aboard the *Anna H*. Neither could mistake the American president, laughing with his companions as he sat at the stern. "Shall we pull closer?"

"No, let's remain here," Armitage said. "There's no point in alerting the security forces, and it's not Mr. Roosevelt we're after."

He trained his field glasses on every boat in sight, then scanned the shoreline. He found no sign of the German. He gripped the gunwale in frustration. Was Schumacher really out there somewhere? Had he come to this place rather than trying to escape? Had he been the man on the railroad trestle during the early hours of the day? If so, had he survived or, as the engineer of the locomotive insisted, been killed?

THE PRESIDENT'S party returned to Birch Island at four o'clock after fishing around Brush, Childs, and Agawa Islands. Their guide, Donald McKenzie, knew these waters, and they had brought in a generous catch. After three days on the water, FDR and Admiral Leahy led the daily pool and were almost even.

The arrival that morning of his close friend and aide, Harry Hopkins, further fueled Roosevelt's exuberance. "Is there any word from Uncle Joe?" he asked.

"Nothing," Hopkins said. "The Russians are pushing to recapture Orel and Belgorod. I doubt he's concerned about anything else."

Roosevelt didn't conceal his disappointment. He had been eager to reassure Stalin and restore the relationship with this ally before Quadrant. Instead, Moscow had recalled its ambassadors from Washington and London, and the State Department had heard rumors through neutral Sweden of contacts between Soviet and German diplomats. It was vital to prevent the Soviets from negotiating a separate peace. Moreover, limiting Stalin's territorial ambitions was crucial to post-war security.

Their discussion turned to Italy. Representatives of the new Badoglio government had approached the British ambassador in Portugal about a peace deal. Roosevelt had proposed making Rome an open city, sparing it from further destruction, but Churchill pushed back.

"What would the Russians say?" he asked. Stalin would view a separate treaty with Italy as "abandoning the principle of unconditional surrender. Rome," he argued, "will soon fall into our hands."

Roosevelt did not want to see the eternal city savaged by war. "I shall write Winston tomorrow," he told Hopkins. "We can't let this happen."

Knowing Stimson's memo was on its way, Hopkins told the president, "Enjoy yourself, because we have a couple of busy days ahead of us." Though he knew the thrust of the war secretary's report, he kept the information to himself.

Roosevelt did as he was told, "enjoying myself immensely," as he cabled Eleanor. Over cocktails aboard the *Ferdinand Magellan*, the men shared "old war stories," miles away from the cares of Washington and the news from overseas.

In three days, however, the American military delegation would leave for Québec for preliminary talks with the British. While he was at peace that Wednesday evening, confident that he was in a safe harbor, Roosevelt sensed he would soon face the most crucial test of his presidency.

As CLOUDS in the eastern sky turned crimson in the reflected light of the Ontario sunset, a lone figure made his way among the docks lining McGregor Bay. He limped, and a ragged sling supported his left arm.

After leaping from the track, yards ahead of the oncoming engine, Jörg Schumacher had landed on his side and lodged against a granite shelf. His bedroll had cushioned his head and back, but his left arm —the one a guard had broken at Bowmanville—hung at his side. The pain was intense. His ankle was swollen to twice its normal size. Blood caked the fabric of both knees. While he had secured the rifle case between his shoulders, his backpack had disappeared, consigned to the inlet along with his flashlight. In the darkness, he had no way of knowing how far he had fallen, much less if there was a way out.

Above him, he had heard shouts of the train's crew members. For the first time since his escape, he weighed whether to respond to their cries and turn himself in. Instead, he crawled to the opposite side of the boulder, concealing himself as best he could. He spent the night curled against its cold surface, unable to sleep and unwilling to risk moving in the dark.

As wisps of daylight hinted at dawn, his position became apparent. He was a third of the way down a steep incline. Below him was nothing but rock, which disappeared into a cascade of water rushing down a low but treacherous waterfall. He could crawl up the slope toward the tracks, but search parties would soon comb the rail bed for his body, if they weren't already.

It made sense to move east and make his way to the crest of what he assumed to be Birch Island, but he was uncertain how his ankle would hold up crawling along the embankment.

In the end, Schumacher settled on a compromise. He scrambled over the rock, using only his right arm for support, until he was out of sight of the railway bridge. He inched up the slope and walked eastward toward the highway. When the train crew failed to find a body, searchers might assume he had survived and put out an alarm. A dirty, bedraggled figure wandering around the island would be reported, and his mission would be over. But he had no choice.

After half an hour, he reached Highway 6, which bridged the inlet over a through-girder bridge. He concealed himself behind a small grove of trees and watched the traffic, primarily military vehicles, cross. He took his time approaching the roadway, walking parallel to the highway, but hidden from view. His ankle ached, and his left arm throbbed.

He came upon a pine-shingled cabin in a small clearing. Four men stood outside, stacking fishing gear in the trunk of a De Soto 4-door sedan. Schumacher waited until the car pulled away, carrying the quartet to where, he assumed, they docked their boat. He spent another ten minutes eyeing the cabin and listening for signs of life. Only then did he peer through the windows, mount the steps, and open the unlocked door.

A box of Red River cereal lay on the counter. Schumacher poured water into a pot on the still-warm stove and searched the cabin while waiting for it to come to a boil. He found a first aid kit behind a knotty pine door in the washroom, holding an assortment of self-adhering gauze and lengths of Ace bandage. Using only his good arm, he dressed the scrapes on his knees and wound the elastic around his right ankle, replacing the kit on the shelf in the bathroom closet. He found a stack of cleaning rags and, using his right hand and his teeth, knotted two together and tied the ends, forming a loop.

He slipped this makeshift sling around his neck and pulled his left arm through it.

Back in the kitchen, he poured cereal into the boiling water and stirred. A bit of coffee remained in the percolator, and he filled a cup upended in the sink.

After finishing breakfast, he washed the pot, coffee cup, and bowl. He poured a small amount of water into the percolator, leaving everything as he had found them. He placed three slices of bread, a small hunk of cheese, and an apple into an empty, grease-stained paper bag from the trash.

Schumacher gave the cabin one more look to make certain there were no signs of his presence and closed the door behind him. At mid-afternoon, he crossed the highway and made his way through the woods to McGregor Bay. Remaining sheltered, he scouted the shoreline until he spotted a marina. Pleasure craft bobbed at their moorings as returning anglers converged on the few open berths.

The German had gone as far as his weary legs would take him for the day. He stretched out behind a thorn bush, his back to a tree. He could no longer risk traversing the island on foot, for he couldn't elude pursuers. His ankle screamed with every step. Pain shot through his body. His left arm was as useless as the Austrian.

What had seemed the best idea—to conceal himself in the trees and take a shot as FDR boarded or left his cruiser—appeared impossible, given his condition. He would have to attack while the president was fishing. But how?

When the last boat came in for the evening, Schumacher ventured onto the dock. All were small craft, a few not even powered, the rest with low-horsepower outboard engines. They might allow him to putt-putt around the bay, perhaps draw close to the presidential party but would afford him no opportunity to get away.

One would have to do.

Schumacher had recognized from the start this might be a suicide mission. He camped out in the woods, awaiting first light, wondering if this night would be his last.

18

AUGUST 5, 1943

Jörg Schumacher arose at first light, relieved himself, ate the apple he'd taken from the cottage, and emerged from the grove of birch trees that gave the island its name. He stepped onto the dock and approached a boat he had selected the night before. It was a 15-foot rowboat with a cedar stripped hull and double action seat, equipped with a Johnson Seahorse outboard motor and two full five-gallon gas tanks. The craft was unremarkable, smelling of dead fish and oil. Its attraction was the extra fuel—that and the fishing rods left aboard that would provide cover.

After placing the rifle, water bottle, and what remained of his food into the hull, Schumacher sat on the dock and eased himself into the small craft. He didn't trust his ankle to support him and could only use his right arm for support. His weight pushed the craft away from the pier, causing him to lose his balance and crash onto the gunwale. Stifling a moan, he crept onto the seat.

He pumped the gas bulb to build fuel pressure, checked the oil bulb to ensure lubrication was flowing into the engine, and lowered the prop into the water. He put the gear in neutral, wrapped the starter cord around the flywheel, and yanked on it. The engine failed to fire. He examined the connections between the tank and the motor, fed a bit more fuel, and tried once more. Again, nothing.

Fearing he'd flooded the motor, he wrapped the cord around the starter again but waited. The sun was up now, and two men passed by, heading to a boat farther out. If it didn't turn over this time, more anglers would arrive, and he would be in a spot.

He gave a mighty prayer to God and a mightier tug to the starter. The motor coughed to life and, as he increased power, hummed.

He crawled toward the bow and unwound the rope from the cleat. As the bow drifted free, he moved toward the stern to repeat the process. An older man wearing a fishing vest and a hat adorned with lures walked onto the dock and stopped above him.

Schumacher had picked the man's boat. How was he to explain himself? He was too lame to scramble out and, if he did so, would move so slowly even this old geezer would catch up.

"I'm sorry," he said, "I must have—"

"Let me help. I see you're flying on only one wing." The man bent down, cast off the rope, and tossed it into the boat. Schumacher smiled, not saying a word.

"Say, isn't that Henry's boat?"

Schumacher beamed at the old man while composing a response in as few words as possible. "*Ja*, he loaned it to me for the morning."

He settled himself onto the seat, slid it back toward the engine, engaged the gear, and motored off before the man could question him further. He didn't look back, knowing that it would fuel his suspicions.

The inlet off McGregor Bay resembled a porpoise traveling west. Schumacher had launched at a point just ahead of the dorsal fin, intending to parallel the coastline toward the blowhole and peak. Instead, he had to pretend he was after fish rather than a man. He headed east toward the dolphin's flukes, toward Wardrope Island.

Once out of sight, he killed the engine, reached for the fishing pole, and cast a line over the side. It took twenty minutes, but the man he'd encountered on the dock soon passed by. "You won't catch much there," he shouted. "The fishing's better out toward the island."

"Thanks," Schumacher replied, wishing he could shoot the nosy parker and be done with him. Only after the man had disappeared from sight did he head back the way he had come, motoring a safe distance offshore. He soon spotted what he was after at the nose of the dolphin, a dock with a ramp whose fresh timbers suggested it had been recently constructed. No one was there at this hour, but Schumacher was patient. He motored out to a point where he could observe without being obvious about it, killed the engine, cast a line into the water, and waited.

A BEECHCRAFT UC-43 Traveler equipped with pontoons leveled off above Current Bay, skimming the gentle waves before settling down. Army Air Force First Lieutenant Edward Kopp was at the controls, his crew chief, Sergeant Charles J. Griffing, alongside him. Built in the previous year, the aircraft was a biplane with negative stagger, meaning that the lower wing extended further forward than the upper wing. The aircraft had been designed a decade before but had since been adapted to serve as military light transport. Three days earlier, Air Corps enlistees had fitted the pontoons, allowing it to function as a courier plane between Oscoda Army Air Force Base and Birch Island.

Kopp maneuvered among the rocks and shoals and brought the craft to a halt. Griffing dropped a buoy, and a Navy runabout tucked alongside the wings to bring the pair ashore. The pilot carried a satchel containing the day's mail, including the packet addressed to Harry Hopkins from Secretary Stimson.

Hopkins opened the document and read it over, closed it in the manila envelope with a string tie, and tapped at the door of the president's suite. "Come in, Harry." FDR knew the rhythm of his trusted advisor's knock.

The two bantered for a moment, and Hopkins handed him the envelope. Roosevelt locked eyes with him. Hopkins typically made some introduction when handing him a paper, explaining what it was, where it came from, and what it conveyed. In this case, his silence served as an alarm.

FDR took a deep breath, reached for his glasses, and read. Hopkins studied his face as the man took it all in. When he finished, the president folded the memorandum, replaced it in the folder, removed his glass, and massaged the bridge of his nose.

"I spoke with the secretary yesterday," Hopkins said. "He's deeply concerned."

"He makes that clear."

"He is convinced Churchill fails to understand the political dilemma we face if we postpone conquering Japan."

Roosevelt smiled. "Perhaps we don't appreciate Mr. Churchill's political dilemma if there is, as he said, a 'channel full of corpses.'"

Hopkins said nothing.

"Harry, Churchill has been fighting this war far longer than we have. They have lost more men in a country less than half our size, so many they've had to consolidate army divisions. And that doesn't include civilians. Churchill cannot afford a bloodbath in the Channel. His government would fall, and there's no telling what would happen.

"Now, if I were to say that to my generals, my words would quickly get back to Stilwell and MacArthur, who are only too happy to abandon Great Britain and focus on Japan. I would lose the presidency, our party would lose Congress, and the world would lose Europe."

He leaned back in his wheelchair and stared out the window of his rail car toward the open water. His voice grew quiet. "I long to tell the American public these truths, but I cannot risk it. I have to walk this narrow path, keeping both Churchill and Stalin together as allies so I can create a lasting peace on both continents."

"I understand, Mr. President.

"Let's go fishing," the president said.

Hopkins couldn't tell what action FDR would take at the forthcoming summit. He would decide only when he was ready while keeping those around him, even Hopkins himself, guessing.

As they left aboard the *Anna H*, neither man knew they were about to hear from the prime minister himself.

———

MARGIE ARRIVED at Pinson's nursing a painful cheek. During the night, she'd bitten herself and had chomped down on it twice during a hurried breakfast. Licking the wound with her tongue, she looked about with uncertainty and asked Rowena how everything was going.

"Fine," she said. "We haven't opened yet."

"I know. What I mean is, has anyone—has anything ...?" Margie stopped. Rowena rolled her eyes.

Calm down, she told herself. *No one knows a thing. Godfrey wouldn't say a word, and he was fine when we parted last night.*

Pinson's had placed a full-page ad of sales items in the *Toronto Daily Star*. When the doors opened at ten, a tidal wave of women swept in. Margie kept busy all morning and forgot her nervousness, although the lesion in her cheek reminded her of the sleepless night she had endured.

She took her lunch in the break room, a peanut butter sandwich and a small box of raisins. Not only did she detect no animosity among the others, a few seemed particularly friendly.

Margie returned to the department in what she expected to be one of her last days there. Did Rowena know Godfrey was moving her next week? If so, she didn't show it, and Margie knew better than to even hint at an impending change.

The afternoon was even busier, and four o'clock came swiftly, only an hour to go before she was to leave for the day. Margie was waiting on an older lady, who didn't know what she wanted, when she looked up to see another woman staring at her. She was tall and slender, with aquiline features. Her hair was bleached to an off-white color without a trace of yellow. She wore a double-strand of pearls and a long, light blue dress that clung to her slight figure. A regal bearing, Margie thought.

She met the woman's icy stare and said, "I'll be with you in a moment." The woman inclined her head. Her face broke into an imperious smile. With a toss of her head, she turned and strode toward the elevator, holding her clutch purse next to her body. Margie watched until the doors of the cage closed behind her.

"Do you?" the elderly woman said.

"I'm sorry. What did you ask?"

She sighed. "Do you have this in lavender?"

"We may. I'll check. But the sales price is only good on the black and white ones."

"Never mind, then." Her hand fluttered as she shuffled away.

Margie looked up to find Rowena staring at her. "Are you all right?" she asked.

"Yes, of course. What's wrong?" Her supervisor glanced toward the elevator. "Who was that woman?"

"You don't know?"

"No, I don't think I've ever seen her."

"That's Mrs. Sperling."

Margie felt her watching for a reaction. "I thought she was ..." Blood rushed to her face. Her underarms grew damp. She clutched her stomach.

"I assumed you knew. I'm sorry. Margie."

She placed her hand on the counter to steady herself. "I—I have to leave."

"Of course," Rowena said and repeated words that had a cruel ring. "I'm so, *so* sorry."

***

TAKING a chance the president would spend the morning in McGregor Bay, Armitage and Cadotte had pulled the boat and launched from the east side of the island. The Ojibwe didn't have to search the inlet. He knew where the president would board the *Anna H* if he fished this bay.

By ten o'clock, they had seen no activity. Cadotte turned the outboard motor up to full throttle and headed out of the inlet, explaining that they had to round the channel at LaCloche Island to return to the Bay of Islands. "It's six miles and will take us some time. Still, it's quicker than pulling the boat out again."

Neither noticed the cedar rowboat lying off to starboard with a single figure, a battered hat pulled over his face, fishing along the far shore, just one among many on the bay this morning.

It took an hour to cross through the channel and head north. From the activity at the train station dock, they realized the *Anna H* and *Mizpah* had departed. Cadotte nosed his craft east, chugging along the top of Childs Island and swinging east around Brush Island. They spotted a floatplane making a gentle arc to the north, and Cadotte followed it. "There are hundreds of islands up here. They could be anywhere."

After an hour of searching, they found the party, not north of Brush Island but farther west. The plane had either been out for a joy ride or was searching for suspicious craft that might be skulking about. Cadotte cut the engine and let the boat drift. The only sound was the slapping of waves against the sides of their craft.

Armitage raised his field glasses and studied the horizon. There was no sign of Schumacher. "But he might be hiding behind any of these islands," he said. *If he's here at all.* For the second time in as many days, he was no longer so confident.

They sat in the boat until midafternoon, then followed the *Anna H,* her companion boat, and three escort vessels at a discreet distance as they returned to the island. If the presidential party had caught anything today, Armitage and Cadotte had not.

They made their way back around Birch Island, pausing at Little Current to refuel. After four o'clock, they entered the inlet. A man approached them in a canoe and called out to Cadotte. The two exchanged a few sentences in Ojibwe. With parting words and a broad wave, Cadotte gunned the engine to life and sped along the north shore. "Someone stole a boat this morning," he called over the roar of the motor and the pounding of the hull as it hit the waves. "Our men are searching for him."

Approaching the marina a half mile to the west, he cut the motor and drifted alongside the dock. Two men stood together, peering out toward the water. One grabbed the line Armitage tossed them. They climbed from the rowboat and introduced themselves to the pair.

One identified himself as Henry Beardsley and explained what had happened. "I got here about ten, and my boat was missing. I thought it might have drifted away, although I'd tied it up good and proper. I rented another boat and went searching for it but saw no sign. I came back a while ago, and George here said he'd talked to the man who stole it."

His companion took up the story, and Armitage asked him to describe the thief. Since the man had been almost prone in the boat during the encounter, George could only guess at his height. The person he described could have been the escaped German or one of thousands of other fair-haired men. "He was pretty beat up. Scratches all over him, and his clothing was torn. He was holding his left arm like it'd been hurt."

"Did he have an accent?"

"I didn't notice. I don't think he said ten words to me." George screwed up his features as though it would help him recall. "Now that you mention it, I think he answered my question by saying 'ja.' Could have been 'yeah,' I suppose, but it sounded more like 'ja.'"

Armitage felt a cold chill pass through his body, certain this was Schumacher. Trying to hide his emotion, he asked George to describe the boat, including the name Bella's Pride. "Your wife?" he asked.

"Naw, my dog. She's dead and gone now."

He didn't know whether it was the wife or the dog that had passed, but it made little difference. He thanked the pair and lowered himself back into the rowboat. "What do you think?" Cadotte said as he clambered in after him.

"It's Schumacher. Who else would steal a fifteen-footer around here when you can rent one by the hour?"

Roosevelt returned from fishing in a joyous mood. He and his companions had enjoyed another perfect day, scudding puffy clouds against a cerulean sky and temperatures in the high seventies. FDR had again caught more fish than anyone else in the party, and he knew they were not sandbagging. "I have little doubt I'll beat you," he told Leahy.

His chief of staff still posed a threat, but with only two more days remaining on the water, the president was confident he'd win the pot. "I feel on top of the world," he said. The week had been good for him, lifting the weight of decision-making and political infighting, creating the illusion he had not a care.

As he boarded the *Ferdinand Magellan*, however, reality greeted him in the form of a cable from Churchill, received and decoded by the Signal Corps officers in the forward communications car. In response to the president's message urging they declare Rome an open city, the prime minister reported that Badoglio's emissary in Portugal had warned of chaos following Mussolini's arrest.

> Every vestige of fascism has been swept away. Italy turned Red overnight. In Turin and Milan, there were Communist demonstrations which had to be put down by armed force. 20 years of fascism has obliterated the middle class. There is nothing between the king and the patriots who have rallied round him and rampant Bolshevism.

Churchill concluded this report with a call to arms. "The sooner we land in Italy, the better. We shall find little opposition and perhaps even active cooperation on the part of the Italians."

It was as Stimson had warned. Churchill was renewing his Mediterranean push, trying to prosecute the war through a drawn-out campaign of attrition.

Accompanying the prime minister's cable was another from US Ambassador John Gilbert Winant, through whom Churchill had transmitted his message. Winant poked holes in the report, suggesting the Italian overture was a German ruse.

As Roosevelt fingered the latter message over his afternoon martini, he saw the ambassador's point. "If Hitler can draw us into an Italian campaign," he told Hopkins and Leahy over the throbbing of the air conditioner, "he will delay any thrust through France, giving him time to regroup and strengthen his western defenses."

Whether Churchill or Winant had correctly read the situation, Roosevelt faced two competing strategies—the cross-Channel thrust advocated by Marshall and the Italian invasion pushed by Churchill and Eden.

True to form, the president gave neither man a sign where his mind lay.

BY MIDMORNING, Schumacher had accepted that Roosevelt wasn't fishing in McGregor Bay that day. Auer had explained how the *Anna H* and *Mizpah* could round the island so the party could board on the opposite bay, but Schumacher had only a general idea where the channel was. He could waste an entire day searching every inlet.

Still, the German couldn't remain where he was. He had stolen this boat, and an alarm could go out at any moment. When he'd left yesterday morning, Auer had complained of shortness of breath and was in no condition to assist him. Schumacher was now incapable of doing it on his own, much less to retrace his steps.

He fired up the outboard engine and, hugging the inlet's south shore, entered the bay. It was full of boats of all sizes this morning, and he passed unnoticed. Auer had supplied an Esso road map, but the scale was too small to provide much detail. He ignored the first three small coves. The channel had to be farther south. He passed Wardrope Island to port and found another inlet just below it. He spent twenty minutes discovering it led nowhere.

A larger island now lay to his left, which had to be Little LaCloche. A long channel appeared to his starboard side, and he motored into it. He passed a lodge to his right, continued another two hundred yards, and found himself at a shoreline. He drifted into the shallows and cut the motor. Beyond the shore, he could hear other craft. Schumacher anchored the boat, waded in, and hobbled forward, treading cautiously due to the uneven surface of the rock beneath his feet.

He stood on a narrow isthmus joining two sections of land, both part of Birch Island. He recalled Auer's descriptions of how the land surrendered to Lake Huron.

Returning to the boat, he continued south while eating his last slice of bread and cheese. A half hour passed, and he entered a waterway between Birch and Little LaCloche, following a line of buoys. The town of Little Current hove into view. From here, Auer had told him, an island led into the channel, and he could take either way around it. He took the northern passage, avoiding prying eyes in the little town. For the first time in hours, he smiled to himself. This was the passage. He had rounded Birch Island.

He turned north toward the railway station but hit on another plan. Rather than searching for the launch area, he needed to find a faster boat. He returned south, hugging the shore of what he now knew was LaCloche Island.

Minutes later, he found a private dock at which a racing runabout was tied up. He anchored nearby, came ashore, and approached it. The German had never heard of a Hacker-Craft. He was unaware that the firm had built the world's fastest powerboats. *El Lagarto*, *Scotty Too*, *My Sweetie*, and *Miss Pepsi* had dominated the competition, winning the Gold Cup in consecutive years.

What Jörg Schumacher did realize, as he eyed the keys dangling from the ignition switch, was that *My Nancy* was a nimble craft that could bring him within range of the president's cabin cruiser before anyone could stop him.

Returning to *Bella's Pride*, Schumacher stripped to his underpants. He started the motor, left it in neutral, and walked it as far from shore as he dared. Engaging the gear, he watched the boat head into the bay toward an uncertain destination.

He entered the nearby woods, standing naked until he was dry, donned his pants and shirt, curled up on the forest floor, wrapped his arms around himself for warmth, and slept. He was now on his own, past the point of no return. Tomorrow would decide his destiny ... and that of the American president.

19

AUGUST 6, 1943

MARGIE GAVE herself one last look in the mirror, picked up her purse, and opened the front door. As she closed it behind her, the telephone rang. Suspecting it was her mother calling, she was tempted to ignore her, but thought better of it.

"Mrs. Armitage?" She recognized the voice of April Humphrey, Godfrey's assistant. "You won't need to come in today."

"Not come in? There was another ad in last night's paper. We will be busy."

The woman's hesitation made Margie grip the earpiece so tightly her knuckles turned white. "You left early yesterday, leaving Mrs. Walter alone. Mr. Sperling had to transfer someone else to cover for you."

"I was ill. I explained the situation to Rowena. I'm sorry. It won't happen again."

Miss Humphrey cleared her throat. "I'm afraid you are no longer needed at Pinson's. We have mailed a check for what we owe you."

"I'm fired?" she said in a choked voice. There was silence at the other end of the phone. "Let me speak with Mr. Sperling, please."

"He's in a meeting at the moment. However, he asked me to express our thanks for your service."

For my "service." Like I'm some sort of farm animal.

"I insist on speaking with him."

"I'm afraid that's impossible. I'll tell him you asked."

"You do that!" She slammed the receiver into its cradle. Ripping her hat from her head, Margie stormed into the kitchen, gripped the counter, and stared out the window, her lips pursed. Five minutes turned to ten while she drummed her fingers on the countertop. Her eyes narrowed, and her mouth set in a hard line of determination.

She reached for the *Daily Star* and turned to the last two pages. Ripping one out, she folded it lengthwise and into thirds, circling one item.

She picked up the phone and dialed a number she knew by heart. She asked the switchboard operator for Godfrey Sperling's office. When April Humphrey answered, she launched into her prepared message without introducing herself. "Tell Mr. Sperling that he is to list me as having resigned, not fired. He is to give me an excellent recommendation to any future employer. If he deviates from this, I will make his life hell. Do you understand me?"

"I can't—"

"You can, and you will. If he asks if this is a threat, the answer is yes. Don't sugarcoat it. Tell him exactly what I said."

She forced herself to calm down and placed a second call.

***

AT DAWN, Jörg Schumacher prowled the shoreline until he saw two couples packing luggage and fishing tackle into a DeSoto Airstream. He waited until the car pulled away, then raided their trash can. Two apples on their paths to extinction, half a loaf of stale bread, and the pickings of meat from a ham bone were enough to sustain him, an improvement over boyhood meals when all the money in the household couldn't buy as much.

His meal finished, he left his hiding place in the woods and crept onto the dock where *My Nancy* was tied up. He sat on the wooden planks, lowered the rifle case into the hull, and eased himself aboard. Crawling forward and aft, he untied the ropes from the cleats and allowed the craft to drift out into the water. The current carried him northward toward the channel.

Once he was out of sight and earshot, he primed the fuel and fired the engine. It caught immediately. At last, something worked in his favor.

All but his physical condition. His left arm was nearly dead weight, but he could use it to brace the rifle if he didn't put pressure on it. His ankle throbbed and was warm to the touch; he wasn't sure whether he'd broken a bone or torn a ligament, but it was still swollen. He wouldn't get far by foot and couldn't defend himself if caught.

The German steered the boat into open water, staying a half mile offshore, close enough to see activity on land but far enough to appear innocuous.

Even as he drifted, he sensed the engine's power. It was like nothing he'd ever experienced on water, although it couldn't compete with his fighter, screaming through the skies thousands of feet above the orchards and pastures of northern France. He steered toward the open bay until the land was just a thin line separating the water and sky and opened the throttle, thrilling to its mighty, unmuffled roar. The horizon disappeared from his view as the bow rose. The boat surged forward until only its rear quarter skimmed the surface. In his exhilaration, he dismissed the pain coursing through his body.

Satisfied, he slowed and made his way north again until he was within sight of the Birch Island railway depot. Both cabin cruisers lay at anchor, ready to take on passengers. He sailed off to a safe distance, cut the engine, removed the rifle from its case, and pulled a fishing cap low over his eyes, a sea hawk preparing to swoop down on its prey.

A LOUD KNOCK at Cadotte's door awakened Armitage. The Ojibwe rose and opened it, chattered in a language he did not understand, and turned to face his friend. "Mr. Roosevelt's cabin cruiser is anchored offshore from the train station. We must pull the boat again and launch on the east side."

They had slept in their clothes, Armitage in a pair of britches and a coarse flax shirt lent to him by his friend. Cadotte handed him a pack containing bread, dried fish, and berries while he carried two Enfield rifles.

During target practice the previous evening, Brandon had shot wildly at first. "I haven't fired a weapon since 1915," he explained.

"You've had no need to," Cadotte replied. "Now you do."

And as he fired more rounds, his decades-old training kicked in. He was now confident he could handle Schumacher if the need arose.

They placed the gear in the back of Cadotte's Ford pickup. "What's this?" Armitage said, spotting an object in the bed of the truck.

"I borrowed a second engine. If we need it, it will get us there faster."

Dawn whispered above the water as they hauled the rowboat aboard the trailer. They stored their gear in the hull and headed back across the peninsula. The launch area into Current Bay was not a dock but a gravel track that disappeared into the water. Cadotte backed the trailer in without a glance at the rearview mirror, as he had the day before. The two men eased the rowboat into the water. Armitage held it in place while Cadotte moved the trailer to higher ground.

A Hudsonian godwit perched atop a spruce tree observing him, sounding its *deew-doo* to unseen companions. Armitage had never seen the bird before. It seemed peaceful, unconcerned by the threats lurking nearby.

Once they were both aboard, Cadotte placed the starter cord around the flywheel, primed the engine, and fired it into life with a practiced pull. They motored south, past the train trestle where Armitage believed his quarry had nearly lost his life. From there, they could see the *Anna H* and another boat, the *Mizpah*, lying at anchor.

"Now what?" Armitage said.

"We wait. If your prisoner is out there, he won't move until the president is in open water. There's too much security here."

The shore bristled with men carrying firearms. Cadotte steered his small craft out into the bay, and the two cast their baitless lines into the water, playing the part of ordinary fishermen.

They lingered for two hours while they nibbled their breakfast. Armitage was too nervous to eat much. He would have welcomed a cup of coffee, but there had been no time to brew it. So he sat, his useless line dangling off the stern, now convinced the German was nearby.

Roosevelt arose early, uncertain what work awaited him before he and his companions could begin their second-to-last day at Birch Island. To his chagrin, the night had brought a slew of cables. One was a terse memo from Marshall outlining a fierce battle raging in Washington over what position the military should take at the Quadrant Conference.

Major General Ray Barker, the American officer second in command at COSSAC, had arrived at the Pentagon to brief the US Joint Planning Staff, only to find the once-supportive team now questioning their commitment to Overlord. A majority now leaned to Great Britain's Mediterranean strategy. Marshall wrote that the Joint Chiefs would meet with Barker that day to formalize their position, even as an advance team departed for Québec.

Roosevelt took his time reading the messages decoded by the Signal Corps five cars forward. The Navy was fighting the Battle of Vella Gulf in the Solomon Islands, and it appeared victory was not far off. But German forces now streamed into Italy to take positions the

Italians had abandoned. "If Winston thinks Italy will be a cakewalk," the president told Hopkins, "he is badly mistaken."

His morning's work done, Roosevelt wheeled himself to the elevator at the rear of the car. The Navy orderly lowered him to the ramp to the dock and helped him up the ramp to the *Anna H.* Hopkins and Leahy followed, the admiral joining the party on the *Mizpah*, where they'd guzzled coffee as they awaited their commander-in-chief.

At 9:15 a.m., both cabin cruisers slipped from their moorings and headed into the bay, escorted by three armed Navy patrol boats.

LIEUTENANT KOPP FIRED the engine of the Beechcraft UC-43 floatplane and maneuvered it away from the moorings. Anticipating an early return to Michigan, Kopp and Griffing had changed the front spark plugs and serviced the aircraft. Now they learned they would not leave until late afternoon at the earliest and might even stay over until Friday morning. As they contemplated a leisurely few hours on the bay, a US Navy officer and a Secret Service agent approached, asking the pilot to take them aloft to inspect the area.

Kopp ordered Sergeant Griffing to stay behind during what he expected would be a short flight and to move their buoy closer to shore. As Kopp started the engine, it seemed to sputter, but it ran evenly once it warmed up. Kopp taxied out to his intended takeoff point, studied the instruments, which showed no signs of malfunction, and checked the magnetos. Once more, the engine sputtered.

"We have a problem," he called over the motor's roar. "I can't risk taking off in these conditions." He made a 180-degree turn and taxied toward his mooring.

As he drew closer to Birch Island, smoke erupted from beneath the dashboard. Still far offshore, Kopp turned off the ignition, the master switch, and the fuel supply. Smoke continued to fill the cockpit.

"Gentlemen, get out on the pontoons," he said. The men followed his instructions while the pilot, standing on the forward wing's leading edge, played an extinguisher on the fire. The flames only increased.

"Inflate your life vests," Kopp ordered. "We're abandoning ship."

While his passengers jumped into the bay, the lieutenant stepped onto the pontoon, scooping water onto the flames. The fire grew closer to the gas tank. Kopp pulled the cord on his own life vest, but it failed to deploy.

Any second, the plane might blow up. Kopp ripped off his faulty vest, leather jacket, shirt, pants, and shoes and plunged in. Behind him, the Beechcraft began to sink. A tower of oily smoke curled into the air as Kopp swam for his life.

On shore, officers and guards saw the column of smoke but no sign of the plane. In the confusion, they shouted at each other. Where was the president? Secret Service supervising agent Mike Reilly raced to the train's signal car and ordered the corpsmen to raise the *Anna H.* The radio operator called the ship three times before getting an answer. No one aboard had been near the radio.

Meanwhile, two Navy enlisted men manned a runabout and shot away from the dock. Sergeant Griffing had just moved the buoy when he heard someone shout, "An aircraft just burned up." He ran onto a dock and waited, his anxiety evident as he rose on the balls of his feet, shielding his eyes from the sun, until the runabout returned with a dripping Lt. Kopp in the bow.

"We don't have the Beechcraft anymore," he called. He jumped into the shallow water and waded in, telling the sailors, "Two men are still floating out there. Forget me and bring them in."

"What happened?" Reilly called out to him. "Did someone fire at you?"

"No, sir. It was purely a mechanical issue."

"Could it be an act of sabotage?"

The drenched lieutenant hesitated, weighing his words before speaking. "I can't say for sure, sir, but I doubt it."

Behind Reilly, the commander in charge of the Navy's operation said, "I've ordered one of the patrol boats back to be on the safe side."

SCHUMACHER STALKED the president's party at a distance, laying off to port and allowing the two cabin cruisers to move well ahead. When they dropped anchor off Childs Island, he faced a decision. Two of the three patrol boats lay between him and the *Anna H*. Even given his speed, he could not run the gauntlet. Nor could he sit there idling. He needed to find an opening. The patrol plane was bound to get suspicious and direct one of the armed Navy vessels to investigate.

He settled on a risky strategy. The German headed *My Nancy* back the way he had come, circling the island to draw ahead of the presidential party. He cruised rather than raced, pretending to be just a Friday pleasure seeker enjoying the August sunshine.

As he rounded the north end of the island, he gave the fishing party a wide berth while surveying the scene through Auer's field glasses. Both cabin cruisers faced away from the island. The *Mizpah* lay to the starboard side of *Anna H*, putting the president's craft directly ahead of him. The patrol boats were off their bow, one to port, another to starboard, with the third positioned between them.

This left one possible ploy. Hugging the shoreline, Schumacher would run in behind *Anna H*'s stern, where the president sat. After he shot Roosevelt, he would be exposed, but in the ensuing confusion, he might be able to make a getaway.

As he began his approach, motoring slowly into position, the patrol boat farthest from him gunned its engine and turned east at high speed. Schumacher spotted a towering column of smoke on the horizon. Something was happening on Birch Island. Had the gunship pulled away to investigate?

The middle patrol boat moved east to cover the position, while the one closest turned to close the gap. Both were headed away from him at full speed.

This was the opening Schumacher needed. He placed the rifle

alongside him and gunned the engine, heading directly for the president's craft.

MARGIE SMILED at the man sitting behind the counter at Eaton's personnel department. "I'm responding to your advertisement for a salesperson in women's shoes."

"Do you have any experience?" the clerk said. He seemed bored, she thought, as though he'd repeated the same list of questions more than a dozen times that morning.

"I've worked at Pinson's since spring. I began as a part-time clerk in millinery. They promoted me to full-time, made me second-in-command in the department, and were about to move me into a management training program."

The clerk gave her his full attention. "Why would you leave Pinson's?"

Margie had thought hard about this question during her bus trip into town. "I like the people there; they've been good to me. But since I do most of my shopping here at Eaton's, I've always felt a bit disloyal."

She allowed herself a small laugh. "When I saw your ad in the paper, I did something foolish. I called Pinson's and gave my notice, then came here."

The clerk frowned, shook his head, and smiled. "That is certainly a commitment." He handed her an application and asked her to complete it on the spot.

As she did so, a woman emerged from the washroom down the hall. "Mrs. Armitage," she exclaimed, "what are you doing here?"

"I'm applying for work."

"You're leaving Pinson's?" Margie repeated her cover story while the clerk listened to the conversation. "Besides, I don't have to change buses to get here."

"I'll have to move my business," the woman said. "The saleswomen there are so stodgy. You really brightened things up. They will miss you."

Margie thanked the woman and continued to work on the application, pretending that she had not noticed the clerk taking in every word of the exchange. He rose from his desk, walked down a corridor, and tapped on a door.

He returned almost immediately. "Mrs. Armitage, Mr. Porter will see you now."

She followed him, wearing a confident smile.

THE TWO FRIENDS trailed the presidential flotilla at a mile's distance to avoid calling attention to themselves. While Cadotte operated the outboard engine, Armitage scanned the horizon with his field glasses. Small fishing boats dotted the bay, and many moved out of the way as the president's party approached.

A half hour into their journey, Armitage called out, "There he is." Cadotte followed the direction in which he was pointing and saw a speck a half mile off.

"How can you be sure from this distance?"

Armitage didn't answer, tracking the boat behind and to port as the rowboat bucked and swayed over the waves. The motorboat turned away, heading in the other direction. "False alarm, I guess." Everyone tall and with fair hair now looked the same to him.

When the *Anna H* anchored, Cadotte moved beyond the flotilla and pulled into the entrance to a cove. Mounting the second engine on the transom, he fired both, leaving them running in neutral, ready to move should the need arise. The two pretended to fish, their empty lines dangling in the water as they had at Birch Island.

It did not take long for a Navy patrol boat to show interest. Armitage was the first to spot it moving toward them and alerted Cadotte, who killed both engines, dropped anchor, and pulled in his line to bait a hook.

"Ahoy," an officer called from the bridge as it drew close. "What's your business here?"

Cadotte raised his pole while Armitage shouted, "We're fishing." He was tempted to ask what they were doing in Canadian waters, but good sense prevailed.

"That's Nick Cadotte," a voice from aboard the Navy vessel called out. An RCMP officer moved forward and waved to them. "He's a member of the Ojibwe council. He's reliable."

"And you?" he called to Armitage.

Before he could answer, Nick said, "Brandon Armitage from Toronto. We're old friends. We served together in the last war. He's on leave from the Veterans Guard."

"All right, men. We have a security cordon here. Stand well off our position."

Both men "aye-ayed" him and went back to their "fishing." The pilot threw the patrol boat in reverse and resumed its place behind the *Anna H.*

Cadotte waited until the vessel was on station, raised anchor, and restarted motors. For twenty minutes, they remained in place. Armitage raised his field glasses to scan the horizon again, but his companion reached out and lowered them. "We're fishing. We don't want to raise their suspicions again."

Armitage looked up every few minutes, scanning the water for signs of activity on other boats. Suddenly, he spotted the same motorboat he had spotted an hour before, hugging the coastline about four hundred yards away. He raised his field glasses and was about to direct his companion's attention toward the craft when the sound of an engine boomed across the water. Turning, they saw a patrol boat racing toward Birch Island. A plume of black smoke curled above the horizon. The remaining gunboats began shifting positions.

As Armitage returned his attention to the speedboat, its bow rose, poised for takeoff as though it were a fighter plane. He shouted to Cadotte, who was already underway, shoving forward the throttles of both engines and racing the three hundred yards it would take to intercept the craft as it bore down on the presidential party.

Brandon raised his rifle and aimed at the onrushing hull. As the rowboat slammed into the waves, he couldn't get a clear shot. Closer the speedboat came, but with its bow raised, whoever was at the wheel didn't see them.

"Look out, Nick." One hundred yards, seventy. Armitage fired one round, but couldn't tell whether he'd hit his target. He pulled back the bolt and slammed it forward again. The powerboat was twenty yards away. It veered to avoid them, but Cadotte raced to intercept it.

Brandon aimed and pulled the trigger, but the shot sailed into the heavens as the speedboat broadsided their small craft at full throttle. He was thrown into the air, the last thing he remembered.

***

"Grab the buoy," a voice called out.

Armitage bobbled in the water, his life preserver true to its name.

"Ahoy, there," the voice repeated. "Can you hear me?"

He turned his head toward the direction of the voice, spitting out a mouthful of water that had rolled over him. Debris surrounded him, bits of plywood and planking. "Nick," he called. "Where are you?"

"Grab the buoy," the voice commanded. Armitage saw one of the two cruisers closing on him.

"Help him," he shouted back.

The crew member stood on the helm. He reeled the life ring back in, hauled it aboard, clutched it in his right hand, and tossed it to within feet of where Armitage lay. "Grab it," he yelled.

Armitage turned his head in the opposite direction and saw, twenty yards from him, Nick Cadotte floating motionless on his back. He stroked toward his friend, pain flaring up his left side where, he presumed, he had landed, putting distance between him and the cruiser.

"Shit!" the crew member called. "What's he doing?"

"Trying to save the other guy," another voice answered. "Mister," he shouted, "leave him alone. We're trying to help you both. Grab the damned buoy."

"Help him!" Armitage called back. Blood was seeping from a wound on Cadotte's head. Armitage didn't know if he was alive or dead, but he knew what would happen to him if he didn't get him out of the water.

He reached his friend as the captain maneuvered the boat toward them. Armitage grasped Cadotte's lift jacket with his left hand and began chopping at the water with his right.

"Let go of him," the sailor called out. "We'll get him. First, we have to get you aboard."

Armitage heard, but ignored him, closing the gap between him and the Anna H as it moved closer to him. He struggled to keep his head above water, taking in mouthfuls as he gasped for air.

The sailor reeled in the life ring and tossed it again, landing it within reach of the Armitage's outstretched arm. He grasped the buoy, still pulling Nick behind him. The sailor pulled them toward the cabin cruiser until both were alongside. Another sailor helped him reach for Armitage, but he repeated his mantra, "Help him. I'm all right."

"He won't let the guy go," the sailor shouted.

An officer joined the pair and took charge. "Pull his friend out first, or we'll never get them in. Let's have some help here."

A slender man dressed in civilian clothes reached over the port side and held Armitage's hand the others hoisted Cadotte from the water. Minutes later, they hoisted Armitage aboard. They wrapped him in blankets and carried him into the cabin, placing him across a cushioned bench. Nick lay across the cabin, and a man hovered over him, listening to his heart through a stethoscope and shining a flashlight into his eyes. A crowd of men dressed in fishing clothes stood watching them.

After several minutes, he turned to Armitage and repeated the same examination. "Don't move," he said. He introduced himself as Dr. McIntyre. "You're safe now. You've had a concussion and taken on a lot of water, but you'll be all right."

"Nick? How is he?" Armitage asked.

"He's badly injured and lost a good deal of blood, but he's stabilized. We're heading to Birch Island to get him to a clinic."

"And the president? How is the president?"

"I'm right as rain," FDR said, wheeling himself into view. "Now, tell us what was going on out there."

And Armitage spilled a yarn so incredible they thought at first he was hallucinating.

20

—————

AUGUST 7, 1943

Roosevelt awoke early, ready to get out on the water for his last day of fishing. Gray clouds lined the horizon. Rain was forecast, and he had no time to lose. His catch was eleven pounds ahead of Leahy's, but he intended to pad it to ensure he would win the pool.

First, however, business loomed. "How are those young men?" he asked Hopkins.

The men were young only compared to the two of them, but Hopkins didn't press the point. "The Canadian officer is sleeping it off in a nearby cottage. His friend has a couple broken ribs and a nasty gash atop his head—you saw how bad off he was—but the tribal clinic expects him to recover."

Roosevelt breathed a sigh of relief. "Let them know how grateful I am. That's some story he told. Is it all true?"

"The Canadians have checked with the prison camp. The man's name is Armitage. He's a guard at the camp, just as he says. There is a prisoner missing. Ontario police say he stole a rifle. He was clearly attacking us. Agent Turner has been over his story. Everything Armitage told us seems to check out."

"And the German?"

"He's escaped, sir."

In the chaos following the collision of the two boats, Lieutenant Manley had shoved the idling *Anna H* into gear and sped toward the shelter of the island. A quick-thinking boatswain's mate wheeled the president inside the cabin cruiser. The skipper of the *Mizpah* interposed his craft between the *Anna H* and the speedboat, but the attacker veered north, with a Navy patrol boat in pursuit. They'd lost him among the islands.

"Let's get him" Roosevelt said.

He poked at his coddled egg and read the first of two telegrams decoded during the night. The first was from Stalin, again begging off from a meeting, citing his "primary duty—the direction of action at the front."

A later meeting, he wrote, "would positively be expedient," but he dashed Roosevelt's hopes for an informal get-together between the two by suggesting they exchange proposals prior to a conference which, he said, should include Churchill. Roosevelt folded the message and finished his breakfast without betraying his disappointment.

The second telegram was from Marshall, informing him that, following Major General Barker's presentation of the COSSAC plan the day before, "the staff revolt ended." The Joint Chiefs, he said, were prepared to insist on the cross-Channel invasion at Quadrant, providing the president agreed.

FDR laid the telegram on the mahogany table, removed his glasses, and rubbed his eyes. He had one last piece of business to conduct, firing off a telegraph to Stimson. "I hope you will lunch with me on Tuesday. Glad to have your memorandum."

With that, he turned to Hopkins and beamed. "Let's go fishing."

As he wheeled himself toward the cabin entrance with his powerful arms, however, Agent Reilly loomed before him. "I have bad news, Mr. President."

Secret Service Agent Greg Turner shook Armitage awake. "We've tracked him."

Armitage had slept fitfully, having been questioned late into the night by agents Turner and Reilly. They led him through every phase of his history with Schumacher and made him repeat it. They probed every aspect of his life before joining the Veterans Guard and checked his bona fides with the Gravenhurst commandant.

"This guy Schumacher," Reilly had said, "sounds like a committed Nazi."

Armitage shook his head. "Like a lot of these young men, he's a patriot but not an ideologue. All he cares about is flying. I once asked him why he worked so hard on his previous escape attempt. He said it was his only way of getting back in the air."

"Then why did he do this?"

"I don't know. It's not like him."

Reilly studied him for a moment. "You sound as though you like the guy."

"He always seemed a decent sort. He's cagey and manipulative but all in the cause of returning home and into the cockpit." Armitage looked down at his hands and, in a quiet voice, said, "He reminds me of my younger son."

Only when the two men had wrung every detail from him did they assign him to a cot in one of the cottages commandeered for the president's visit. Armitage spent most of the night reliving the story and wondering what had become of the German. Reilly had told him the speedboat had outrun the Navy vessel. A patrol plane continued the chase as Schumacher turned west around Brush Island and weaved his way through the archipelago. He had beached *My Nancy* off the mainland near Whitefish Falls.

"Where is he?" Armitage asked as Turner shoved a mug of hot coffee toward him.

"We don't know where he is, but we know where he's been. After the alert went out, a resident reported seeing a man limping up River Road toward Camp Manitou at dusk. The OPP began a house-to-house search during the night."

Turner sported a slight smile. "An hour ago, they stumbled onto a cabin owned by an Austrian immigrant named Auer. He's dead, so he can't tell us anything. His car is missing, so we think your man is on the run again. Reilly will remain with the president while I head to the cabin. Do you care to come along?"

Armitage was already pulling his boots on. "I thought you would," Turner said.

As soon as she felt Sarah would be awake, Margie called the young woman. "Can you come for lunch?" she said. "I owe you for what you did for me yesterday."

"I'd love to, but not for your thanks. You would have done the same for me."

"'The saleswomen there are so stodgy. You really brightened things up,'" Margie said. "That was brilliant."

The two women laughed at the ruse they had engineered.

"And you're certain this manager of yours, Miss ..."

"Rowena Walter. Yes, I am. You had only to hear the sarcasm dripping from her voice when she told me how sorry she was." Margie didn't know how the woman had learned of the affair or how she'd passed word to Mrs. Sperling. An anonymous phone call? A letter? It made no difference. She had shown her distaste for Margie in recent days and struck out whenever she found the opportunity. Margie could make trouble for her by reporting her suspicions to Sperling, but to what purpose?

"Have you heard from your husband?" Sarah asked.

"No." She bit down on the word like a cherry pit.

Margie had thought of little else in the past six days. Twice she'd called the camp and asked for him. The officer had been polite, saying he was on an assignment of some sort, but declined to give details. Was he telling the truth? Brandon didn't conduct missions. He was just a guard. Was this the officer's flimsy way of telling her he refused to speak to her?

She walked the three blocks to the market, picked up a can of tuna, some fresh tomatoes, green beans, and lettuce, and returned home, enjoying the sudden breeze that presaged an afternoon of thunderstorms.

As she opened the front door, she stooped to collect the letters and flyers the postman had dropped through the slot. She continued into the kitchen and put the groceries away without taking the time to look through them.

Only after stringing the green beans and adding them to a pan of boiling water with two eggs, washing and draining the lettuce, and quartering four tomatoes did she turn her attention to the mail. She set aside the light company bill, tore open the envelope from Pinson's, kissing the paycheck, and examined the letter bearing the Sudbury postmark. The address was in Brandon's handwriting. What was he doing there?

She opened the envelope with trembling fingers and smoothed out the letter.

My darling Margie,

The commandant has sent me to Sudbury to carry out an assignment. I cannot tell you more but should return by this weekend to take a few days of leave and talk with you in person.

I traveled to Toronto yesterday and thought of coming by, but I wasn't sure I could find the right words.

I came there to visit Jeanne Canavan, the woman to whom I was engaged before we met. It was not a social call. It was part of my assignment. I realize that sounds unlikely and wish I could explain, but I hope you will take my word for it.

From the moment I set eyes on her, I realized we

had nothing in common. I once loved a girl, but I don't know the woman I met yesterday. Perhaps she is the same, and I have changed. Captivity will do that to you. So will marriage and responsibility.

She invited me to stay for lunch, but I declined, not because I am virtuous, but because I had no interest in renewing our acquaintance.

I love you, you see. At the time we met, I was at a low point in my life. It was not just that I had lost Jeanne; I was physically and emotionally crippled.

I had returned to a world I no longer recognized. I had no purpose. The bank refused to take me back. You will recall how others looked down on returning prisoners. Their sons and brothers had died in France and saw being captured as a sign of cowardice. Even your mother once suggested I had sat out the war.

I passed people untouched by the conflict who carried on as though nothing had happened. They did not want to hear about my years in captivity, nor did I wish to tell them. I had exchanged one form of prison for another, this one within myself.

From the moment we met, all that changed. I stopped thinking about myself and began caring about someone else. Five minutes of conversation with you, and my self-absorption lifted.

You had a new person living inside you. What a joy, I thought, to welcome this creature and embrace it as my own. I settled into my government job and made the best of things. Not the career I wanted, but a path forward, a way to provide for my new family. We were happy, you, Henry, and I. When Dickie came along, life was complete.

I was as concerned as you when the boys left last year. You think I sent them. I did not. I had been through war and wanted no part of it for them. But you know our Henry. When he set his mind to something, no one could stop him. And where he went, so went Dickie.

When we thought both were dead, something snapped. I returned to that dark place. I wanted revenge. That's why I enlisted. I tell myself I joined the Veterans Guard for them, but it was for me.

You say I sought redemption, to be seen as a hero rather than a disgraced prisoner. Perhaps you're right. Whatever my motivation, I thought only of myself. I left you alone, unable and unwilling to share your grief.

I now realize how selfish I was. By denying you the love and support you deserved, I encouraged you to find it elsewhere. Whatever has happened between you and your lover is my fault. Not yours.

Margie, I love you and want you back more than ever. The war is turning. The Germans have lost North Africa and Sicily. Russia is recapturing her land and her people. We will march on Berlin and crush this evil regime. Perhaps not this year, but soon.

Then Henry will return. Time will have changed him. He may be broken, as I was. He will need us—his mother and his father. And we will need each other. If *you will have me back, I promise to be there for you and for him.*

　　With all my love,
　　Brandon

A burning smell penetrated her tears. Rushing to the Emerson stove, she grabbed the pot from which the water had evaporated. The hot handle seared her hand, and she dropped it onto the floor. She fell to her knees, the pot imprinting itself on the linoleum, and broke down sobbing.

Two ARMED RCMP officers stood outside the log cabin nestled in the woods near Whitefish Falls, their stern presence contrasting with the surrounding forest's tranquility. A light wind ruffled the trees, signaling an imminent change in the weather. The stirring leaves mingled with the sounds of water tumbling over rocks in a nearby stream.

They introduced themselves to Armitage and Turner as Staff Sergeant Jason Devlin and Trooper Olivier Dufresne. "After we alerted you," Devlin reported, "we discovered a shortwave receiver, transmitter, and what looks like a codebook hidden under the bed. An inspector is on his way down from Sudbury. We think this guy was a German spy."

Turner nodded, as if he'd suspected something of the sort. "I don't care how resourceful your prisoner is," he said to Armitage. "He had to have help to come as close as he did."

Brandon thought about the transmitter he'd discovered at Gravenhurst, the staged brouhaha above the swim area that had aided Schumacher's getaway, and the role Pamela Canavan had played. "He had plenty of it," he said. "This conspiracy came from the top."

"We'd like to take a look inside," Turner said.

"I've been told not to admit anyone until our inspector arrives," Devlin countered.

"I realize I have no status here," Turner said, "but this prisoner has escaped from your prison camp and attempted an assassination on your territory. He's on the run, and I'm trying to help you catch him before he causes more harm."

The staff sergeant rubbed his cheek and looked toward the side as though determining whose orders to follow. "I suppose it's all right, but don't touch anything."

Turner followed the sergeant into the structure, Armitage trailing behind him. Trooper Dufresne remained on guard outside.

The cabin had a single living area, at one end of which was a wood stove. An aging sofa dominated the room. A camp bed and chair flanked the stove, while a small table with two chairs faced them on the opposite wall. A hunting rifle hung over the front door. To the left, three fishing rods rested in a wooden stand. Right of the door, beneath an empty hook on the wall, a metal box held tackle, lines, hooks, and flies, and beyond that stood a tall, narrow bookcase with four shelves. Armitage glanced at the titles, about half of which were works of fiction in German. Most of the English volumes were nonfiction, a history of Canada, a dictionary and thesaurus, timetables, maps, and an operating rulebook for the Canadian Pacific Railway.

Adjacent doors at the rear of the room led to a single bedroom and kitchen. A pump handle hung over the metal sink. There was no indoor toilet. A rustic, spartan home like those nearby, used as summer getaways.

Or had been, for the owner lay in the middle of a tattered rug before the sofa.

"By my guess, he's been dead at least two days," Devlin said. "The district coroner is on his way and should give us a more accurate time of death. There's no sign of foul play."

"Natural causes, you think?"

"A heart attack, aneurism, or something of the sort."

"How did you connect the German prisoner to this place?" Turner said.

"A neighbor saw a man fitting his description drive off in Auer's International Harvester pickup right after dawn."

Turner looked around him. "His rifle is undisturbed. Do we know if he took any other weapons?"

"His neighbor says that, apart from his truck, the only thing missing is his ring of keys."

"Which he'd need for the vehicle."

"Not that kind," Sergeant Devlin replied. "He was a retired railwayman. He kept his rail keys on a hook above the door."

Turner raised his eyebrows, and Armitage explained. "Railways lock up everything—baggage and mail cars, oil and pump houses, signals and switch stands. Rail workers are never without their keys. Lose them, and they're in big trouble."

Recalling a distant memory, Armitage continued, "My mother used to grab my dad's keys before he'd go out drinking with the boys. He had lost them once. After that, she took charge."

In other circumstances, the story would have elicited chuckles, but no one was laughing now. Why had Schumacher taken a set of Canadian Pacific keys? What did he have in mind?

He stood at the small table, his hand brushing the cover of a thick volume, *Official Guide of the Railways*, the only printed material not in the bookcase. "May I open it?"

Devlin frowned, considered for a moment, and waved him on.

Armitage turned the pages with the eraser end of a pencil. "Hello, what's this?"

Agent Turner moved alongside him to see what had attracted his interest.

"A map is missing," Armitage said. He turned back a page, then forward again to display the map following, pointing to an indentation. Someone had borne down hard on the missing page before removing it.

Turner ran his finger over the spot and smiled. Turning to Devlin, he said, "Where around here could we find another copy? The nearest library?"

Armitage interrupted. "Any station agent will have a current copy."

"The station in Espanola is closest." Devlin gave rough directions.

Turner massaged his chin with his right hand. "We need some help," he said. "Ask your superior officer if you can come along with us. I think I know what Herr Schumacher is planning."

<hr>

SCHUMACHER KEPT the speed of Auer's pickup at thirty-five miles per hour as he turned east-northeast on Highway 17. As Sudbury disappeared behind him, he stopped fidgeting and darting glances in the rearview mirror. He had passed two police cars in the city, and neither had paid attention to him. He no longer felt conspicuous. Just another farmer driving his nine-year-old utility vehicle into town for supplies.

With his tension ebbing, the pain in his ankle reasserted itself. The skin had been an inky blue when he'd unwrapped it this morning, deeper than a normal bruise and surrounded by flaming red blotches. It had become infected.

He couldn't risk seeing a doctor. The word would soon be out that a German prisoner was on the loose. But the pain was constant. He had to keep his foot on the accelerator, yet the ankle screamed at him, demanding he shift position. The throbbing wound telegraphed his heartbeat to his brain. He shifted his weight from one buttock to the other, changing his right leg's angle of attack.

Alongside him on the passenger seat lay the map from Auer's dog-eared railway guide. If the instructions he'd received from the SS last night were accurate, he had chosen an ideal spot. He only needed to find the turnoff.

Past Callum, the highway turned eastward and then towards the southeast as it rounded lakes and passed through hilly terrain. He was in no rush. He had hours to get into position. After passing through a quiet town called Markstay, he pulled onto a side road, opened the door, and dangled his legs out of the cab.

He thought about Auer. When he'd returned to the cabin, hoping the man could help him, he'd found him sprawled on the floor. The Austrian had complained of shortness of breath and dizziness the evening he left, and his face had a gray cast. Schumacher had pressured him, saying, "We're in this together. If they catch me, they catch you. I'll wind up in detention. You won't get off so easy." He had suffered an attack of some sort. Had it been too much?

He dismissed the thought. If Auer had fallen ill while he was still with him, he couldn't have done a thing about it. He had a mission to perform.

He stepped from the pickup and took a few tentative steps. The pain was more intense now than earlier in the day. He relieved himself and returned to the truck as a gentle rain fell. He executed a clumsy turn on the narrow dirt road and returned to the highway.

Schumacher drove for another half hour, reducing his speed as he passed through Verner. Ten minutes beyond, after rechecking the map, he turned right onto a gravel road. The rain fell harder now; the cold seeped into the pickup like an uninvited passenger.

Two miles south, he came to a railway crossing marked only by a crossbuck. He crossed over it, but after picturing what he intended to do, he returned to the north side of the track, facing the highway.

A hayfield lay to his right. He would have preferred to drive into it to conceal the pickup, but with the rain now falling in torrents, he worried he'd mire the vehicle in mud. Instead, he found a small turnoff that led to a locked gate. It offered no concealment but was off the road.

He turned off the engine, hooked Auer's key ring around his wrist, shouldered his rifle, grabbed a crowbar from the back of the pickup, and limped toward the tracks as the rain became a downpour.

ARMITAGE AND TURNER stepped to the Espanola Canadian Pacific station's ticket window and asked to see the agent's copy of the railway guide. The man gave him an odd look, since the agent held the same publication in his left hand. Turner had insisted on taking it, forcing Sergeant Devlin to radio the inspector for permission.

Seeing Devlin and Dufresne standing behind them, the station agent shrugged and returned a moment later with a duplicate. Armitage turned to the missing page. It depicted the rail lines east from Sudbury to Sturgeon Falls.

Opening Auer's copy, Turner tore out the page that had followed the missing map, aligned it over the page from the station agent's guide, and bore down on the indentation with a pencil, breaking through the paper. He lifted Auer's copy and studied the location now marked on the agent's map. It lay on a railway line east of Sudbury, bordering Lake Nipissing.

"How far is this?" Agent Turner asked.

The station agent scratched his forehead, about to answer, but Sergeant Devlin said, "About ninety miles. We know where it is."

Back in the RCMP squad car, Turner contacted Mike Reilly. "We know where Schumacher is. It's safe for the president to fish this morning, but his trip home may be a different story." He explained what Schumacher intended to do.

"The old man won't be happy about this," Reilly said.

"He'll be more aggrieved if we can't find Schumacher."

"Agreed. By the way, tell Armitage not a word of this to anyone."

Turner glanced at him. "He's with me. He got the message."

Sergeant Devlin reduced speed as the patrol car passed through Kirk and southeast toward Lake Nipissing. Most of the signs were in French. Trooper Dufresne explained that French-speaking families had migrated here from Michigan's Upper Peninsula in the last century to preserve their language. Armitage found the story fascinating, but he could tell Turner, sitting alongside him in back, was paying no attention.

The rain fell harder. Armitage telegraphed prayers to Devlin, who pressed his face against the windshield as he tried to find the road through the deluge.

As they passed through Verner, Agent Turner said, "Careful now. We're near the turnoff."

"We still have a little way to go," Devlin replied.

Armitage suppressed a smile at the presumptuousness of the American who thought he knew more about rural Ontario than the officers who patrolled it. Turner appeared unchastened, leaning forward to direct the pair, but they found the turnoff before he did and headed south.

"Slowly, now," he said, but Devlin had already reduced speed. Anything faster would have shaken the Chevy apart on the rugged road. It was difficult to see a thing, as the wiper blades couldn't keep up with the downpour. The sky was so dark it could have been late evening rather than mid-afternoon.

The gravel road seemed to lead nowhere. "Shit," Turner said. "You call this August? I didn't come dressed for it."

"We may have a spare jacket in the trunk," Dufresne said from the passenger seat. "Hold on. There it is." An I-H pickup was parked on a stub of farm road to the left, blocked by a fence. The Mounties got out of the cruiser, guns drawn, and approached the pickup. Turner and Armitage exited the cruiser and crouched behind it, ready to open fire if the need arose.

"No sign of him," Devlin said as he returned with water draining off his hat, "but he's around here somewhere. The rail map is on the front seat."

The waterlogged quartet retuned to the cruiser.

"Continue up to the crossing," Turner said. As though on cue, they heard a locomotive rumble in the distance. Devlin drove to within sight of the crossbuck sign and pulled to the side of the road. The engine, billowing smoke, chugged by at high speed, pulling flat-cars laden with logs. They waited in the car, the windshield fogging from their breath as the long train passed, leaving only when the caboose crossed in front of them, a red lamp hanging from its rear platform.

"Let's split up," the agent said. "Dufresne, you come east with me. Armitage and Devlin can head west. One of us should watch the track while the other keeps a lookout for the German."

Armitage shook his head. The secret service agent treated the Canadians as though they'd done nothing during their careers but guard moose crossings.

The two pairs separated, Turner armed with a mean-looking semi-automatic weapon, Armitage carrying the Colt M911. "Wouldn't you prefer a rifle?" Devlin said.

"I don't intend to use it." Devlin scowled, and Armitage rushed to reassure him. "I will if I have to, but I know this guy. I hope I can reason with him and end this without bloodshed."

That seemed to satisfy him, and they started up the track. "You're limping," Devlin said. "Are you hurt?"

Armitage was surprised the man hadn't noticed before. "A long time ago," he said, "and the story is even longer."

They trudged forward through the downpour. Since he knew Schumacher, Armitage took the point, but he couldn't see a thing with the rain falling. His eyes darted back and forth between the field on both sides and the track itself. The grade rose. They were at the foot of an incline of some sort. They walked for ten minutes until Armitage halted, the officer nearly running into him. "Look here."

Devlin followed him off the roadbed and to the muddy track where Armitage pointed at a row of boot prints. "He's hurt."

Devlin studied the impression. The tread of the left food made a deep impression in the soil, while only the right heel made an imprint. "He's limping," Armitage said, a man who knew all the signs.

"Which means he won't have gotten far."

"Maybe. You don't know the guy. He's relentless." He looked around for a moment. "We should stay off the tracks. We're vulnerable on the roadbed."

Devlin grunted in agreement, and they took another hundred steps. "We know he's west of the grade crossing," he said. "We should alert the others so they can join the hunt."

Armitage sniffed the air like a hunting dog. "You go after them. I would only slow you down."

Devlin cleared his throat as though considering. "All right, but don't go any farther." As he backtracked, Armitage took a hundred more steps. Schumacher's boot prints disappeared in gravel that had cascaded off the roadbed.

When he'd ventured two hundred yards more, the rain relented. Giving a silent prayer of gratitude, he spotted a switch stand ten yards ahead. To his left, another set of tracks peeled off to the south, a spur leading toward Cache Bay. Through the rising mist, Armitage could see the grade ahead continue a steep climb.

Ignoring Devlin's instructions, he approached the switch stand. It was unlocked, but the points—the rails at the switch—still headed westward.

Peering at the track as it disappeared uphill, Armitage envisioned what was to happen. Roosevelt's train was to come thundering down the grade. As it approached, Schumacher would emerge from wherever he was hiding and, as the front wheels of the car passed over the switch, shift the track. The front wheels would continue forward as the rear wheels veered onto the siding, causing the *Ferdinand Magellan* to crab sideways and career off the track."

He should go back for help, but something kept him standing there. Roosevelt was out of danger. Agents Turner and Reilly had seen to that. What remained was to bring Schumacher in.

"You can come out now, Jörg."

He heard no response.

"Three armed officers are with me. You're trapped." He took a few steps forward, his Colt pointing at the underbrush to the south of the roadbed. "Schumacher?"

Behind him, Armitage heard the unmistakable sound of a safety of a rifle being disengaged, followed by a bolt pushing a round from the magazine into the chamber.

"Drop it," Schumacher called out.

Armitage's chest muscles tightened, and his breathing constricted. He shivered as blood retreated from his hands and feet.

He'd been a damned fool, consumed by the mechanics of what Schumacher planned and paying no attention to the man himself. Armitage lowered his Colt and turned. The German stood off to the side, holding the Ross with his right arm, aiming it at his chest. He saw the barrel droop and realized the man was injured. A rivulet of rain dripped from the long barrel.

"It's over," Armitage said.

"Over for you, perhaps, but not for me."

Dangling the Colt by the trigger guard, Armitage nodded toward the tracks. "You plan to derail Roosevelt's train. If the impact doesn't kill him, you will."

"Very good. How did you learn all this?"

"It doesn't matter. The point is, you won't succeed."

"And why not?"

"Because he's no longer coming this way." The German looked at him open-mouthed, then smirked, unwilling to fall for the suspected ruse.

"You had it right. Instead of heading south toward Hamilton, he planned to return via this northerly route to travel down the Ottawa River, take in the scenery, and visit the prime minister at the capital. But with you on the loose, his security detail has vetoed his side trip."

"I don't believe you."

"I don't care what you think. He's not coming. And one more thing." Schumacher didn't speak, but his expression said, *What?*

"That rifle won't fire. You laid it down when you unlocked the switch. Look for yourself. It's soaked and muddy. That renders it useless. Believe me. I know."

Schumacher examined the Ross, a weapon he knew by reputation.

"Jörg, I don't want to hurt you. It would be like shooting my son." The German seemed to consider that. "Haven't we done enough to each other in this war? Hand me the rifle."

Schumacher hesitated. He looked down at his swollen ankle. It wouldn't allow him to outrun even this cripple. Heaving a long sigh, his body bowing in defeat, he dropped the Ross and hobbled back toward the crossing.

Armitage holstered his Colt and retrieved the rifle, aimed in the air, and pulled the trigger. The explosion nearly knocked him off his feet and sent his prisoner sprawling. "Sorry," Armitage said. "The one time I was certain this piece of shit wouldn't fire, it did."

As Schumacher tried to rise to his feet, Armitage said, "You're hurt. Grab my hand. That's it. Lean on me."

With their arms draped around each other, the two men, captor and captive, stumbled back the way they had come.

AT 10 P.M., the engineer released the brake and eased forward on the throttle. The locomotive pulling the *Ferdinand Magellan* and the rest of the six-car train inched away from the railway station at Birch Island.

In his car, Roosevelt, who seldom complained, sulked. He had spent an hour pleading with Mike Reilly to restore his planned trip along the Ottawa River. "Now that the man's recaptured, let me have this last day of beauty and peace."

The secret service agent was firm. "Mr. President, we've changed everything. The Canadian Pacific has spent the day rerouting traffic, and we've canceled the arrangements in Ottawa. We can't put it back together on such short notice."

Roosevelt inclined his head as though to say, *Can't you?*

"Maybe next year, Mr. President."

He let out a petulant sigh. "At least I won the pool." He laughed as he wheeled himself into his bedroom for a long night's sleep. Roosevelt still hadn't shared with Hopkins, Leahy, or Marshall whether he would hew to their advice or give in to Churchill.

21

AUGUST 8-31, 1943

BRANDON CALLED Margie to let her know he would be home in a few days. He first returned to Little Current, taking up a post at Nick Cadotte's bedside at the tribal clinic. Examining the wound in his friend's head, Armitage said, "You've been scalped."

Nick coughed, suppressing a chuckle. "Don't do that. It hurts when I laugh."

On his second day, Cadotte felt well enough to walk the narrow hallway. Brandon supported him for a few steps, but Nick waved him off, making his way alone. He was discharged the following day.

Armitage accompanied him back to his cabin at Whitefish Bay. He cleaned up the place, which Margie would have been surprised to see, bought provisions, and spent the night there. The following morning, he bid his friend goodbye and took the train north to Sudbury where he checked in with Sergeant-Major Gibney.

"I hear they caught your prisoner," the OPP officer said.

Armitage was at first amused by his use of the pronoun, but something told him not to pursue the matter. "Yes," he said.

"I suppose you've read it was President Roosevelt we were protecting at Birch Island." Now that Roosevelt was safely back in

Washington, Canadian newspapers trumpeted his visit. "So you see why we couldn't spare the manpower to join in the search."

Armitage assured him he understood, though none of this made sense. Gibney seemed unaware of the attack on Roosevelt and certainly not any role Armitage had played in preventing it.

That afternoon, he took the train to Toronto, arriving home a bit after nine. After closing the door and dropping his duffel bag, he collapsed into Margie's arms and wept, something she hadn't seen him do in all the time she'd known him.

She pulled away from his embrace, staring at his bedraggled figure. "What's wrong, Brandon? Where have you been?"

"It's a long story," he said, smiling to reassure her. "The main thing is I'm fine now. And I love you."

He repeated that he loved her, apologized for his indifference, and begged for her forgiveness. "But I'm the one who broke my vow," she said.

"I promised to love," he said, his voice cracking, "and that I did. But I also promised to honor and cherish, and I have not."

They spent the night holding each other and made love with an intensity neither had brought to the marriage before.

"When Henry returns, he'll be a changed person," he told her over breakfast the following morning. "He won't face the rejection I experienced. His friends won't turn their backs on him. Employers won't shun him. Those days are over."

Holding her hands in his, he said, "But he will feel a mix of emotions. Guilt that he survived while his comrades did not. Anger at his missing years. A dark hole in his psyche he can't fill. He may lash out at us, close the door to his room and not come out for days. We must be patient. He needs to know we're here for him."

"And we will," she said. "Why didn't you tell me what you were going through when we met?"

"Selfishness," he said. "I've spent years thinking only of myself. That's over. I'll never keep a secret from you again. I promise."

"Nor will I," she said.

ON THE DAY following the conclusion of the Quadrant Conference, President Roosevelt made his postponed trip to Ottawa. Governor General Alexander Cambridge and several other dignitaries met his train as it arrived.

After several days of rain, the weather was glorious, helping to account for thirty thousand Canadian well-wishers who turned out to greet him at Parliament Hill. It was, the President's Log claimed, "the largest crowd ever to welcome a distinguished visitor to Ottawa, even exceeding the welcome accorded King George VI and Queen Elizabeth."

The president was wheeled to the Peace Tower platform where, at noon, the carillon tolled "God Save the King." FDR's friend, Prime Minister Mackenzie King, introduced him. Standing in his leg braces, Roosevelt addressed the crowd.

"We did not choose this war," he said. "War was violently forced upon us by criminal aggressors who measure their standards of morality by the extent of the death and destruction they can inflict upon their neighbors."

Turning to the just-concluded conference, he said, "The Combined Staffs have been sitting around a table talking things over, discussing ways and means, in the manner of friends, in the manner of partners, and may I even say in the manner of members of the same family.

"We have talked constructively of our common purposes in this war—of our determination to achieve victory in the shortest possible time—of our essential cooperation with our great and brave fighting allies."

As he had done in past public statements, he papered over eight days of rancorous discussions. On his return from his fishing trip, he had met with Marshall and Stimson. Both were concerned when Harry Hopkins reported Roosevelt's reaction to Stimson's memo had been "inscrutable."

Stimson had drafted a second memorandum, calling the Anglo-

American differences over strategy "a vital difference of faith." He argued it was time for the president to assume leadership of the Atlantic Alliance. The military needed clear direction, which they were not getting from London. Given Churchill's reticence, Stimson feared the invasion could not succeed unless an American was in command.

When they met on August 10, Roosevelt told Stimson that he had read his report with interest. As Marshall had predicted, by putting his assessment in writing and not pressuring him, the president had adopted the position. "I have come to much the same conclusion myself," he told Stimson. An hour later, with the Joint Chiefs in attendance, he reaffirmed his commitment to Operation Overlord. As to his guardedness in communicating his decision, he said. "I never let my left hand know what my right hand is doing."

The die seemed to be cast, but just to be sure, Roosevelt wanted nineteen US divisions moved to the United Kingdom, trained, equipped, and ready to fight by the following May, in advance of D-Day. Marshall promised the Commander in Chief this could and would be done.

Stimson and Marshall still feared the persistent prime minister would turn FDR's head when he visited Hyde Park, but they need not have worried. Three days later, as the two leaders sat beneath a tree overlooking the Hudson River, Roosevelt informed the prime minister of his decision. Churchill seemed to acquiesce, but he soon pleaded with Roosevelt to accompany him by train to Québec, giving him one last chance to change the president's mind. He refused, saying he had to return to Washington for important business before the conference.

At the Citadel, Allied planners wrangled. Admiral Brooke opened the meeting by insisting that while operations in Italy should take the cross-Channel operation into consideration, "giving Overlord overriding priority is too binding." Marshall countered that anything less risked making it a subsidiary operation that could doom its chances for success. He hinted that unless the British affirmed the invasion strategy, the US might shift divisions and material to the Pacific.

The British Chiefs came around, with the proviso that the Italian campaign would continue. On August 17, the Allies took Sicily. The US side gave in to invading Italy, provided transferring divisions for Overlord could proceed.

Churchill learned of the compromise on his arrival. Confronted with a *fait accompli*, he caved.

On the following day, Roosevelt told the cheering crowd on Parliament Hill, "We have arrived, harmoniously, at certain definite conclusions. I am not at liberty to disclose just what these conclusions are. But, in due time, we shall communicate the secret information of the Québec Conference to Germany, Italy, and Japan. We shall tell it to them in the only language their twisted minds seem capable of understanding."

One year after military dithering had cost the lives of 916 Canadians and the capture of 1,946 more at Dieppe, the Allies committed to an action that would end the war in Europe and hasten the downfall of the Japanese Empire. Roosevelt would not live to see it, but he would have his way.

THAT AFTERNOON, Armitage visited Gravenhurst to pick up his belongings. Shortly after his return home, he had petitioned the Veterans Guard to be released, an offer that had been promptly accepted without so much as thanks for his service.

When he arrived at the camp, no one acknowledged his absence. No one seemed aware of the role he had played.

"I'm sorry you have to leave us," Lieutenant Morrison said, avoiding eye contact. "It's unfortunate things turned out this way."

Armitage gaped at him. And then he got it. For some reason, Ottawa had made it seem he'd failed in his mission and been cashiered for his troubles.

"There is an endless line of volunteers," he replied noncommittally.

"I hear they captured Schumacher trying to board a freighter in Montreal."

"That's what I read," Armitage said, playing along with Ottawa's hastily concocted cover story.

Why, he had wondered, put Schumacher in Montreal rather than Sudbury? Once again, he reached the logical conclusion. There had been no reports about the attack on Roosevelt. Neither Gibney nor Morrison knew about it. By planting the story that Schumacher had been captured in Quebec rather than Ontario, the government was putting distance between him and the president's trip. But why?

And the cover story had been designed only to account for Schumacher, not for him. They'd made him a scapegoat. He'd gone off chasing Schumacher in the wrong direction and tied up forces needlessly in the process.

So be it. He thanked Morrison, turned on his heel, and collected his few belongings, preparing to walk back to the railway station.

Corporal Smith stopped him and offered to give him a ride. Armitage thanked him but refused. The secret service had ordered him not to speak of what had happened at Birch Island, and Smith would pepper him with questions he couldn't answer. His time in the Veterans Guard was over, a closed book. What mattered now was his marriage. And their son.

***

JOSEPH GOEBBELS BURIED his head in his hands. He had listened as President Roosevelt addressed the crowd in Ottawa, promising to "deliver a message" to Hitler. It was no propaganda trick. Roosevelt was alive. The Québec conference had proceeded as planned. The British and Americans were united. There seemed no way he could drive a wedge between them.

No one had heard from the German flyer. The Canadians had reported his recapture two weeks before, but Himmler said he had not returned to the Gravenhurst camp. Had he made it to the Canadian island? Had he even attempted to carry out his mission? Or had he made straight for Montreal to stow away and return home?

If the Canadians had recaptured him, as they claimed, why had he failed to turn up at any of the other camps? What of the Austrian agent at Birch Island? Himmler said his handlers in the Third Division had heard nothing from him.

Goebbels could answer none of these questions. He knew Roosevelt had triumphed over Churchill at the conference. There might still be an invasion of Italy—Allied bombing of the Rome marshaling yard seemed to promise that.

But Goebbels knew the Allies would focus most of their strength on Northwest Europe. France, Norway, Denmark, the Low Countries. No one knew where the Allies would land. Only that they would, and with overwhelming force. They would sweep across the Continent, aiming straight for the German heartland while the Russians came at them from the East.

Nothing would stop them.

ON THE LAST day of the month, Margie was preparing breakfast when the doorbell interrupted them. "I'll get it," she said.

The man at their front door was not in uniform, but he was clearly an official. "You must want my husband," she said before he could introduce himself.

"Yes, Mrs. ..." But Margie had already hailed Brandon, who emerged from the kitchen.

"I'm Mr. Smythe," the man said. Though he tried to adopt a Canadian accent, he failed to conceal his British origins. Why was he masquerading as a fellow countryman?

"You're Brandon Armitage? Is there somewhere we might speak? In private?"

"I have no secrets from my wife."

"I'm afraid I must insist."

"Then you can leave."

"That's all right, Brandon. I have work to do." Margie glared at the intruder and retreated to the kitchen.

Smythe waited until Armitage had seated himself, then pulled a chair close to face him. "What's this about?" Armitage asked.

"Three weeks ago, an American Secret Service agent instructed you not to tell anyone what occurred at Birch Island. Do you recall this?"

"I do."

"And have you done so?"

"No."

"Not even your wife?"

"She's curious, of course."

"Have you told her, Mr. Armitage?"

"I said I hadn't."

Smythe—Armitage assumed his name was anything but—let out a long, satisfied sigh. "Very good. You're not to do so. Not now. Not ever."

"Why not?"

He looked directly into Brandon's eyes. "Because nothing happened. A German prisoner escaped. We captured him trying to leave the country."

"Where is Schumacher?"

"We are holding him at a prison, and he will remain there. That's all I can tell you."

"And the girl?" Smythe's face was blank. "Pamela Canavan. What's become of her?"

"I know no one by that name."

"I get it," Brandon said. "If something had occurred while the American president was at Birch Island, it would have embarrassed the US and Canada—particularly since I warned both security services about the threat Schumacher posed. Thus, it's better for all concerned if the incident never happened. And since nothing happened, no one can be prosecuted for causing it. Is that it?"

"Hmm. Something like that." The man arose. "So not a word to anyone. Have I made myself clear?"

"Perfectly." Armitage followed him to the door, closing it behind him. Neither said goodbye.

"What was that all about?" Margie said as he entered the kitchen.

Armitage poured two cups of coffee and motioned her to a seat at the table. "I promised you I'd keep no secrets from you."

She nodded.

"So you must tell no one what I'm about to share with you. Do you promise?"

"I do."

He held both her hands in his as he began to speak.

ACKNOWLEDGEMENTS

While this is a work of fiction, it is based on a historical incident. In August of 1943, just prior to the Quadrant Conference, Franklin Roosevelt departed Washington for a weeklong fishing trip in Ontario, a visit suggested to him the year before by his friend, E.F. McDonald. As my friend Philip Padgett recounts in his excellent history, *Advocating Overlord: The D-Day Strategy and the Atomic Bomb*:

> The fishing party departed Birch Island by train at 10 p.m., August 7. [The] original plan had been to make a circle to return along the beautiful Ottawa River and through Canada's capital. However, there had been a security alert. An escaped German prisoner, Peter Krug, had been recaptured earlyAugust 5 near the railway in North Bay, Ontario, through which Roosevelt's returning train would have passed. FDR's train instead retraced its route through Ontario, then directly back to Washington.

In an email to Phil as soon as I read the passage, I wrote that one of the book's incidents, which I did not identify, had tantalized me by its potential for a novel. Phil responded that he knew what part of his story I meant and began showering me with background information on Krug's escape.

The rest, as they say, is history. Even while finishing a previous novel, *Novak's Mission*, I began immersing myself in the background to FDR's trip, the fascinating story of Canada's incarceration of German POWs for Great Britain, the sensitive negotiations between England and the US on strategy in the European theater, the thoughts and motivations of Goebbels, Churchill, Roosevelt, and those around them—down the proverbial rabbit hole.

I am grateful to Phil for sharing hundreds of pages of research he compiled for *Advocating Overlord*, timelines, notes of secret service agents at Birch Island, correspondence between the principles, and much more. He also directed me to an out-of-print copy of a history of Camp XX, *The Gilded Cage* by Cecil James Porter.

Another longtime friend and public media colleague, Thomas Hurley, a licensed radio operator and executive director of the Massachusetts Airport Management Association, provided invaluable assistance in explaining how the German prisoners could have built a transmitter and receiver from parts, and how their transmissions could have been discovered by another radio operator.

On the Quora website, Edward Pickett told me the story of how Canadian families learned of the death of a member in military service during the war. David Currey, a former railway man, went out of his way to help me explain how a railway switch operates. Michael Schlueter, a Canadian Army officer, helped with forms of address for Canadian non-coms during the war. Harold Zwanepol and Steve Weatherbe provided information on how and when Canadians first learned of the Dieppe Raid. Steven Haddock and Rob Archer described life in Toronto during the war years. Ronald J Brown and Mark Jones gave me information on the Anglican Church.

Other Quora members who filled in gaps in my knowledge are Les Howie, Bill Mahaffy, Robert Crooks, Norm Soley, Dean Bliejer, Erich Eisenmenger, Michael Baumgartner, John Robillard, and Bob Weiss.

Two Norwegians, Ivar Kristvik and Eirik Randsborg, provided the *tyskertøs* insult.

The Old Mill Family Restaurant in Gravenhurst told me about the now-defunct Sloane's Restaurant. The staff at the Gravenhurst Public Library answered questions about the town, matters I would have researched in person had not the COVID pandemic prohibited travel.

To compensate for my inability to visit the Canadian sites in person, I turned to Matthew Godden of Thames Valley Wordworks.

Matthew reviewed my entire manuscript, making numerous suggestions for improvement, all of which were incorporated into the finished story. My account of much of Northern Ontario's francophone population being linguistic refugees from Michigan was new to him, but much of the flavor of the area came from him. Thank you, Matthew.

I am deeply indebted to David Volk, who edited the final manuscript. His attention to detail directed me to things that were unclear, saved me from confusing several minor characters, and corrected many grammatical errors. David is co-chair of Pittsburgh South Writer's Group whose members reviewed scenes in the book covering technical details.

Finally, Toronto's Laura Boyle or lauraboyledesign.com, produced the cover art, as she has done for all of my books. She does great work and is a joy to work with.

My life partner, Julie Lewis, provides support and privacy while I write. I love you, "Jubie."

ABOUT THE AUTHOR

James H. Lewis is the author of four previous novels, including the Chief Novak series of police procedurals. A sixth, *Belonging*, a family drama, originally released on Kindle Vella, will soon be released in book form.

A former journalist, public media executive, and consultant to non-profit organizations, Lewis also works as a copywriter for nonprofit clients. Lewis is a member of The Author's Guild, Pennwriters, and Pittsburgh South Writer's Group. Having lived all over the United States he now makes his home in Pittsburgh.

facebook.com/JamesLewisAuthor

twitter.com/Pitt_JimLewis

amazon.com/~/e/B07JMWL8NF

goodreads.com/James_H_Lewis

bookbub.com/authors/james-h-lewis

linkedin.com/in/pittjimlewis

www.ingramcontent.com/pod-product-compliance
Lightning Source LLC
Chambersburg PA
CBHW021134310726
48971CB00002B/323